BATTERSEA, 1957

Chapter One

'Mum, I've got something to tell you. Neville has asked me to marry him.' Hazel stood in the doorway, ready for an argument.

Cora Butler wasn't surprised at the news. Her middle daughter had been courting Neville Parrot for a year, but as she didn't think he'd make much of a husband, she said, 'I hope you didn't say yes. You'll never be rich if you marry him.'

'Money isn't everything.'

'It is when you've hardly got two pennies to rub together,' Cora snapped. She knew what it was to struggle and wanted better for her daughter. After losing her husband during the war Cora had been left to raise three girls on her own. It had been so hard. She'd had to do anything to earn a few bob to feed them, and along with cleaning she'd taken in washing and ironing. Her back was permanently damaged from bending over the bath for hours on end, rubbing at the soaking laundry, and her knuckles were scarred from using a scrubbing board. Even though the war had ended twelve years ago she still felt the effects of it every day.

'I don't care about money,' Hazel protested. 'I love Neville and I'm going to marry him.'

Cora's lips tightened and, gathering her thoughts, she walked across her tiny front room to the window. The room was as immaculate as she could get it, seeing as there were three of them living there, but nothing in it was new or close to it. She flicked back the lace curtain to gaze out onto another cold, miserable January day in Ennis Street. All the houses were the same, basically two-up, two-down, narrow, terraced, flat-fronted, and bleak. As bleak as her mood. She had hoped that her daughter would find a way out of this ugly working-class area, but Neville offered little chance of that. The streets were so close together she could hardly see the sky when she looked up. The houses opposite were a bit bigger because of the way the road curved but they were still nothing to shout about.

With a sigh Cora dropped the curtain and turned to her daughter again. Of her three girls, Hazel was the prettiest, with auburn hair that fell in natural curls to her shoulders. Her femininity was marred only by her big-boned build, making her look formidable, but with green eyes, a pert nose and full lips, she nevertheless turned men's heads. Hazel could have taken her pick, but instead she'd fallen for Neville Parrot. His family lived in one of the houses opposite them, and they had moved in eighteen months ago when his father got a job on the railway. They seemed nice enough and Neville was a good-looking lad, but he probably earned a pittance in the local paint factory. 'You've fallen for his looks, but looks ain't everything. As I said, you'll never be rich if you marry him.'

'We'll both be working, so we'll be fine. I'm going to carry on at the café.'

'Yeah, until kids come along,' Cora commented. 'You'll feel the pinch then.'

'Mum, stop going on about it. Can't you just be happy for me?'

Cora saw that Hazel's eyes were flooding with tears, something she rarely saw from her tough daughter, and though Cora was hardened from the life she'd had to live, she nevertheless felt a twinge of guilt. Hazel's eyes had been bright with happiness when she'd announced that Neville had asked her to marry him, but now they were pools of pain. 'Yeah, all right. I'm sorry, love. I just wanted better for you, but if you're happy, then I'm happy,' she said, and then, trying to lighten the mood, added, 'Mind you, it's just as well I didn't name you Polly.'

'Why's that?' Hazel asked.

'Think about it. You'd be Mrs Polly Parrot,' Cora said and chuckled.

Hazel laughed, happy again now, but as pain shot across Cora's back, she hurried to sit by the fire once more where she could warm it a little, taking the chance to hold out her aching hands to the flames whilst she was there.

Alison Butler, Cora's youngest daughter, scurried along Ennis Street, her shoulders hunched as though expecting an attack at any moment. It wouldn't be physical – it rarely was, although she got the occasional shove or push from behind – but it would be verbal and hurtful. Hardly a day went by when something along those lines failed to happen. Her fears came to fruition as two boys of about eleven darted up in front of her.

'Watcha, horse face,' mocked Jimmy Small.

'My dad said she's got a face that could win the

13

Epsom Derby,' Ian Young said.

'Yeah, that's a good one,' laughed Jimmy.

'Come on. Gee up, horsey,' Ian urged. 'Let's see how fast you can gallop.'

Alison kept her head down, hiding her pain. She had suffered name-calling all her young life, at school, on the streets, and it never seemed to stop. She knew only too well that her looks weren't anything to write home about – growing up with such pretty sisters had made that only too clear – but she could never understand why so many people were so keen to point it out, with thoughtless cruelty. She picked up her pace and reaching her front door she dashed inside before closing it quickly behind her. Only then did she give vent to her feelings and was unable to hold back a sob of distress.

As the door opened directly into the front room, she could see that her mother was sitting on one side of the fireplace, her sister on the other. Both stared at her. It was her mother who spoke, though her tone was uncaring. 'What's wrong? Don't tell me. I can guess. Someone's been calling you names again?'

Alison nodded, finding that her throat was too constricted to speak.

'With a face like that, it ain't gonna stop and you should be used to it by now,' Hazel said scathingly.

Alison knew that Hazel was right. It was what her sister had told her for as long as she could remember. She should be used to it and did her best to ignore the name-calling, but today, with cramping pains in her tummy signalling her time

14

of the month, the two boys had got to her. But she wasn't about to tell Hazel. She knew better than to expect any sympathy from that direction.

'Anyway, wait till you hear my news,' Hazel went on. 'This'll stop you looking so miserable. You'll never guess.' She looked expectantly at her younger sister.

Alison shook her head, still unable to speak.

'Neville's only asked me to marry him!' Hazel exclaimed. 'And of course I said yes. What do you make of that? Aren't you pleased for me?'

'That's ... that's ... lovely,' Alison stuttered. She wasn't surprised. Hazel had been going on and on about Neville ever since they'd started going out together and never missed a chance to remind her younger sister that she stood no chance of getting herself such a good-looking boyfriend – or any boyfriend at all. Alison secretly longed for a boy-friend of her own but as she was too shy to have real friends of any kind she didn't see much hope for the future. Hazel had no false modesty about her own good looks and never failed to point out that Alison had drawn the short straw in that department. True to form she made the most of the moment now.

'You might at least try to look happy for me,' she said. 'It isn't as if you're going to be getting married any time soon yourself. Look at you – who'd have you? Long streak of misery that you are. Well, you can buck your ideas up and help me when I need you. There's going to be loads of pre-parations to sort out for my big day.' She beamed in delight. 'We're going to have a do that every-one'll remember for years to come.'

15

'Now hang on a minute.' Cora sat up straight, ignoring the painful twinge in her back. 'Let's not get ahead of ourselves. You've only just got engaged. Plenty of time to talk about what sort of wedding you'll be having. You don't need no big do. Just think what that'll cost. You won't want to be wasting money when you're starting out. Setting up a home sets you back a fair bit, I can tell you.' Privately she was already dreading Hazel moving out and losing the wages she brought to the household. Every precious penny counted.

'Don't be like that, Mum.'

Hazel could always win her mother round in a way that Alison never managed. Somehow she always knew what to say to get her own way – it was second nature to her, and Alison couldn't work out how she did it. Once Hazel made up her mind about something there was usually no stopping her.

'You wouldn't want me to skimp on my wedding, would you? You want to be proud of me, don't you? You want me to be happy? And we're both working so we'll save towards it, starting today.' She turned to her sister. 'Everyone will have to muck in to help as much as they can. No excuses, Alison, you're doing this for me and I don't want no lip from you.'

Blimey, thought Alison, that was rich coming from her bully of a sister. She had never dared give her any lip. She didn't give anyone lip, it wasn't in her nature. Hazel stood up. Although she was tall, she was still a good way shorter than her younger sister, who always tried to hide her embarrassing height by rounding her shoulders and looking

16

down. Hazel did the exact opposite, standing straight and proud and flaunting her assets for all they were worth. 'I've got to get ready. Me and Neville are going out to celebrate. Don't wait up.' She ran up the narrow staircase that led off the front room, with just a curtain to hide it from the living area. The stairs led to a tiny landing, with doors to two small bedrooms, one for Hazel and one for Cora. A third door opened into a box room which Alison used as a bedroom, in which there was scarcely room enough for her to lie down.

'Looks like it'll be just you and me stuck here together, then,' said Cora. The idea depressed her. Try as she might she just could not bring herself to love her youngest daughter. The very sight of the girl reminded her of all the trouble she'd been through, the hell of losing her husband in the war and then the nightmare when she found he'd left her pregnant after what turned out to be his final leave. Her other two daughters had been old enough to go to school and she'd have been able to get a decent job to keep them all if it hadn't been for the unwanted arrival of this last girl, who'd been nothing but a disappointment and a burden from the word go. She'd been a sickly baby and couldn't be left alone for a minute. She'd been the wrong shape for hand-me-downs from her sisters almost from the start – where did she get that stupid height from? Looking at her daughter now, Cora sighed. She'd loved her husband but struggled to find a trace of him in Alison. The girl had ugly buck teeth, a long face, and plain mousy hair that hung in rats' tails. There was no sign of her father's looks, still less of his good humour and

17

high spirits. Back in the days when they'd been courting, Cora had been swept off her feet by Jack Butler's charm and determination to make the best of things no matter what, and she'd responded in kind. It was only what had happened after he'd been killed in action that had turned her bitter and exhausted. Deep down she knew it was unreasonable but she couldn't help blaming Alison for all of it. Groaning at the pain in her back and the arthritis in her hands, she pushed herself to her feet.

'Right, I reckon I'd better write to our Linda to let her know the news. Don't suppose she'll be visiting to hear it for herself seeing as she was only here last week. We'll just have to hope I catch the last post.'

'Maybe she'll come again when she hears,' Alison said, her eyes lighting up. She loved her eldest sister, who'd always stood up for her against her mother's indifference and Hazel's constant bullying. 'We can't expect her to make the journey all the time. Not when she's so far away down in Kent and she's got little June to look after.'

Cora's expression softened. Her three-year-old granddaughter was the apple of her eye and could do no wrong. Linda had done well for herself, marrying truck driver Terry Owens and moving from the crowded terraces of Battersea out to the wide spaces of Kent, but the icing on the cake was the arrival of June. There wasn't anything she wouldn't do to protect the little girl.

'Well, maybe Hazel's latest will bring them back here sooner than usual,' Cora said. 'Right, enough of you standing around doing nothing. Go and take those filthy factory overalls off and then get yourself in the kitchen to help with the dinner. Those spuds won't peel themselves and my poor hands won't stand it, so it's all down to you.'

Chapter Two

The factory wasn't far away but Alison always arrived tired and out of breath from scurrying along the street trying not to be noticed. It never worked. The following week, on Friday morning, two of the paperboys from the local newsagent-cum-corner shop had been the ones to torment her. The fact that her mother worked in the same shop didn't deter them.

Now she made her way to the small canteen to grab a warming cup of tea before starting her shift. It was freezing outside and her own house was little better, as Cora always said there was no point in lighting the fire if nobody was going to be home. 'Look who's here,' called Ron Small as she approached. She forced herself not to turn and run away. Ron was the father of young Jimmy Small and had an even crueller way with words than his son. 'Watch your milk, folks. One look from her'll curdle it.' He laughed at his own joke, though some of the women standing around the tea urn glanced at him sharply. 'Cheer up, love, it might never happen.' He gave a heartless chuckle and moved off.

'Don't you pay him no mind,' said Betty

Shawcross, handing Alison a cup. 'Not exactly God's gift himself, is he?' She buttoned her overall. 'Empty vessels and all that. Nobody takes him seriously and neither should you.'

'Thanks,' said Alison nervously. Even though many of the women she worked with were kind to her, she couldn't help feeling that this might change at any moment, although she'd been working with them for several months. She just wasn't used to it. The only person who'd ever been nice to her was her big sister Linda, and these women hardly even knew her. She found it hard to know what to say to them, as she'd always felt safer staying in her shell. She sometimes wondered if she should try to make friends with them but as she'd never really had any she wasn't sure how to start.

'Come on, we've been called to a meeting outside the foreman's office,' said Marjory Weekes. 'All of our section is to report there in five minutes. So give me a cuppa sharpish. If this is about laying people off then I'm going to get one last drop of tea out of them.' She pulled off her bright headscarf and dug in her pockets for her factory regulation cap.

'Don't say that, you'll frighten the girl,' said Betty protectively, noticing how alarmed Alison looked, and hoping Marjory was talking her usual nonsense. None of them could afford to lose their job. They weren't that well-paid but it was regular work, nine to five. It was typical Marjory, speaking before she thought.

Alison shuddered. She dreaded what her mother would say if she came home without work. The

20

best day of the week was when she brought back her wages and handed them over to Cora, who was always so pleased to see the money that she'd almost be pleasant to her youngest daughter. It was the only thing that didn't make her feel completely worthless, and she knew how much her mother relied on her contribution.

There was a commotion at the door as a young woman rushed in. Vera Jewell was cutting it fine as usual, shaking out her shiny curls and unbuttoning her fashionable mac in one fast and fluid movement. She caught Alison's eye and grinned. They were almost the same age and Alison had managed a few conversations with her without being rebuffed, which was a welcome novelty. She wondered if she might be able to make a proper friend of her if she could only hold her nerve.

Vera joined the group of women as they made their way along to the meeting. Alison was trying to look on the bright side. Maybe it was a new rule they all had to know about, or a change to the machinery. She hoped it wasn't going to be something difficult. Learning something new always made her extra clumsy. Once she got the hang of something she was fine but the thought of everyone looking at her for the first few goes made her nervous, then her hands would shake and she'd make a mess of it.

'Morning, ladies,' said the foreman, even more careworn than usual. 'I won't keep you waiting. Some of you will have heard the rumours going round that we've lost the Pagett's contract. I'd love to be able to tell you it's a load of tosh but sad to say, it's true.' There was a gasp at this. Clearly it

21

was news to most of them. 'Right,' he went on briskly, obviously keen to get it over with. Sweat was beginning to appear on his balding head. 'You're not daft. You'll have worked out what that means – we can't keep all of you on without those orders coming in. So it's last in, first out.' He glanced at a piece of paper he'd been holding. 'Mrs Tullis, Miss Jewell, Miss Butler. That's you. Come into my office, please. The rest of you – back to work.' He turned and opened his office door.

Vera turned and pulled a face but Alison shut her eyes in horror. This couldn't be happening. What was she going to do now? It was all she could do not to cry out in despair.

'You all right, love?' asked Betty, briefly touching her arm in the kindly way she had with everybody. 'You've gone all pale. Don't take on. You'll be fine, a hard worker like you, young, fit and healthy. You'll have no problem getting something else. An' anyway, you'll be better off away from the likes of that Ron Small.'

Alison made an effort to pull herself together and nodded grimly. But a little voice inside her head told her it wasn't going to be quite as simple as that.

'I might've flamin' well known it was too good to last,' snapped Cora as she came through the door. 'Useless lump like you. What was it you did to get the sack? Knock something over, clumsy great thing that you are?' Cora hadn't had to wait until she got home to hear the news. One of the blessings of working in the newsagent's was she

22

managed to pick up all the gossip as soon as it started, and Vera Jewell's mother had been straight in there the moment she learnt her own daughter was out of a job. Winnie Jewell had been incensed on Vera's behalf, wanting to make an official complaint, claiming the foreman had been unfair and that her daughter was an innocent victim who deserved to be taken back. But Cora wasn't having any of it. Secretly she was surprised Alison had lasted as long as she did. She was also sure that Vera Jewell, whose lipstick was always bright scarlet, couldn't be described as innocent in any way.

'I didn't do anything,' Alison protested, going to put the kettle on in the vain hope a cup of tea would keep her mother quiet. 'It was last in first out. Betty Shawcross said I was a hard worker. I'll get a good reference. I didn't do anything wrong.'

'Well, you needn't think you can sit around here on your arse all day,' Cora warned her. 'You've got to earn your keep and more besides. I'll need your wages more than ever if that sister of yours insists on marrying that good-looking layabout across the road. She says she's in love! What's that got to do with anythin'?' she snorted in derision as her youngest passed her a cup.

Alison raised her eyes to the ceiling but said nothing. Even if she did get another job, and that would be a miracle, she'd have to shell out towards Hazel's wedding. As if her cruel sister deserved any help towards her perfect big day.

'Neville works hard, Mum,' she pointed out. 'And he's really keen on Hazel, anyone can see that.' She might not like the idea of helping to-wards the wedding but she had nothing against the

23

young man himself – at least he was never mean to her.

'He works in the paint factory,' Cora said. 'Where's he going to go with that? He'll be stuck in the same place on the same pay year after year, and your sister won't like that one bit. I raised her to expect more. Course, you can expect that, but Hazel...' Cora broke off, gripped with disappointment for her beloved middle daughter. She could have done so much better for herself. Cora knew that Hazel's expectations were high and feared Neville Parrot was never going to be able to make her happy, whether she loved him or not. Clearing her throat, she pulled herself together. 'She could have done like our Linda. Look what she's managed – to get away from here, out into the fresh air, husband who could run his own business one day. That's what I scrimped and saved for. To give you girls a better start.' Grimly she set her cup down on the chipped Formica table and slumped back, fearing the future.

Early on Saturday morning there was something to cheer Cora when she heard a knock at the door and, opening it, in stepped Linda, holding her daughter by the hand. Cora gasped in amazed delight. Unplanned visits from her eldest were few and far between.

'Say hello to Granny and Auntie Alison, Junie!' Linda smiled at the effect her arrival had had. 'Isn't it lovely to see them so soon after our last visit?' She began to take off her new winter coat. 'Sorry to just drop in on you but I had to come as soon as I heard Hazel's news.'

Cora leaned over to kiss the little girl on her head

of golden curls. 'This is a nice surprise for Granny! Didn't think I'd be seeing you for ages.' Slowly she arched herself back upright, struggling to hide her pained expression from her granddaughter. She didn't want to let on just how difficult it was to bend to greet her.

'We couldn't stay home after getting your letter,' Linda assured her mother. She smiled brightly at Alison. 'Is that kettle on? I'd love a cuppa.'

Alison quickly refilled the battered old kettle and set it to boil once more. Having her big sister drop by was a real pleasure. Smiling back, she took in her eldest sister's appearance. Even though Hazel was the prettiest of them, people always noticed Linda. Her thick brown hair was in a long bob, and her warm brown eyes sparkled at seeing her younger sister. She had on a neat twinset with pearl buttons that clearly hadn't come from the local market, which was where the rest of the family were forced to buy their clothes.

'So tell me all about Hazel's news!' she demanded. Alison obligingly filled her in on as many details about the engagement as she could, and Linda nodded approvingly. Finally she was satisfied.

'How are things otherwise?' she asked, setting down her cup. 'What's changed round here since last week?'

Sighing, Alison knew she had to confess her latest disaster and decided she'd better get the announcement over and done with before her mother could give her version of events. 'Bad news yesterday,' she said sadly. 'I lost my job. They had to lay three of us off because our biggest customer

25

cancelled their order.'

'Oh, that's really bad luck.' Linda went round the cramped kitchen table to hug her sister. 'You must feel terrible. But it can't have been your fault, so nobody can blame you.'

'No, I know, and that's what everyone at work said,' Alison replied. 'But I can't help feeling I'm to blame.'

Nobody had heard Hazel coming downstairs, but now she stood on the threshold of the room, her expression thunderous. 'Blame?' she repeated. 'Blame for what? What've you done now?'

'Nothing, I've done nothing,' said Alison desperately, knowing what was to come. 'But as I was last to join the factory, I'm out of a job.'

Hazel stood stock-still and silent but her eyes were flashing.

'Hazel, we came all the way to congratulate you as soon as we heard your news,' Linda said hurriedly. 'Didn't we, June? Say congratulations to Auntie Hazel.'

'Con ... con...' the little girl began, moving across to her aunt, confident of another hug.

But Hazel barely registered her niece, or her big sister. She stared in disgust at Alison. 'God, you really are useless,' she hissed. 'How dare you? You bloody well knew that we need every penny for my wedding. You did this on purpose, didn't you? That's exactly the sort of spiteful thing you'd do. Well, I'm not standin' for it.' She started to edge her way across the kitchen.

'Hazel!' Linda cried. 'Don't be like that. It's nobody's fault. You leave Alison alone. Really, stop it, you're frightening June.' The little girl had

26

backed away and was now cowering behind a chair, unable to understand why everything had gone so wrong so quickly.

'Now, Hazel, we know you're disappointed,' said Cora, unable to be cross with her middle daughter. 'Alison will get another job and we'll sort things out. Don't be such a daft mare and calm down.'

But there was no stopping Hazel when she was in a temper, and this time she felt she had just cause. She flew at her younger sister, and if Linda and Cora hadn't been there to hold her back she would have knocked her to the ground. 'You make me sick!' she shouted. 'All you had to do was hang on to that flamin' job for a few more months but you couldn't even do that, could you? What's the point of you? Why are you even alive? We'd be better off without you!'

An ear-piercing cry filled the air as June began to howl, not sure what was going on, but deeply upset that the people she loved most in the world were so angry with each other.

Alison made good her escape while she could, before Hazel broke free and came after her again. She knew from plenty of past experience that this was the safest thing to do. If only she could escape, like Linda had. She often dreamed of someone sweeping her off her feet, like in the magazines some of the women had brought to work. But what man would ever rescue her?

Chapter Three

'You should've seen her,' said Hazel later that evening. She sat up straight against the faded velvet banquette. 'Standin' there saying she wasn't to blame. Honestly, you've no idea what it's like livin' with her, puttin' up with her day in day out.'

'We're going to be fine,' said Neville, trying to calm Hazel down. He'd dressed up for his night out, in his most stylish shirt and jacket. He was a good-looking young man with thick dark hair and laughter in his eyes. He didn't mind that he was shorter than Hazel – most men were. 'We've been through all this. I'll get some extra shifts. Nobody likes the night shift, they're always asking us to sign on for extra hours then. Pay's better an' all. You'll have your big day.' His eyes shone at the idea of the most gorgeous woman in Battersea walking down the aisle to marry him. Sometimes he still couldn't believe his luck. The moment he saw Hazel he knew she was the one for him and now she'd agreed to be his wife. Life didn't get any better than this.

'I know.' Hazel made an effort to calm down. Neville loved her, and that was what mattered. He was the best-looking man she knew and even better, his family were new to the area so didn't know what sort of childhood she'd had. She shivered at the memories of hand-me-downs, always being short of food, always cold, her mother permanently pinched from worry about the rent and whether they'd be evicted. All the kids she'd been at school with knew about it and would have teased her more if they'd dared, but she'd always had a fierce temper and nobody tried it twice. The worst thing was when one of the girls in her class recognised Hazel wearing one of her own dresses that had been given away as jumble. Hazel had had to put up with weeks of snide comments, bringing home the truth that while her classmates weren't well-off, she was the lowest of the low. She dreaded it when these scenes from the past forced themselves into her mind and the feelings of shame came rushing back. She hated this; she liked to be in control of events and the recollections of that childhood when she'd been ashamed so often threatened to overwhelm her. She remembered how it was only when she'd started to grow up and fill out a bit that the jibes stopped. Suddenly everyone wanted to get to know her – or at least the boys did. But Hazel wasn't stupid. She knew she'd be better off waiting for the right one and didn't allow any of the others to take liberties. Now she'd found him, and she was going to put the misery of her past behind her. Neville was exactly what she'd been waiting for.

She took a sip of her sherry as she glanced around. 'Are you sure this is all right, me being seen out in a pub? I don't look like a tart in here, do I?'

'You never look like a tart,' Neville said. 'You look like a proper lady. And that's what a lady would drink. Why, don't you like it?'

'Not sure.' Hazel thought it tasted like woodchips soaked in sugar but wasn't going to say so. She knew Linda had sherry at home, and she was doing all right for herself, so this is what she would have to learn to like. She'd always refused to go into a public bar, but this was a secluded little snug. She couldn't have sat at home after what had happened, and Neville's family were lovely but there were a lot of them in a house not much bigger than her own. As well as his parents, he had a sister almost the same age as him and a younger brother who never shut up, and who shared Neville's cramped bedroom. When she and Neville got married she had every intention of ending up somewhere better than either of their families. She wasn't exactly sure how they'd do it but she had every hope that they'd get away and improve their lot. He'd promised her he'd give her anything she wanted and she trusted him to mean it. Somehow they would find a way to make it happen. Just because they were young and only starting out didn't mean they'd live like their parents on Ennis Street for the rest of their lives.

'Can't beat a pint of beer,' smiled Neville. 'But when I start my overtime, I'll cut down. That way we'll save even more. You're going to look like a princess.'

'Really?' Hazel suddenly felt like crying. He was so good to her.

'My princess. You'll knock 'em dead, you'll be so beautiful, and I'll be the proudest man in Battersea. Just you wait and see.'

'Oh Neville, we're going to be so happy.' Hazel couldn't help a sob. The events of the day had been too much, but soon she'd be married to this man who loved her and spoilt her, and she was going to have the sort of life she'd always dreamed of. The future was bright, and nobody was going to take that away from her.

Despite her aches and pains, Cora loved her job at the corner shop. It was the best she'd ever had. She could sit down behind the counter when they weren't busy and best of all she got to hear every piece of gossip before anyone else. Her boss was delighted to have such a reliable employee and pretty well let her run the place as she thought fit.

This morning she'd made sure the paperboys left on time for their rounds with all the right newspapers and magazines, and was about to start on the ledger. If she didn't keep it up to date, it took ages to add everything up at the end of the day, and she wanted to get home as soon as possible. She didn't want any more fights breaking out between Hazel and Alison. Hazel had admitted she'd been overwrought, what with wanting all the help she could get to pay for the perfect wedding, but Cora knew it could all flare up again if she wasn't there to keep the peace. For the hundredth time she cursed Alison under her breath for losing that factory job.

The bell over the door rang as Winnie Jewell came in, followed by a sharp gust of freezing wind.

'Shut that!' Cora exclaimed. 'That's coming straight from the Arctic, that is.'

'At least you're warm in here,' shivered Winnie, rubbing her chapped hands. 'What've you got

31

round that counter, a heater? I can smell the paraffin from here.'

'You need it, I can tell you.' Cora was in no mood to take nonsense from the woman. 'What can I do for you? Got your delivery all right, did you?'

'I fancied something a bit extra,' said Winnie. She patted her plaid headscarf. 'Now our Vera's at home in the daytime I thought I'd get her a *Radio Times* so she can have a bit of a treat, listen to programmes in the afternoon. Not that she'll be doing that for long. She got herself a new job yesterday, up Arding and Hobbs. She starts next week. Cleaner place than that old factory and a better class of people.' She stopped. 'No offence, of course.'

'None taken.' Cora would bide her time and get the woman back for that one. Even if Alison left a lot to be desired, Winnie Jewell was hardly a cut above the rest. As for her daughter Vera, she wondered if Arding and Hobbs knew what they were in for.

'Here you go.' She reached across and took a *Radio Times* from the pile.

'Thanks.' Winnie began to flick through the pages. 'Might as well take a look here where it's warm. Vera's favourite is "The Goon Show" but I think it's a load of old nonsense. Here we are, there's one this week. Don't know what she sees in it but it makes her laugh.'

'I have to agree with you there,' said Cora. 'Nothing but smut and stupid noises. You'd think the BBC had better things to put on. Not that my girls have much time to listen to such things.'

32

'Oh?' said Winnie. 'I'd have thought your Alison would have all the time in the world these days.'

Cora hated it when anyone caught her out. 'No, because we're all going to be working every spare hour God sends to make sure our Hazel has a perfect wedding.' She enjoyed the look of surprise on the other woman's face. News must not have got round yet. 'Yes, Hazel has got engaged to Neville Parrot, and we're very happy for them.'

'Oh, he's a nice-looking bloke,' said Winnie with approval. 'Polite too. She's a lucky girl.'

'And he's a very lucky lad,' said Cora instantly. 'Our Hazel could have had her pick, but it's young love, and who am I to stand in their way.'

The two women fell silent for a moment. Then Winnie remembered something. 'Where's she getting her dress?'

'We haven't decided yet,' Cora replied. She wasn't about to start discussing the finances of the big day, or the fact that the dress would have to be home-made with material from the market.

'Well, you know that shop that does wedding dresses and evening wear down towards Wandsworth?' Winnie asked. 'Always got a lovely frock in the window? Well, they're a girl short and Vera was going to see them about it, but then she got the job at Arding and Hobbs. That's much closer of course. But would Alison be interested?'

'She might,' said Cora, trying not to seem too keen. 'I'll tell her about it. That's if she hasn't found something already, of course.'

'Of course,' said Winnie, playing along. 'Well, better not keep you. I'll be off.' She struggled to open the door against the freezing gale.

Cora sighed as the door slammed shut. Winnie could be irritating and she had a massive blind spot when it came to her wayward daughter but it was good of her to mention the job vacancy. She would definitely make sure Alison went to see about it tomorrow. Even if it was very different to what the girl was used to, it couldn't be that hard. She might even get a staff discount. Now that would be very useful. Smiling with anticipation, Cora pulled the big ledger back towards her.

Next day Alison trudged down the hill towards Wandsworth, wondering if this was a good idea. She hadn't had much choice. Her mother had come home full of Winnie's suggestion and what a good thing it would be if she got the job at the dress shop. Hazel had leapt on it immediately, delighted at the idea of such elegant clothes at bargain prices.

'But you don't know that,' Alison had protested. 'They might not agree. They'd probably still be too expensive. And I haven't even got the job yet.'

'Don't be such a killjoy,' Hazel had flared. 'Don't you want me to look smart? I could get a wedding dress and a going-away outfit.'

'Going-away outfit?' This was the first Cora had heard of it. 'Going away where? And why do you need a special outfit for it? You've got a perfectly good coat already.'

'Oh Mum, that won't be any good.' Hazel pulled a face. 'Everyone has a special suit to go away in. And of course Neville will take me somewhere, he just ain't said where yet. I couldn't possibly wear my coat. It's not even new. I need something smarter. Did you see what Linda had on the other day? That was new this winter, and she didn't even have anything special to wear it for.'

'That's because her Terry earns a decent wage,' snapped Cora. 'I keep telling you, but you don't listen. When you get to Linda's station in life, you can have all these luxuries. The rest of us have to get by as best we can.'

Alison cringed as she remembered how Hazel had flounced out, leaving her to deal with Cora, who of course said it was all her fault. So now the pressure really was on her not only to get the job, but to get a big discount as well. Anything less would leave her mother disappointed and her sister furious.

The hill down to Wandsworth was longer than she remembered. Maybe she should have taken a bus but until she knew when her next wage packet would be in, Alison didn't want to spend anything more than she had to. She didn't want to be accused of sponging off the household. At least she didn't have to worry about the schoolboys around here, as it wasn't likely she'd run into anyone she knew. She thought some people were looking at her oddly but couldn't be sure as she avoided meeting their eyes. As usual, she withdrew into her shell, making no contact with anybody – the only way she felt safe. There was no point in going looking for trouble, especially when it seemed to find her so often.

By the time she reached the dress shop, she had blisters on both feet. She stood outside, mesmerised by the frock in the front window. She'd never seen anything like it. A slim mannequin was placed against a background of deep purple velvet, which made the silvery whiteness of the frock even more special. It had a full skirt and the bodice was embroidered with tiny white stars, only visible when she looked very closely. Glancing down at her own dull skirt poking out beneath her gabardine raincoat, she felt drabber than ever.

Gathering her courage, she pushed open the door and stepped inside.

The place smelt of flowers. Alison turned around and noticed a big display of roses arranged in a cut-glass vase.

'Beautiful, aren't they?' said a voice, and an extremely elegant woman came out of the back room, brushing an imaginary piece of lint from her dark sleeve. 'Can I help you?'

Alison was at a loss for words. She tried to picture herself in the woman's place, with eyebrows so finely drawn and hair sprayed into neat waves.

The woman tried again. 'Can I help you?'

Alison wished the floor would open up and swallow her. Finally she said, 'It's about the job.'

'The job?'

'My mum was told you had a job going.'

'Does she want to work in this establishment?'

'No,' Alison said. 'It's me. I need a job.'

The woman's expression didn't change but she looked her up and down, very slowly. The silence seemed to go on forever. Finally she said: 'You?'

Alison nodded, blushing.

'Have you any experience at this sort of thing? Are you familiar with this quality of product?'

'No ... not really,' Alison stumbled, 'but you

see, my sister's getting married, and she wants a wedding dress and we thought...'

'I see,' said the woman. She brushed her sleeve again, quite deliberately. 'Well, I'm not sure that you'd be suitable. I don't think you're quite what my customers expect when they come for a fitting.'

Alison wasn't sure what to make of that. 'Why? What do you mean?'

The woman sighed. 'We sell only the finest formal wear. Our customers expect to be assisted by someone who exhibits everything that is associated with such products – elegance, finesse. To be blunt, when I look at you, that is not what I see.'

Alison felt like running out there and then but forced herself to stand her ground. 'I can get different clothes.'

'No, no, no,' said the woman. 'Or rather, yes, that would help, but it's what you do with what you wear as much as how you wear it. What would be the point of giving you a couture jacket? You'd never notice the shape of it if you stand like that all the time.'

'I know I'm too tall,' Alison began, 'but I can't help...'

'That's not what I meant,' cut in the woman. 'Your height is an asset. Many would love to be as tall as you. But when you round your shoulders and stare at your feet all the time you ruin the whole effect. You must project style and poise. Style and poise.'

Alison looked at her as if she was speaking another language.

'So you see, my dear,' said the woman, moving towards the door, 'until you understand what I'm talking about, and I can see that you don't, this is not the place for you. I must detain you no longer. I wish you luck in your search for more suitable employment.' With that, she ushered Alison back onto the freezing pavement and shut the door firmly behind her.

Alison was totally humiliated. It was one thing to be insulted by her family, the local children and the men at the factory. That was bad, but she was used to it. This felt different. She couldn't help her height. She couldn't help having ugly, worn-out clothes. Staring ahead up the hill, she knew she'd have no choice but to drag herself back up to the top, in the useless shoes that weren't made for walking, and which had been a waste of time.

Close to despair, Alison knew that she should see if any other places around here had cards in the window advertising jobs, as she wasn't down Wandsworth way very often, but she'd lost the will to search. She knew she couldn't go straight home – even if Cora was still at work, her mother would be bound to hear from someone that her youngest had been in all afternoon and then there'd be a huge row and she'd be accused of not trying. Her mother and sister had a point – she was as useless as they said, and without the kind women at the factory nobody was going to make her believe otherwise. She couldn't go to a café – she dared not spend the money for a cup of tea or a bun. There was nothing for it but to walk the chilly streets until it grew dark, and then she would have

38

to face Hazel's anger when she told her there'd be no cut-price wedding dress after all.

'Drink up, Nev!'

The news had got out about his engagement and all his mates from the paint factory who weren't on the late shift had insisted on taking Neville to the pub to celebrate.

'Commiserate, more like,' said Dennis Banks, one of the older ones, who loved to tell them all about his success with different women every weekend. Neville grinned. He didn't believe half the tales – some of them sounded physically impossible. But he wasn't going to turn down the offer of a free pint.

'Yeah, what d'you want to get yourself shackled for so young?' demanded Nobby. Nobby was prematurely bald and had slightly bulging eyes, so Neville reckoned he hadn't had too many chances of being shackled himself.

'Nobby, ain't you seen her?' said Bill Stevens. 'You should be so lucky. She's a real looker, is Nev's bird. Oh, she'll tire him out, she will. He'll be a shadow of his former self. But he'll be happy with it. Won't you, Nev?'

'Never happier,' beamed Neville. It was true. He'd had two and a half pints, he was engaged to the most beautiful woman in Battersea, and here were all his mates, wishing him well. They were in the smoky public bar, and things were just beginning to get raucous, but he didn't mind. He felt as if he didn't have a care in the world.

'Do you know what to do on the big night?' Dennis went on. 'Shall I give you some tips? I got

39

lots of those...'

'Yeah, like don't let your sister go down a dark alley with Dennis,' interrupted Bill, setting down his glass on the worn wooden counter. 'Another, young Nev?'

'Don't mind if I do.' Nev ignored all the nudging and tried to focus on the pint before him as all the lights from the bar and brass from the surrounds seemed to be shining extra brightly. He wasn't really worried about his wedding night, even though he hadn't had much experience. His mates assumed because he was a good-looking bloke that he'd had plenty of women but it wasn't true. He'd been cooped up sharing a bedroom with his younger brother for most of his life and there hadn't exactly been many opportunities to break away, and God alone knew there wasn't a spare inch of space at Hazel's house. Even though she had a room to herself there was no chance of a bit of slap and tickle with her mother and sister living in such close quarters. Still, he loved her and she loved him, so what could go wrong? He certainly wasn't going to be asking Dennis for tips.

'Not in a hurry to get married, are you?' Nobby asked. 'No big rush, is there? You ain't expecting the patter of tiny feet?'

'Get away, Nobby.' Nev pretended to be offended. 'My Hazel's a respectable girl. There won't be no hurried wedding for her. She wants the best. And I'm going to give it to her.'

'Oh, we'd all give it to her,' Bill laughed. Some of the others joined in, especially those who appreciated Hazel's finer points.

'That's enough, boys,' said Frank Dalby, their

40

foreman. 'Leave the lad to have his drink. No call for insulting the lady. Time enough for insults when you're married, and I should know.'

Frank's wife was famous for giving as good as she got, but nobody really had a bad word to say about Marian Dalby, who had been known to bake fruit cakes for her husband to take in to the lads on late shift, in case they got hungry as the hours of the night wore on. Nev thought that if his marriage was as happy as Frank's then he'd have no cause for complaint. Even so, he couldn't quite see Hazel cooking for his workmates.

But that didn't matter. Here was Dennis giving him a new pint, there were all his friends raising their glasses to him, and Hazel was going to be his wife. Neville Parrot was on top of the world.

Chapter Four

Hazel was on her lunch break from the café where she worked. She wasn't really hungry, as she'd had a huge bacon sandwich after the breakfast rush had died down. 'Can't have you wasting away before your big day,' her boss had said. Not much danger of that, thought Hazel. Still, she knew Neville liked her curves, and it was up to her to make the most of them.

Now she found herself wandering towards the street market, which was busy with shoppers out for a bargain. Housewives crowded round the food stalls, some with small children. One boy, whose

41

socks were falling down, reached for an apple and his mother immediately smacked him on the ear. 'I've told you before,' she shouted. 'Put that down now.'

Hazel shook her head and walked on. She hadn't had many apples as a kid, or at least not ones to eat as a treat when they were out shopping. Cora made apple crumble, eking out the fruit with lots of oats, but there hadn't been the money to spare for much else. Not that there had been much else available, thanks to the war and food rationing. She hurried away as the boy began to cry.

There were several stalls selling clothing and bolts of material, and she couldn't help but be drawn to one of them. 'Morning, Hazel,' said the stallholder. It was Joe Philpott, who'd known her family for years. 'Is the good news true, then? You and Neville are getting hitched?' He was a big man with a round face, and she'd never seen him anything other than smiling. How he did it, she couldn't imagine, standing out here in all weathers, dealing with grumpy customers, half of which were always trying to get something for nothing. It was bad enough in the café but at least you were indoors, and always had the kitchen to escape to. Out here, there was no avoiding any-one.

'That's right,' she said. 'He popped the question and I said yes.'

'Has he given you a ring then?' Joe wanted to know.

'Not yet, we're going to choose something to-gether,' Hazel said hurriedly. She didn't want any-one thinking Neville was too cheap to buy her one.

'He didn't want to risk getting the wrong size. I'd have been really disappointed if he'd done that.'

'Quite right too,' Joe agreed. He stamped his feet on the cold ground. 'Will you be looking to do a spot of dressmaking before the day itself? Who's doing your dress? Are you having brides-maids?'

Hazel bit back her irritation at his persistence. She was careful to keep her temper in check in public and liked to present a respectable front. There was no point in being rude to Joe, par-ticularly if she might have to come to him for cut-price material in the near future. She desperately wanted a proper long white dress from a shop but since Alison had failed to get that blasted job, letting them all down, she knew it might not happen. Yet again she cursed her sister for being so useless.

'Not sure yet,' she said blithely. 'We only just got engaged. We haven't decided on many of the details. But I expect we'll be needing something. Will you keep your eyes out if anything good comes along?'

'It would be my pleasure,' Joe assured her, smil-ing more widely than ever. He watched as Hazel turned and made her way further along the mar-ket. What a fine-looking young woman she was. That Neville was one lucky sod. He'd better treat her right. God knows that family had been through terrible times when the girls were little. Still, look at Hazel now. It just showed that even if life dealt you an unfair hand, you could still come out fighting. That's what he believed himself. It's what kept him coming back to his stall on the coldest days of the year.

Hazel paused at the hardware stall, trying to remember if her mother needed anything for the kitchen. A familiar face looked at her and she had to think for a moment who it was. Then it came to her – it was one of Neville's colleagues from the paint factory. Bill, that was his name. 'Hello,' she said.

'Congratulations, Hazel,' said Bill, putting down the toolkit he'd been inspecting. 'Good to know you're making an honest man of that Neville at last.'

'Someone's got to do it,' she said. 'Not at work today, then?'

'I'm on the late shift,' Bill explained. 'Pay's better. Not so many distractions either. Cuts into your social life but I reckon it's worth it.'

'Good idea,' said Hazel. She pushed back a wave of her auburn hair. 'Neville's going to do more late shifts and overtime so we can save up.'

'Yes, he told me he was thinking of doing that,' said Bill. He glanced at his watch. 'Nice to see you but must be going.' He waved and moved on. If he had a woman like Hazel to go home to he wouldn't be working lates. Neville must be mad, leaving a bird like that to amuse herself every evening. Still, it wasn't his worry.

Hazel noticed a set of knives going cheap and reached across to take a better look at them. They seemed like decent quality for the bargain price and she knew their old ones at home were in a sorry state, with loose handles and blades worn thin from years of sharpening. She'd take them back as a peace offering to her mum for having

44

lost her temper in front of her niece. She was sorry about that now, and hadn't wanted to frighten the little girl. Bringing these home would show she could think of others, not just of herself. Pleased at having such a clever idea, Hazel got the stall-holder to round the price down still further and set off back to the café, carrying her bargain.

Someone pushed open the door to the shop and set the bell ringing. Cora hurriedly looked up from the counter, where she'd been reading the *Daily Mail*. She'd been enjoying the story of the new princess in Monaco. She'd always been a Grace Kelly fan and now the former film star had a daughter who was born a princess. Sighing, Cora put from her mind her worries about her own family.

Then she realised she recognised the figure who'd just walked in.

'Fred Chapman!' she exclaimed. 'Haven't seen you for ages. Where've you been hidin' yourself?'

'Cora Butler, as I live and breathe,' said Fred, wheezing as the warm air hit him. He was a short man with a balding head and a face red from the chilly January weather. His hands were large and coarse, from heavy lifting and hard work, but his smile was genuine and lit up his plain face. 'Didn't realise you worked here. You don't look a day older than when I last saw you.'

'Couldn't have been that long ago then, Fred.' Cora gave him a straight look. 'But how have you been keeping? Have you still got that butcher's shop on Falcon Road? And how's your mother?'

Fred's expression changed. 'That'll be why you

45

haven't seen me in a while,' he said. 'Mother died last year and I've been trying to get things sorted ever since. It hasn't been easy, what with it being just me to do everything and keep the shop going too. But she hadn't been well for ages so I couldn't have wanted her to go on the way she was.'

'A blessing, then,' said Cora. Privately she thought it was just as well. Old Mrs Chapman had been a proper harridan, bullying her mild-mannered son and taking out her disappointments on anybody stupid enough to go near her. Cora remembered many years ago, when her husband had still been alive, going round to the flat above the shop and getting her head bitten off for nothing more than saying hello. Jack Butler had been good friends with Fred Chapman before the war, despite being a few years older, but that had made no difference to the spiteful old woman. Looking at Fred, she wondered where the time had gone, realising that he must be in his early forties now.

'Maybe,' said Fred, rubbing his hands and looking around. 'So how long you been here, then, Cora?'

'The job came up just when me back got too stiff to take in the laundry, and I have to say it suits me down to the ground,' beamed Cora. 'And how's business these days?'

'Not so bad,' said Fred, who was never keen to talk shop when he was away from work. He didn't like to blow his own trumpet for fear it would change his luck – his business had flourished in the years since rationing ended. The reason he was away from the premises now was that he was having some new fridges installed, the very latest models, but he didn't imagine anyone would be very interested in that. 'You should stop by sometime, Cora. Are you still getting your meat from the market? You should come to me instead. I won't charge you the earth, you being an old friend and everything.'

'That's very kind of you, Fred,' said Cora, delighted at the thought of a bargain piece of good-quality meat. 'My girls eat me out of house and home. I've got a day off early next week so maybe I'll come and see you then.'

'I shall look forward to it.' Fred reached into his pocket for his change. 'I only came in here for a pack of Lucky Strikes. So bumping into you again is an unexpected bonus.' He took the cigarettes and offered one to Cora.

'No thanks, can't stand the things,' she replied. There had been no money for luxuries like tobacco for many years and now she'd got out of the habit. Besides, she didn't want to end up wheezing like Fred. Shaking her head as he went through the door, she wondered how someone as sour and bitter as Mrs Chapman could have such a friendly son. Pity he looked the way he did. Then again, she should know all about children who didn't resemble their parents. She turned back to the story of Princess Grace with her new daughter, a world away from the overcrowded house and the useless out-of-work girl in it.

Alison had forced herself to have another attempt to find work. She'd gone up and down all the roads around Clapham Junction, trying the shops, the offices, even the station itself. It wouldn't be so bad to be behind the scenes somewhere, in a back room where she didn't have to face the public. She had her reference from the factory and it said she was a reliable worker, but it did no good. Nobody was hiring, or that's what they said as soon as they saw her. 'Try again in a few weeks, love,' said the woman in the ticket office. 'You never know. Don't give up.'

Easy for her to say, thought Alison. She had a warm office, friendly people to chat to and she probably had a loving family at home as well. Why did some people have all the luck? When she'd been younger she'd thought all families were like her own but now she knew differently. She wished her mother and Hazel would stop picking on her and yet she knew she was so awkward she probably deserved it all.

Rounding a corner she was dismayed to find two of the paperboys from the newsagent's coming towards her. 'Look, it's horse face!' shouted one, pulling his hand out of his pocket to point at her. A shower of coins fell onto the pavement.

'Horse face, horse face!' called his friend, pretending to gallop. 'Imagine seeing that when you look in the mirror! Nay-y-y-y!'

'Why aren't you at school?' demanded Alison, too fed up to ignore them. 'What's all that money? Have you been stealing from my mum's shop? She'll get the police on you if you do that.' Even though Cora wouldn't care about them teasing her daughter, she'd be down like a ton of bricks if any of them had been putting their hands in the till.

'No we ain't. We won the money in the penny arcade and don't go telling your mum any differ-

48

ent,' said one boy menacingly as he shoved her against a wall, while the other one scooped up the coins.

Alison pushed him away and grimly turned for home. Her sleeve had ripped where the boy had gripped it but she already knew that she wouldn't say anything – not because she was frightened, it was far from the worst thing that had happened to her, but because she was ashamed. Being pushed around by a boy half her size and half her age – she didn't want anyone to know about it. All it had done was make a miserable day even worse. But the most worrying thing was, she couldn't see how her life could ever get any better.

Chapter Five

'Good weekend, Nev?' asked Nobby on Monday morning. 'Were you out down the pub? Making the most of your final months being young, free and single?'

Neville rubbed his eyes. He didn't want to admit it but working back-to-back shifts over the past couple of days had been more tiring than he'd thought. He'd had hardly any sleep and, worse still, he'd hardly seen Hazel. But it was going to be worth it, to give her the wedding she so badly wanted. 'Did a spot of overtime,' he said. 'Saves me spendin' the cash down the boozer.'

Nobby raised his eyebrows. He didn't believe in working weekends. Nothing kept him from the pub on Friday and Saturday nights; that was the whole point of going to work – to have the money to sink a few pints with his mates. 'Don't you go wasting your youth,' he told the younger man. 'These are the best years of your life, these are. Plenty of time for overtime when you're hitched.'

'I'll bear that in mind,' said Neville, keen to get away from Nobby, who he found annoying at the best of times, even when he wasn't half-asleep on his feet. He turned to hang up his coat. 'Right, back to me usual station.' He dragged himself over to his bench.

Nobby pulled a face. Seemed as if young Neville wasn't cut out to be the life and soul of the party after all. 'Suit yourself,' he muttered.

'What's up?' asked Bill, unwinding his scarf in Chelsea colours.

Nobby shook his head. 'Probably nothing,' he said. 'That Neville's missed a weekend down the pub so he could do overtime. Funny way of enjoying yourself, ain't it?'

'That'll be his bird,' said Bill. 'I bumped into her last week down the market and she said he was going to do more shifts. They're saving up.'

'Bloody hell, he don't want to be dancing to her tune already.' Nobby didn't like the sound of that. 'Time enough for all that, that's what I told him.'

'I take it you were down the Queen Vic as usual, then,' said Bill, not wanting to start the week with Nobby in a bad temper. 'I went to the game. Bloody freezing it was too.'

'That's why you want to spend your weekend in a nice warm pub,' Nobby told him. 'You take my

50

advice next time and read about your game in the paper somewhere where you can sit by the fire and have a drop of beer.'

'That's called my own front room, mate,' said Bill cheerfully. 'But love my mum as I do, you can't beat the terraces on a Saturday. We'll agree to differ, shall we?'

Nobby pretended to agree. But he wasn't happy.

Cora stood on the sawdust-covered floor of Fred Chapman's butcher's shop, nodding her head in approval. 'You ain't done bad for yourself even with all the upset of your mum passing away,' she said. 'You keep this place in good nick, I'll say that much.'

Fred nodded as he wiped his hands on his butcher's apron. He could tell it was tighter than ever but try as he might, his waistline kept on growing. Not like Cora. She was skinny as a rake, always had been. 'Now you need feeding up a bit,' he said. 'How about a nice piece of brisket? Or some chuck steak?'

'My girls would be thrilled,' said Cora. Usually she would have offal or oxtail, and make it go further by cooking lots of pearl barley or potatoes with it. What a good job Fred had needed that pack of cigarettes when he did.

'Look, you can have this bit and I'll add the rest of the tray as well.' Fred leant over the counter and began putting the bright red meat into a bag. 'This was left over as a customer ordered it but never turned up. So you'd be doing me a favour.' It was a lie but Cora didn't need to know that. He

51

could tell she wouldn't want charity. 'And how are the girls? They must be all grown up now.'

'Linda's married, living down in Kent, and got a three-year-old,' said Cora, her face lighting up at the thought of her beloved June. 'She's done well for herself. Hazel's just got engaged, nice enough boy but never going to set the world on fire. Still, he loves her and that counts for somethin'. As for Alison...' She looked heavenwards. 'May God forgive me, I don't know what to do with that girl. She's seventeen now. She's not long got the push from the factory she was at and can't get nothing else, just when we got the expense of the wedding to cope with. She don't seem to have no get up and go. Just sits around moping.'

'Really?' Fred tried to think of the last time he'd seen Cora's daughters. It would have been well before his mother had her final illness. Even so, he didn't remember Alison being useless. He could tell from Cora's expression that this was a sore point and didn't want to get himself involved in something he'd regret; it wasn't like him to make rash decisions. But the coincidence seemed too good to miss.

'Really,' Cora said bitterly. 'Though I says it as shouldn't, she's got no vim at all. I can't understand who she takes after. You know what Jack was like.'

'I do,' said Fred at once. 'He was a good man, Cora, a man in a million. He was like a big brother to me and I know how tough it was for you when he was killed.' He paused and made up his mind. Jack had stood up for him on many

52

occasions when he was growing up; now was his chance to pay him back by helping his family. 'I just found out my shop girl is leaving Battersea. Says her folks want to get away.'

'Can't blame them,' said Cora instantly. 'I'd do the same if I could.'

'But it leaves me short,' Fred went on. 'I can't run this place on my own, not and keep up standards. I don't know if your Alison would be interested, but I need someone to start tomorrow. She wouldn't have to know the business, I could teach her everything. I just need someone I can trust, and I could trust her, couldn't I?'

You could trust her to spoil your day, Cora had to stop herself from saying. Then she gave herself a shake. This was an ideal offer. It might not bring Hazel the wedding dress of her dreams, but they would all eat better than they'd done for years and it would get Alison out from under her feet. 'I have to warn you that she ain't improved in looks or temperament at all,' she said. 'She might scarc off your customers so you'll want to keep her out the back. But credit where credit's due,' she added, hoping she hadn't said too much and made him change his mind. 'She's reliable, that's what her reference says.'

'There you are then,' said Fred. 'I don't need someone with film star looks round here. If she can add up orders and sweep a floor, that'll do me to start with. And from what I remember she's a bright girl.'

'Well, I'll get her to come down tomorrow and you can see if she's suitable. She should be very grateful. You're a good man, Fred Chapman, and

53

don't think I don't know it.'

'So we'll be happy all round,' beamed Fred. 'You get that nice bit of beef home and have a slap-up meal. I'd stew it, myself. Tasty as can be when it's stewed. And I'll see your girl tomorrow.' As Cora saw herself out, Fred hoped he'd done the right thing. But surely the daughter of his old friend couldn't be all bad. Her mother was just tired. He knew how difficult it was to be cooped up with a family member all day every day. As for the girl, he'd find out soon enough what she was really like.

'A butcher's?' said Alison as they were sitting at the dinner table that evening.

'What's wrong with that?' demanded Cora. 'There's no room for you to be la-di-da, it's a good honest job so make sure you're there first thing tomorrow.'

'But I don't know anything about it,' Alison said. She was terrified of the idea. A shop – talking to people who'd be whispering about her as soon as her back was turned. What if she got it all wrong? And there would be blood from the meat everywhere.

'What do you need to know about it?' Hazel was scornful. How typical of her sister to make a fuss before she'd even started. 'You ain't got to kill anything. You just shove it in bags and take people's money. Even you must be able to manage that.'

'But the blood...' Alison began.

'Don't tell me you mind a bit of blood,' Cora said. 'You know where meat comes from. You're happy enough to eat it.' She looked pointedly at

54

Alison's empty plate. They'd all enjoyed the stew. Fred had been right – it had been a very tasty piece of beef and they hadn't eaten that well for ages.

Hazel wasn't going to back off. 'You know we need the money. And you haven't exactly been flooded with job offers, have you? So that settles it. End of.' She got up to help clear the table. 'Come on, pass me your plate. I'm in a hurry as I'm going to see Neville. He's got a night off at last.'

Alison was silent as she did as she was asked. She tried to remember what Fred Chapman was like. She'd seen him when she was little but that wasn't much help. Had he brought them sweets? It might have been someone else. Yet it was a rare enough event for it to have stuck in her memory.

'Don't just sit there, help your sister,' snapped Cora.

Alison slowly got to her feet. 'Did Fred once bring us sweets when we were kids?' she asked.

Cora thought for a moment. 'Don't know. But it's the sort of thing he'd do. He's a kind man, Fred is. You're lucky.' Then she laughed. 'At least you won't be struck dumb by his good looks. He's shorter than you are, twice as wide, nearly bald and wheezes like he's just run all the way from the park up to Clapham Junction.'

'You'll be the perfect pair!' crowed Hazel. 'Short fat Fred and long tall Alison with the face that could sink a thousand ships. You'll draw the crowds, you will. People will come for miles.' She finished stacking the dirty dishes. 'There you are, your turn to wash up. I'm off.'

'Maybe I'll be good for business then,' Alison said, trying to persuade herself that this might turn out all right, despite her sister's comments. 'I must be good for something.'

'First time for everything,' said Cora dismissively.

Chapter Six

Falcon Road was busy, full of people going to work, heading for Clapham Junction or coming from there, or waiting for buses to take them up the hill. Alison huddled in her gabardine mac, wishing she'd put on her worn-out coat, which although shabbier, was slightly warmer. Would it be any better in the shop? If there was raw meat around it would probably be cold. Just what she needed on a day like this. As she reached the door it started to rain and she hurried inside, chilled to the bone.

At once she was hit by the smell. It made her want to run outside again. But before she could turn to leave, Fred Chapman came through the plastic curtain that divided the shop area from whatever lay behind and smiled in welcome. She was trapped.

'Alison! Well, look at you,' he said, looking up at her – he was quite a bit shorter and she could see the top of his nearly bald head. 'Grown so tall! I hope we can get you an apron to fit. The last assistant was much smaller than you.'

Marvellous, thought Alison. I've done something wrong already. What a good start.

But Fred was fussing round and found something he thought would do. 'You take this and come through to the back. We won't open until nine so we've time for a cup of tea and to get you settled in.' He pushed his way through the curtain and gulping, trying not to breathe too deeply, Alison followed him.

There were two enormous fridges on the right but on the left, a door led into a surprisingly cosy room. A gas fire was on full and Alison was irresistibly drawn to it, holding out her red hands to warm them. Fred was making himself busy at a small counter in the corner, where there was a kettle and various tins. 'Tea, sugar, and the milk's in here,' he said. 'This big one's for biscuits. Fancy a digestive to settle your stomach?'

Alison nodded. 'How did you know?'

'Happens to lots of people,' said Fred. 'You get used to the smell, you know. I've just been separating some cuts of meat. So that's what you smelt when you came in. Can't tell in here though, can you? So if it gets too much to start with, you come in here. Here's your tea.'

'Thanks, Mr Chapman,' said Alison, shyly sitting down, wrapping her hands around the mug.

She helped herself to a biscuit and began to feel better.

'You'd better call me Fred,' said Fred. 'Otherwise I shall be getting above myself. We won't do too much today. You can just watch me and get to meet some of the regulars. You probably know

57

lots of them.' Alison was dreading having to come face to face with so many people every day, but said nothing. She knew that everyone whispered behind her back as soon as they saw her – somehow she'd have to deal with it as best she could. 'You might weigh me out some sausages in a bit. That won't be too bad, will it?'

'No,' she said. 'I think I could do that.'

Fred gave Alison all the easy things to do in the morning, showing her how to use the big scales, the till, where the change was kept and what went where in the giant fridges. He kept her away from where the big carcasses were hung and didn't ask her to cut anything except sausages. He was quietly surprised at how quickly she seemed to pick things up and assumed her nervousness was down to being new at the job. He had no idea how awkward she always felt around people. She'd much rather stay in the back where no one could see her.

Alison avoided any of the building beyond the fridges as she had no wish to see the raw, bloody meat any more than she had to. By the time it made it to the front of the shop it was in smaller chunks and just about bearable, not so different from the kitchen at home. She was afraid Fred would ask her to try the big slicer on which he cut the ham and corned beef wafer thin, as it looked like a quick way of losing her fingers, but he didn't. She also managed to avoid most of the customers to begin with but by mid-morning, trade was hotting up.

'Oh, so this is where you're working now, is it?'

Alison had seen a woman come in wearing a large plaid headscarf against the rain but hadn't realised it was Winnie Jewell. 'Hello, Mrs Jewell,' she said, smiling weakly.

'Dress shop didn't work out then?' demanded Winnie, pulling off the scarf and sending a shower of raindrops onto the sawdust on the floor.

'No, no, that was no good...'Alison began, embarrassed at the memory of the horrendous interview.

'Can't say I'm surprised,' Winnie said. 'They're very posh in there.' She gave Alison an appraising look.

'Well, their loss is my gain,' said Fred grandly, passing behind the counter with a tray of something shiny Alison didn't want to examine too closely. 'What can I get you today, Mrs Jewell? Your usual kidneys?'

Alison took the opportunity to escape through the plastic curtain. She was sure that Winnie Jewell had set her up to fail and had come in here to rub it in. She could hear Fred making conversation with the woman – he had her eating out of his hand. Good, let him deal with her.

The shop door banged shut and Fred came through to find her. 'So you know Mrs Jewell?'

'Yes.' Alison wondered what was coming next.

'Maybe you'd like to stop and talk to her next time then,' suggested Fred.

'Maybe.'

Fred shook his head. 'Treat them well and they'll come back for more. It don't matter what she might have said or done before, she's a customer now and that's different. Remember that.

You're wearing that apron – that deserves re-spect.' He looked her in the eye and she felt as if she was shrinking. 'Come on then. If you can quickly sweep up that wet sawdust and put down new before the lunchtime rush begins, we can think about what we'll have for our own lunch. Did you bring anything in?'

Alison hadn't even thought about that. 'No, I didn't know...'

'That's all right then,' said Fred. 'I expect you don't fancy a steak and kidney pie?' Alison nearly gagged. 'How about you go up the road for fish and chips for both of us? On me, for your first day.'

'That would be lovely. Thank you very much, Mr Chap ... Fred.' Alison was relieved. She risked a small smile. Her nerves had made her hungry and she had only just noticed, but the thought of meat in any shape or form would have been unbearable.

She quickly swept up the old sawdust, now soggy and lumpy, and put down fresh before any new customers could come in. Then she grabbed Fred's money and her mac. She stopped outside the neighbouring shop's awning to fasten it against the rain, which was still falling hard.

Someone stepped out from the doorway. It was a young man in the brown overalls of the iron-monger's. Alison immediately noticed he was good-looking – not as good-looking as Neville, but his hair was very dark and so were his eyes. He was shorter than her, but so were most people. He took a second glance at her and grinned.

'You working next door?' he asked.

'That's right.' Alison didn't want to appear shy so kept her answer short. She was taken aback that he had bothered to speak to her at all.

'We're going to be neighbours, then. I work in here. I'm Paul, by the way.'

'Hello, Paul, I'm Alison.'

'Going out in this weather?' he teased. 'I wouldn't send a dog out in that.'

Alison moved a little closer to him to avoid the rain that was being driven sideways under the awning, almost afraid of her own daring. 'Going to get Mr Chapman's lunch,' she said.

'Got you at his beck and call, has he? You want to watch that. It'll be unpaid overtime next,' said Paul, with an air of authority.

Alison could feel herself blushing. 'No, it's not like that. He's a very good boss. I'd better be off.' She straightened her shoulders and forced herself out into the downpour.

Paul watched her go. He'd noticed how she blushed when she came closer to him and then was in a hurry to get away. He'd only been in the job two weeks himself and had been bored witless for most of that but now it looked as if there might be some fun to be had. If she was that shy after such a brief conversation then she couldn't be very experienced with men. With looks like that he bet most lads of his age avoided her. Well, for him at least, things had just got much more interesting on Falcon Road.

Alison was impressed. Fred had installed a Baby Belling oven in the cosy side room and so his fish and chips could keep warm while she ate hers;

61

they couldn't eat together during the busy lunch period. She sat in the armchair next to the fire, finishing her chips. This might not be so bad after all. Fred had been as kind to her as Betty Shaw-cross at the factory, and slowly she began to feel that she might not fail at this new job. As long as she could stay away from the carcasses she'd be all right.

Fred came through from the shop and put on the kettle. 'I'm starving,' he said. 'Are you all right to go out the front for a bit on your own? If there's anything you need then shout.'

'I'll be fine,' said Alison, getting to her feet.

While the next half an hour was busy, it was mostly people she didn't know or who were vaguely familiar faces – none of those who'd taunted her so regularly. They usually wanted something quick for this evening's tea. Now she understood why she'd spent much of the morning weighing sausages: nearly all of them wanted a pound or half a pound, and all she had to do was reach for a bundle she'd separated earlier and put them in greaseproof paper. This was easy. Now and again she even talked to customers beyond 'can I help you?' Maybe this would all work out. And there was that nice-looking man next door who hadn't been rude to her. Slowly she began to relax a little.

Fred finished his fish and chips and came through the door just as Marian Dalby came in. Alison knew who she was – Neville had talked about her, saying his foreman was married to the best baker in Battersea, and didn't have a bad word to say about her. She looked as if she enjoyed plenty of her own cakes, as she was plump and round-faced, smiling even though her coat was wet. 'Mr Chapman!' she exclaimed. 'I see you've found yourself a new assistant. Let me see … you're Hazel Butler's sister, aren't you?'

'That's right,' Alison said. 'She just got engaged to Neville Parrot, who works at the paint factory.'

'That explains why my Frank came in so late from the pub recently,' said the woman, shaking the raindrops from her curly hair. 'He said they'd been toasting the young couple. Well, he seems like a nice lad. Now, Mr Chapman, I'm laying on some food for my brother's birthday and I'll be needing some pork chops. What can you do for me?'

'I have the very thing for you,' said Fred instantly, 'but I don't have many out front. Alison, could you fetch the rest? Out the back, the room on the right past the fridges, you'll see a big box with a red lid. It's not heavy.'

Alison set off into the back of the building and found the right door, just after the opening to the yard. It was much colder out here. She sniffed as her nose threatened to drip, then opened the door.

The smell hit her at once: the smell of blood but far stronger than she'd ever come across it. Hanging from the ceiling were the dead animals, with their shiny red flesh and yellow fat all exposed. The lifeless head of a pig almost brushed against her as she gasped in horror. Choking, she slammed the door and ran towards the yard. She threw open the big wooden door and made it outside just in time before her guts heaved in terror and she was violently sick.

Chapter Seven

Alison felt she had ruined everything. She was sure that she'd get the sack again and things would be worse at home than ever. But Fred assured her they hadn't heard a thing in the shop and when he'd eventually fetched Mrs Dalby's pork chops himself, she'd been happy and gone on her way. Apparently lots of people were sick at their first sight of a whole carcass, close up. But, he'd reminded her, they had the luxury of an indoor toilet at the back of the building so next time she had better use that. 'Good job it was raining hard,' he said.

Alison wasn't going to let herself down again and resolved to get used to what was in the back room. The next day she forced herself to go inside and look at the pigs and sides of beef, and managed to stay there for thirty seconds before running out again. Hanging over the toilet, she closed her eyes and swore she would become accustomed to it. She'd have to.

Over the next week Fred patiently explained about the different cuts of meat and what they could be used for. 'People don't just want to buy the beef or whatever, they want to know what they can do with it,' he told her. 'Have you done much cooking?'

'No,' said Alison. 'Mum and Hazel always say I waste good food when I try. Besides, we never had much meat at home. Up till now, that is.' Her mother and sister had always made it clear that her lack of cooking skills was just one more way that she was a failure around the house. But Fred had been slipping her odds and ends to take back – the remains of a tray of mince, the last two sausages that wouldn't make a half-pound, pigs' trotters that looked far pinker than the ones her mother sometimes bought from the market. Cora had been delighted and Hazel was triumphant – every penny saved on food meant more for her wedding fund. However Alison still didn't like handling the stuff. The cool feel of the trotters had turned her stomach. As for liver and kidneys, she didn't think she'd ever manage to eat them again.

'I reckon you should try a spot of cooking, then,' suggested Fred. 'I've got the Baby Belling. You could do us something for lunch. If the shop smells of home cooking I reckon that will make the punters buy even more.' He was pleased with the idea. The girl looked as if she could do with fattening up and this way he'd get a good meal at lunchtime as well as the one he always made sure to cook himself in the evening. He'd be doing her a favour too; she'd need to be able to cook when she got married, when the time came.

He had abandoned all thoughts of marrying himself. He'd been in no position to do so when he first took over the family business, as it had been in a bad state and it took him all his time and energy to turn it around. Then came the war, when his flat feet had kept him out of the armed services but he'd spent every spare hour as an ARP warden. Some of the sights he saw in those days made him wonder if he could ever bring himself to care for another human being – there were so many dreadful ways to lose a loved one. The pain of families when he told them their nearest and dearest had been killed by buzz bombs, or crushed when a shelter collapsed stayed with him still. There had been a few grateful widows during those years, but it was no time to think of anything more than a brief affair to hold the everyday horrors at bay.

After that his mother, always bullying and difficult, had got worse and worse till it became clear that she wasn't only rude and brutal but terminally ill as well. Fred had done his duty, shutting his ears to her comments as he looked after her in the flat above the shop, and secretly, he'd been heartily relieved when she died. So here he was, a bachelor in his early forties, with a quietly thriving business and premises in a prime location. But he was under no illusions about his looks. He'd been called pig face and worse, thanks to his round, stubby nose and face that went red with the slightest exertion, and he knew his prospects of romance were poor. So he concentrated on enjoying his food, getting along with his customers, and making a success of the shop. He tried not to think about what he might be missing out on. He told himself that if he was lonely then it was a price worth paying, and most days he almost believed it.

Alison was dubious about the whole cooking idea but she was beginning to realise that when Fred set his mind to something, he wasn't easily put off. So she gave in. Sometimes she would fry something quickly during the lunch hour – bacon and eggs, sausage and beans. Other times she would chop up the meat and vegetables for a casserole in the morning and put it on to stew so that it was ready when they needed it. She got a sweet feeling of satisfaction the day that Winnie Jewell came in and commented that something smelt good. As Fred had guessed, she bought more than her usual that day.

The only downside to cooking lunch was that she had fewer excuses to go outside and catch a glimpse of the young man who worked next door. She saw him now and again, if she had to go on an errand to the post box or bank – Fred had decided she was trustworthy and would sometimes send her to fetch the change. But there had been no more conversations under the awning.

A few weeks after she'd started working at the butcher's, Fred was sorting through the drawers underneath the counter, pulling out odds and ends, but not finding what he was after. 'Drat. There's no string left,' he said. 'That won't do. You go next door and get us some more. Take it out of the petty cash.'

Alison hurried off at once.

The hardware shop seemed dim compared to the bright white tiles of the butcher's. At first she could hardly make out if there was anyone else there, as the shelves seemed to extend forever into a dark back area and the counter was lit only by a weak bulb. Not a very good advert for their lighting department, she thought.

Then someone cleared his throat. 'Yes, young

lady?' An elderly man was behind the counter, stooping over it. 'Is there something you wanted?'

Before she could answer, the door opened once more and in came a middle-aged woman, dressed as if she worked in an office. 'Good morning,' she said. 'I've come for the Denman and Sons order.' Alison recognised the name of one of the oldest solicitors' firms and of course the old man turned his attention to the new customer. 'Mr Lanning!' he called. 'You're needed at the front counter.'

Paul emerged from the gloom, wiping his hands on his brown overall. He grinned wickedly. 'Good morning, miss,' he said. 'And how may I help you?'

Bravely Alison made herself smile back. 'I'd like some string please.'

'What sort of string? Garden twine? Parcel string? We've lots of string. If it's string you're after, you've come to the right place.' Even in the semi-darkness she could see his eyes were twinkling.

'Oh, not garden twine,' she said. 'Definitely not that. String suitable for tying around cuts of beef. And parcels of greaseproof paper.'

'Ah, that sort of string. Well now, you're in luck. Seeing as we are so close to a butcher's we make sure to keep that kind in stock.' He made his way to a set of drawers and pulled open one of them. 'Here you are. Do you need a paper bag?'

'No,' said Alison, feeling a blush creep up her face. 'I'll put it in my pocket.'

'If you'd care to come over to the till, miss,' he said, grinning even more wickedly. As he took her money and gave her back the change his fingertips brushed her palm. She was sure he did it deliberately, and right under the eyes of his boss and the formidable office lady. It was all she could do to get out of the shop in one piece.

Well now, thought Paul. I've made her run away again. Even in the half-light of the hardware store he could tell she'd gone bright red. Maybe it was time to step things up a little and not to wait for events to take their course. He was tired of not having a woman. He didn't want one perman-ently – or not one who looked as odd as this one did. But he needed the practice. She couldn't get many offers with those looks. She'd be grateful. He liked the idea of taking advantage of that.

'We've picked the date for the wedding, Mum,' said Hazel. She was so excited she couldn't even wait to get her coat off. 'Second Saturday in Sep-tember. So that's seven months to get everything ready.'

'And where's the money to come from?' asked Cora. She still hadn't got through to her daugh-ter that a big wedding was a waste.

'You know Neville's been working all hours,' said Hazel. 'He ain't taken me to the cinema for weeks cos he's been on extra shifts every week-end. He's so tired he can hardly stand. And I'm only taking Sundays off from now on. So that'll all add up.'

'And it helps that I'm bringing home decent food,' Alison said, wishing they'd acknowledge her efforts.

'That's as may be,' snapped Cora, 'but it's only offcuts. Fred couldn't sell that stuff. So don't you go getting above yourself, thinking you're bringing us home something special.' In truth she wouldn't be without the extra supplies and she'd got used to them very quickly but that was no reason to be soft on her youngest. 'See if you can get something this weekend. Linda's bringing June up for Sunday tea. A bit of ham for sandwiches would be a start.'

'I'm sure that will be fine.' Alison couldn't do enough for her big sister and niece. 'Fred wouldn't object to that.'

'I suppose you're going to measure Linda for a bridesmaid's frock?' Cora said, busying herself laying the table. 'Here, Alison. Make yourself useful and do this.'

Alison looked up from her seat by the fireplace. 'And am I going to be a bridesmaid?'

Hazel glared at her. 'Why would I want you to spoil the wedding pictures? Linda's different, she'll look the part, but you'll only depress people. Besides, God knows how much material we'd need to make you a frock. If you were normal height there'd be no problem and we could use the same pattern for both of you but no. You're too tall and you're a weird shape.' She threw her handbag to the floor.

'It'll seem odd though, won't it?' Alison went on. She didn't particularly want to be a bridesmaid, it would make her the focus of too much attention, but she knew how to rile her sister. A little spark of new confidence made her do so now. 'Is Neville's sister going to be a bridesmaid too? Cos if she is it'll look a bit funny if I'm not one too.'

'Of course Kathy's being a bridesmaid. She'll

look really pretty. Which you won't.' However, Hazel hated the thought of doing the wrong thing in public. It didn't matter how rude she was to her sister behind closed doors – she wanted to be seen to be respectable and nothing must spoil that impression. 'I'll think about it but don't push your luck. And if – *if* – I say yes, you'll have to stand at the back.'

'Obviously,' said Alison, setting down the salt and pepper. 'As I'm going to be looking over all of your heads. Including Neville's.'

'Give it a rest,' Cora shouted. She'd had enough. 'I'm sick to death of hearin' you go on. I don't know what's got into you. Don't you dare ruin your sister's big day.' She almost groaned as her back gave her a painful twinge. Standing over the stove hadn't helped. 'Alison, you dish up while your sister puts away her work things. And less of your lip.'

Alison dished up a meal for the second time that day, giving herself the smallest portion as she was still full from lunch at the butcher's. She liked eating in the middle of the day – it gave her energy to work hard all afternoon. She found herself enjoying it more and more, as long as she didn't have to cut up offal. She had at least stopped being sick at the sight of it or the smell of blood, and now her appetite was back with a vengeance. She had also started to chat to the customers and found herself even bantering with some of them – she couldn't have imagined doing that a few weeks ago. It made it more difficult to put up with her mother and sister, though. She was more and more tempted to answer back, which she'd never have done before.

71

Still, Linda and June were going to be here on Sunday. She could look forward to that at least. And maybe, just maybe, she would see Paul again tomorrow.

'I don't know what you think you're smilin' at,' Cora snapped, seeing a dreamy look pass across her youngest daughter's face. But Alison didn't care. There was no way she'd mention him to her mother, but already she was thinking of what items they might be short of so she could make an excuse to pop in to the hardware store as soon as possible.

Chapter Eight

'It's your round, Paul,' said Paul's best friend, Kenny Parker. They'd been in the pub since six o'clock and this would be their third pint. Paul was in no hurry to go home. He shared his flat with his father and two older brothers, and it was a tip. He hated the place but his father was adamant they couldn't afford anything else, even with all of them working. Paul guessed that was because his father spent everything at the dog track, or if he couldn't go there in person, at the bookies. It had been the same ever since his mother had died. This was the fourth place they'd moved to since then and each had been worse than the last.

'Same again, mate?'

Kenny nodded.

'Here you go.' Paul set the drinks down on the

sticky table-top. 'How's work?'

'Same old,' said Kenny, sipping the bitter and smacking his lips. 'Turn up at nine, leave at five, paid on Friday. Not much more to it. How's yours? Been there a few weeks now, ain't you?'

'It's all right,' Paul said. 'The boss is ancient and he can't see what I'm doing half the time. Can't say it's anything to get excited about.' He raised his glass and drank. 'I might get some fun out of the girl who works in the next shop though.'

Kenny looked up, interested. 'What's she like? Should I be jealous?'

Paul wondered whether to wind his friend up and make Alison sound more than she really was but decided he would get caught out in the lie too easily if Kenny decided to pay Falcon Road a visit. 'Nah, probably not. She's not much of a looker.'

'Then why are you bothering?' Kenny asked. 'What else has she got going for her?'

'She's got good tits,' said Paul, which he hoped was true, although her mac hadn't given him more than a rough idea. Still, he'd passed away several boring hours in the hardware shop imagining what might lie beneath. 'And I reckon she's got really long legs. She's tall, see. But her face ... no, you don't want to know about it. Her teeth are horrible and so's her hair.'

'Bit of a mare then,' said Kenny. 'So you better keep yer eyes on her tits and legs if you don't want to be put off.'

'Well, I can do that easily enough,' laughed Paul. 'She'll be desperate for me, you wait and see. She'll be begging me for it.'

'Bet you she won't,' said Kenny. He'd heard all

73

this before and to the best of his knowledge no girl had ever begged Paul for anything.

'Bet you she will,' said Paul, suddenly serious. 'It's February now and I bet you five bob that before March is over I'll have had her.'

'You're on.'

'I shouldn't even accept that as it'll be like taking candy from a baby,' said Paul, finishing his pint with relish. 'But I know you'll be offended if I say no. Five bob, end of March, she'll have been begging me for weeks.' He was certain he was right. And if she didn't beg him, he'd have her anyway.

'Nice sandwiches, Mum,' said Linda. 'June, have you tried one? Eat something so Granny can see you like her food.'

'Oh, she can have some cake if she'd rather,' said Cora, giving her granddaughter a cuddle. 'You'd enjoy that, wouldn't you, Junie? Try some of this.' She put a small slice of jam sponge on a plate and June eagerly took it from her.

'What sort of material are you thinking about for our frocks, Hazel?' asked Linda, who'd spent the last half-hour upstairs with her sisters, getting measured up. 'Did you have a colour in mind?'

'Something to go with my hair,' said Hazel, pushing an auburn wave back over her ear. She was very proud of her hair but knew she'd have to avoid reds and pinks. 'Probably green or blue. Suppose I'll have to see what Joe Philpott's got going. He said he'd keep an eye out for something nice for me.'

'He'd do that, he's got a soft spot for you,' said

74

Linda. 'What about your dress? Will ___ et that fabric too?'

'I'm still hoping I can buy one,' said ___. 'Of course if Alison hadn't messed up her j___ ___ter-view at that place...'

'Then you wouldn't be eating ham sandw___ now,' said Alison. 'And we can all enjoy this wh___ as it's only you who gets to wear a big wh___ wedding dress.'

'Can I have a special dress?' asked June. She wasn't sure what they were talking about but she did like getting new clothes.

'We'll see,' said Linda, 'but you can't go getting jam over it.' She wiped her daughter's face with her handkerchief. 'That's better. Maybe you can have a frock trimmed with the same pattern that Mummy and Auntie Alison will be wearing.'

Hazel knew that June would steal the show if she was a flower girl and couldn't work out if that would be good or not. Would it take attention away from her? 'We've got to get enough for Kathy's dress as well so I ain't sure if there will be enough...'

'Don't worry, I didn't mean you'd have to fork out for another one,' said Linda, helping herself to another sandwich. 'I only meant if there were scraps left over we could make a bow or a ruffle or something like that. If it's a problem then Terry will be happy to pay. He's doing really well at the moment.'

'That's good,' said Hazel, secretly seething th___ Terry was, yet again, such a success. She felt s___ Linda was only saying it to emphasise how l___ Neville earned by comparison. That was so u___

– he ldn't even join them for tea because he
was g extra shifts this weekend.
is e lucky, I know,' said Linda. 'Not everyone
is ood provider like my Terry.'
a sure we can manage something for June,'
ca said. She'd love to see the girl be part of the
ceedings. 'Maybe a little waistcoat and hair-
ind?' She ruffled her granddaughter's golden
urls. 'Blue or green would go with her colouring.'

Hazel decided that having Linda, Kathy and
now June as her attendants would make it less
likely everyone would notice Alison so much.
'You're right, Mum,' she said. 'She'll look gorgeous. Could you do that, June? Maybe hold a
special bunch of flowers at my wedding?'

June smiled happily, enjoying being the centre
of attention.

'How's the new job, Alison?' asked Linda.
'What's it like working for Fred?'

'He's been very kind,' said Alison. 'All the blood
and stuff turned my stomach to start with but I'm
getting used to it. I haven't been sick for ages.'

'For God's sake, you never told us that,' exclaimed Cora. She wondered that her daughter
hadn't been sacked on the spot. 'You need to
toughen up and fast, my girl. If his customers
find out you've been throwing up round the back
they'll stop coming and then where will you be?
Well, you're used to being out of work, but think
f poor Fred. You don't want to ruin his business
en he's been so good as to help you out.'

'm sure it's hard to get used to it to start with,'
Linda.

'Big girl like you, being sick!' Cora went on.

'I just said, I haven't done that for ages,' protested Alison. 'You should see what it's like with all that dead meat in one place. The smell of it is disgusting. But I'm getting much better. Fred said so.'

'I'm sure you are,' said Linda. 'I don't know how I'd have managed. And you bring home ham like this, so there's a bonus.'

'Fred asked to be remembered to you,' said Alison. 'He's been teaching me to cook as well. Says one of my lunches sets him up for the rest of the day.'

'Sets him up for food poisoning more like,' snapped Hazel. 'Or have you suddenly improved? He's too good to you by half.'

'Maybe you're practising to become a housewife,' Linda gently teased. 'Is there a boyfriend on the horizon you've been keeping quiet about?'

'Of course not,' said Alison, hoping she wasn't going to blush. She realised she'd been blushing quite a lot since the visit to the ironmonger's. 'Don't be daft. Who'd look at me?'

'True,' said Hazel at once.

But you don't know everything, thought Alison, not even tempted to rise to the bait this time. Someone has looked at me. And he seems really nice. What's more, I'm going to make sure I see him tomorrow.

Cheeky tyke, thought Cora, shooing the last of the paper-boys out of the shop early on Monday morning. He'd had the nerve to ask her where her ugly daughter was as he hadn't seen her around

77

for a few weeks. Suppose he'll be taking the mickey out of some other poor sod, she said to herself, looking up at the sky. As March approached it was getting just a bit warmer and signs of spring were beginning to appear. She couldn't wait. She'd had enough of being cold and her back and hands were always worse during the winter.

Flexing her fingers at the idea, she made her way round the shop making sure all was in order before the first customers arrived. Often she thought this was the best bit of the day – everything in its place, all the boys out of the way, nobody to disturb her peace and quiet. But she knew she'd hate it if nobody came in all day and there was no gossip. That's what gave the job its spice.

It wasn't long before Winnie Jewell set the doorbell ringing. 'Morning, Cora!' she called.

'You're early, Winnie,' said Cora.

'I need some aspirin for my Vera before she goes to work,' explained Winnie. 'She's got such a headache, poor love, and I can't send her out looking miserable to Arding and Hobbs. You know, they expect better from their staff than that.'

Probably got a hangover, thought Cora. 'Poor girl,' she said aloud.

'That's just what I thought,' said Winnie, getting out her purse. 'How was your weekend? I had my sister Beryl round and she's having such trouble, I thought she was never going to leave.'

'Really?'

'It's her neighbours,' Winnie went on. 'I told her not to move down that way but would she listen? She's not that far from the power station and it's not a patch on her old place, though the rent ain't bad. As for her neighbours, well, the place is filthy. I said to her, you got to be careful, what if they get rats? They don't empty their bins and their back garden's like a junk yard. If they get rats then they're bound to come over the fence and into her kitchen. Think of that. And she's got young kids. What if they get bitten? Then she'll wish she never left her old place.'

'Sounds dreadful,' said Cora, interrupting Winnie's incessant chatter. Ennis Street might not be much but at least everyone put their bins out on the right day.

'It's because they haven't got a woman to look after them,' Winnie explained. 'There's four grown men in that flat. A father and three sons. All the boys are working so they can't be stupid. But they ain't got no idea how to keep a place clean. That's not what the main trouble is, though. Gambling, that's what's caused all their problems.'

'How do you know that?' demanded Cora.

'It's common knowledge,' said Winnie. 'The father is always down the bookies. Takes his lads in with him sometimes. Throws away all their money on the horses or the dogs. He's ruined his family, hasn't got time for anything else. They say his wife died and you know what, I'd say it was a blessing. If my Peter started gambling I'd have to throw him out. I can't be having that.

'Quite right too,' agreed Cora. She'd no time for gamblers either. There was nothing wrong with the odd flutter on the Grand National but that was where it stopped. She'd seen people get sucked into it, always believing they'd strike it lucky if they gave it just one more go. No, that was the quick road to ruin.

'As I said, when Beryl came round yesterday, she didn't want to go home.' Winnie shook her head. 'Says her life isn't worth living with those Lannings bringing the place into disrepute. I told her, go and report them to the landlord. But I don't know if she will. That landlord takes ages to get off his backside and do anything.'

'That's landlords for you,' said Cora.

'They don't like putting themselves to any trouble, do they? Not as long as their rent's being paid.' Winnie sighed. 'Anyway, better be getting back. Nice talking to you.' She put her aspirin in her bag and left.

Cora didn't envy Winnie's sister. Bothersome neighbours were a curse in these streets where the houses were so tightly packed together. Everyone knew each other's business simply by hearing it all through the walls or open windows. She thanked her lucky stars that they'd had no trouble for a while. She'd lived in Ennis Street for so long that she knew everyone's histories.

As if on cue, her next customer was Neville's mother, Jill Parrot. She didn't know the woman that well, but if they were to be family then that would change. She liked the look of her. Jill kept herself looking smart, even though you could tell her clothes weren't top quality.

'Good morning, Mrs Butler!' she said. 'Clearing up, isn't it? We might get a nice day after all.'

'Call me Cora. We can't be having all this Mrs business now your Neville's going to marry our Hazel.'

'I'm sorry we've not had a chance to get to-

80

gether to celebrate the engagement. I'm afraid I've been down with a lousy cold. We're so happy that Neville is going to marry Hazel. She's a lovely girl and he's working every hour God sends so they can have their perfect wedding,' Jill said, smiling.

'That's lovely, isn't it?' Cora smiled back. 'Mind you, Hazel's got her hopes up for a big do. I hope they don't bite off more than they can chew. She's going to have June all dressed up too, from what they were saying yesterday. Though I have to say, for a three-year-old she's beautifully behaved, so there'll be no trouble. And she's so little that she'll hardly need a scrap of material. Not like Alison.'

'Your youngest certainly is tall,' agreed Jill. She could sense the impatience behind Cora's remark but couldn't really see what was wrong with the girl. She'd always found her perfectly polite. Of course she wasn't as pretty as her sisters, especially Hazel, but then, not many young women were as fortunate to have looks like that.

'Hazel was thinking of blue or green for the bridesmaid's dresses. Will your Kathy like that?'

'I'm sure she will,' said Jill. 'She's lucky, being dark like Neville, she can wear most colours. That comes from my Lennie. It's all right for some. I'm too pale to get away with strong oranges and yellows, for instance.'

'I think we're safe to say Hazel won't choose orange,' Cora replied. 'With hair like hers she knows there are colours she has to steer well clear of. Linda can wear anything and look good in it. Whereas Alison looks terrible in everything.'

81

'Oh, I'm sure that's not true,' said Jill, slightly shocked. It would help if the girl stood up straight, or tried to do something with her hair, but she sensed she'd only make things worse if she said that. She hastily changed the subject. 'Neville was saying that Hazel's only taking one day a week off from the café from now on, to save up more money for the big day. That's going to be hard work for her.'

'It is, but when she sets her heart on something there's no changing her mind,' Cora told her. 'She'll be on her feet six days a week and dead beat on Sundays. I suppose you're only young once but where she'll get the time and energy to organise everything she wants I do not know.'

Jill beamed in anticipation. 'Well, there's nothing I like better than a good wedding, and I'm not bad at organising if I say so myself,' she said. 'So it looks as if it'll be down to you and me.'

Chapter Nine

Alison was a couple of minutes later leaving for work that morning and she was pleased to see that meant she was walking down Falcon Road just when Paul was winding open the hardware shop's awning.

'Nice day for it,' he said, giving her a cheeky wink.

She blushed immediately. 'Yes, looks as if we

82

might get a bit of sun for once,' she managed to reply.

'Suppose that means you'll be out walking with your boyfriend, then.'

She went even redder. 'Oh no, I haven't got...' she began, but a call from inside the shop interrupted her.

'Mr Lanning! We haven't got all day.'

Paul raised his eyebrows. 'See what I have to put up with,' he said quietly. 'Bet you feel sorry for me, don't you?' He turned his spaniel eyes on her and she felt her heart beat faster. 'Best be off. Don't work too hard.' He disappeared inside into the gloom.

Alison took a moment before turning towards the butcher's. What a start to the week that was. Should she take it as an omen? Why had he said that about her having a boyfriend – was he winding her up or might it mean that he liked her? She didn't want to get her hopes up too much but surely he wouldn't have said it otherwise?

Alison wouldn't have been so happy if she'd known what was really going through Paul's mind: that he didn't even have to set the bait for her, she was his for the taking. It was all going to be too easy.

Fred looked up as Alison pushed open the door. He smiled at the sight of her – she was almost cheerful. 'Good weekend?' he asked. 'Did your sister come like she said she would? Did she like my ham?'

'She did, and everyone loved your ham.' Alison hung her mac on the coat hooks by the plastic curtain, brightening at his interest. 'We got measured

83

for our bridesmaids' dresses. Hazel doesn't really want me to be one but she sort of had to agree. She'd look bad otherwise and she won't risk that.'

'I'm sure you'll look beautiful,' said Fred, and meant it. He knew Alison didn't get on with her middle sister but he saw a different side of her. When she forgot to be nervous or shy she was the ideal assistant: a fast learner, good with the customers, good with money, and not a bad cook either, now that he'd taught her some of the basics. She was beginning to blossom and he was delighted to see it.

'I'm going to have a full-length frock,' Alison went on, 'and Hazel's on about ordering special bouquets of flowers for us all. Ta-da! You wouldn't recognise me.' She twirled on the spot with her arms outspread.

Fred smiled again, and wondered what had brought on all this. She didn't seem the sort of girl to get so excited about a new dress. Usually she seemed so sensible.

'Sounds like it'll be a real day to remember. Now, sorry to bring you back down to earth, but we're due a delivery of chicken this morning,' he told her. 'You don't have to do anything with them, they'll all be nicely dead and plucked already, but if I'm out the back and Mr Reynolds arrives in his van, that's what it'll be about so give me a shout.'

'All right,' said Alison. She was happy enough to check the order as long as she didn't have to look into the birds' eyes. That gave her the creeps, and she'd almost thought about giving up eating chicken, but she liked it too much. 'What does Mr

84

Reynolds do with all the eggs he must have?'

'No idea,' said Fred, pausing as he emptied change into the till. 'Why, do you fancy some for lunch? You can always ask him.'

'Not particularly,' said Alison. 'But I was just wondering. You know, people come in here and buy their ham or their bacon or sausage, and all those things go well with eggs. So wouldn't it make sense to sell eggs as well?'

'Suppose so,' said Fred dubiously, 'but where would we put them?'

'There's plenty of room,' she insisted. 'You don't see it because you're used to how everything is laid out, but you could put the slicer closer to the till. There'd be plenty of room on the counter if we did that.'

Fred thought for a moment. Maybe it wasn't such a bad idea. She was right, there was lots of space, and perhaps he'd become blind to how much of it was wasted. Now he had his big fridges, things that had once been kept on the old cool tiled shelves had been moved into them, and he'd simply allowed everything else to spread out. It wasn't efficient, and that bothered him. He liked to be as efficient as possible – that was what made a business a success.

'I do believe you've got a point,' he said. 'So if we are to sell eggs, what do we do next?'

'Find out how much Mr Reynolds would sell them to us for,' said Alison at once. 'Find out how often he could bring them.'

'And?' Fred was enjoying this.

'And work out how much we would sell them at,' she went on. 'Like we do with the meat. Work out a percentage to make sure we sell at a profit.'

'And?'

That stopped her. 'Isn't that everything?'

'We need to know that we can sell them for the same price, or less than, the grocer's. I can't remember what I paid for eggs the last time I did a bit of shopping.'

'When we have a quiet spell I could pop along and check.'

'Yes, good idea. When Mr Reynolds turns up we'll ask him about his prices and availability. After that you can run along to the grocer's.'

Alison was happy to agree and, as she was longing to see Paul again, she began to plan an excuse to go into the ironmonger's too.

Later that day, in Kent, Linda was cutting bread for sandwiches, thinking there was nothing like the smell of a freshly baked loaf – even if that made it harder to slice. June was playing with her teddy bear in the corner of the kitchen. They both looked up when they heard the door open.

'Terry! I didn't expect you home for lunch.' Linda wiped her hands on her apron. 'Shall I make you a sandwich too? We were just about to have ours, weren't we, June?'

Terry stepped around the table and kissed his wife. She had hardly changed since he'd first met her – still smart and pretty enough to turn all the men's heads, and you wouldn't think she'd had a kid to look at her figure. She kept herself well and he liked that in a woman. He was the envy of his mates and that was no bad thing either.

'Can't stop for long,' he said. 'I just needed to

86

pick something up. But it gives me a chance to see my little princess.' He bent down to June's level and gave her a quick hug. June giggled in delight.

'Not like you to forget anything,' Linda commented, stacking the slices and reaching for the butter. 'There's nothing wrong, is there?' She tried not to imagine what it could be. She prided herself on being sensible but she knew if anything happened to Terry's job driving the lorries, the whole respectable life they'd built for themselves away from Battersea would crumble. She didn't intend to allow that.

Terry ran his hand through his dark blond wavy hair. There was no doubt where June got her looks from – they had the same colouring, down to the bright blue eyes. Terry was well aware of his physical appearance but he only had eyes for Linda. He'd seen the mess some of his mates had got into over women – that wasn't for him. The two of them made a strong team and he was about to be in a position where he could make it even stronger.

'Nothing's wrong at all,' he said easily. 'They still think I'm the bee's knees at the depot. But I might be able to do a bit extra. How do you like the sound of that?'

'Will it mean you being away more?' Linda hated it when Terry had to travel long distances. 'You know June likes you here at her bedtime. You have to think of things like that.'

'No, it's all local,' Terry assured her. 'One of the benefits of living in Kent is so much is on your doorstep. Some extra goods might come up that need looking after and transporting.'

'Looking after?'

'They might not be suitable for the usual warehouse,' Terry tried to explain without actually giving away too much. He scanned the shelves for the packet he'd forgotten to take into work that morning and reached over to pick it up, but there was no escaping Linda's questions.

'So where would they go? What are we talking about?'

Terry knew he had to proceed carefully. One of the things he loved about Linda was she was so quick on the uptake, but at moments like this it made everything more difficult. He didn't want to lie – she always knew when he was lying and it made things worse. But what she didn't know wouldn't hurt her.

'We're talking about a few boxes,' he said. 'I reckon they could go in our shed. They wouldn't be there long and they wouldn't be in your way. You wouldn't even know they were there.'

'Except if I needed to go into the shed.'

'But you hardly ever do. You leave this to me. It's all work, nothing to do with you.'

'Boxes of what? June, why don't you take Teddy and make him wash his hands before lunch?' Linda was proud of the fact they had an upstairs bathroom but now she was extra thankful as she didn't want the little girl to overhear what she suspected Terry was about to say. June headed off up the stairs and Linda turned a direct look on him.

'All right, Terry, boxes of what? Do you mean stolen goods?'

'No, nothing's stolen. It'll be all sorts. But mainly from France.'

88

'Are you talking about smuggled stuff, then? It's to avoid paying duty, isn't it?'

Terry sighed. He hated to think what she'd be like if she was in the police. Criminals wouldn't stand a chance. 'Look, it'll be all right...'

'I don't want you to get involved in anything illegal, Terry,' Linda said. 'That puts everything we've achieved at risk – you, me and June. You always said you wouldn't do anything dodgy and I know you've had offers. But you can't do anything to damage our family. Promise me you won't.'

Terry could never say no to his wife, but he knew that this opportunity wouldn't come along twice and it would be worth what he saw as a very small risk. Last week a man had approached him, making it clear he was part of a larger operation. They'd once been customers of the haulage firm he worked for, and kept an eye out for anyone who might be useful to them and who'd appreciate the chance of a little extra on the side.

'We'd get compensated for our trouble,' he said. 'Really, it makes sense. The docks are just down the road with ferries going to France. We're in the ideal place to take advantage of that. Just think, we'd be able to move to a bigger house if we're careful.'

Linda shut her eyes. She was tempted. She wanted another baby more than anything and she was damned if she was going to raise her own children in the overcrowded conditions she'd been brought up in. Terry had found her Achilles heel. She knew it, he knew it. She felt sick at the thought of losing everything but if this was their big break... Terry wasn't a chancer, she told herself. He'd have thought it all through and weighed up the odds.

'I don't want you doing anything dangerous,' she said, furious that she might break into tears at any moment. 'Nothing that'll threaten what we've done so far. I want to be proud of you, Terry, not afraid for you.'

Terry reached out and hugged his wife tightly. 'I'd never put you in danger, you know that. I love you far too much. I just want us to do well. And I know you want another baby.' He hugged her even tighter. 'I do too. We could make a start right now if you like. We'll have our family in a lovely big house, Linda. I promise you it'll be all right.'

Linda hugged him back then pushed him away. 'You daft sod. Look what you've made me do.' She wiped her face. 'June'll come in and see at any moment.' Hurriedly she splashed her cheeks with water at the sink. 'Be careful, Terry. I trust you, of course I do. But make sure you only deal with people you can trust too. Nothing stolen.'

'No, it's nothing like that, I told you.' Terry made for the door once more, juggling the packet from hand to hand. 'Just think of it as a grey area. That's all it is. A grey area.'

Alison had set off to find out what the grocer charged for eggs. She was enjoying the sense of freedom and the fact that Fred trusted her to do this. Since she'd started her job at the butchers, things were starting to look a little brighter.

When Alison went into the grocer's, she purchased a packet of biscuits while surreptitiously taking note of the egg prices. She then hurried back, desperate to make time to pop into the ironmonger's.

There was no sign of the old man at the counter but Paul was there in an instant, his overall sleeves rolled up to his elbows. She couldn't help noticing the dark hairs on his arms and hoped she wasn't staring. 'Hello again,' he said. 'I was just doing a spot of lifting round the back. The boss isn't up to it but it's no trouble for me.'

'No, I suppose not,' said Alison. She could imagine he was strong, and stopped her train of thought before it could go any further.

'But you haven't come in here to hear about that, have you?' He gave her his cheeky grin. 'What can I do for you?' He raised his eyebrows and she had to giggle.

'I just want a nice big nail to hang my coat on.'

'You don't want a nail. You want a hook. Come this way and I'll see what I can find,' Paul said, leading her into the gloomy interior of the shop. He stopped at a row of dusty drawers and, opening one, he pulled out a brass hook. 'Here's a nice one. Perfect to hang a coat on.'

Before she knew how it had happened, Alison found herself pressed against the shelves behind her. Paul was so close that she could smell his skin and hear his breathing as he asked, 'Would you like to buy it?'

'I ... think ... so...' She couldn't meet his eyes, afraid he'd see her turmoil.

There was a clatter from the front of the shop. 'Mr Lanning! Where are you, please?'

Paul gave a short laugh. 'He always does this. Just when things were getting interesting. Come on.' More loudly he called, 'I'm with a customer. We're just going to the till.'

She had no choice but to follow him as he quickly moved towards the counter, twisting to avoid the various boxes of seemingly random items stacked in odd places along the shop floor. She couldn't think straight. What had just happened? Was it all in her head?

Blindly she handed over the money and again felt that deliberate touch of his fingers against the skin of her palm as he gave her the change. 'I'll see you out, miss,' he said. The old man nodded in approval and began to make his stooped way away from the counter once more.

Paul grandly opened the door for her. 'Do you bring sandwiches in for lunch?' he asked casually.

'No,' she said, 'I usually eat with Fr ... Mr Chapman. We've got chicken casserole today.'

'Pity,' he said.

But when she turned to ask him what he meant, he'd already shut the door.

For the second time that day she stood under the awning not understanding what was going on. She was annoyed that she was at a disadvantage, having had so little experience with men. Then she gave herself a shake. Whatever was going on, she decided she'd enjoy it for all it was worth.

Jill Parrot sat at her kitchen table, several sheets of paper in front of her. There was nothing she liked better than a project to organise. They had about six and a half months to plan the wedding and she couldn't wait to get started. With Cora, Hazel and Neville working full time and beyond, she was the best person to step in.

She made several headings: Guests, Venue, Catering. Then she divided the remaining space into six columns, one for each month. How long would it take to decide on a venue and how much notice did they need? She wrote a target date in pencil. When it had been confirmed she would write over it in pen. Maybe she should colour-code it according to who was going to do what. Should she assume that it would be at the local church and then they could use the hall? She'd better check. Neither she nor her husband Lennie had any special ties to the parish, and her children would only go to church if it was Christmas, Easter or a special event. Cora was born and bred here, though, and might have strong views.

Jill didn't mind as long as the young couple had a good day and a proper celebration to start their life together. She smiled as she remembered her own wedding day – how happy she'd been. Neville had come along a year later and Kathy not long after that. Neville was a hard worker, she'd give him that, and such a good-looking lad. Kathy was the brains of the family; she'd got herself a job in an office and was planning to work for the civil service. Jill hoped her daughter wouldn't put everything into her career and delay having a family of her own. It wasn't that she objected to women working – she just didn't want the girl to miss out. Office jobs were all very well but she couldn't see how that would match the satisfaction of keeping a house, even a small one, and raising children.

Sighing, she thought of her youngest. Richie at fourteen was rock-and-roll mad. He drove them all crazy by playing his records at top volume, which meant they could be heard in every room and probably through the neighbouring walls too. There would be trouble with that one day. And the music was terrible, not what she thought of as music at all. She could only hope he'd grow out of it soon.

Well, she wasn't going to let that spoil her plans. Gathering her pieces of paper together she decided the next thing would be to go through her lists with Hazel, Neville and Cora. Then she would really get to work. This was going to be an unforgettable day.

'Kenny, you are going to lose your money, mate.' Paul grinned wolfishly at his friend as they stood at the bar early that evening waiting to be served. They didn't usually come to the pub on a Monday but Paul had had enough of the filthy flat. After a weekend of heavy losses his father was in a worse state than ever and was liable to fly into a violent rage at the least thing. Paul intended to put off going home for several hours by which time the old bugger would be asleep or in a drunken stupor – he didn't care which.

'You sound pretty sure of yourself.' Kenny was convinced Paul was all mouth and no trousers when it came down to it. He'd been friends with him since they were at school and had never known him to have a proper girlfriend. It wasn't for lack of trying but there was something about

Paul when you got to know him that seemed to put the girls off. Maybe it was down to his mum dying when she had. He didn't seem to know what to do with a girl beyond flirting – which, Kenny had to admit, he was quite good at. 'So how is the ugly bird, then?'

'She's like putty in my hands,' Paul said, signalling to the barman for two pints. 'I don't even have to try. She's after me all the time. If I could only get rid of my boss for a bit I could have her against the storeroom door.' He paused at the thought. That would be perfect – it would be dark enough not to have to look at her face and then every time he was sent to the storeroom he could remember what he'd done. He almost spilt the drinks at the idea.

'You filthy sod.' Kenny raised his glass. 'To you getting the sack. Because you will. You said yourself that your boss never lets you alone for a minute, and a minute wouldn't be long enough even for you, mate.'

'Shut up,' said Paul easily. 'I'll think of something. She ain't worth losing a job over. I'm not prepared to go short of cash for her. But I won't have to. She'll follow me wherever I ask her. So maybe the storeroom will have to wait.'

'And who said romance was dead,' Kenny sniggered. He didn't want Paul to lose his job – that would put the kibosh on their nights down the pub, which were more important than any stupid girl. 'I'll want a full report, mind. You seen what's under her coat yet?'

'Mind your own business.' Paul had been certain he could have got beneath her horrible mac

95

earlier in the day if his boss hadn't called him. She'd been trembling in front of him. What a pushover.

'That's a no, then,' said Kenny triumphantly. 'Never mind, spring is round the corner. Be able to get a good look then, won't you? All those lovely girls taking off their winter gear and going round in tight jumpers. Maybe the ugly bird will be one of those. Reckon she'll wear one of those low V-necks? You can see everything that's on offer with one of those. We said end of March, didn't we?'

'I won't even need that,' said Paul confidently. He didn't intend to wait much longer. If she was as keen as she seemed he wanted to take full advantage of it.

'Are you coming down the pub, Nev?'

Neville was so tired he was swaying on his feet. It was eight o'clock and after working all weekend, he'd just done more overtime. Now all he wanted to do was to get home, eat his dinner and then collapse into bed.

'No, not this time,' he said. 'Mum always does a stew on Mondays and she'll be keeping it warm for me.'

'Seeing the lovely Hazel after, are we?' asked Bill. 'Maybe taking her down the Granada?'

'Nah, staying in,' said Neville, smiling weakly. They hadn't been to the cinema for weeks. He knew he had to keep saving to come anywhere close to meeting Hazel's high hopes.

'Time enough for staying in when you've settled down,' Bill teased him. 'You know what they say, all work and no play...'

'Makes Neville under the thumb already,' Nobby cut in.

'Leave it out, Nobby,' said Neville, irritated. 'It's Monday night for God's sake.'

'Yes but when was the last time you came down the pub on a Friday?' Nobby asked. 'See what I mean? Dull boy, Neville. Don't you go letting them women tell you what to do. Once they realise they can get away with that, there's no stopping them. You have to be firm from the beginning. Show them who's boss.'

As if you'd know, thought Neville. The only women Nobby went near were on the pages of the smutty magazines he kept in his locker. 'Sorry to disappoint you, lads,' he said. 'But I don't miss Mum's stew for nothing. If you can't keep your mum happy then what's the point?'

'True,' said Bill. 'Off you go, then. But maybe come with us on Friday or you'll never hear the end of it.'

'Good idea,' said Neville, and headed for the factory gates. He missed going down the pub with his mates. It wouldn't hurt to join them at the end of the week. He never said he would give them up completely and he was sure Hazel wouldn't begrudge him one night off. All she wanted was for him to be happy.

Chapter Ten

Over a week had passed, and on Tuesday morning Cora pondered Jill's ideas as she sat behind the newsagent's counter. She'd been impressed by the level of planning her neighbour had suggested and was almost reassured they could afford it all. As long as everyone kept their jobs and nobody did anything stupid they should be all right and Hazel could have her big day almost exactly as she wanted it – although the wedding dress would have to be home-made. Jill turned out to be good at dressmaking as well, for which Cora was grateful. She could do it if she had to but her hands were so stiff and painful, any kind of sewing soon became agony. Jill had a Singer sewing machine. So that was sorted out.

Cora had volunteered to have a word with the local vicar as she knew him best. Hazel had been christened at his church but wasn't exactly a regular member of the congregation, especially as Sunday was now her only day off. Cora went every now and again, more for the social side than anything else; it was a sure way of seeing people who didn't come to the shop. As long as it wasn't too cold and wet everyone would gather in the churchyard after the service, exchanging small talk, and Cora often picked up snippets that were invaluable. Thanks to one overheard conversation, she already had a good idea of what the going rate for the church hall was, and didn't intend to be overcharged when the time came.

She looked up as Winnie Jewell came in. 'Morning, Winnie.'

'Morning, Cora.' Winnie didn't look like her usual chipper self. Cora didn't have to wait long to find out why. 'I'm flippin' well worn out, I am.'

'Why, Winnie, whatever's the matter?' Cora was keen to know the reason. The entertainment from all the local gossip was one of the main reasons she enjoyed her job. 'Would you like me to make you a nice cup of tea as it's quiet?'

'Would you, Cora?' Winnie brightened a little. 'I won't say no. I'm glad to be out of the house.'

Cora kept a kettle, some mugs and milk in a cooler in a corner behind the counter and she soon had a hot drink ready. 'You take your time, Winnie, and tell me all about it.'

'It's my poor sister.' Winnie blew on her tea. 'You know she's having a dreadful time with the neighbours. It's got much worse. This weekend they were all fighting and she could hear everything through the wall. The old man was drunk and swearing something dreadful, and our Beryl has young kids. Well, they could hear the lot. They've started using some of those words and they got in trouble at school for it. Beryl's at the end of her tether. Also, she thinks they've damaged the wall throwing things at it. Sounded as if the father was trying to kill one of the boys. All over a racehorse. I don't know what to advise.'

'All you can do is listen, Winnie.' Cora hoped there would be more. This was payback time for Winnie's snobby remarks about her bloody Vera

99

working at Arding and Hobbs.

'Beryl would like to stay at my house, but I just haven't got the room. All we can hope for is that her neighbours will quieten down. If they don't, she'll just have to report them to the landlord.'

'That's what I'd do,' said Cora. Thank God her neighbours weren't anything like as bad. She knew young Richie over the road played his music very loud but it never went on late. She could always go over and have a word with Jill about it if she needed to. She wouldn't get sworn at if she did, either – she'd never heard Neville or any of his family be rude or coarse.

'They were at our place until the kids' bedtime on Sunday night,' Winnie went on. 'I fed them and everything – Beryl's not happy using her kitchen what with the worry about the rats. It's enough to shred your nerves. I don't know what Vera's colleagues will say if they get to hear about it.'

'I'm sure they won't, Winnie. Anyway, it's not your kitchen that's got rats. If you ask me, it's good of you to do so much for your sister.'

'You've got to look after your family, that's what I always say,' Winnie said as she drained the last of her tea and asked to buy ten Woodbines. 'That was a lovely cuppa and it was good of you to make it for me, Cora. You must be bored to tears with hearing about my sister's problems with the Lanning family.'

'Think nothing of it, Winnie,' said Cora, smiling as she completed the sale, at the thought of this nice bit of gossip that she could pass on.

Alison tried to time her arrival at work to coincide with Paul putting up the awning but she was disappointed. As she drew closer to the row of shops she could see the old man, Paul's boss, arranging the last of the boxes outside. He nodded briefly but didn't look as if he was in the mood for conversation.

'What's up with him?' she asked Fred as she hung up her coat. 'Looks as if he got out of the wrong side of the bed this morning.'

Fred was weighing out some mince. 'He said his assistant is off sick today so he'll have to do all the lifting himself, and he's not really up to it any more. Takes its toll after a while when you're his age.' He didn't sound very interested and so Alison didn't ask if he knew how sick Paul was. 'Here, take this and put it out the back in one of the fridges. There's room on the bottom shelf.'

Alison took the tray of mince, wondering if Paul was really sick or if he'd just fancied a day off. She wouldn't put it past him to fake it, as she knew he got bored standing around in the ironmonger's with just the old man for company. I must find a way of going in there and seeing him more often, she thought. She began to daydream about how much he'd enjoy her company, and what they might talk about. Would he like to know about Hazel and her plans for the wedding? No, maybe that would put him off. She didn't want to jump the gun. He'd probably think she was reading too much into their few encounters. But all the same she'd like to know more about him, about his family, what he did when he wasn't at work.

'Alison, are you back there?' called Fred. 'I

could do with a hand out here.'

Shaking herself out of her fantasy, she realised she'd been standing by the back door for ages, imagining how things would be the next time she saw Paul. Well, it didn't look as if it was going to be today. She'd have to put those hopes on hold. It didn't hurt to daydream though.

Hazel had been rushed off her feet in the café all morning. They were one person short and the result was she hadn't sat down since the start of her shift. At least she'd had an early night last night and so had plenty of energy. That was one good thing with Neville doing so much overtime and not taking her out as often – she didn't stay out late and wake up feeling as if she'd already done a day's work. She told herself she should be glad about that but couldn't help the resentment at having to stay in with her mother and sister every evening. It was enough to make anyone depressed – her mother's constant whinging and Alison's long face staring into space for hours on end. Roll on the day when she and Neville had their own place and didn't have to put up with her family any longer.

'All right, Hazel? How are the wedding plans?'

It was Joe Philpott from the market. He headed for the corner table which had a big padded bench down one side. He was so big he found it hard to sit on the usual chairs and his long legs barely fitted under the table.

'Coming along fine, thanks,' she smiled. She reached in her apron pocket for her notepad and pencil. 'What'll it be today, Joe?'

'I was going to have just a cup of tea,' he said, 'but now I'm here and there are all those lovely kitchen smells I think I'll have a bacon sandwich as well.' His mouth watered at the thought of it.

'Cup of tea and a bacon sandwich coming right up.' She wrote the order on her pad.

'Still not bought you a ring, then?' he said, glancing at her left hand.

Hazel tried not to show how irritated she was. 'We've been too busy to go and look for one. Nev's working every shift he can and the only day off I get is Sunday. By the time I'm finished here every day I'm too spent to go trailing round the shops and Nev would still be at the factory anyway.' For a moment she felt sorry for herself. Then she straightened her shoulders. 'Still, it'll be worth it.' Who needs a ring anyway, she thought as she made her way back to the kitchen. It'd be nice but I'd rather have the big wedding.

The kitchen always made a point of serving local customers quickly, knowing they usually could only spare a few minutes to take a break, so Joe's sandwich was ready almost at once. Hazel took it over with a big mug of tea. 'There you are, Joe. Extra large to keep you going out there. Is it busy today?'

'Not bad for a weekday,' he said, squirting ketchup over the bacon. 'This is exactly what the doctor ordered. My compliments to the chef. So, Hazel, you thought any more about bridesmaid's dresses?'

Hazel brightened. 'Yes, Neville's mother is going to help out. So we're going to have our sisters in full-length dresses, and our Linda's little girl is going to have some of the material to make up a waistcoat to match.'

'Chosen your colours?'

Hazel nodded. 'Blue or green. I'd like pale colours best.'

'You stop by the stall after your shift and I'll show you something I reckon you'll like,' said Joe. 'We've got some gorgeous taffeta in, lots of shades, and not too dear. If you're buying for all those frocks I can do you a discount.'

'Would you, Joe?' Hazel gave him a huge grin and flicked her hair over her shoulder. 'You're a star. Tell you what, I'll nip back to Ennis Street and get Nev's mum. She knows all about dressmaking and she'll know what will suit the pattern. You'll like her.'

'See you later then.' Joe raised his mug and Hazel hurried off to the next customer. She'd forgive Joe for going on about the ring if she could get some decent material at a knockdown rate. That would mean her own dress could be even more special.

Linda had had a couple of days to get used to the idea of Terry bringing home boxes to store by the time the first lot arrived. There weren't many, and if she hadn't known what he was planning to do then she might have missed them altogether. He arrived home later than usual, when it was already dark, and went at once to open the garden shed. Only a couple of minutes later he was coming through the back door, a big grin on his face.

'Piece of cake,' he said, kissing her. 'You'll hardly know they're there and they'll be gone before the end of the week.'

'You make sure they are,' said Linda. She still wasn't happy about it. 'I don't want June or her friends going in there and finding them.'

'You don't let them, do you?' Terry hadn't thought of that. He hadn't asked many questions but some of the boxes sounded as if they contained glass bottles. His guess was they were brandy. He didn't want his daughter getting her hands on them.

'I don't but you never know what can happen.' Linda was if anything over-protective of her little girl but even she didn't have eyes in the back of her head. Terry didn't know what it was like to try to run a house and look after a lively three-year-old at the same time. 'They go outside to play and there's no knowing what they'll do. They've gone in there sometimes before I caught them and brought them out. I tell them not to and they aren't being naughty, they just forget. It's bad enough that there are sharp tools in there, but now if there are boxes...'

'I'll fit a new lock on it at the weekend,' said Terry hastily. He kicked himself, realising he should have thought of this before. If anything went wrong there would be very unpleasant consequences. His contact had made that abundantly clear.

'Good idea,' said Linda, but she thought that her husband's boast of them hardly knowing the boxes were there was already untrue. Now she'd be worrying that there was something in there that would harm her daughter. 'In the meantime I'll keep her out of the garden. Maybe she can go and play at her friends' rather than them coming here for a few days.' Then she bit her lip. It sounded like she begrudged having June's friends round. She didn't – she just didn't want any of them asking questions, seeing something they shouldn't or, worse, getting hurt.

Terry noticed she'd gone quiet. 'Chin up,' he said. 'Remember why we're doing this. It's for our family. We'll get that big house and fill it.' His eyes sparkled. 'Shall we make a start tonight? Have a nice early bed?' He hugged her again and allowed his hands to wander down her back and gave her bottom a squeeze.

'Stop it, Terry!' Linda pushed him away, trying to keep it lighthearted. Normally she'd pretend to be shocked but secretly loved the thought of an early bed. They'd get June off to sleep and then it would be just the two of them. She still fancied Terry as much as when they were newly-weds and she knew how lucky she was. Plenty of her friends complained they found sex a chore or their husbands were getting bored of them, or even having affairs. Linda loved Terry with all her heart and was absolutely confident he felt the same. She fought against the doubts filling her head. But somehow the boxes in the shed were casting a gloom over her mood. She tried to smile and look enthusiastic as she made her way over to the oven but her heart wasn't in it.

Grimly she set the water to boil to cook the potatoes she'd already peeled that afternoon. She usually prided herself on having a meal ready for Terry almost as soon as he set foot through the door and she didn't intend anything to spoil that routine. If he worked hard outside their home then it was her job to keep him well fed and wanting for nothing. She threw in a couple of pinches of salt, angry with herself for getting upset probably over nothing. She couldn't complain – she'd agreed to this and it would get them what they both wanted in the end, so they'd all benefit. She should be glad of it, not feeling like crying into the vegetables. But she couldn't stop thinking about the boxes in the shed.

Chapter Eleven

Paul woke up to the sound of arguing. It was a moment before he could clear his head of sleep. Then he remembered. His dad had had an even worse loss on the track than usual and his two older brothers had had a go at him. That had been on Monday night, after he'd gone to the pub with Kenny. He'd misjudged it – everyone was still awake when he got back and shouting the place down. His dad had tried to hit his oldest brother and by bad luck Paul had been in the way. It wasn't a case of heroics – he'd been trying to get out of the flat, but he'd been too slow. One moment he was trying to reach the front door, the next his father's fist had landed in his stomach and he was lying in agony on the filthy hall floor. He'd been sick at once all over the ugly rag rug that was already covered in mud and God knows what else. Then he'd collapsed, winded and unable to move.

Next thing he knew he was in his bed – one of his brothers must have carried him there. His dark hair smelt of vomit and his stomach felt like it was on fire. For two days he'd stayed where he was, barely able to shuffle to the sink to clean himself up. There was no way he could have gone in to work, let alone lifted anything while he was there. One of his brothers went past the ironmonger's and told the boss he was sick without explaining what it was. He thought he might lose his job but decided on balance he was safe. The old man liked him for some reason. He'd talk him round once he was able to get back on his feet.

Now it was the third morning and there was another argument going on. Paul couldn't believe it. While he'd been lying in bed, wondering if he'd ever eat properly again, his father had taken the last of the housekeeping and gone to the bookies. He'd lost the lot. He was shouting excuses, claiming that it was the only way they'd ever get back their losses.

The brothers were having none of it and shouting back. Someone slammed a fist against a wall. They were in the next room but Paul could hear it all. This was a madhouse. He couldn't stay in it for one moment longer. The dark and gloomy shop would be better than this. If he moved carefully it didn't seem to hurt quite so much today. He'd manage it if he took things slowly. At least once he'd done up his shirt there was no sign of the damage his father had inflicted – for a drunk old man he packed a deadly punch. Paul wouldn't have thought he had it in him, but now he knew differently.

Gradually he edged his way around the bedroom, stepping over piles of unwashed clothes and mouldy cups and plates. He made an effort to look as normal as possible, dragging on his work trousers and flinching as he bent to find his shoes. He felt in his pockets and to his relief discovered what was left of last week's wages was still there – his father hadn't got hold of it and he was going to make sure it stayed that way.

The more he moved, the better he felt. He was going to be all right. Quietly he let himself out of the house, not wanting to get involved in yet another family argument. Once he was a safe distance down the road, he paused and took out his cigarettes. Lighting one he drew in the tobacco and sighed with pleasure. It was his first one since Monday evening and his head swam a little, which felt good.

He was furious with his father. Why should he have to live like this, in a stinking flat, just because the old bastard couldn't control his gambling? It had been getting steadily worse for the last few months. His friends didn't have to put up with this. They had normal families, ones that ate together, in clean houses, which they stayed in for years without having to do a moonlight flit every now and again. Yes, the men went to the pub but they didn't come home and hit their adult children or at least not without good reason. Paul wondered what would have happened if he'd been more prepared. Would he have hit his father back? He was almost as tall as the old man and far, far fitter. The way he felt now he wouldn't have been able to stop himself. He would have pounded his face until it was unrecognisable. Even then it wouldn't have been enough to take away the red hot anger inside.

Somehow he was going to have to try to go about his work as normal and keep his temper with the stupid customers with their stupid requests. If that stuck-up woman from the solicitors came in he didn't know how he'd avoid losing it. Everything about her drove him mad – her affected voice, her matching gloves and handbag, her scarf in its little gold ring. Well, he didn't think so. He'd like to show her just how worthless she was. He'd slap her about and then... He stopped himself. He couldn't go further at the moment, not with stomach muscles that screamed in agony if he stretched or bent over. But when he was feeling better he'd show them. Or he'd show somebody. He knew exactly who. That ugly bird in the butcher's. She'd be perfect – she followed him around with her big doe eyes as it was. Better, he'd win the money from Kenny and he could hide that from his father. It was March tomorrow – the timing would be spot on as long as he didn't take too long to recover.

Stubbing out his cigarette he resolved to get it over and done with as soon as possible. He needed the money. Even more he needed to show someone who was boss. He needed to get rid of the anger flooding his veins like poison before it drove him insane.

Alison was delighted to see that Paul was back at work at last, but he didn't seem inclined to talk. He was little short of rude. She couldn't help feeling disappointed as she'd watched for him all week, wondering if they would have any of the conversations she'd imagined in her daydreams. She'd fantasised that they would spend their lunch hour together, or he'd ask her to go for a walk with him after work. Sometimes she relived the moment by the shelves when she'd thought he was going to touch her before the old man broke the spell shouting for his assistant. Her imagination finished the scene in ever wilder ways, which left her confused and excited at the same time. What if they'd carried on, ignoring the old man? What might have happened? She could hardly breathe when she thought about it. Her face was very hot.

'Snap out of it, Alison,' said Fred. 'I don't know what's got into you this past couple of days. Get your head out of the clouds and your feet back on the ground, my girl. We've got a busy morning ahead of us.'

'Sorry, Fred,' said Alison, embarrassed. Thank God he didn't know what she'd been thinking about. She hoped there was no clue to it on her face. She didn't want to annoy him – she liked working with Fred more and more.

'I see your young friend next door is back,' Fred went on.

'He's not...' she began.

'His boss said he's had a bad stomach upset so don't you go catching anything from him,' said Fred sternly. 'We can't have anything infectious round here. Our hygiene has to come first at all times.'

'Of course,' said Alison, thinking how unfair it

was. As if she hung around with Paul long enough to catch anything. She'd only exchanged a handful of words, and Fred didn't know about half of those. She supposed the old man had been talking. Even so, she and Paul could hardly be said to be friends. At least not yet. Chance would be a fine thing.

She looked up and saw Fred was grinning. He'd been teasing her.

'We've got our first lot of eggs in,' he told her. 'If I start making space for them near the till, you can check them to make sure there's no cracked ones. Then maybe you can write a sign. We'll keep a careful eye out, and see who buys them and how many. You might want to make a note.'

'All right,' said Alison. She supposed she should feel pleased. This was her idea after all. But all she could think about was Paul.

'Maybe we should fill the shop with smells of home cooking, to encourage people,' Fred continued. 'Fry an egg or two out the back, that sort of thing.'

'I'm not sure the smell of fried egg would work,' said Alison. 'Might put people off. It sometimes makes me feel sick. I reckon the smell of bacon would be better. Make their mouths water.'

'Let's try that, then.' Fred had thought she'd be more enthusiastic and want to do more, as this was her project. Maybe he'd been kidding himself that she was coming to enjoy the work at his shop. He reminded himself she was only seventeen – he couldn't expect her to love the place like he did, to pour all her energy into making it a success. Go easy on her, he reminded himself. Most of the

112

time he had to admit he valued her company – she was getting better with the customers and she'd taken to the job far more quickly than he'd expected. He hadn't felt so optimistic in ages, but he wished he knew what was bothering her. Maybe her difficult sister had been having a go again, or Cora had been unkind in some way. He just didn't know.

'Hello, Paul.' Alison forced herself to be casual as she came back from the post office that lunchtime. 'Sorry to hear you've been ill. Hope you're feeling better.'

Now that she'd cornered him by the ironmonger's door, Paul had no alternative but speak to her, though he wanted nothing more than to buy some sandwiches and find somewhere quiet to eat them. The morning had been harder than he'd thought – he was in considerable pain and hadn't realised how tired that would make him, not to mention irritable. He knew he was only just holding it together.

'I'm fine,' he said shortly. The sight of her face, full of concern but with those awful buck teeth, wasn't doing much for his recovery. He stared at her tits instead and felt a bit better. Soon, he thought, soon. Then he winced as another spasm shot through him.

'Are you hurt?' she said, all anxious now.

God, he had to get away from her. He couldn't breathe. 'It's nothing,' he said. 'Just a tummy bug. It's gone now but I'm not quite over it. I didn't want to miss work though. Don't like letting the boss down.' He made himself smile. It wouldn't hurt to have a comment like that get back to the miserable old sod, who clearly hadn't really believed he was sick until he clapped eyes on him this morning.

'Are you sure you should be here?' she asked, still not getting out of the way. 'Maybe you should go home. I bet your boss wouldn't mind.'

That was the last place he needed to be. All he wanted was to buy something bland to eat and then retreat to the dark, damp little storeroom at the back for some peace. It didn't seem too much to ask. Gritting his teeth he managed to reply and not just push past her.

'I'll think about it,' he promised. 'Right now I'm going to get some fresh air and walk to the end of the road and back. That'll set me right. So don't let me hold you up.' With that he was free, hurrying away towards the corner.

Alison stared after him, feeling let down. That had been nothing like the way he spoke to her in her fantasies. He couldn't wait to get away. Then she told herself not to be stupid. He had only just come back to work after being ill and he obviously wasn't right yet. That was all it was. As soon as he was truly better they'd be back to how they were before. She could see it now. She couldn't wait.

Hazel was waiting for Neville outside the factory gates when he finished his day shift. She'd checked with his mother and for once he wasn't doing overtime so she made sure to get there well before they all came out. There he was, with Bill and Nobby. They were digging him in the ribs and she could hear their raucous laughter. Then all three noticed her.

Neville's face immediately split into a big grin and Bill nodded with a small smile. Only Nobby looked disapproving. Well, she wasn't going to worry about an ugly mug like him. From what she could gather he wasn't much use at anything. She had to admit that beside his balding colleague Neville was better looking than ever. She was lucky.

'Look who it is.' Bill dug Neville in the ribs again.

'Here to make sure he gets home all right?' asked Nobby. The words were innocent enough but there was an edge behind them that she didn't like. She could see what he was implying. She ignored him.

'Thought I'd catch a few extra minutes with you.' She beamed at her handsome boyfriend. 'We're both working so hard I hardly see you.'

'You shouldn't have.' Neville sounded a bit embarrassed but she could tell he was pleased. She took his arm and gave it a squeeze.

'Come on, Nobby,' said Bill. 'Let's not get in the way. See you tomorrow, Nev, and remember you're coming down the pub with us after.'

Hazel raised her eyebrows as the other two headed off.

'Boys' night out, is it?'

'Not really,' said Neville. 'They keep asking me and when I say no, they have a go. So on Monday they asked again and obviously I'm not going to go drinking at the start of the week. The easiest thing was to say I'd go out on Friday. I'll still be up for the early shift on Saturday though.' He

115

looked at her and saw her face was clouding over. 'I'm not going to spend all my wages so no need to worry. It's just a one-off.'

'But Neville, like I said, we hardly see each other,' Hazel protested. 'Now when you do have a night off you're going out with your mates. Don't you want us to be together? Go out and have some fun like we used to?'

'Of course I do,' said Neville, confused by the turn this had taken. 'That's why I'm working so hard. Why we're both working so hard. It's just one evening down the pub. I won't even stay that long.'

'No, no, don't come back early on my account,' snapped Hazel. 'Not when your precious friends mean more to you than I do. No point in short-changing them of your company.' She could feel her temper building inside her. All these days of dashing around in the café, barely having a break, running herself ragged and only having boring Sundays off, no real shopping – it was beginning to get to her. And now she wasn't even going to see her fiancé on Friday night. 'They're clearly more important than I am.'

'Don't be silly, Hazel...' he began.

'Silly? Silly, is it?' She rounded on him. 'I don't think so. I'd say you're thoughtless and selfish. When are you going to take me out? When are we going to buy a ring? People keep asking and I have to say no, we're waiting to find the perfect one and haven't seen it yet. I can't very well tell them the truth, can I? That my boyfriend would rather be down the pub with his mates than seen out in public with me?'

Neville stared at her flashing eyes and the set of her mouth and thought he was looking at a stranger. This wasn't his Hazel. He had no idea what to say to calm her down. Finally he took hold of her shoulders.

'Tell you what we'll do,' he said. 'If we set off now we can make the early show at the Granada. You'd like that, wouldn't you? My treat. Then on Saturday I can get a break between the early and late shifts and meet you when you finish at the café. We could go looking for a ring then. How would you like that?' He held his breath, waiting to see if it would work.

Hazel looked at him suspiciously. 'Are you sure you can spare the time?'

'Spare the time? Are you kidding? I'd walk barefoot over broken glass for you,' he said. 'I'd walk backwards. You just say the word. There's nothing I wouldn't do for you. You're the most precious thing in my life.'

Suddenly she felt ashamed of doubting him and losing her temper. 'I know,' she sniffed. 'It's being so tired, that's what it is. I'd love to go to the pictures. I don't even care what's on. I just want an evening with you, like we used to have. It feels like ages since we did anything like this.'

'It is,' he agreed. 'Come on, let's dash home to eat our dinner, then I'll pick you up afterwards and we'll head up the hill. Give me your hand. There. Now people will know I'm proud to be out with you. My princess.'

Wiping her eye with the back of her glove she told herself to buck up and not to be so stupid. He loved her, she loved him. There were bound

117

to be a few ups and downs. Nothing was going to be handed to them on a plate.

'Come on then,' she said, catching his elbow and almost running towards Ennis Street. Her kitten heels clacked on the pavement as she hurried him along. 'Let's see if we can catch the trailers and everything. I want to make the most of a rare night out with the best-looking man in Battersea.'

Chapter Twelve

Alison spent Friday trying to catch a glimpse of Paul to see if he seemed any better but hardly got a moment to herself all day. For some reason the butcher's was busier than she'd ever seen it. Everyone was coming in wanting meat for the weekend and they kept running out of stock in the front of the store and having to go to the fridges or the back room to fetch more. Fred had no choice at one point but to ask her to deal with her pet hate: liver and kidneys.

'Sooner you start, sooner you'll finish,' he said abruptly. He couldn't afford to be soft about this. He knew she couldn't stand the feel of them but she had to learn. 'Just pretend they're sausages or mince and sort them like that. I don't want you shaking with nerves and having it all slithering about out front when someone wants a pound for steak and kidney pudding.'

Alison pulled a face as she turned her back but knew he was right. She'd avoiding touching them since her first day and the thought of doing so had got worse and worse. She just had to get on with it. Gingerly she approached the pile of kidneys, shining dark red in the pale morning sun. They wobbled as she lifted the tray. She tried not to look as they shone and jiggled when she carried them towards the scales.

'That's it,' said Fred encouragingly. He'd never had a problem with it himself. Meat was meat – you simply had to accept it came in different colours and textures. He saw a kind of beauty in it, the way you could cut different pieces and use them for different meals. He liked to think nothing was wasted. Now he was keen to pass on his knowledge, but he'd have to get Alison over this hurdle first.

'Ugh, give me a nice sausage any day,' she groaned. 'I don't mind eating it but this is horrible.' Still, she managed to weigh out a pound and slide it into a small dish. 'Right, and the next.' Slowly she forced herself to work through the whole tray until she had a row of dishes each with its shiny maroon pile. 'There's just this bit left over.'

'Sure you don't want that for lunch?'

'You're joking. I'm never going near it again.'

'But you did well,' he said seriously. 'I know you don't like it. But you haven't had to run out the back once. See? You're getting better at this. On your first day I thought you were going to spend all the time being sick. Now you're a seasoned professional.'

'Not quite.' Alison still couldn't get used to receiving compliments, even though Fred always commented when she'd done something right. They were a novelty and she wasn't quite sure what she should say. She was pleased though. A few weeks ago she couldn't have done it. Fred was good at teaching her and putting her at ease, she realised. It felt good to have learnt something.

Around the middle of the afternoon the door opened and in came Jill Parrot. 'Hello, Alison! I'd heard you were working here. Oh, what lovely kidneys. Don't they look delicious? I'll take enough for a pie for all my lot at home. We're having a treat as my Lennie got a bonus for all his overtime. Better make it a pound and are those leftovers? Them as well. I don't know where Neville puts it all.'

Fred nodded in satisfaction as Alison wrapped the parcel and cut some steak too, chatting to Jill all the while. The girl was doing well. She'd got over whatever was bothering her earlier in the week and had the makings of a good assistant yet.

By the time they came to close up for the day, what was left of the early sun had gone and the clouds were threatening again. 'Typical,' said Fred, wiping down the counter. 'Usual weekend weather. You got any plans, Alison?'

'Not really.' She was leaning over the counter, trying to see if Paul was winding in the awning next door. 'Might have to go over to Jill's if she's got the patterns for the bridesmaid's dress.' There he was. She grabbed her coat. 'Right, I'll be off then. Have a good weekend, Fred.'

'Give my regards to your mother.'

'I will.' She hurried through the door and then reminded herself not to be too flustered. Taking a deep breath she sauntered over to where Paul was taking in the last of the boxes. 'Are you feeling better today, then?'

Paul glanced up and immediately noticed the eager gleam in her eyes.

'Not too bad. Better than yesterday.' It was true. He couldn't have managed the boxes before. He was almost back to normal and he smiled. Time to start the weekend with a bit of fun.

Alison grinned shyly and looked away. 'I think it's going to rain.'

'Of course it will. It's Friday.' He pretended to hesitate. 'Are you walking up the road? Hang on a mo and I'll come with you. I'll just leave my overall inside.'

'All right.' Alison felt herself blush and wished she didn't do so every time he spoke to her. As he disappeared through the ironmonger's door the first few spots began to fall. She turned to glance up at the sky. It was getting darker and darker.

'Here we are.' Paul was back, shrugging into his overcoat. She could see it was almost as worn out as her mac. 'Let's get away before our bosses call us back.'

'I don't think mine would,' Alison felt bound to say. She didn't spot Fred at the window of the butcher's as the pair of them began to head away from the row of shops.

'Mine definitely would,' Paul said. 'He's mean like that. If he can stop anyone enjoying them-selves then he will. It's how he is. Doesn't believe in having a good time. Not like me.' He drew ahead and faced her. 'What about you? Do you like a good time?'

'Well, I...' She wasn't sure what to say. What did he mean by a good time? A trip to the cinema, or even to a dance hall? Was he about to ask her out? She'd never been dancing but perhaps her luck was turning. She couldn't read his expression though. The rain began to fall harder.

The pavement began to shine like pewter with all the raindrops. As the rain got harder, the water started to flow down the street, picking up rubbish and carrying it into the gutter. Alison wasn't sure she wanted to go very far in this weather. She had dreamed about looking her best for Paul and if she was to go on her first trip with a young man, she didn't want to be soaked through. Her feet began to squelch.

They were passing the entrance to an alleyway, narrow and dark from the tall buildings to either side, but drier than the pavement. 'Here, let's shelter.' He pushed her inside. 'That's better. Don't want to ruin your hair now, do we?' He caught hold of her straggling hair and tugged her towards him. She gasped. What was he doing? Was this normal? 'What were we saying about a good time? Are you going to show me a good time?'

'What ... what...' Alison wasn't sure about the way this was going. She'd fantasised about getting up close to him but he was hurting her. 'Hang on, let go, that's...'

He stopped her by clapping a hand over her mouth. 'Shut up. No need to talk. Don't put me off.' Suddenly his hands were all over her, pawing her, opening her mac, pulling up her skirt, fumbling beneath. She tried to break away but he was too strong. All his frailty of yesterday had gone.

She was pinned against the slimy wall of the alley and couldn't get him off. He was breathing heavily, almost grunting. Then she felt something strange and very painful. He was inside her, pushing, pumping, making her feel as if she was being ripped open. What was he doing? This was nothing like she'd imagined. This was agony. His breath was red hot on her skin. His mouth was on a level with her neck and she hated the sensation. Finally she freed herself enough to scream.

At once he pulled away and slapped her hard. 'Shut up. I told you. Shut up.' He fastened his trousers in a hurry. 'Stupid bitch. What are you screaming for? You've been begging for this for weeks. Don't pretend you haven't.' He grabbed her chin and almost spat in her face. 'Don't you go saying anything about this. Nobody will believe you. And if they do I'll say you begged me for it and I did it out of kindness. Look at you. I'm taking pity on you, I am. Who else is going to fuck you? So you just stay quiet. Right, I'm off. Things to do, people to see. And remember to keep that mouth of yours shut. You don't want to make me angry. I'll be sure to hear about it if you try to tell anybody.' And he was gone.

Alison sank to the ground, barely registering that it was covered in stinking rubbish. She trembled with shock. Her face stung, her insides had been torn apart. What had he done? Is this what Hazel had taunted her about, what men did to women? Even though she worked with carcasses all day she didn't know much about what bodies did. This didn't feel right. This wasn't what she wanted. She couldn't understand how fun, flirty Paul had turned into a monster in the blink of an eye.

Slowly she made herself stand up. She couldn't stay here, she'd freeze. She tried a few steps to see if she could walk and found that she could, though she didn't know how she managed it. All the lower pieces of her body felt as if they'd been rearranged.

Gradually she wandered to the mouth of the alley and out into the rain, where the water fell on her face and cooled it. She did up her mac. One button was missing, but she could mend that. She didn't know if she could put everything else right. She felt as if all her dreams had been thrown to the filthy ground and trampled on. Her hopes for a romantic future had been based on nothing. She was what she had always been – the ugly sister, the worthless one. She was back where she'd started, only feeling even more stupid for believing her life was changing for the better. As she headed for Ennis Street she resolved to tell them nothing. Not because Paul had threatened her, but because she would never bear the shame.

Chapter Thirteen

'I still don't see why you want to let Neville waste money on an engagement ring,' Cora complained. 'Thought you weren't meant to be spending money, and that's why you're working all the time. Look at you now, worn to shreds. That's what happens when you stay out late and get up and do a

124

full shift. Burning the candle at both ends, my girl. Can't go on like that. And now you're off gallivanting, wasting money on a ring.'

'Leave it out, Mum.' Hazel was too pleased to be really cross. She and Neville had had a lovely evening at the cinema, then they'd gone for a drink and sat in their favourite snug. Tomorrow he would take her round the jewellers. She didn't care if she was tired. Her mother was just jealous. 'What's for tea?'

'What does it look like?' Cora could understand that her middle daughter didn't want anything to do with getting a meal ready after spending all day serving food to other people but it was no excuse for being soft in the head. 'If it looks like a pie and smells like a pie, odds are it's a pie. Although if your sister had come home on time and brought us something like she ought to, we could have had a better one. Still, it'll be good enough if I say so myself.'

'I'm sure it will.' There was no sense in Hazel winding up her mother, or she might get dragged into helping in the kitchen. She could do without that. 'I'm going to wash my hair if dinner's not ready yet. I want to look my best for tomorrow.' She made her way out of the kitchen just as the front door opened and Alison walked in. She was drenched.

'Don't just stand there dripping all over the place, you great drowned rat.' Cora sighed in exasperation. 'Get that coat off and bung it in front of the fire. Here, you lost a button?'

'Maybe,' gasped Alison. It hurt to talk where she'd been hit but she wasn't going to admit that.

125

'Clumsy as ever. Hang about, what've you done to your face?'

'Slipped on a wet bit of pavement,' Alison lied. It sounded plausible on a night like this.

'Careless as well as clumsy. Hope you haven't torn your clothes.' Cora turned away from the sight of her youngest, hair hanging down and water falling off the ends, with her hangdog face soaking wet. It was enough to drive anyone to despair. 'You brought home anything from Fred to keep us going over the weekend?'

'No, sorry, we were flat out all day and ran out of nearly everything.' Alison turned to go upstairs.

'Bloody marvellous,' Cora snapped. 'Now I'll have to go to the market to get a bit of meat for our Sunday roast.'

Alison shut her eyes briefly to cope with the pain in her throbbing face. At least this would give her mother something else to complain about. All her survival instincts screamed at her to try to carry on as normal and so even though she wasn't hungry she said, 'Is that pie for tea?'

'Yes. I been slaving away ever since I got back from the newsagent's. It's steak and kidney.'

With a hand over her mouth Alison ran up the stairs.

As soon as Neville came into the café on Saturday afternoon, Hazel was ready to go. She'd hung up her apron early and was all set to leave as soon as she saw him. He barely had time to wave to her boss before she dragged him out of the door.

'I want to show you something,' she explained.

'Steady on, Hazel, what's the hurry?' Neville

was still feeling hung-over from the night before. His mates had made sure he stayed for the whole evening, plying him with pints and then with shots of whisky, which he wasn't used to. At least he hadn't had to buy anything, but he didn't know how he managed to get up in time for the morning shift. Now the last thing he wanted to do was to be dragged around the jeweller's shops. But he knew he couldn't back out. Hazel would never forgive him. Her heart was set on this and, whether they could really afford to or not, he had to keep her happy.

'I don't want them to start packing up.'

'Who?'

'The market stalls. You're going to love this.'

Neville very much doubted it but didn't have much choice. Hazel was forging ahead like a galleon in full sail, sweeping him alongside her. He wondered what could be so urgent, as he tried to keep up.

'Here we are,' she said as they reached the market. Some traders were already shutting down as the flow of customers had started to dry up, but Joe Philpott's bolts of material were still all on display. 'Hello, Joe. See, I told you I'd bring him along.' She nudged Neville. 'Joe's got something special for us. Haven't you, Joe?'

'I surely have,' said the big man, noticing that Neville was much less keen than Hazel though he was doing his best to hide it. 'Some lovely taffeta for your bridesmaids. It's a shade that will set your hair off perfect, Hazel. Not quite blue and not quite green. Sort of turquoise. There. What d'you think?'

Hazel turned to Neville in great excitement. 'Isn't it the bee's knees? Your Kathy will look fabulous in that and so will Linda. Even Alison might not be too bad. I'll get the exact lengths off your mum and pick it up on Monday, as long as you're happy.'

'I'm happy,' Neville assured her. He was glad she was pleased even if he couldn't see what the fuss was about. At least it wouldn't cost them an arm and a leg.

'And there's more,' Hazel went on, excited that she was getting what she wanted, even if it wasn't quite the expensive dress she'd first dreamed of. 'Show him, Joe.'

Joe reached underneath the stall and emerged with another bolt of material, this time white and lacy. 'Only got this one lot left, so you'll need to make up your mind.'

Some of the neighbouring traders had come to a stop and were looking on. Neville wasn't sure what he was meant to say. 'It's very nice... It's lovely,' he added, catching Hazel's eye. Then it dawned on him. 'You'd look like a real princess in that, Hazel. This is for your dress, isn't it?'

'As long as your mum can make it from this amount of material,' she said anxiously. 'It'll be touch and go. But it's just what I've been dreaming of. I've kept an eye out for ages and there hasn't been anything as good as this.'

'If anyone can do it, my mum can,' Neville assured her. He felt his spirits rise. His gorgeous Hazel was going to get the dress that she wanted after all. 'Why don't you bring her along on Monday? She'd love to help out and make sure you buy

128

enough stuff.'

'Will you set it aside until then, Joe?' asked Hazel. She wanted to cry, it was all working out so well.

Joe nodded, packing the precious material safely away under the stall. 'It'll be my pleasure.'

'And now we're off to look for the ring,' Hazel announced.

'Good luck then,' said Joe and some of the other traders nodded. Neville could see they all thought the world of Hazel and wanted her to have the best. He felt his heart swelling in his chest.

'Let's go,' he said. 'Only the best for my princess.'

Hazel had never been so happy.

On Monday morning Cora was at the counter as usual, glad of a sit-down. She was relieved to get back to work after the weekend. Hazel had been impossible, all excited about finding her material and Neville taking her shopping for the blasted engagement ring. Cora wanted her daughter to be happy but still couldn't see the point of extravagance. In the event they hadn't come home with anything but Neville had been hinting heavily that Hazel was to expect a surprise. She'll have a surprise when she sees what sort of a place they'd be living in on his pay packet, Cora thought darkly. He was a nice enough lad but he lacked ambition and had no real get up and go to him. His sister was different – she could see that girl going far. But Neville? She doubted it.

'Cora!' It was Winnie. 'Thank God you aren't busy.'

'I only just sat down,' Cora said.

'I've got to tell someone. You'll never guess.'

'Go on.' Cora could see there would be no stopping the woman.

'It's Beryl's neighbours. They was shouting and fighting all last week and she nearly called the police on them. She wouldn't normally want no bother but it was that bad, she was at her wits' end. Then yesterday it all went quiet and she thought they was sleeping it off. First thing this morning the landlord's banging on her door and she hasn't seen him round their place for months. Wouldn't usually get his hands dirty but soon as it looked like he might lose money he was round like a shot.'

'Lose money?'

'Yes. They've only gone and done a bunk. No sign of any of them. But the state they left the place in! He won't be able to get anyone else in there for I don't know how long. It's filthy, there are holes in the walls, and just like I said, there's rats all over. How they lived like that I don't know. Those Lannings are a disgrace. So now nobody knows where they've gone. The landlord had the cheek to ask Beryl if she knew. She said to him, do I look like the sort of person who would associate with the likes of them? So he's none the wiser.'

'And it was gambling, you said?' Cora needed to get all the details straight.

'Horses and the dog track. Beryl heard it all. The old man blew everything on one last bet and lost. His boys didn't take kindly to it and they've been arguing for days on end. So they couldn't

130

pay the rent or anything else and now they've done a runner.'

'Your poor sister,' said Cora. 'What a worry. And her with little kids.'

'It's been awful for her,' Winnie said. 'At least now she'll have a bit of peace. He'll have to do the place up, and that'll mean he'll be a bit more careful about who he lets move in next time. He won't want anyone that rough again. She might get some decent neighbours at last.'

'The least she deserves,' said Cora. 'Can I get you anything, Winnie? Or did you drop in to tell me the news?'

Winnie put her hand in her pocket. 'I've only gone and forgotten my list. That's what it's been like these past few days. I'll take a packet of short-bread for the time being and come back later if I need more.' She handed over the money and put the biscuits in her big net bag. 'I'd best get on.'

Drawing her warm cardigan around her, Cora watched the woman go. That was a good start to the morning. A pity nobody she knew would know who this family who'd done a flit were, but it was a choice piece of gossip none the less.

Ten minutes later, Jill Parrot came in, a large parcel under her arm. 'Hello, Winnie. I've just come from the market with Hazel. We went there together when she was on her break and look what we bought.' She put the parcel on the table and carefully unwrapped it.

'This is the famous turquoise taffeta, I suppose,' said Cora. Hazel had gone on and on about it at the weekend and she'd got fed up, but now she couldn't help a flutter of excitement as Jill pulled

131

back the last of the brown paper. 'Oh, it's lovely. I'll give her credit where it's due, that girl can pick a good material.'

'It is, isn't it,' beamed Jill. 'And look what's underneath. We'll have to be careful as there isn't much leeway, but as long as we don't make any big mistakes...'

'This is for Hazel's dress?' Cora fingered the delicate lace and felt a tear come to her eye. Stop it, you daft old fool, she told herself. But she was thrilled that her daughter was going to get her big white dress after all. 'I don't know what to say. It's so fine. She'll look like something out of the magazines. You're doing her proud, Jill. I can't thank you enough.'

'Well, it's Neville's big day too,' Jill pointed out. 'He wants nothing more than to make Hazel happy. If I can help with that, I'll be more than pleased.' She began to rewrap the parcel again. 'Don't want to get newsprint or anything on this. There's not an inch to spare. She wanted you to see it at once though.'

'Oh, she's a good girl.' Cora sank down on her stool, almost overcome with emotion. 'I can't believe she'll be gone soon. And I have to say, you are good neighbours. I know you aren't from round here but you've been nothing but kind to us.'

'Thanks, Cora.' Jill tied the string tight around the bundle, careful not to damage it.

'Talking of which,' Cora added, 'there's been a right to-do down towards the power station. You won't know her but Beryl – that's auntie to Vera Jewell that Alison used to work with – she had awful neighbours and now they've done a bunk.'

132

'Vera Jewell? I think Neville's mentioned her.'

I bet he has, Cora thought. 'Yes, apparently it was all about gambling debts. A family of four disappeared overnight. Dreadful, isn't it?'

'Sounds like it,' agreed Jill. 'We should count our blessings. There but for the grace of God and all that. Right, I'd better get this home and start thinking about patterns.'

'Yes, we've a lot to be thankful for,' said Cora, wondering who she could pass the news on to next. It never hurt to have a good piece of gossip to spread.

Chapter Fourteen

Alison dreaded the thought of going to work on Monday morning but there was no getting out of it. She couldn't pretend she was still feeling the effects of falling on the wet pavement. Nobody had questioned her story as the weather had been filthy on Friday night but she wasn't going to risk it.

She stayed in bed as late as she dared, deciding that she'd rather arrive after nine than see Paul opening up the shop next door. Her mother and Hazel had left earlier than her as usual, so she didn't have to face them at least. Slowly she forced herself to get ready, carefully washing her bruised face, wincing at the rough flannel. But that was nothing to the agony she felt inside. Disappointment and betrayal were mixed with an awful

133

sensation that she'd asked for what he'd done to her, that it was all her fault. All her life she'd been told she was to blame for everything bad that happened to her, so this was no different.

Approaching the row of shops she felt her heart hammering in her chest. Somehow she had to act normally, to carry on, just to get through the next few hours. What if Paul came out to do the awning like he often did? There was no sign of him however and the boxes that were usually stacked outside the ironmonger's were nowhere to be seen. She hurried past, fearful he would come out.

Fred gasped when she went in. 'Whatever have you gone and done to your face, Alison? That looks painful. Have you put anything on it?'

'Slipped on the pavement in the rain,' she muttered. 'I'm all right really. Looks worse than it is.'

'You should have put a raw steak on it,' said Fred. 'Pity you weren't here when it happened.' He looked at her directly. 'On Friday, was it?'

'Yes, in that cloudburst. But can you see my mum wasting good steak on a bruise?'

'No, you've got a point there.' He knew there wouldn't be much steak to spare in the Butler household. Still, he couldn't help remembering what he'd seen through the shop window when the girl had left on Friday night, chatting to the lad from next door. Fred had had little to do with the young fellow but something made him instinctively distrust him. He was too cocky, too full of swagger. However he kept his suspicions to himself.

The morning passed in its usual way. Mondays were often quiet as people had Sunday roast left over to eat as cold cuts or make into other meals to eke it out. Fred and Alison got on with sorting out deliveries and restocking the front counter, putting out the eggs that were beginning to prove popular, and stopping to serve the occasional customer. Alison was glad of the routine and relieved she didn't have to make much small talk. She was still in shock at what had happened and while the physical pain was slowly fading, her heart felt like it was breaking. She blamed herself for being so stupid as to think someone might actually like her. She should have known better. But why had he seemed so friendly when he'd hated her all along? She couldn't understand it and the riddle went round and round in her head.

It was almost lunchtime when the doorbell went and the manager of the ironmonger's came in. Fred looked up. 'Hello. We don't often see you in here.'

'No,' said the man, who seemed rather embarrassed. 'My wife does all the shopping. I haven't come to buy anything.' He cleared his throat. 'I don't suppose you've seen my assistant this morning? Mr Lanning?'

'No, can't say as I have,' said Fred.

'I wondered if you knew anything, miss,' said the man. 'You seemed to get on well with him.'

Alison blushed bright red. Surely he hadn't worked out what had happened? 'Not really. I spoke to him now and again, but I don't know him very well. I haven't seen him today.'

'Well, it's most inconvenient. He might have let me know if he was ill again. At least last week his brother came in to tell me but I've not had a word this morning. Most irregular.'

'Perhaps they've all come down with the bug,' Fred suggested. 'I'm sure he'll turn up.'

'He'd better have a good excuse or he'll find himself out of a job,' snapped the man, before turning abruptly and leaving.

Fred shrugged as the door slammed. 'Bit odd, but he's got his knickers in a proper twist, hasn't he? Funny old sod.'

'Mmmm,' said Alison but her mind was whirling. Had Paul stayed away to avoid her? She'd hated the thought of seeing him again but assumed he would turn up and act as if nothing had happened. He might even threaten her again. Part of her was beginning to feel relieved that she wouldn't have to endure that, or at least not today.

'Right, let's get stuck in to parcelling up this pork,' said Fred. He looked at her carefully, but she didn't seem to notice.

Alison did as she was asked and tried to concentrate, but now she was more confused than ever.

Neville had worked an extra night shift at the paint factory over the weekend in order to have the Monday afternoon off. Now he knew what ring size Hazel wore and what sort of things she liked he could buy her what she wanted. They'd looked at loads of beautiful rings on Saturday and she'd found it hard to choose. It was true many were beyond his budget but there had been a few places with items that he could have stretched to. Now he was on his way back to one of them, selling secondhand jewellery, which was within his price

136

range. He didn't think Hazel would mind it not being new. It was more important that it looked right.

He walked quickly past Clapham Junction, dodging the crowds of people that were always coming and going around the station whatever the time of day, and made his way along past Arding and Hobbs, head down against the wind. He turned up his collar as he went and almost bumped into someone coming out of the huge store.

'I'm so sorry...' He stopped. The figure looked familiar. She was wearing a tightly belted rain-coat, high stiletto heels, and very bright lipstick.

'Neville Parrot, isn't it?' The young woman met his glance with her sparkling blue eyes. 'I'm Vera, Vera Jewell. Are you still at the paint factory? I know some of your colleagues there.'

'Of course. I thought I knew your face.' Neville grinned, as it wasn't only her face that was fami-liar. Her curvy body was unmistakable, even though he'd never seen it up close. Then he reminded himself what he was meant to be doing this afternoon.

'I used to work with Alison Butler,' she went on. 'You're going out with her sister, aren't you?'

'That's right. We're getting married. In fact, I'm just going to buy her the engagement ring.'

'Really?' Vera's face broke into a big smile. 'Congratulations. Where are you buying it? In here? I could get you a discount.'

Neville shook his head. Even with a discount he knew the prices in the department store would be beyond him. 'Nah, we've seen a few we like in a

137

little place round the corner. She wants it to be special, you know, so she's pointed out a few and now I'm going to pick the best one.'

Vera nodded. 'She's a lucky woman. Most men wouldn't know how to do that.'

Neville shuffled his feet. 'Well, I don't really know much about it either, but it's what she wants.'

'Don't suppose you'd like some help with the final decision?' offered Vera. Then she checked herself. 'Sorry, you probably think I'm being really cheeky. But I love looking at jewellery and now I'm working in there I've got a better eye for colour and style. Everyone says so.' She gave him another little smile.

Neville hesitated. What harm could it do? He knew Vera had a bit of a reputation but that was likely put about by men she'd turned down. She seemed perfectly friendly, not at all the manipulative schemer some of his colleagues had described. 'Are you sure you've got time?' he said.

'Yes, it's my lunch hour.'

'In that case I'd be glad of your help,' he said. They set off towards the second-hand jewellers and Neville decided everyone had got completely the wrong idea about this woman.

Alison arrived back after work with a bag of pork offcuts to keep her mother quiet. There had still been no sign of Paul and his boss had come into the butcher's on two further occasions. By the time he'd finished Alison felt as if she was being accused of hiding something. Even though she'd denied knowing where he was she thought she'd probably sounded guilty as she had something much worse to hide. If only they knew. But she would rather die than tell anyone what had happened. Fred had looked at her oddly several times but she'd assured him there was nothing wrong. She was certain he would sack her on the spot if he found out. She was damaged goods now. He most likely wouldn't want to be tainted by having her anywhere near the shop. She was desperate for sympathy but dared not hope for any. The pain was so great though that she didn't know how she would bear it on her own.

'Here, look what Fred sent for you,' she said as Cora turned to see which of her daughters it was.

'Pork? Oh, that's good of him.' Cora was all smiles. 'He's a nice man and don't you ever forget what a kind deed he did taking you on. I only hope he doesn't live to regret it. You make sure you're a credit to him.'

'He says I'm learning fast,' Alison said. She knew her mother would never believe that she could be good at something, so she was wasting her breath, but Fred's confidence in her was the one way her life had improved. Carry on as normal, she reminded herself. Don't give her cause to suspect anything is wrong.

'Like I said, he's a nice man.' Cora made room for the pork in her crowded kitchen. 'He won't go saying you're useless even if he thinks it. Now come and show me your new skills by chopping those veg.'

Alison sighed. Her mother was never going to change. She took off her mac and washed her hands at the sink, noticing how shabby everything

139

was compared to Fred's gleaming surfaces. Her mother scrubbed and scrubbed but it was a losing battle. There was no way on earth the kitchen would look smart. The utensils were battered from many years of use, the cupboards needed a fresh lick of paint and most of the crockery was chipped. Wearily she reached for the peeler, with its wonky handle.

Suddenly, Hazel burst in.

'Good, you're here, Mum.' She ignored her sister. 'Neville's coming over in a minute. He's got it, he's got it.'

'Are you talking about your ring?' Alison said.

'What else would it be?' Hazel shot back.

Cora wiped her hands. 'That's lovely. Will he want some tea?'

'No, his mum is doing something. He's just going to pop over. He won't be long.'

Almost immediately, there was a knock on the front door.

'We'll do this in the front room,' Cora decided. 'Come through, Hazel. You too,' she added as an afterthought, gesturing to Alison. She followed them, thinking how this was rubbing salt into her wound. Hazel's boyfriend was doing all the right things while her own brief hopes of someone to love had been snuffed out.

Neville came in, carrying a small velvet bag in midnight blue. Hazel could barely contain her excitement as she took it and reached inside. She gasped as she opened the matching velvet box.

'Oh Neville, it's beautiful.' She lifted out the ring and Neville slipped it onto her fourth finger. 'It fits perfectly. It's that one we saw, isn't it? It

140

was my favourite but I didn't like to say.'

Cora took her daughter's hand and looked closely at the ring. 'Those little blue stones on either side of the big one are gorgeous. You are clever. They'll go with the bridesmaid's dresses.'

'They're aquamarines,' said Neville. 'They're related to emeralds. I thought they'd go with the sort of colours you wear most, Hazel.'

Cora was impressed. 'You know a lot about these things, Neville. I'd never have thought it. You've really looked into this.'

Neville beamed, glad he'd stored away those facts. He knew he had some work to do to win Cora's approval and this had been a good step towards it. He kept quiet about how Vera had won over the old jeweller, getting him talking and even persuading him to reduce the price. He didn't want Hazel to think him a skinflint, but it was always a relief to get a bargain, as the wedding costs were mounting up. It hadn't been the same man they'd seen on Saturday so he hadn't known who Neville was buying the ring for. He'd assumed Vera was the fiancée and they'd gone along with it. Neville knew he could never have made such a good choice on his own or have learned about the stones. He definitely didn't have Vera's way of bargaining – she'd charmed the jeweller, who'd found her irresistible.

Hazel waved her hand in front of Alison's face. 'What do you think?'

'I love it,' said Alison, doing her best not to let her emotions show. 'It's beautiful.'

'Bet you wish you had one like it,' Hazel said, her eyes glittering. She turned to her sister and hissed quietly, 'Better make the most of this as you'll never have one of your own. A pity, but there it is.'

'Well done, Neville,' said Alison, forcing herself to ignore the thoughtlessly cruel taunt. She was used to this sort of thing but wondered if the young man had realised how spiteful his bride-to-be really was.

'I'd better be getting back to Mum, she's doing bubble and squeak.'

'Oh, that reminds me.' Cora's thoughts flew to her conversation with Jill that morning. 'I was telling her earlier. Winnie Jewell came in first thing and her sister's family have been having a really tough time of late. I said to you, didn't I, Hazel? Awful trouble with their neighbours.'

'Winnie Jewell? Yes, you did say,' said Hazel.

'Did she say how Vera's doing?' asked Alison. She'd often wondered how her former colleague was getting on, and missed her cheerful way of making light of any problems. It would have been fun to have got to know her better before that awful day when they'd been sacked.

'No, I didn't ask her,' said Cora, not pleased at having her story interrupted. 'I've got no interest in that girl. No better than she should be, that one.'

'She's a right tart,' agreed Hazel. 'You want to keep away from the likes of her, Neville. She'd have her grasping hands on you in a flash given half a chance. Go on, Mum.'

Neville caught his breath in relief at not having to reply. He'd half-thought about sharing the story with Hazel, thinking they'd have a good laugh

142

together about the old jeweller making such a mistake. Now he was glad he hadn't mentioned it. He'd keep that secret to himself.

'It was Winnie's sister Beryl who had the problem,' Cora went on. 'This family next door were the lowest of the low, filthy habits and disgusting language. There weren't no mother, just three grown lads and a drunken father who gambled away all their money. The place was a disgrace and they were always fighting. Beryl could hear the lot. Well, guess what. They've only gone and done a flit.'

'No!' Hazel's eyes widened. She loved a bit of gossip as much as her mother. It was always good to hear about someone worse off than herself.

'Poor woman,' said Neville. 'We won't ever get in a mess like that, Hazel.'

'I should think not,' said Cora. 'You come from a respectable family. Not like those Lannings.'

Alison thought she must have misheard.

'Did you say Lannings?'

'Yes, that was their name. Why, do you know them? How on earth would you know someone like that?'

Alison felt her blood run cold. She stuttered as she replied. 'That's the name of the assistant in the ironmonger's next door to Fred's shop. It might be a coincidence though.'

'Might be,' said Cora dubiously. 'Not a common name, is it? I'd have thought a respectable shopkeeper would think twice before employing someone like that. I'm surprised at him.'

'Well, it's not as if it was Fred who made the mistake,' said Neville. 'I really had better be off.

143

Hazel, let me see your hand one more time to check I got it absolutely right. If I say so myself that is a good ring. You look even more beautiful now and I didn't think that was possible.'

Alison took advantage of the moment to run upstairs to her tiny box room. She couldn't stand one moment more of all the lovey-dovey behaviour but more importantly she needed a moment to think about the bombshell her mother had dropped. She could hear Cora tutting and Hazel saying 'Leave her, she's just jealous', as she threw herself on her narrow bed. Good, let them think that. She had far more urgent matters on her mind. So Paul was gone for good. He came from a terrible family. In one way that was just as well – he'd never have been a proper boyfriend and she was well rid of him. She should be glad. But she'd hoped for so much. It didn't matter that she'd got it wrong. For once in her life she had dreamed of this being someone who would love her and who she could love back, and now it wasn't going to happen. It was never going to happen. She was ugly and worthless and everything about her was useless. How completely stupid she had been to imagine it could have been different.

Hugging her pillow she tried to stifle the sob that rose unstoppably in her throat. She'd been too shocked to cry after he attacked her on Friday. Now all the sorrow and fear and hurt came flooding out and she wept as if her heart would break. Her fantasies of a boyfriend who would take care of her were nothing but ashes and she didn't think she would ever get over it.

Chapter Fifteen

Linda had almost forgotten the reason why there was a new lock on the shed. True to his word, Terry had made sure the boxes were collected only a few days after they'd been delivered and she hadn't had to see any of it. June had been intrigued by the shiny new lock for about three minutes and had then lost interest. It was as if it had never happened.

That meant she wasn't particularly pleased when Terry made his announcement a few weeks later. 'I've said they can use our shed again.'

'Who?' she asked, at first misunderstanding.

'Best you don't know any names,' he said at once. 'What you don't know can't hurt you. And it'll only be for a few days, like before.'

Then it dawned on her what he was on about. 'Must we, Terry? You know I didn't like it last time.'

'But you liked the extra money in the bank,' he pointed out. 'That's all saved away for our moving-house fund. This way we'll be able to add to it.'

'I know, I know.' Linda couldn't deny it. 'But do we really have to? Maybe there's another way to save up. Now June's that bit older, perhaps I could get a part-time job...'

No. Absolutely not. No wife of mine is going to go out to work. We always said I'd be the pro-

145

vider. June needs you at home, not out messing around in an office or shop. We don't want her looked after by strangers – who knows what habits she'd pick up? My family are at the other end of the country and it would take too long to get her to yours. No, you can't be leaving her at this tender age.'

Linda sighed and twisted the tea towel she was holding round and round in her hands. 'I know that's what we always said. I don't want to have anyone else look after her, not really. I'm just trying to think of a way we don't have to put ourselves at risk.'

'Life's a risk.' Terry put his arms around her. 'Sometimes you just got to take a chance. And this will be worth it, believe me.'

'What? What's different this time?' Linda had picked up on his tone of voice, the one he always used when he was trying to avoid telling her the full story.

'Nothing. Not really. It'll be a bit more stuff, that's all. It will all fit, there's no problem with that. Don't you start worrying over nothing.'

'It's not over nothing, is it? You just said it was more stuff. Do you know what it is?'

'Best we don't ask,' he said seriously. 'It won't be stolen, it won't be dangerous. It's not going to explode or anything. It'll just be luxury goods to bring people a bit of pleasure that they wouldn't otherwise have had.'

'Because they couldn't afford to pay the full price, you mean.' Linda broke away from him and started to pace around the kitchen.

'Something like that, yeah.' Terry didn't think

that was so bad. As long as that was all it turned out to be. His contact had floated the idea that they could do even more business if Terry was willing to take care of other goods, but hadn't specified what. Terry hadn't agreed but hadn't said no either. He reckoned he would think about it if this next job went as smoothly as the first. That had been money for old rope. If they wanted another baby they'd have to save up fast and it wasn't going to be easy on his wages, reasonable though they were. They had standards to maintain.

Linda tried to think it through rationally, but she was afraid. She'd put her anxieties to the back of her mind but now they broke out. What if the boxes were found? What if Terry was sent to jail? That would bring everything crashing down and what would she do then? She couldn't bear to return to Battersea. Everyone would know she had failed and blame her for daring to leave her old life behind. She loved her new life and wasn't prepared to sacrifice it. But she also wanted the new house and a baby to go in it.

'Stop it, love.' Terry reached for her, preventing her from pacing any more. 'You're working yourself up and you don't need to. I'll take care of everything and nobody will be any the wiser. It's not yet anyway.'

'When will it be?' she asked. She didn't know if she was glad it wasn't tomorrow or if it would be better quickly over and done with.

'They're not sure. Something to do with the tides. Probably end of next week. They'll let me know. Then maybe you can arrange to be out for a few hours.'

147

'A few hours? How much are we talking about?'

'I told you, only what will fit in the shed. It won't take that long, I only said that so's you'd have time to go somewhere and not see anything.' For the hundredth time he cursed his wife's quick wits. Usually he loved that about her but sometimes he wished she'd just let something pass without questioning every aspect of it.

Linda nodded, only slightly pacified. She wasn't really convinced. 'Promise me you'll be careful.' She shut her eyes, trying to get rid of the feeling that something would go wrong. 'Promise me that you'll walk away from all this if it starts to get dangerous. I don't want you getting hurt.'

'Nobody's going to get hurt.' Terry was pretty sure it wouldn't come to that. Not for a pile of boxes.

'Promise me.'

'All right, all right, I promise. It's all going to be right as rain. You won't know they're there and if you take June with you then she won't ask awkward questions. And we know where she gets that from.' He smiled at his wife, teasing her.

'It'll serve her well,' she said. 'She won't let anyone walk all over her. I was thinking, maybe I'll go up to see Mum. I haven't been for ages and when she last wrote she said Hazel's got a lovely new engagement ring. That would be a good reason to turn up. June will like that too.'

'That's the spirit,' said Terry. He didn't like to see her down in the dumps. This would solve everything.

'Oh my good God, whatever is that noise?' Cora

148

could hear it even before the door to the Parrot house opened and the music grew twice as loud.

'Come on in,' said Jill. 'I'm sorry about this. It's Richie's latest favourite. Someone called Elvis Presley. Awful, isn't it?'

'I don't know what to say.' Cora stepped inside and Jill hurriedly closed the door. 'You can't call it music, can you? It's just noise. I don't know what he sees in it.'

Jill led her through to the small but immaculately clean back kitchen, where she had her latest wedding plans laid out on the table. 'Here we are. It's a bit better in here. He'll get tired of it soon and then we'll all be able to think straight again.'

Cora sat on one of the ladder-back chairs and then turned as Kathy came into the room. She couldn't help noticing how smart the girl was, with her dark wavy hair just long enough to lie on her starched white collar, which matched the elegantly thin white belt around her tiny waist.

'Hello, Mrs Butler. Mum, I'm going out with some of the girls from work later, so don't worry about me if I'm not back at the usual time.' With a smile she was gone.

'Lovely girl, your daughter,' sighed Cora. Sometimes she wished one of hers worked in an office so they could look like that. Not that Alison would be anything like as stylish as Kathy – but when she brought back her bloodied aprons to be washed, Cora shuddered to touch them. 'Hard worker too. Mind you, our Hazel has been going non-stop with only one day off a week. If she runs around much more she'll be too thin for her

149

wedding dress.'

'Oh no, we can't have that. All these dresses have to be exactly right and I can't be altering them at the last minute,' Jill said. 'We'll have to feed her up more. I've got a book of McCall patterns and they're very careful about getting the size right. So none of our girls is allowed to change shape in any way until after the second Saturday of September.'

They started going through the lists of what was to be done and when, checking everything was going to plan. September was still six months away but there was so much to do in between. Finally they had done as much as they could and sat back to take a break. Jill went to the kettle and filled it.

'We had a letter from our Linda this morning,' Cora told her. 'She's coming up for a day at the weekend and bringing June. They haven't been to visit us for ages. Maybe I can bring them over so they can see the material. June'll be thrilled.'

'That's a good idea.' Jill set the kettle to boil. 'Must be hard having her living away like that.'

'I can't complain,' Cora said. 'She's bettered herself. She's done well. She's never been no trouble to me. I look at her and I think I done all right. Hazel too. Wish I could say the same for Alison but there's always one.'

'She's not so bad,' Jill replied, pouring the boiling water into the teapot. 'If she stood up straight and had a different haircut it would do wonders for her. Kathy's good with hair – shall I ask her?'

'No, no, that would be a waste of her time,' Cora assured her. 'I wouldn't want to impose. God knows I've tried suggesting improvements but it just falls on deaf ears. She's not interested.'

Jill wanted to get off this awkward subject. 'You heard any more about that family that did a moonlight flit? Has anyone seen anything of them since?'

'No, not that I know of.' Cora shook her head. 'Turns out one of them worked in the shop next to the butcher's so Alison knew him a bit. He's never shown his face since. Left his boss high and dry. He's trying to get a new assistant but no luck yet. Some people have no consideration.'

Before she could go on, the volume of the music rose still further.

'Right, I've had enough,' said Jill, setting down her cup. 'Excuse me, Cora. I need to go and have a word with that young man upstairs. Just because he's mad about rock and roll doesn't mean we all are.'

Cora sat and listened as the music abruptly stopped but Richie carried on singing 'Hound Dog'. Then there was a yell of, 'Oh, Mum!'

'I'll give you crying all the time in a minute,' Jill shouted. 'You'll have something to cry about if you carry on like this. I'll take that record player away and tell your father, then you'll be sorry.' The voices faded.

Cora nodded. That was only right and proper. She wished Jack had been around to help her with the girls, but she'd had to do everything. It would have been nice to share the trials of three growing children. Maybe he would have been able to sort Alison out. Then she thought it was unlikely. The girl was impossible.

Chapter Sixteen

Alison tried to work at her usual speed the next Monday morning, knowing it would be the quietest time of the week, but she couldn't find the energy. She felt completely worn out and couldn't see the point of anything. Wearily she transferred cuts of pork and beef from the back of the shop to the front, dragging her feet, feeling every tray was a dead weight.

She'd so looked forward to Linda's visit. Her big sister was the one person in the world who'd always stood up for her and who didn't blame her for being so awkward. Linda might have understood if Alison could have got up the courage to tell her what had happened that Friday night. But that hadn't happened.

From the moment she and June had arrived it was nothing but plans for the wedding. If it wasn't arrangements for the dresses it was exclaiming over Hazel's engagement ring. Alison had hardly been able to get a word in edgeways, let alone a moment to confess to her big sister. It had been a huge disappointment.

There had been a moment when they were both on their own in the kitchen when Linda had asked her if she was all right. That would have been the time to say something – but then June had come running in and any chance of comfort from her big sister had vanished.

She should have known it was a false hope. Nobody could help her carry her burden. It had been her fault for daring to dream Paul really liked her, that she could have a boyfriend like all the other girls did. Telling Linda wouldn't have altered that. Although the bruises had faded, in her heart she was deeply hurt. That hadn't even begun to heal. She wondered if it ever would.

Grimly Alison went from shop to storeroom, listening to Fred talking to the occasional customer, knowing this state of everlasting misery was how things were going to be. There was nothing to look forward to except a bleak future and she'd been stupid to think otherwise.

Over the next few weeks Alison grew more and more tired and barely spoke unless she had to. She lost all interest in food and the cosy lunches with Fred petered out. She made up an excuse of not wanting to put on weight before the wedding as the dress couldn't be altered. Fred went along with it but was sure there was more to it than that.

He knew Alison wasn't one to put herself forward but over the time she'd worked for him he'd seen her start to come out of her shell and how naturally easy she could be with people when given a chance. It worried him that these days she avoided speaking to the customers unless there was no way out of it. And she barely chatted to him at all. He knew he was far older than her and that she wouldn't look on him as a friend and yet he couldn't help feeling snubbed. They'd built up a good working relationship – or at least he

153

thought they had. He'd found her a real companion, with opinions and ideas that he suspected she never shared with anyone else. She'd begun to smile and when she stopped worrying about everything it turned out she had a quick sense of humour too. Maybe he should ask her outright if there was something wrong. But what did he know about young women? Even if she did confide in him, he wasn't sure he'd know what to say. It wasn't as if he'd had much experience of women at all, unless he counted his domineering mother. He certainly didn't know what the modern girl might have to worry about.

So he said nothing. That didn't stop him growing ever more concerned, as Alison's face got thinner and thinner and her eyes developed dark rings beneath them. Was she ill? Was that what was alarming her and making her behave so differently?

She also seemed to be back where she started when it came to dealing with offal. Several times now he'd seen her hurrying to the back of the shop and then a door would slam and there would be the unmistakable sound of someone being sick. If this went on he was going to have to say something, as it was affecting the way they worked. He had to be able to rely on her to pack and serve whatever was in the store. She couldn't pick and choose. He couldn't be out the back checking deliveries wondering if she was going to leave a customer in the lurch as she ran off to the toilet. Business would suffer and he wasn't having that.

Alison had seen the look on Fred's face when she'd returned to the counter. She was beginning to suspect she might have more to worry about than an angry boss. Even though she was naïve she wasn't completely ignorant. When she'd been working at the factory several of the women had been pregnant and had talked about their symptoms. One in particular had had to be sick several times each morning and had treated everyone to a full description every time. Alison had thought it was enough to put anyone off having a baby.

She remembered when Linda had been expecting June. Four years ago she'd been too young to pay that much attention especially as Linda had recently moved down to Kent, adamant that no child of hers would be born in Battersea. But her big sister had been up to visit a lot in those early days and had talked to Cora about how hard she was finding pregnancy. Alison had listened to the list of sickness, tiredness, being off her favourite foods, swollen ankles, disturbed sleep, and pitied her big sister. Of course when June arrived everyone had been delighted. But Linda's circumstances were very different.

She forced herself to count back to when she'd last had those stomach cramps she always got when it was her time of the month. It hadn't been long after she'd started working for Fred and she'd been too embarrassed to ask if she could sit down for a bit when they'd got really bad. Paul had raped her at the beginning of March. She counted on her fingers the weeks that had passed. Her heart sank when she realised it all added up. She'd been too miserable to notice at first. She'd assumed her overwhelming tiredness was down to being so depressed about Paul's terrible betrayal.

A baby. Was that really what was happening to her? How would she know for certain? How could she cope with a baby? Where would she live? She was pretty sure Cora wouldn't want it in her house. Her mother would be mortified at the disgrace of it. Cora had very plain views about girls who let themselves get taken advantage of before marriage and never hesitated to voice them. Alison couldn't even begin to imagine what she'd have to say when her mother found out.

She tried to be practical. Would she be able to carry on working? What would Fred say? She didn't know what he thought of unmarried mothers but she knew he was very against anything that was bad for business. Once word got around she was sure she would be a liability to him. Even if he was kind, how hard would it be to work once the baby was born? Cora had told her often enough what it had been like in the war, having to hold down two or three jobs to keep the wolf from the door with two little girls and herself as the unwanted extra nuisance. She'd been dropped off with neighbours much of the time. They'd been willing to help out because Cora had been left a widow. Alison knew she couldn't count on anyone helping her.

What would it be like to have Paul's baby? Every time she looked at it she would be reminded of that stinking alley, the shock of realising what he was doing. How could she live with that? Would it have his eyes? She'd adored those eyes once but now she knew how cruel they could be. How could she love a child who looked like him?

But as the days went by, she realised that maybe

there was a way around it. Perhaps she didn't have to have the baby. She'd heard whispered conversations about people who got rid of their unborn children. There had been a woman at the factory who was rumoured to have done it. She'd been mysteriously off sick for a few days and had returned, gaunt but determined, saying nothing. The word was she had a husband but he beat her and she didn't want to bring a child into a household like that. Some had condemned her and others had been sympathetic. Alison thought it couldn't have been worse than being unmarried and going through with it.

But how would she find out about such a thing? She didn't have any friends to advise her. Her family was out of the question. Who did she know who might be able to point her in the right direction? She didn't know enough about any of this.

Alison bit back a sob as she faced the fact that there was nobody she could turn to. She had to find out what was happening to her but she was totally alone.

Cora was delighted. She'd been to see about hiring the church hall in September and had managed to get it at what she knew was a very good rate. She'd emphasised the fact that she was a widow but, though poor, her daughters were respectable and hard-working. She'd also mentioned that the Parrots were exactly the sort of family they wanted to move to the area – prepared to help out and muck in with anything, even though they weren't local. She'd painted the picture of Hazel

157

and Neville as the perfect young couple who just needed a little helping hand to start their life together before becoming pillars of the community. The church warden couldn't have been more obliging. They'd settled on the price and Cora had put down a deposit. She congratulated herself on a job well done.

She decided she would treat herself to a trip round the market. Normally she only rushed from stall to stall, haggling for what she needed, never taking much notice of what else was there. Now she walked slowly along, enjoying the spring sunshine, eyeing the goods on offer. The thought struck her that Hazel would soon be wanting new items for when she set up home with Neville. Perhaps they would be given some as wedding presents but they would have to buy the rest. It was a bit early to start yet but it wouldn't hurt to look. Also, for the first time there would be some spare room in her own house. She'd become so used to the cramped space she hadn't really considered what it would be like once Hazel left and took all her clothes with her. They took up more room than her own and Alison's put together.

Cora groaned to herself. She'd be stuck with Alison and nobody else to break the tedium. She wasn't looking forward to that. With Hazel there was always something to talk about – where she'd been, who'd been in the café, what was happening at Neville's factory. But with Alison there was nothing. She never brought back any decent gossip from the butcher's, even though she must hear lots of it. Too dim to work out what was worth repeating and what wasn't, more than likely. She had no friends and never went anywhere. She might earn her keep by bringing home her wages and the offcuts and leftovers, but as a companion she was worse than useless.

'All right, Mrs Butler?' called Joe Philpott. 'How are the dresses coming on?'

Cora smiled at him. 'They're going to be lovely. Jill Parrot is very clever with her sewing machine. I wish I was half as good at dressmaking as she is.'

'Hazel tells me you've made lots of her stuff and you've taught her everything she knows.' He winked. 'And she's a stunner. So you must be pretty good yourself.'

'Oh, nonsense,' said Cora but she was flattered. She hadn't had a bit of a banter for ages.

'Tell you what, why don't you take a look at my trimmings.' Joe brought out a big box. 'See anything you fancy? What about these pearl buttons?'

'Joe Philpott, if those are real pearl then I'm a Dutchman.' She picked up a packet of rickrack binding in different colours. 'Now this is more like me. I could use some of this when I'm making up a frock for my granddaughter. She's three already, you know.'

'You don't look old enough to be a grand-mother,' said Joe. 'I'd never have believed it if I hadn't heard it from your own mouth. Why don't you choose a couple of colours and have them on me. On account of your family being such good customers of late.'

Cora beamed. 'That's very good of you. I'll take you up on that before you change your mind. That pretty primrose yellow and the pale blue. They'll

159

suit her best.'

Joe popped the wavy binding into a paper bag and handed it over. 'There you go.'

Still smiling broadly, Cora wandered along the other stalls, thinking this was her lucky day. After all she'd been through over the years, she was well overdue a change of fortune.

Chapter Seventeen

The walk from the butcher's to Clapham Junction was almost too much for Alison. She had to hurry as she only had her lunch hour to complete her mission, but it left her gasping for breath by the time she reached her destination. Not eating much didn't help. All she really felt like was small pieces of dry toast. Anything else made her sicker than ever.

On the corner at Clapham Junction was the grand entrance to Arding and Hobbs. She glanced at it nervously. She'd hardly ever been there, never having had the money to afford their prices. She remembered going in a few times as a child, although what with the war and clothes rationing it was much quieter back then, and Linda had taken her there a couple of years ago. She knew it was huge inside and that it was easy to get lost. She'd have to keep her wits about her as she didn't have time to lose her way.

It seemed as if half of Battersea had come to the big department store at lunchtime, as the press of people going in and out of the big doors threatened to overwhelm her. Alison put her head down and concentrated on keeping going. She was here for only one reason and she couldn't allow herself to be distracted or fear the crowds. Her idea might be a crazy one but she knew she had to try.

She had to find the floor with ladies' wear. Once there she had to hope the person she was looking for was on duty. There was no guarantee that she would be, but Alison couldn't think of another way to see her. It had to appear casual. She just had to keep her fingers crossed she wasn't on her lunch break as well. She knew it was a long shot and she might be making too much of what had been a brief acquaintance but she'd always hoped it would turn into something more. Well, now was the time to put the idea to the test.

This must be it. She was surrounded by elegant clothes far finer than anything she'd ever worn. Wide-skirted dresses in every colour imaginable hung from hangers, and further away she could see a rack of the new sack dresses, none of which would be in her size, she was sure. She dared not touch anything and just prayed her awkwardness didn't show on her face as she tried to blend in with the other customers. How she would love to have clothes like this. Such a dream seemed farther away than ever. If her fears were right soon all she would be able to fit into would be her baggiest jumpers.

Then she saw the familiar figure. She made her way cautiously across the floor, and came to a halt by a rack of blouses. She carefully chose one with a scalloped collar and lifted it on its hanger, as if she did this sort of thing every day.

'Can I help you, madam?'

'No thank you, I'm...' Alison looked up, feigning surprise. 'Vera! Fancy seeing you here!'

'Alison Butler! I was only wondering the other day how you were getting on,' said Vera, smart in her shop clothes and without the usual bright lipstick. 'Are you here to choose something for your sister's wedding?'

Alison wasn't surprised she'd heard about the big event. Winnie had probably passed on the news after a gossip session with Cora at the newsagent's. That was how Alison had learnt where to find her old colleague. Most likely all of Battersea knew about the wedding by now.

'Not really. I've got to wear a bridesmaid's dress. I wish I could just go in normal clothes but there's no escape.' Alison didn't allow herself to think about what would happen if this conversation failed and she had to tell Hazel why she couldn't be a bridesmaid. She'd deal with that later. Otherwise she would break down completely. But the good thing was her former colleague seemed as friendly and open as ever, and hadn't cut her dead.

'Did Hazel like her ring?'

'Yes, she ... how did you know about the ring?' Alison was so surprised that she forgot what she'd come to ask.

'Didn't Neville say?' Vera's hand flew to her mouth. 'Oh God, I've gone and put my foot in it. Don't worry, it was all perfectly innocent.'

'What was?'

'Well, I happened to bump into him when he

162

was going to choose the ring and he was all of a dither so I asked if he needed a bit of a hand. I went along to help him pick the right one. You know what men are like, haven't a clue about that sort of thing.' Vera raised her eyebrows.

'He didn't say,' Alison told her. She was stunned by this piece of news. 'I ... I won't mention it to Hazel.' She knew what her sister and her mother thought of Vera and could imagine what would happen if they found out. They'd never believe it was as innocent as Vera claimed. If Alison spilled the beans then she was sure somehow she'd end up getting blamed for it.

'How are you getting on?' Vera asked. 'Anything's better than the factory, isn't it? Those miserable old men always trying to get you in a corner and cop a feel. Dirty sods. There's none of that in this place.'

That had never happened to Alison but it reminded her of why she was here. 'I'm glad to be out of there,' she said truthfully, 'but I've got a bit of a problem. Actually, you might be able to help me. Is there anywhere we can talk without everyone listening?'

'Not really. But I could meet you after work if you like.' Vera glanced up. 'Would that be all right? I finish at five today.'

Alison took a deep breath. Of course. It had been silly to think Vera would be able to get away when the store was so busy. But she hadn't said no outright. That was good of her – it wasn't as if they'd had the chance to get to know each other properly before. 'Would you? That's really kind of you. I finish at five too.'

'We'll do that then.' Vera nodded. 'I'd better go. The supervisor's always on my case, thinks I spend too much time chatting as it is. Five-fifteen, that café outside the station? See you there.'

Alison flew out of the door of the butcher's at just after five. Usually she helped Fred to clear up but she didn't want to miss Vera, who only had a short distance to go to the café. Fred watched her, wondering what the urgency was. It was the fastest he'd seen her move for ages.

After walking as fast as she could, Alison arrived at the café, breathless. There was no sign of Vera. Frantically Alison's eyes swept the room. There were young couples gazing at each other over the Formica tables, some old men who looked as if they'd been in there all afternoon, a few professional types grabbing a quick snack before the long train journey back to the suburbs. But no Vera.

Hesitantly Alison took a seat at one of the few vacant tables. The heat and smells of cooked food were making her feel sick again and her head swam. She gripped the edge of the table. Up to today she'd been sick only in the mornings. Please God don't let that change now.

There was a gust of cold air as the door opened and Vera burst in, red lipstick freshly applied, coat belted tightly to show off her figure. Every male head in the place turned. She ignored them all. 'Sorry I'm late. That supervisor drives me nuts. You'd think the world was going to end if I left as much as a speck of dust on the underwear shelf. Still, I'm here now. What are you having?'

'Just a cup of tea,' said Alison, hoping she'd be able to keep it down.

'I fancy some of that cake,' said Vera, pointing to a rich fruit loaf on display at the counter. 'I get ravenous in there on my feet all day. Sure you don't want any?'

Alison shook her head, trying not to gag.

'All right, just the one then.' Vera smiled to catch the attention of a passing waitress and placed their order. 'Not bad in here, is it? So, what was it you wanted me to help with?'

Alison looked around to check there was nobody in there who might know who she was but couldn't see anyone. She'd better say her piece and get it over with. She was so nervous she hardly knew where to start.

'I've not been very well,' she said abruptly. Then it all came out in a rush. 'I've been sick a lot, I'm tired all the time, I'm losing weight, I can't think straight.' She gasped. 'I don't know who to ask what's going on. When I happened to bump into you...' She paused as she told the white lie. 'I thought you might know what it all means.'

Vera waited as their teas and cake arrived. She sipped her drink and lifted an eyebrow. 'I see. If you don't mind me asking, have you missed your monthlies?'

Miserably Alison nodded. 'Twice. I didn't think anything of it at first. But now, what with being sick all the time ... it's not just the smells at work, everything sets me off. I couldn't handle the kidneys and stuff to begin with and my boss got used to me running out, so he still thinks it's that. But I think it might not be.' She couldn't meet

165

the other woman's eyes.

Vera toyed with her cake and then set down her fork. 'Right. That only sounds like one thing to me. Are you having a baby?'

Alison couldn't stop a tear from escaping. 'I'm afraid I might be. I'm not making it up, am I? Those are the symptoms, aren't they?'

Vera nodded. 'Sounds like it. You can miss your monthlies for lots of things but adding it all together ... when did you and your boyfriend do it?'

Alison almost laughed. 'He wasn't really my boyfriend.' She caught Vera's expression and hurriedly corrected herself. 'I thought he might be, once. He was nice and everything to start with. But then ... then ... it was almost dark and he pushed me ... and forced me. I couldn't stop him.' She shuddered at the memory. 'And now he's gone and disappeared. So I'm stuck.'

'Can't you tell your mum?' Vera asked. 'Hang on, no, I suppose not. What about your sister?'

'Not likely,' sighed Alison. 'She'll say I've done it deliberately to ruin her wedding. You're the first person I've told. There isn't anyone. My big sister might help but she's away from home and I can never get her on her own for a minute.'

If Vera was surprised she didn't show it. After a moment she patted the back of Alison's hand. 'You poor thing. That's such bad luck. You mustn't blame yourself. These things happen.'

'Thanks.' Alison wiped her face with her hanky. 'But I do blame myself. I shouldn't have been so stupid. It's my fault for trusting him.'

Vera tutted. 'It isn't. You just said you didn't have

166

no choice. So it's his fault, no two ways about it. But it's you what has to bear the consequence. Not fair, is it?'

Alison shook her head. Now that she'd finally told her secret she felt drained. 'Please, eat your cake. Don't let me spoil it.'

'You daft mare!' Vera touched her arm. 'Don't say such things. I'd love to help you more but I'm not sure how.'

'You've listened to me and didn't blame me,' said Alison. 'That's more than I deserve. But I was thinking. Remember back at the factory, there was that woman who was having a baby – and then she wasn't?' She dropped her voice. 'Do you know how that happened? What did she do?'

Vera's eyes narrowed. 'Yes, I remember. But don't you go thinking of such a thing. It's dangerous, and illegal. You could die and they won't lift a finger to save you. Costs a bomb as well. Believe me, you don't want to go anywhere near that.'

Alison's last flicker of hope disappeared. 'Is it that bad? Don't you know anyone?'

Vera shook her head and her eyes flashed. 'No, I don't. And if I did I wouldn't send you their way. I'm serious, they'd kill you and not care. I wouldn't go near them if I was in your position. Which I haven't been.'

'I didn't mean...' Alison began, anxious not to offend Vera even though she was on the brink of despair.

'I'm not stupid,' Vera said, slowly lifting her cup and then putting it down again. 'I know what people say about me. As it happens, they're wrong. Just because I wear makeup and dress the way I do doesn't mean I drop my knickers for anyone who asks. I like a bit of fun, so what? Doesn't everyone? It makes me sick, the way they all sit on their tight little arses and whisper behind their hands and nudge each other when I come near. Thinking they're better than me. At least I'm honest about it. Two-faced old bags.'

'I didn't mean anything by it, Vera,' said Alison. 'I knew you'd tell me what was what, that's all.'

'Well, I'm telling you now to stay away from those back-street bodgers,' Vera said, calm again. 'It's the best advice I can give you. I'm sorry I can't do more, I wish I could. Look, I better be going, but come and see me any time. You can always leave a message for me if I'm not on duty. Don't go doing anything silly – promise me.'

Alison smiled weakly. It was strange to think that this woman who everyone was so rude about could offer kindness so willingly and yet her own family, always certain they were doing the right thing, wouldn't hesitate to throw her to the dogs. 'Thanks,' she said. 'I'll be all right. At least now I know.'

Vera picked up her big handbag. 'Always better to know what you're up against, that's my motto. See you around.'

Alison wished she could be as sure. It seemed that whatever way she looked at it, the future was impossible. If she couldn't get rid of the baby, then what was she to do?

Chapter Eighteen

Neville had met Hazel after work and had taken her to the cinema. They couldn't spend every night at home, saving money. He wanted to spoil her a bit, to show her how proud he was to be seen out with her. The evenings were getting longer as it was late spring, with summer just around the corner. The sun was setting as they wandered back towards Ennis Street, and Hazel paused outside a shop window.

'Look at that tea set,' she said. 'Isn't it lovely? We could have something like that when we're married.'

'My mum said we could have her old one,' Neville told her. He couldn't see what the difference was. It was something to drink tea out of, and he didn't really care what the cups and saucers looked like. There was no point in wasting good money on such things when there were so many important wedding preparations on which to spend their hard-earned cash.

'That's nice of her,' said Hazel, trying not to grit her teeth, 'but that one there is more modern. See those shapes and colours? That's what's fashionable. Linda's got one very like it.'

Neville nodded, thinking that he was going to have to get used to that idea. He was hearing more and more of what Linda had and how perfect it all was. He hadn't realised Hazel was quite so keen to have everything her sister had, or even better.

'Let's save up for it then,' he said. 'We can start off with what Mum gives us and then put a bit away each week. Anyway we'll have to find somewhere to live first.'

Hazel pressed her nose against the shop window. 'They've got some cushions as well. I can't wait to start making a home together.' She turned and smiled invitingly. He drew her into his arms and kissed her.

'I'm more interested in what we have in our bedroom,' he breathed, unbuttoning her coat and pulling her to him around the waist. 'Let's think about that first.'

She snuggled closer and then pulled away. 'Time enough for all that when we're married.' She didn't want to be thought common, canoodling with her boyfriend in a shop doorway in the fading light. But the wedding night seemed like ages away. Sometimes she hated having to wait.

'We'll have a beautiful bed,' he went on, 'and we'll never want to leave it. I'm going to make you so happy…' He reached for her again and kissed her more and more desperately, his hands moving under her coat. For a few moments she gave in, then wriggled out of his arms.

'What if someone sees us?' she hissed. 'Let's walk on.' She held his hand and found she was trembling with suppressed passion. Why did the other girls have all the fun? Perhaps she should just give in. But she'd never bear the shame if anyone found out or, worse, if she got caught out and fell pregnant.

'Where shall we live?' he said after a moment.

'We could start putting our name down with the landlords. I'd like to be close to Mum.'

Hazel sighed. What she really wanted was to be in a better area, even if somewhere like Kent was out of the question. She knew they couldn't be too far from the paint factory, but they could do better than Ennis Street. Also, while she could see it would be useful to be near their families, she didn't want them dropping in every spare minute of the day. She was looking forward to some privacy alone with Neville as God knows they had precious little of that now.

'Maybe not too near your mum,' she suggested. 'I mean, nothing against her, or the rest of your family, but I want it to be just us.' She squeezed his hand tightly and turned to look at him meaningfully.

'So do I.' He could barely get the words out. 'I can't tell you how much I want to be alone with you in our house. September seems like ages away.'

'Only a few months now.' She started to walk on again. 'We could find somewhere a bit further from the factory, further away from the power station. That wouldn't be too bad, we could still see everyone.'

Neville wasn't sure. He reckoned he would miss his mum's home cooking and had thought they might drop by for a meal whenever they could. He also didn't want to have to spend ages getting home if he was on night shifts.

'Not too far from the factory,' he said. 'Remember I'll still have to do lots of overtime if we're setting up house and buying new stuff. You don't

171

want me arriving home dog tired. I want to save my energy for other things...'

'Yes, but we'll want to have somewhere as nice as we can afford,' she insisted. 'I don't want a cramped place like Mum's. Linda's house has lots more room in it and she's thinking of going somewhere even bigger. I don't want to live in a hovel.'

Neville wondered if Hazel actually knew how much flats in the area cost, as he was pretty sure that was all they could manage, even if they both carried on working long hours. But he didn't want to disappoint her. 'I won't let you live in no hovel,' he assured her. 'Nothing but the best for my princess.' He stopped and kissed her once again. 'Come on, we've still got time for a drink. How about a visit to the pub before last orders?'

Hazel looked at him standing under the street-light and thought once again how gorgeous he was. But all the same, she'd have to put her foot down about where they lived. She was desperate to have a nice home away from the crowded terraces of her childhood, where the only view was straight onto row after row of houses just like her own. She sensed Neville would live next to his mum if she let him, and she wasn't going to settle for that. She couldn't wait to get him alone in their own place. September seemed longer away than ever.

'A drink would be lovely,' she said, hugging him and breathing in the scent of his neck. She'd force herself to have another sherry. After all, Linda liked it.

'Your idea to sell eggs has been a great success,' Fred said to Alison a few days later, as the latest delivery arrived. 'Look, this is twice what we took that first time. Some days we can't keep up with demand.' He grinned broadly, wiping his hands on his apron. Nothing made him happier than a successful business move. He wished she was as pleased as he was, but he couldn't even raise a smile from her. 'It's all down to you.'

Alison tried to sound interested. 'Thanks, Fred. It's nothing.'

'It's not nothing. Good ideas are money in the bank. Good ideas are what keep this place going.' He wanted her to understand. 'Not everyone has them. You can wait for years for an idea that works. You must have a talent.' He waited to see if she reacted.

Alison smiled wanly. 'Beginner's luck.'

Fred bustled around the counter. 'Don't be so hard on yourself. You have to learn to take a compliment. I'm not making it up, you know. How about a nice omelette for lunch? We haven't done that for ages.'

Instead of accepting with enthusiasm Alison turned green and ran through to the back.

Well now, thought Fred. That wasn't about handling offal. They hadn't sold any all morning and she hadn't had to move any in the storeroom. A tummy bug? It was possible. There was always something going round, but he hoped he'd impressed upon her that if she was sick she mustn't come in. There could be another reason of course.

He thought about it. She'd been awful when she'd first started the job, running off to be sick

173

every five minutes, but then she'd improved. She hadn't complained about cutting up all manner of bits of animal that would have turned many people's stomachs. Then it had all started up again.

He didn't want to ask her outright. Maybe he'd got this wrong. He hoped he had. But he could hear her now out the back, running a tap loudly to try to cover the other noise. It might work for the customers but it didn't fool him.

He thought about what he knew of her. She never mentioned friends and had certainly never said anything about a boyfriend. Then again, why would she? He was only her boss. She probably thought of him as ancient. Also, he knew her mother and she wouldn't want any snippets to get back to Cora. He was fond of his old friend's wife but knew she had a fearsome reputation as a gossip. All the more reason for Alison to keep her secrets.

He was equally aware of what Cora thought of her youngest daughter, and – from comments Alison had let slip – what Hazel thought as well. Fred didn't agree. Alison was bright and funny and good company once you got past her awkwardness. All right, she wasn't a looker like her sister, but she had other things in her favour. He'd come to count on her around the place. If he could see her special qualities he supposed a young man might too.

So what were this young man's intentions? Was he going to stand by her and do the right thing? Maybe she hadn't told him yet, or maybe he was as scared as she was. Alison was only seventeen.

Perhaps her young man wasn't much older. Perhaps he needed someone to talk him round, point out that he couldn't leave her in the lurch when it was as much his fault as hers. It was no laughing matter to have a baby when you weren't married.

The more Fred thought about it, the more certain he was that this was what was wrong with his assistant. He made up his mind. He'd have to say something. She wasn't just his employee, she was his old friend's daughter too, and he wasn't around to look after her any more.

After a while Alison emerged, her hair even more straggly than usual, her face white. 'Sorry, Fred. Must be something I ate.' She wouldn't meet his steady gaze.

He wasn't prepared to accept that. 'Seems to me as if you've been eating lots of things that don't agree with you,' he said. 'In fact, you've been doing that for quite a while. Strange thing is, I never see you eat anything. You're wasting away. Are you sure nothing else is wrong?'

Alison shook her head and looked away. 'I'm all right,' she muttered. 'I had a big breakfast before I came in.'

Fred took a breath. He didn't want to pry. Yet this couldn't go on. He had a duty to say more. 'Are you?' he asked. 'I don't think you've been overeating at breakfast every day for these last few weeks. That won't make you tired and listless. That's not like you. You were lively and you learnt everything fast. You even chopped up liver.'

Alison gulped and turned her back to him.

'Look, I don't want to stick my nose in,' Fred

went on doggedly. 'But I've got to say something. I don't think you're well. Have you been to a doctor?'

'I hate doctors,' Alison said quietly, her voice catching.

'But you should go. You can't carry on like this. People will notice.'

'I'm putting off the customers, am I?' she cried. 'That's exactly what Mum and Hazel said would happen. It was only a matter of time.'

'No, no, that's not what I meant.' He clumsily tried to touch her shoulder but she shook him off.

'I don't want to hurt your business,' she choked. 'You've been nice to me. I'll go.'

'No, you mustn't go.' He was doing this all wrong. 'I don't want you to go. I just wondered if there was anything else wrong. Anything I could help with. If you wanted me to have a word with your young man…'

'No!' she shouted. 'I'm all right. Just leave me alone.'

He couldn't bear to see her so upset. 'Listen, I don't mind. Sometimes it's better man to man. Make him understand that he can't just leave you to face the music…'

'You've no idea what you're talking about! I tell you I'm all right! There's nothing more to be said!'

'Alison, stop, think for a moment…'

She had grabbed her coat and was running for the door. 'I'm all right! I'm all right!'

She dashed out into the street, nearly knocking a customer off her feet.

'Goodness, whatever's wrong with her?'

Fred forced himself to make light of it. 'Oh, she saw a big spider out the back. You know what some people are like about them. She'll be back once she's calmed down. What can I get you? We've got a lovely bit of pork belly at the moment.'

As he went through the familiar motions of cutting the meat and wrapping it, he wondered what he should do. Ought he say something to Cora? He couldn't just do nothing, not when Alison had more or less confirmed his suspicions. But he didn't want to land her in hot water either. 'Here you are,' he said, with his best shopkeeper's smile. 'See you soon.'

Wiping down the counter, he realised he'd have to wait and see. He couldn't force the girl to accept help, no matter how concerned he was for her welfare. But if there was a young man out there who'd let her down, he wasn't going to stand for it.

Chapter Nineteen

Alison almost ran down Falcon Road, desperate to put as much distance between herself and the butcher's as possible. She was glad it had started to rain – it made her tears less obvious. The few people who were out in it had their heads down, taking no notice of her. She hunched over more than ever, trying to stifle her sobs.

She turned off the main road and wandered on

more slowly now, not caring that she was getting soaked. A few more turnings and she was by the river. She could see the hulking shapes of the wharves. The buildings across the water were shrouded in drizzle, grey masses against grey clouds. If she walked along the bank a bit further she'd be at St Mary's church. Her family never went there but she had an idea that Fred did. She couldn't see the point of it all. God hadn't answered any of her prayers so far and she certainly wasn't going to spill her heart out to a vicar. She remembered hearing that the church had homes for people like her – unmarried mothers who needed to give birth to their babies in secret, away from gossiping neighbours and shamed families. She shuddered. She didn't want to go to any such place, but she didn't want to go through this alone.

Should she trust Fred? As she grew calmer she thought hard about it. He'd been kind so far and even though he'd asked those intrusive questions he hadn't ordered her to leave. But what could he do? He was a middle-aged man with, if her mother was to be believed, no experience of women except for an old harridan of a mother. Would he know about doctors who could help her? But Vera had said that was illegal. Even if her friend hadn't told her what she wanted to hear, Alison believed her. The image came to her of a blood-soaked couch, sharp instruments all around, and a girl lying in the middle of it, rolling in agony. She didn't think she had the nerve to risk it, let alone the money.

As the fine rain continued to fall she realised she

was getting colder. Good. Maybe she could catch pneumonia and then she might lose the baby. Then she couldn't be blamed for killing it but the result would be the same. Perhaps she could manage it so that her mother and Hazel wouldn't find out. She could say it was a heavy case of the monthlies. She'd tell Fred he'd been mistaken and she'd been ill after all. That would mean Vera was the only other person who knew, and she wouldn't say a word.

Alison opened her coat so that the rain would soak her apron and blouse beneath it but as fast as the shower had started it stopped again. The sun came out and instead of getting drenched, Alison began to dry out, steam rising off her coat. The weather was warming up with the advent of summer and usually she would have been pleased, but now it had spoiled her one desperate idea. She'd have to get something other than pneumonia, or else wait for the next heavy rainstorm. She shrugged. It was the best she could come up with.

Gazing over the churning water she decided she'd have to put a brave face on it and at least act more cheerful even if she didn't feel it. If she went on like this even her mother might notice eventually. She'd stop wallowing in misery and get on with earning as much at the shop as she could, just in case her plan didn't work. Then when it rained again she'd find a reason to be out in it for a long time and let nature take its course. Plenty of women lost babies when they were ill, after all.

Taking a deep breath she turned her back on the river and began to retrace her steps. The old lanes between the water and the main roads shone with raindrops and for a moment she stopped to take in how lovely they looked. The sun was out and the early summer greenery was swaying in a gentle breeze. If only things had been different. She could have looked at this scene and enjoyed it properly. She hardly ever took a moment to see what was around her. She was so used to her mother saying how awful the area was and Linda telling them how marvellous Kent was in contrast that she went along with them. But there were spots in Battersea that she loved, and this was her home. She just had to get through the next few weeks and hope that nobody noticed anything until she had a chance to put her plan into action.

'You go on in and play, then Mummy will be back for you this afternoon.' Linda was dropping off June at the home of one of her little friends. She was a sociable child and loved having friends round and now some were inviting her back to their houses. Linda was glad of the break some-times although she was very particular about who June went to play with. She didn't want her associating with just anybody. They might as well have stayed in Battersea if she mixed with some of the kids round here.

As soon as she'd turned the corner into her own street Linda's smile faltered. She was trying to put on a good front but inside her emotions were in turmoil. For a few weeks she'd thought the longed-for second baby was on its way and she could hardly contain her joy. This is what June really needed: a brother or sister. Only children were lonely, it was well known. And it was so tempting to spoil her. She knew Terry would love a son, to play football with and teach all about lorries, though he'd be more than happy with another daughter as well. She'd been on the point of telling him last night.

Then she'd felt the dreaded cramp in the stomach and it had all come to nothing. She'd sat in the indoor, upstairs bathroom that they were both so proud of and wept in disappointment. She'd been so sure; she'd felt more tired, her breasts had seemed larger and more tender, her mood was different. She thought her appetite had changed too. Now she didn't know if she'd imagined all of it and it was simply that her monthlies were very late or if she had just lost what would have been a baby.

She told herself not to be so silly. They had plenty of time. She was only twenty-four. Women far older than her had babies. She and Terry had years ahead of them and goodness knows they enjoyed trying. That wasn't the problem. So why was she so depressed about it? These things happened.

Because, said a little voice in her head, if you were pregnant then Terry might not take all these risks storing the boxes. He wouldn't dare to upset you. He knew how much she worried every time the consignments arrived, and how she'd noticed they were getting bigger and staying on their property for longer. The good thing was the payments went up each time. Yet she'd be quite happy to draw the line under what they'd saved. There was enough for a bigger place now. It wouldn't be a

181

mansion but it would have an extra room for the new baby when it came.

The sooner that baby showed signs of arriving the better. She hated the way it wasn't under her control. She loved having everything go to plan. June had been conceived within a year of their marriage and had been born bang on time. That had lulled Linda into a false sense of security. Everything she'd wanted, she'd worked hard for and it had all fallen into place. Though she never admitted as much, even to herself, she'd assumed this would continue. Now it looked as if she was wrong.

Snap out of it, she told herself. Usually she had no patience with mopers. It's just a minor setback. Don't go making yourself a nervous wreck. Everyone says you have to be relaxed to fall pregnant. You've got to keep calm. Don't make trouble where there's none.

She laughed to herself. She had to be patient. And anyway, Hazel would have been furious if she'd fallen pregnant and couldn't fit into her bridesmaid's dress. So there was a bright side after all. Heaven help anyone who did anything to ruin her sister's wedding.

Over the next few weeks Alison did everything she could to make herself ill while trying to behave normally. Every time it rained she managed to get soaked – but as the weather got warmer there were fewer and fewer showers. If a customer mentioned having a cold or a bug she made sure to serve them and to keep them chatting for as long as possible. She didn't catch anything.

One Saturday afternoon she slipped out and went to the local library, where she checked all the medical encyclopaedias. Not surprisingly they didn't give any clues to how to get rid of unwanted babies. She tried flicking through various novels instead, and that was more useful. There was something called a gin bath. Did that mean taking a bath in gin? It sounded expensive. She read on and saw that the heroine took a very hot bath and drank a bottle of gin while she was in it. That sounded more like it.

Having a bath at home was complicated, as there wasn't a bathroom in the house. A tin bath hung in the outside toilet. This had to be moved into the kitchen and then filled with water heated on the cooker. Usually they didn't bother and washed standing up at the sink. Still, it sounded as if it would be possible.

Alison walked for some while up the hill from the library until she found herself in an area near Stockwell where nobody would know her, and managed to buy a bottle of gin. She'd have to make up an excuse to Cora why her contribution to the household budget was less than usual as it took a big chunk out of her wages. She could say that Fred had made her buy some new aprons out of her own money. That would do.

By the time she got home it was early evening and Cora was slamming down a plate on the table in front of her almost as soon as she got through the door. 'Where've you been? You can have this on your own. I'm going over to see Jill, as some of us are working hard for your sister's wedding. We'll be busy all evening so there won't

183

be no afters if you don't make it yourself.'

'I don't mind,' said Alison, hiding her bag behind the chair. 'Where's Hazel?'

'Gone to see Neville. For once he ain't working the late shift and they're making the most of her having a day off tomorrow to have a night out and I don't blame them. So you're on your own, unless you got any other plans.' She looked critically at her daughter. 'Which I don't suppose you have.'

'I might have a bath,' said Alison.

'Well, wash your hair while you're at it. See if you can do anything to make it less like rats' tails.' With that Cora picked up her handbag and headed out.

Alison was relieved. She quickly ate the spam fritters Cora had made and then set about putting water on to heat. She dragged the tin bath off its rusty hook and into the kitchen where it took up all the available space. While waiting for the water she tried her first sip of gin.

It tasted disgusting. She didn't think she'd be able to manage much of it but wasn't sure how much she needed to drink for it to work. She deliberately poured a glass to finish off before getting into the bath.

She started off by sipping it slowly but found it too horrible, so held her nose and gulped back the lot. It burned her throat and she thought it wouldn't stay down but she steadied herself and waited. After a few moments she thought she'd be all right. She was very unsteady but somehow managed to tip hot water into the bath, strip off and sit in it.

Maybe this was why you had to drink gin. She'd

never normally be able to stand it this hot. Her head swam. How long did she have to stay in here? It was sweaty and uncomfortable – if she hadn't had the gin it would have been painful. She couldn't bear to dip her head in it to wash her hair. Then a wave of nausea hit her.

Stumbling, she grabbed a towel to wrap around herself just in time and made it to the outside toilet. She vomited up the spam fritters and the gin in one agonising heave. Panting, she rested her head against the cool wall, thinking that she'd been sick more often in the past few months than in the rest of her life put together. She wondered if that meant it wouldn't work. She ought to drink more and top up the water but she couldn't bear it.

Eventually she made her way back inside and slowly emptied out the bath before hanging it back up. Alison desperately wanted to throw away the gin but realised she'd never afford it again so hid it at the back of a kitchen cupboard. Then she went upstairs and collapsed on her cramped bed, the tiny room going round in circles, as she waited for something to happen.

She woke in the morning with a pounding head. Cautiously she glanced under the covers. Nothing. It had all been for nothing. There was not a drop of blood to be seen.

Chapter Twenty

Fred was at war with himself. He didn't know what to do for the best. After Alison had run out in tears he'd vowed to keep his big mouth shut. By rights it was none of his business. Yet he didn't really believe that. In some way he felt responsible for her. It wasn't just because she was his assistant. It was more that she didn't have a father to look out for her interests. Also, he admitted to himself, her mother and sister didn't seem to like her very much or be inclined to help her. Furthermore he genuinely liked and admired the young woman, who'd become such an asset to the shop.

He noticed that the weight she'd lost had started to come back, and then that she'd begun to show a bump. As June turned into July it was definitely making an appearance. Perhaps he was more aware of it because he saw her tying her apron every morning. She fastened it more and more loosely as the weeks went on, but in that moment before tying the ribbons he could see the little curve.

Sometimes he would ask her if she'd been to see a doctor yet, but she'd shake her head and refuse to talk about it. He wondered if her mother knew. No, something would have happened if she did – Cora wouldn't have accepted such a bombshell. But hadn't she noticed? The girl's hair was shining, her skin was blooming, and she was wearing clothes that were baggier and baggier. It seemed obvious to him and he was just a middle-aged man who knew very little about young women's bodies. Surely her mother or her sister would spot something? Did they pay that little attention to her at home?

The one good thing was that the sickness seemed to have passed. Alison was back to her capable self around the shop, cutting up liver without a murmur. It was only now and again when he caught her staring into space with a hopeless expression that he'd have known anything was wrong. She had grown more and more quiet, chatting to customers if she couldn't find a way out of it but not volunteering any comments as she'd begun to do only a few months earlier. It made him sad to see the change in her. She was closing in on herself again, just when she'd been doing so well.

Should he tell Cora, prepare her for the news? Would she take it better coming from him? But then again he didn't know the circumstances or if there was some unknown young man waiting in the wings. Just because the girl never mentioned him didn't mean anything. He could be away doing National Service. If he was going to have a conversation with her mother then he should find out the facts. Yet every time he tried to raise the subject Alison clammed up and after several attempts he was none the wiser.

On the surface they were nearly back to their old companionable ways. 'What are you doing this weekend?' he asked as one Friday afternoon drew to a close. Fred was quite pleased with himself.

187

When he'd worked out how much it would cost to employ Alison, he'd found it cheaper to employ a lad on Saturdays, allowing Alison to have the weekend off. 'Cinema, maybe? Have you seen *Funny Face* yet? They say that Audrey Hepburn's marvellous in it.'

'No, I haven't been for ages,' she replied. The truth was she'd hardly ever gone to the cinema. Her mother had never had the money to take them, she'd been too young to go with Linda before she left home, and Hazel didn't want to be seen out with her. A handful of times some of the women from the factory had asked her along and she'd enjoyed herself, but the last thing she wanted was to see other people's romances paraded in her face right now. 'I'll probably just stay in. Might treat myself to something at the market.' She'd taken to buying men's shirts in a large size, making sure they were from one of the stalls well away from Joe Philpott and his mates. If she chose plain ones they weren't so very different to the blouses she'd worn before. As long as she did her own washing then Cora or Hazel had no reason to suspect anything. Somehow she'd convinced herself that she could keep up the pretence that nothing was wrong and that this would continue up to the baby's birth. Beyond that, she hadn't thought.

'It's got Fred Astaire in it too,' said Fred. 'I like him. I used to fancy myself as a bit of a dancer when I was young.'

'Did you?' Alison couldn't hide her surprise. Fred was the last person she could imagine on the dance floor, let alone moving like Fred Astaire.

'I did,' said Fred, keeping a straight face. 'Sadly

188

nobody else rated my efforts. I knew all the steps but that wasn't enough. Then the war came and Mother got ill, so that was the end of that. I used to love all that going out and dancing, it was a right laugh and took my mind off things, but her needs had to come first, it was only right. I had to hang up my dancing shoes once and for all.'

'That's a shame,' she said. 'You should try it again some time. It's never too late.' She smiled as she picked up her coat that no longer quite reached around her middle.

To hear her talk like that, thought Fred when he was alone clearing up in the shop, you would think nothing was wrong. He swept the old sawdust into neat piles and began to put down new for the next morning. It couldn't continue. It was the calm before the storm.

Alison found herself alone in the house that evening. Cora had gone to see Jill, and Hazel needed to sort out some details about bridesmaid's duties with Kathy, and had made it very clear that Alison's views wouldn't be welcome. 'Kathy's got common sense, which is more than you have,' Hazel had told her, 'so we'll just let you know what we decide.'

Exhausted, Alison made her way back down the narrow stairs towards the living room. As she did so her foot caught on the edge of the tread and she had to catch hold of the banister to keep her balance. As she stood shakily at the foot of the stairs she wondered if this could be the answer to her problem. Hadn't she read somewhere of a woman losing her baby after a fall? Would she have

189

the nerve to try it? But what if she backed out now – would she dare to risk everyone finding out about her shameful secret?

Trying to think straight through her misery, she climbed back up towards the dim landing. She might never get such a chance again. The trick would be to fall far enough to cause a miscarriage but not so hard as to really hurt herself. When she was little she used to play at jumping from the stairs but that was a very long time ago. She'd twisted her ankle once and Cora had been furious. Cora's anger would be worth it though. She could easily put up with the pain from the fall if this got rid of the baby. She shook her head. She'd have to throw herself from at least halfway up. In the half-light it seemed impossibly high up and her courage failed her.

Then she remembered the hidden bottle of gin. If she had some of that she would feel braver. Quietly, hoping that Cora or Hazel didn't decide to come home early, she found where she'd tucked the green bottle and drank a slug straight from the neck. It tasted no better than the last time but she knew she had to manage it somehow. She made herself take another swig, and another. That was better. She felt very unsteady now. Carefully she returned the bottle to its hiding place.

Slowly she made her way back to the chosen step. The walls around her were starting to spin, so she tried to focus on the doormat. She'd aim to land there. Pushing away her growing despair she closed her eyes and launched herself forward as hard as she could.

There was an agonising crack as her knees hit

the bottom step, then she felt the scratchy coir of the doormat against her face. She thought she might be sick but that passed. Alison lay there, staring at the patterns the streetlight made on the walls and lino, in an effort to stop her head from spinning. She lost track of time. Her legs and cheek were very sore but she couldn't feel anything else happening. How long would it take?

Finally she realised she'd have to move. She was blocking the door where she was, and the last thing she wanted was for her mother or sister to find her collapsed on the doormat. Wincing at the pain in her knees she dragged herself back up the stairs and fell onto her mean little bed. Now she just had to wait. Slowly sleep overcame her and she gave in, utterly tired out with the emotional strain of pretending all was fine when inside she wanted to scream for help.

A noise from the street woke Alison in the middle of the night and she sat up, trying to work out why she felt so ill and why her head was pounding. Then it all came flooding back to her. Cautiously she felt between her legs and the bedsheets underneath but there was nothing. All that effort and no result, just like before. A sob burst from her throat but she choked it back, not wanting to wake anyone. She couldn't afford for them to hear her distress. Her knees were on fire, her head was splitting and her stomach heaved at the unaccustomed gin, but the bump was still there.

'Don't you think you can lie in today,' Cora shouted up the stairs. 'You have to do my shopping this morning and then this afternoon you're needed round at Jill's. She's cut out your frock and now she has to adjust it before sewing it up.'

Alison dragged herself out of bed with a groan, avoiding the sight of her swollen belly. Her headache had faded but her knees were stiff and bruised. Her face felt raw from where it had slammed into the doormat. She could barely stand to start with but after moving around a little they weren't so bad. At least her skirt was long enough to cover them. If she hurried now she could get the grocery shopping over and done with and maybe manage to drop in on Vera to say hello. She'd done this a couple of times since they'd met in the café, only ever managing a quick conversation in between Vera's customers, but it broke up the day. She felt she deserved this treat after the agony of the night before. To think she'd wondered about trying to get to know Vera when they worked together but had been too shy – and now they'd ended up friends thanks to the most unlikely of reasons.

Alison skipped breakfast as she was trying not to eat much, thinking she could keep the weight off that way. Also, she still felt sick from the gulps of gin. Cora didn't notice or, if she did, never commented. She was probably just glad to have more bacon for herself and Hazel. Alison often felt the only way she'd really please her mother was to become invisible.

The queues at the baker's and grocer's were longer than normal and there was no time for a detour via Arding and Hobbs. She couldn't move as fast as usual because of the pain in her legs.

192

Disappointed, she returned with her bags of goods, to find Cora fussing round the kitchen. 'Jill wants you over there at half two. If you're quick you can have a sandwich, and make me one while you're at it. Use some of that ham you brought back yesterday.'

Alison did as she was asked, making only half a round for herself. She was ravenous now but in her confused logic she hoped she could hide the growing bump by cutting down on what she ate. Resolutely she pushed away her plate. 'All right, I'll be off then.'

'Hold your horses,' said Cora. 'I'm coming too. I know Jill will have done a good job but I want to make sure it's all to Hazel's liking, as she probably won't finish at the café in time to see you.'

I can't see Hazel hurrying to see me for any reason, thought Alison, as she sat at the kitchen table while her mother ate her ham sandwich. She stopped halfway through to add more Branston pickle.

'I'll give Fred his due, he does lovely ham.' Finally Cora finished. 'What's got into you, ants in your pants? It's only over the road. We'll be there early.'

'She won't mind us being early,' said Alison, anxious now to get the ordeal over with. She hated showing her body to anyone at the best of times and she certainly didn't want her mother scrutinising it now. She'd have to think of a story to explain the latest bruises. Not to mention her growing waistline.

Jill was waiting for them in her front room, which was scarcely bigger than their own but was

193

somehow much more cheerful. It helped that Mr Parrot must bring home a decent wage, but it was more than that. There were bright cushions everywhere, and a well-placed mirror made it seem lighter and brighter. It felt like a room where people were happy. Music sounded from upstairs.

'More Elvis?' asked Cora. 'Hasn't he grown out of it yet?'

'I wish it was Elvis,' sighed Jill. 'Richie's gone off him. He plays someone called Little Richard now – it's even worse. He screeches along and we don't know what to do with ourselves, it's driving us crazy.'

'I don't know why he doesn't like a nice British boy like Tommy Steele,' said Cora. 'I don't mind him. And he's from quite near here too. Lovely lad. Not like this American rubbish.'

Alison rather liked what she could hear coming through the ceiling but knew better than to say so.

'Right, Alison, do you want to go upstairs and change?' Jill asked. 'Here it is – mind the pins. You can use Kathy's room, that's the equivalent of yours over the road. Will you need a hand?'

'She'll be fine down here,' said Cora. 'We don't want to put you to no trouble. It's nothing we haven't seen before so she can change down here. You've got net curtains, so no one passing by can see anything. You won't frighten anyone, Alison.'

Alison took a deep breath. This wasn't what she wanted at all – there would be no chance to cover up. But she couldn't see a way around it. Reluctantly she unbuttoned her shirt.

'Is that new?' asked Jill. 'I haven't seen it before.

It's quite plain, isn't it?'

'Oh, I got it for work,' Alison said hastily. 'No point in wearing anything fancy there. You never know what you might get on it.' She undid the waistband of her skirt, which she'd stretched with extra elastic, hiding this as best she could.

'Let's try the frock, then. If you lift your arms up and bend your legs so you're at my level, I'll slip it on you.' Jill picked up the turquoise fabric, carefully making sure the pins didn't catch on anything. 'Over we go ... and just tug it gently. Ah, it seems to be a bit stuck. Nasty bruises you have on those knees – did you fall over? Hit your face as well, did you? Stand up straight and I'll try again. No, it's still not budging. I wonder if I cut it wrong?'

'I don't think so,' said Cora, her expression a mixture of horror and disgust.

A deathly silence fell. Alison knew she was blushing and stared at the ceiling, willing the thumping sounds of Little Richard to make it fall in on them.

'Alison,' said her mother finally, 'what's that?'

'What's what?'

'That. That bump. The bump in your belly.'

'I've got a touch of indigestion.'

'Indigestion? You haven't eaten enough to feed a fly. Indigestion my arse.'

Jill gasped, not fully realising what was going on. Then she moved from the window and saw what the fuss was about. 'Alison? What's this?'

'I've got an upset tummy, it's nothing,' Alison said, closing her eyes against the look on her mother's face.

'It's not nothing.' Cora's voice rose sharply. 'I know exactly what that is. Do you think I'm stupid, my girl? Do you think I don't know a fallen woman when I see one? A filthy little tart? That's what you are, a filthy little tart. My own daughter. Gone and got herself a bun in the oven and never so much as a word about it. So what have you got to say for yourself now your secret's out, eh? What's your excuse?'

Alison said nothing, desperately willing her mother to stop, but she continued her tirade.

'How did you manage that? You actually managed to get a man to come near you? Was he blind? Who is it? Is he going to make an honest woman of you?'

Tears fell down Alison's face but still she said nothing. There was nothing to say. All Cora's ranting and raving wouldn't change anything.

'Answer me, you little trollop!' Cora swung her daughter around to face her. 'Who's done this? Who've you let do this? Who does he think he is? Who do you think you are, ruining our family's good name?'

'Now, Cora, I'm sure Alison can explain,' said Jill, horrified at the way her friend had changed. The lively, chirpy neighbour had become a screaming monster who she barely recognised. No wonder the girl was petrified.

Cora ignored her. 'When I think of all I've done for you! You've never been anything but a burden and yet I've fed you and clothed you and given you a roof over your head. You've wanted for nothing and this is how you repay me. Well, you needn't think you're bringing a baby into my

196

house. You're a disgrace, to me and your dear late father and your sisters. You've let us all down. You're an ungrateful little strumpet and you've no one to blame but yourself.'

Alison stood stock-still, waiting for her mother to finish. She couldn't go on forever, she'd have to draw breath at some point. But just when she thought things could get no worse, the front door opened.

'What's going on, Mum? I could hear you yelling from outside,' said Hazel, red-faced from running back from the café so she could check on how the dress was coming on. She was greeted by the sight of her beanpole sister standing in the middle of the room, barelegged, her taffeta frock halfway over her body, tears running down her face. On one side was Jill, her hands up to her face with an expression of horror. On the other was her mother, hair and eyes wild, looking fit to kill.

'Hazel.' Jill took a deep breath. 'We weren't expecting you so soon. Let me just say...'

'She's pregnant,' yelled Cora, stabbing a finger at Alison. 'Yes, you heard. Your gormless little sister has disgraced herself and brought shame to us all. I wish I didn't have to tell you, Hazel, but it's true. Look at her.' Alison cowered at her mother's sharp glance.

For a moment Hazel just stood frozen, but then her face infused with colour. She strode across the room in two steps and slapped her sister hard across the face.

'You little bitch. You've done this deliberately, haven't you? You've done it to ruin my wedding because you're jealous.'

197

'I'm not jealous, and I didn't get pregnant deliberately. I ... I was...,' Alison cried, sobs racking her body as she broke down, unable to go on.

'Whose is it?' demanded Hazel, gimlet eyes trained on her sister. 'Who would possibly want to do it with you? Tell me his name and I'll bloody kill him.' She grabbed her roughly by the arm.

'It won't do you any good,' Alison wept. 'He's gone. He doesn't even know. His family disappeared and I've heard nothing since.'

'Oh no.' It dawned on Cora who she meant. 'Not those good-for-nothing gamblers? Not the Lannings? You let one of them ... you're carrying a child from that bad lot... How could you? How could you do this to your family?'

With a loud cry Alison wrenched the bridesmaid dress off, scattering pins all over the floor. There was the sound of tearing fabric but nobody tried to save it. She then threw on her skirt and shirt before fleeing out of the front door.

'And don't come back!' Cora cried after her. 'Don't you dare think you can show your face round here! You're nothing but a tart and a slapper and you've disgraced us all!'

Jill Parrot stood by her kitchen counter, waiting for the kettle to boil. She was in shock, unable to take in what had just happened. She tried to make excuses for Cora, although she was horrified at the behaviour of the woman she'd begun to think of as a friend. She hoped she'd have reacted differently if Kathy, God forbid, found herself in such a position. Then Hazel had hit her sister. She would never have believed it if she hadn't seen it. But she had to make allowances. They were both upset and obviously neither had had the slightest idea beforehand.

What would Neville do now? He'd have to be told. Would he feel tainted, marrying into a family that had been disgraced? She didn't know what to advise him. People would be bound to talk when they found out and everyone associated with Alison would be under scrutiny. Then again, he wasn't marrying Alison, he was marrying Hazel, and he loved her. It shouldn't matter what her sister had done, but she knew not everybody would see it like that. It was bound to affect them.

As for the lovely dress ... she knew it was the least of their worries but when she'd heard that fabric tearing part of her had wanted to cry too. She'd spent so long carefully cutting it to Alison's unusual size, and had looked forward to seeing how it fitted the girl. She'd wanted to make her something special, something she realised her mother and sister never did. Now there would be no need. She wondered if she should feel angry at her, for doing this damage to them all, but couldn't find it in her heart to do so. She felt deeply sorry for her.

Cora came through into the kitchen. 'I'm sorry, Jill, I really am. All your hard work on that lovely frock. Well, she won't be wearing it now.' She shook her head. 'You could have knocked me down with a feather. Alison of all people. I never thought she had it in her. Never so much as whispered anything about a boyfriend. Now it turns out he's done a runner. Can't say I blame him.'

Jill sighed. 'Cup of tea? And would Hazel like one?'

'No, that's kind of you, but I won't,' said Cora. 'Hazel's already gone so she can see Neville between shifts. She'd rather he heard it from her than anywhere else. I better get home. I got some thinking to do.'

'Well, if you're sure, Cora.' Jill was slightly relieved to be rid of the woman when she was in this mood.

Cora almost ran across the street, not trusting herself to say another word. She was beyond anger. To think that one of her daughters could have stooped so low. Never in all their years of poverty had she let them do anything shameful. Money couldn't buy you a good name. They had been brought up to know right from wrong and how they should behave. Perhaps she hadn't drummed into Alison hard enough what she should and shouldn't do where boys were concerned as she'd found it hard to imagine the need would arise. Linda and Hazel had always had boyfriends and yet neither of them had got into trouble – they were very strict, never risking their reputations. Now Alison had brought ruin to their door. Their name would be muck.

Cora hardened her heart. If Hazel's happiness was at stake then she wouldn't let Alison wreck it. The girl had made her own bed and would have to lie on it. Clearly she thought she was big enough to make her own decisions. Well, now she'd have to learn to live with the consequences. Her youngest daughter wouldn't be getting any help from her.

Chapter Twenty-One

Alison found herself retracing her steps down to the river, where she had wandered after the row with Fred. That seemed like ages ago. That was when she'd come up with the stupid idea to make herself ill to try to lose the baby. A fat lot of good that had done. She knew that she was stuck with it. Now that the truth was out, she had to face the facts. She was having a baby, her family had thrown her out and she was on her own.

The sun shone brightly and seemed to mock her. Now and again she saw people wandering along, most likely on their way to Battersea Park. There were couples holding hands, or young families, parents taking care of their small children. She couldn't ever remember Cora showing such tenderness to her. She'd been a nuisance from the start. She'd never been wanted by anyone except Linda. Fred said she was learning the job well but he could always get another assistant. People like Mrs Shawcross or Vera were kind but they'd be like that to everyone. She wasn't special, she had never been number one to anybody. As for Paul, she shuddered. He had raped her!

So it was just her and the baby she didn't want, the creature she'd tried to get rid of, but not very well. Who would care if both of them lived or died? Would anybody miss them? The more she thought about it, the more the answer seemed clear. No.

Her thoughts turned to stories she'd read in the papers. People threw themselves under trains. She recalled Hazel coming back from somewhere, when she and Neville had just started courting, and they'd been delayed by an accident: a person under a train. At the time she couldn't imagine how someone could hate the world so much they'd want to end it all. Now she knew how they felt.

Would she be able to do it? There was no shortage of train tracks around Battersea. They snaked along the river and up to Clapham Junction and beyond. She could pick one. There must be one that was easy to get to – from a bridge or a siding. They were busy all day and into the night with constant traffic. It wouldn't take long to find somewhere.

It would be easier if she had a drop of gin first. She'd hated the taste but it had made sitting in the boiling hot bath or the pathetic attempt to fall downstairs just about bearable. That would be hard as she'd run off without her handbag or coat, so she had no money. If she'd been Vera she could have been bold and walked into a pub and sat at the bar until a man offered to buy her a drink. She didn't have the nerve to try it though.

Maybe she'd be able to slip a bottle into her bag if she went into a busy shop. Late Saturday afternoon, there would be lots of shoppers about and she might get away with it. But what if she got caught? Then she'd have the shame of being arrested on top of the pregnancy. That would be all over Battersea in two minutes flat. All those men from the factory and boys who used to tease her would snigger and say told you so. Look at her, she was bound to come to a bad end.

She walked further, not really paying attention to where she was going, the river on her left, the sun behind her. She realised she was hurting all over from her useless leap from the stairs. Ahead were some benches and she sank gratefully down on one before realising where she was. It was the churchyard at St Mary's. The pointed tower reached high above the columns of its porch, and the clock showed half past five. She'd been wandering around for nearly three hours. No wonder her feet felt like they were on fire – she'd only just registered that but it hardly mattered.

She stood up again and gazed over the low wall to the river. She could see the north bank clearly today. Red buses were going along the embankment. Their passengers would be going home from shopping or heading off for a Saturday night out. They'd be looking forward to showing off what they'd bought or meeting up with family and friends. It felt like a world away.

Beneath her the river churned, blue and grey, bits of wood floating along in the current. She wondered if that was what the sea looked like. She'd never seen it. Trips to the seaside were for other families, not hers. She never would see it now. There was no future for her or this creature she carried inside her.

Nobody was around. The passengers on the north bank wouldn't be able to see her clearly and if they could, they wouldn't be able to do anything in time. She braced her hands on the top of the wall and found it was quite solid. She scrambled up and it was surprisingly easy. Balancing on the top she looked up at the sun. No more sitting out in the sunshine for her. No more anything. She was as worthless as everyone had always said and they'd all be better off without her. They'd be glad. No more horse face, no long streak of misery, no unwanted burden. She didn't need gin now to soften the blow. Her mind was made up. This was it. Taking a deep breath, she gathered her courage to jump.

'Alison!' said a voice. 'What the hell are you doing?'

Chapter Twenty-Two

'Right, lads, one hour's break and those of you who are signed up for the late shift come back after that,' said Frank Dalby, the foreman. 'My Marian's done a ginger cake for your tea break later so no skiving off tonight.'

'Time for a swift half in between shifts, Nev?' asked Dennis. 'I'm goin' for a quick one before getting ready for a big night out.'

Neville hesitated. He was tempted, and it was Saturday after all, but he wasn't as quick with the machinery after a drink. A half would be all right but he knew from past experience they'd buy him another, and then he'd come back and make mistakes. So far he'd got away with it but he knew Frank had his suspicions. He didn't want to lose his overtime.

'Go on, Nev, just a quick one round the corner won't hurt.' Bill nudged him. 'I'm coming back for the late shift as well so I won't let them get you drunk. Let your hair down a bit, why don't yer.'

As they made their way out into the yard Neville could make out the silhouette of someone waiting at the gates. Before he could say anything Nobby was laughing.

'Look who it is. Someone's come to pick you up, Nev, to make sure you don't go off enjoying yourself.'

'Leave it out, Nobby,' growled Neville. He wondered what was up. If Hazel had come to the factory then there must be something wrong. He hoped his parents hadn't been taken ill.

'Tell her she'll have to wait as you're gonna go down the pub with your mates,' said Nobby. 'You don't want to miss out on your one bit of enjoyment for the weekend. She can see you any time.'

Hazel was waving frantically.

'I'd better see what she wants,' said Neville. 'Sorry, I'll have that half another time.'

'Ooh, look at him, under the thumb already and not even married,' jeered Nobby. 'Gawd knows what he'll be like once he's tied the knot. You run along now and keep the little lady company. Don't mind us.'

Bill shrugged into his jacket and glanced at his colleague. 'Stop giving him grief and come down the pub. I'm in a hurry even if you aren't.'

Sullenly Nobby turned away. He didn't hold with the way Neville was always at his girlfriend's beck and call, even if she was a stunner. She should be taught her place and he wondered if Neville would ever be up for doing that.

'Hazel, what's the matter?' Neville said, taking one look at her expression. 'It's not Mum, is it? Or Dad? Is everyone all right?'

'No, we bloody aren't all right,' she hissed, catching hold of his arm. 'Your mum and dad are fine, Neville. Don't get all het up about them. But wait till I tell you what we've just found out.'

'What? Don't keep me guessing if it's really bad.'

'Not here,' she said. 'Wait till we're out of everyone's hearing. Then I'll explain.' Her jaw was set with fury as she drew him down the street before she gave him the news.

Alison nearly fell off the wall. She hadn't heard anyone approaching and in her state of anxiety the shock was enough to make her stumble badly. Fred immediately jumped forward and took her arms, steadying her.

'Get down here,' he said gruffly. He didn't know what to say. He'd been convinced she was about to throw herself into the water. He was shaking, realising he'd got to her just in time. Now he had to persuade her to come back to the church path where it was safe. 'It's not a long way down, look, I'll help you.'

'No, no.' Alison was shaking even more. She'd been so determined to jump, to put an end to it all. How could she get rid of Fred? She didn't know if she could be so brave again. It was now or never. She had to do it, there was nothing left for her to live for. 'Leave me alone,' she whimpered. 'Let me do what I've got to do. It's the only way. Go home, leave me alone.'

'I won't do that, Alison.' Fred drew himself up to his full height. 'I don't know what you think you're doing up there but it's not right. You could fall and hurt yourself. I can't let you do that. Come back down here before there's an accident. Look, step here, on this big stone.' He tried to keep his voice calm but he felt panic begin to rise. What if she slipped? She was far too tall for him to lift down by force. He glanced around to see if there was anyone nearby to help but there wasn't.

'No, Fred, I've got to do this,' she cried. 'Let me go. I don't want you to stop me. It's for the best, really it is. You have to believe me. Nobody will miss me and it's better all round without me. Go away.'

Fred wanted to cry himself but knew that would be the worst thing to do. 'I'll miss you, Alison.' He tried to make her laugh. 'I don't want to train another assistant to cut up kidneys. What if they keep being sick? What'll I do then? Who will talk to Winnie Jewell?'

It didn't work. Alison stared at him as if he was mad then tried to twist away, but couldn't free herself from his grip. She lost her footing and fell, not into the water but off the wall onto the path, landing on the ground and pulling Fred over as well. Sobbing, she tried to get away, but now he was on the same level he caught hold of her and wouldn't let go. He was stronger than she'd thought. Slowly she felt the fight ebb out of her. All her resolution of a few moments ago drained away and she collapsed weeping on the ground.

Once he was sure she wasn't going to do a runner, Fred dragged himself into a sitting position. He gently patted her shoulder. 'Come on, get up,' he said. 'You can't stay down there. You'll get your shirt all filthy.'

'I don't care,' she sobbed. 'What does it matter how I look or what I do? Nobody gives a toss whether I live or die. I want to die. I was going to jump just then. Why didn't you let me get on with it?'

'You're young, you've got your whole life ahead of you,' he said seriously. 'You can't leap into the river when you're only seventeen. I don't mind what you've done to get to this state, I don't want to see you die. Come on, I'll take you home.'

'I can't go home.' Alison gave another racking sob. 'They've found out I'm having a baby and thrown me out. I don't want to see them again anyway. They hate me, always have. I'd rather be dead than live under their roof again.'

Fred sighed. He supposed they were bound to react like that though he'd hoped for better from Cora. It would be down to the shock of it. 'They don't mean it. They'll be worried where you are. They'll be a bit surprised by the news, that's all. Look, I'll come with you, help explain.'

Alison laughed bitterly. 'They won't be worried, or at least not about me. All they can think of is I've ruined their reputation and it'll spoil the wedding. I tried to tell them ... what happened...' She burst into more tears. 'It's not what they think. I didn't want this, I didn't have a choice, he forced me and hurt me badly too.

208

They wouldn't believe me anyway so what's the point? They won't believe you either. They think I've disgraced them on purpose and they'll never forgive that.'

Fred's heart went out to her, this poor strange girl with her awkward ways and shabby clothes. He pulled her to him and began to rock her, trying to stop her crying. 'Listen, it'll be all right. You can't see the wood for the trees at the moment but things will settle down. They won't stay angry forever.' His mind went back to a rainy day at the beginning of March. He'd wondered then what had gone on, especially when she'd shown up with a bruised face after the weekend. Now he blamed himself for not trusting his instincts. He'd known something was badly wrong then but hadn't wanted to pry. If he'd followed his gut feeling, everything might have been different. She was only a girl; he was meant to be a man of the world, and if anyone was to blame then it was him.

Fred took a deep breath, and knowing that he had to somehow bring back a sense of normality, he said, 'Now come on. What you need is a cup of tea. I tell you what we'll do. You'll wipe your face and give me a smile. Then we'll go back to the shop and have a drop of tea and a slice of cake. Things will look brighter by then. You can have a bit of a sit-down upstairs if you like. Listen to the radio for a while. Give everyone time to calm down.'

Gradually the sobs grew quieter and she was still. 'All right,' she said in a muffled voice. 'I'll come back to the shop. But I'm not going home. They won't want me and I don't want them.'

'We'll see,' said Fred, certain that her family couldn't be so cruel as to refuse her in her hour of need. 'You don't have to decide anything now. Just come with me. There you are, up we get. Stretch your legs. Now hold on to me.'

He offered her his arm and she gave a small smile. 'I'm too tall, Fred. It'll look strange.'

'No, you're exactly right as you are, it's me who's too short,' he said. 'We don't care what anyone thinks, do we? Let them think what they like. Good luck to them.' He started to lead her out of the churchyard, back along the winding old streets to the bottom of Falcon Road.

Alison suddenly felt so tired she could hardly walk. Everything seemed unreal. She was meant to be dead by now, but here she was, walking through the twisting narrow streets in the early evening sunshine, holding on to her boss's arm. The bump was still there and she still hurt all over from throwing herself downstairs. This couldn't be happening. Fred was acting like this was all part of a normal day, rescuing his assistant from killing herself and inviting her back for tea and cake. Whatever was he thinking really? She'd worry about that later. Now she had to concentrate on putting one foot in front of the other, so that she wouldn't collapse to the ground.

Fred guided her along, ignoring the suspicious glances some people threw their way, deliberately not reacting when one or two of them nudged their companions. He supposed they would look odd, her so tall and him so short and stocky. It didn't matter. All he cared about was that Alison hadn't jumped into the Thames and killed herself and the baby she carried.

'Here we are.' He unlocked the door beside the one to the shop. 'We'll go straight up to the flat. It's more comfortable there. If we go into the shop someone might see the light on and think we're still open. You need a good rest, that's what.'

He led the way up a steep flight of stairs and she wearily followed. At the top was a corridor and she turned into a room that must have been directly above the shop itself. It was a large living room with two big windows, letting in all the sunshine. She registered that it looked nothing like their living room at home, but didn't have the energy to work out what was different. There was a big sofa, that was what mattered. She sank onto it and before she knew it she had escaped into sleep.

'Well, how did he take it?' Cora demanded as soon as Hazel came in. 'He hasn't called it all off, has he?'

Hazel shook her head despondently. 'No, he wouldn't do that. He's sad for me of course. Doesn't want it to ruin our big day. Anyway I'm glad he heard it from me. Some of those men he works with are right old women when it comes to gossip. He was going down the pub with them between shifts when I met him and one or two were giving me filthy looks. I don't want them casting aspersions about us, I'll have a right go at them if I need to.' She looked around. 'Any sign of that little tart? Has she dared to show her face?'

'I should think not,' snapped Cora. 'I ain't havin' her in this place again, dragging us all down to her level. I don't know where she's gone

211

but she can stay there, wherever it is.'

'Good riddance.' Hazel was relieved, thinking that her mother might have softened. She certainly didn't want Alison back in the house, taking up more and more room as her pregnancy progressed, with all and sundry able to see for themselves what state she was in.

'We'd better let Linda know what's going on,' Cora went on. 'She mustn't hear it from anyone else either. Heaven knows what she'll have to say about it. She's always had a soft spot for your sister but this will make the scales fall from her eyes. It'll be a horrible shock for her, poor love. She was always so strict with Terry when they were courting, she won't be able to imagine what her sister was thinking. And Alison was living here while she was carrying on with that useless little toe-rag. The nerve, the bloody nerve.'

'Maybe Linda will ask Alison to live with her,' Hazel suggested. That at least would keep her out of harm's way.

Cora bristled. 'I wouldn't have thought so. She won't want her new friends to see the sort of trouble she's left behind. Not when she's worked so hard to better herself. I won't be suggesting it and don't you do so either. I'm going to give myself a day to calm down before I write to her as I don't trust myself to think straight when I'm this het up.'

Hazel pulled a face. 'Don't you think she'd want to help her out?'

'She'd love to help if she could I'm sure,' said Cora, 'but it's a terrible idea. We don't want June seeing such a shocking example. Bad enough to know it goes on but in her own family! No, she can't have that. The trollop will have to make her own arrangements and that's all there is to it.'

Chapter Twenty-Three

Fred sat in one of his two new armchairs, the untouched Dundee cake in front of him. Alison had been asleep for two hours. He wondered if he ought to send a message to Cora to let her know her daughter was all right, but he didn't want to leave in case the girl woke up. He was afraid that if she came to and saw she was alone she might take off again and harm herself. He couldn't live with himself if that happened. For the time being she was his responsibility and he had to look after her.

It didn't mean he had to starve though. He reached out and picked up the knife he'd taken out to cut the cake, and the noise of blade on china made her stir. Slowly she sat up, confused and disoriented.

Trying for normality again, Fred asked, 'Do you fancy that slice of cake?', cutting into it and helping himself to some.

Alison wasn't totally sure where she was but Fred seemed to be there so it was probably all right. Groaning then she remembered what had happened. She'd tried to kill herself but had failed. She couldn't even do that right. 'Where am I?'

'In my living room above the butcher's,' he

said. 'Don't worry, you can stay here till you're ready to leave. You've slept for ages. You must be hungry.'

Alison realised he was right. She'd had nothing since the half of a ham sandwich hours before. Now there didn't seem to be any good reason not to eat, as the bump wasn't a secret any more. 'Thanks, I'll have some.'

'Good, you'll like it,' Fred beamed, passing her a slice on a delicate plate. 'Now you're awake I'm going to get a note to your mum to say where you are. She'll be concerned.'

'She won't,' said Alison. 'You don't know her like I do. She won't care.'

'I'm going to do it anyway,' said Fred. 'There's a young lad who lives opposite who's always glad of an extra bob to take a message. Many's a time I've thought of a delivery I need after the post has gone and he's always happy to help. So I'll ask him. Won't be a mo.' Quietly, he slipped out.

Alison finished her cake, and eating for comfort too now, cut herself some more. She didn't think he'd mind. As she ate it, she took in the room where she was sitting. Even though she was tired and distressed she was surprised at what it was like.

The furniture was sparse but looked new. It was obviously not utility, the only modern type she had ever come across. It had spindly legs and shiny surfaces, and there were cushions with very strange shapes printed on the fabric. It all felt a bit empty, as if there had once been more things there but they'd been taken away.

She puzzled at this new side of Fred. This must

have all cost a lot. He was careful with his money in the shop and always happy when they made a good profit but he never seemed to have much more than anyone else she knew. He certainly never said anything about furniture or fashion. She decided she quite liked it but couldn't understand why he'd got it. Maybe he shared the flat with someone? Did he have a lady friend she didn't know about? It didn't seem likely – he could never have kept that a secret from her, as whoever used the flat would have to come and go right by the shop window. She had never given much thought to what the flat upstairs was like but she hadn't imagined it would be like this.

The downstairs door banged and Fred's footsteps echoed on the stairs. 'That's all sorted out,' he wheezed. 'He'll go round and if your mum wants to send a message back, she can. If she doesn't then no harm done. Ah, I see you enjoyed the cake.'

'Thanks.' Alison looked round. 'Fred, your living room … it's not what I thought it would be like.'

Fred seemed embarrassed, shuffling as he returned to his armchair. 'The new stuff, you mean? Do you like it?'

Alison paused for a moment. 'Yes. Or at least I think so. I haven't really seen anything like it. It was just a bit of a surprise.'

He nodded. 'When Mother died, I decided to have a good old clear out. We had things she'd got from her parents and grandparents and it was all dark and miserable. This is a big room but you'd never have known it with all that in it. So I thought, Fred my lad, you can make a new start. I haven't got very far yet. It needs more to make it like a home, but it's a beginning.'

Alison nodded. She felt like that about the grim and worn-out items at home. She'd have chucked out the lot if it was up to her – and if she had the cash to get replacements. That wasn't likely to happen now.

'Are you sure you don't mind me being here?' She realised how late it was. 'Aren't you going out? Or expecting company? It's Saturday and I don't want to be in your way.'

Fred laughed. 'No, I'm not going anywhere. I hardly ever do. And I'm not expecting any visitors. So don't worry.'

'Don't you?' Alison thought she was the only single person in London who always stayed in and spent Saturday night on their own, from what her sisters and everyone at the factory said. 'What about the cinema? You're always telling me I should see this film or that. You must go out then.'

'Sometimes I do,' Fred admitted, 'but not very often. Not at the weekend anyway. People think you're strange if you're on your own on a weekend evening.'

'Don't you have any friends?' The question was out before Alison realised what she'd said.

Fred shook his head ruefully. 'I suppose that makes me seem like a sad old sod but I got out of the habit. I had plenty when I was younger like your dad, for instance. He was a good lad. We used to go out and get up to all sorts. But then there was the war, and then Mother was ill and needed me around all the time. Before I realised it everyone I used to know was either dead, moved away or stuck at home for one reason or another. Anyway, I've got the business to think of. That takes up all my time. Sometimes I'm up here doing the books into the small hours.'

'You should have said!' she burst out. 'I could do more in the shop and then you could do the books in working hours. You don't need to work all night on them.'

'I don't mind,' he said. 'I like it. They keep me company.' He shuffled his feet again. 'That's enough of my lack of social life. I can't last all evening on a piece of cake. I need some proper food. What do you say to a meal and a glass of beer? Sorry, you probably don't drink it. Ginger beer? Yes? Good. You make yourself comfortable and I'll get busy. Here, let me turn the radio on for you.'

He began to potter around the kitchen, taking out pans and finding glasses. All the while he kept an ear open for the messenger boy in case he brought word from Cora. He had been certain she'd reply. But as the time wore on, there was nothing.

Some hours later, Fred sat at his desk and tried to concentrate on his accounts. Usually he found it soothing but tonight he couldn't seem to think straight. He was too unsettled by the strange events of the day.

He and Alison had eaten and she'd insisted on washing up, so he let her. She was clearly worn out so he'd shown her to one of his spare rooms and said she could stay as long as she liked. She'd

217

seemed surprised again by the modern style of the furniture and décor, which pleased him even though he was worried about her. He was very embarrassed to lend her a T-shirt to sleep in, but she'd been too tired to care. He'd made her promise to call out for him if she needed anything, then left her to sleep.

There was still no word from Cora. He couldn't understand it. If it had been him... He laughed grimly to himself. He wasn't likely ever to be in such a position. But what did this make him now – would people talk if they realised she had spent the night in his flat? Not that he could have done otherwise, but would it sully her reputation still further? Then again, the gossips would really have their work cut out to imagine any scandal between the awkward girl and her short, balding boss. He felt responsible because of his friendship with her father, and that was good enough. He wouldn't allow her to roam the streets, especially in her condition.

What she said had hit home. It was true that he didn't really have friends. He'd convinced himself he was happy enough, building up the business, content to spend his evenings with his accounts. But now he could see it through someone else's eyes, it did strike him as sad. What sort of man preferred lines of figures to human company? There was nothing wrong with him – he was free to do as he liked once the shop was shut. He knew his looks weren't up to much and he'd never been very popular with the girls even when he was young, but he'd stopped trying. Years of dealing with his difficult mother had led him to retreat into his shell, glad of the peace and quiet. Yet she was dead now. He'd managed to throw out her cluttered old furniture but he hadn't done anything about his habits.

Now he could see how sad he must appear to the outside world. If he admitted it, he was lonely. He didn't want to spend the rest of his life with just his accounts to turn to. He'd enjoyed this evening in a funny sort of way, having someone there to cook for, to fuss over. He couldn't remember the last time he'd done that.

He also had to admit he liked having Alison around. She was the opposite of his mother, who had thought she knew everything and shouted her views at anyone daft enough to come near. Alison was quiet until you got to know her but then she turned out to be smart and funny. He was sure there was still more to her, but she was so unused to having anyone take her seriously she kept much of her personality under wraps. Even in the current circumstances she managed to be good company, amusing and observant, asking the sort of questions that nobody else would. In fact, she reminded him of her father – she had all the qualities of a good friend. If things had been different maybe that's what she would have been. He realised just how much he would have missed her if she'd succeeded in her tragic plan to kill herself. His life would be darker, duller and lonelier without her.

He closed the accounts book in front of him as the idea struck him. At first he dismissed it as plain crazy. It would never work. But once it was hatched the idea wouldn't go away. He tried to

219

forget it as it was so ridiculous. As the minutes went by he began to ask himself if it was really possible. It would be risky even to contemplate it and he might be laughed at for the very suggestion. And yet ... and yet... It would solve everything, for him, for Alison and the baby, and for Cora. If only they'd agree.

It might seem mad, but the solution was simple: he would marry Alison. She and the baby could live with him here in this flat. It was too big for one person and he rattled around in it, wondering how to fill the space he'd made. She would help him, and the baby could have its own room. He could take care of her, as her father would have wanted him to do. Then she wouldn't have to face the scandal of being an unmarried mother and the baby wouldn't be called a bastard. It would be better for both of them, if he could make her see it that way.

Fred's thoughts continued to turn. Cora would surely be delighted. She'd get rid of the daughter she plainly had little time for and the family name wouldn't be disgraced. Hazel's wedding could go ahead with no cloud hanging over it. So she would be easy to persuade.

Alison might not be so keen though. Perhaps she had dreams of a romantic wedding and a gorgeous young husband, and he knew he was far from that. But given what had happened to her she wasn't in a position to choose. He'd offer her security and a roof over her head, even if it wasn't exactly a love match. He could provide for her and the baby. He wasn't sure how he felt about having to raise another man's child but that would be the price he paid.

He thought he'd enjoy getting to know her better. He admired her strength of character, knowing what she'd had to cope with, and it would be a joy to see the lighter side of it when the time was right. As for the physical side of marriage, there would be nothing going on while she was pregnant. He wasn't so cruel as to imagine there would be. Yet he hoped that after the baby was born they would grow to care for each other. He missed the sensation of a woman's arms around him. Those encounters during the war were all a long time ago, but he'd enjoyed them while they lasted, even though he'd known they were only temporary comfort. He remembered the women had seemed happy enough. Maybe he could show Alison he wasn't such a sad old sod after all.

Chapter Twenty-Four

On Sunday morning Cora decided she had better show her face at church. Now that they'd booked the hall for Hazel's reception she wanted to make sure she kept in the stewards' good books. It also wouldn't hurt to have some of the congregation on her side when the news about Alison got around. The daughter might be a disgrace but the mother was a fine church-going woman. That was the impression she wanted to give. So she put on her best coat, found her one good hat and set off.

If anyone asked her how her family was doing

she'd just talk about Hazel and all her plans. There was no need to mention Alison. No point in inviting trouble, she thought grimly. It would be upon them soon enough. So the girl had taken refuge with Fred yesterday, and he'd been soft enough to let her. More fool him. He'd only be tainted by sheltering a fallen woman. If he wanted to help her, that was his lookout. She didn't intend to make that mistake.

After the service Cora exchanged pleasantries with a handful of people she barely knew and then left, figuring that she'd done her duty. She'd said only enough to appear polite, and that would just have to do. At least she had a nice piece of beef to roast for Sunday lunch. It might be her last one for a long time if Alison wasn't going to be bringing home the offcuts any longer. The selfish girl hadn't thought about that either. It was one more reason not to let her come home again.

When Cora returned home from church, Hazel was still in her dressing gown, sitting at the kitchen table. 'Fred was here,' she said, spreading butter on her toast.

'What did he want? If he's come to ask me to forgive your sister and take her back, he's got another thing coming.'

'He didn't say,' Hazel replied. 'Just that he wanted to speak to you. I told him you were at church and would be home later so he's going to come over in half an hour. I'll leave you to it. I want to paint my nails.'

'Waste of time, you only chip them working at the café,' Cora pointed out. 'If you had a nice office job like Kathy you could keep your nails

222

looking beautiful but when you're in and out of that kitchen all day they don't stand a chance.'

Hazel shrugged. 'That's why I want them looking right on my one day off. I'm seeing Neville this evening. At least I've got a gorgeous boyfriend unlike Kathy. Men hear what she does for a living and they get scared off. They don't want a career girl. So who's having the most fun?' She grinned. 'A typewriter won't keep her warm at night, will it?' Hazel liked Kathy well enough but she was getting fed up of the way her mother always compared them. Kathy had neat hair, nice clothes, good job prospects, and could do no wrong. Hazel knew she'd be bored stupid in an office and didn't envy her future sister-in-law, she just wished her mother would shut up about her.

'Go on then.' Cora took off her coat and hat, hung them up and started to prepare the vegetables to go with the roast as her daughter ran upstairs. She sighed – Hazel wouldn't want to help with the cooking if she'd just done her nails. So it was all down to her, as usual.

She'd almost finished peeling the carrots when Fred arrived. Wiping her hands, she showed him to the armchair in the front room and waited to hear what he had to say. She wouldn't offer him tea until she learnt the purpose of his visit. She adjusted the lace curtain to make sure nobody could see them.

Fred wondered how to begin. He'd had it all prepared in his mind but then when Cora wasn't in he'd been thrown. Now he couldn't remember how he'd planned to broach the subject. He hadn't seen Alison that morning so she had no

223

clue what he was doing. If it all went wrong with Cora then she need never know. But he was struggling to find the right words.

Cora broke the silence. 'Out with it, Fred. If you've come round here to ask me to let Alison come home, you're wasting your time. I meant what I said. She ain't bringing her disgrace to our door. That's final.' She folded her arms, determined not to weaken. It was all right for him – he wasn't family. He could walk away and carry on as if nothing had happened. He wasn't facing the ruin of everything he'd worked so hard for.

'Well, Cora...' Fred shook his head, hesitating. 'That wasn't quite what I was going to say.' What was wrong with him? He did business deals all the time, negotiating prices and deliveries and with far tougher figures than Cora Butler. He forgot his prepared speech and came straight out with it.

'What if I marry Alison?'

For once Cora was at a loss for words. This was the last thing she'd been expecting. Her jaw dropped and her eyes widened. Finally she said, 'What?'

'I want to marry Alison. That way we all win. She gets a roof over her head and the baby's. Your family doesn't have its name dragged through the mud. I get a wife and maybe a business partner too.' Fred nodded. That last bit sounded good.

'Has she put you up to this?' Cora demanded. It was such an outlandish idea that she couldn't believe Fred had come up with it voluntarily.

'No, of course not. I haven't asked her yet. I thought it proper to ask you first,' Fred said, disappointed again at Cora's reaction. She was always determined to think the worst of her daughter. The years of hardship had evidently changed her from the fun-loving young woman he'd once known.

'You actually want to marry Alison? When she's carrying another man's child?'

'Cora, I know it's not the ideal start to a marriage,' Fred said. 'It's not the way I'd have chosen. But that's how things are. I can't stand by and watch her life ruined. She deserves better than that. This way she gets a ring on her finger and she can carry on working for as long as she's able, if she would like to. She'll want for nothing, I'll promise you that.'

Cora was slowly realising that he was serious. It began to dawn on her that this really would be a way out of an impossible situation. 'You'd marry her, knowing about her like you do?'

'She'd be doing me a favour,' he insisted. 'An honour. I know I'm not the husband she'd have dreamed of but I can give her a comfortable life.' Even now he didn't spell out to Cora how well his business was doing and how he'd be able to spoil Alison. He was too cautious to boast. 'She's a hard worker and we get along fine day by day in the shop. So I have every hope we could do so as husband and wife.'

Cora wondered if he could possibly find her youngest daughter attractive but didn't want to risk him changing his mind by asking. 'You're sure? You aren't pulling my leg?'

'You know I wouldn't do that,' he said. 'Not about an important thing like this. I'm serious, Cora. All I need is your agreement and then I'll go back to ask Alison, to see if she'll say yes.'

'You have my permission, and she'll say yes all right,' said Cora instantly. 'She'd better bloody well agree. It's far more than she could expect. You are a good man, Fred Chapman. I only hope you don't live to regret it.' Her eyes shone. Fred had his own business and nobody to spend his money on – it was respectability far beyond anything Alison could have hoped for. Cora could have hugged herself in delight. As the smell of her Sunday roast wafted through to the front room, she imagined having succulent beef every time she felt like it. They'd all benefit from this, as long as Alison said yes.

'I won't regret it,' Fred said with certainty. 'I've never been more sure of anything in my life. Now I have your permission I'll go back and ask Alison to be my wife.'

'Then bring her back here,' said Cora. 'This changes everything. She can't stay under your roof if she's to be a respectable wife. She'll have to come back home, but we'll let everyone know that you're engaged. Then even if her bump starts to show they'll have less to gossip about. When are you thinking of getting married?'

'I'll have to discuss that with Alison,' said Fred, feeling that the situation was rapidly slipping away from him. Cora had gone from angry suspicion to planning the wedding in less than five minutes. He felt it might not be quite so simple. There was still a lot to sort out but at least he'd got Cora's blessing.

'Keep your fingers crossed for me, then,' he said, now anxious to leave. 'I'll be off.'

'Bring her round as soon as you can,' beamed Cora as she watched him go down the street, keeping an eye out for any movement of the net curtains at her neighbours' windows. They'd have something to stare at soon enough, she thought happily. And not what she'd been afraid of yesterday either. This was going to give everyone the surprise of their lives.

'Bring who round?' asked Hazel, coming down the stairs, her nails gleaming a dramatic dark red. 'You haven't given in, have you? She's not moving back in after all she's done, is she?'

'Wait till you hear the news,' Cora told her excitedly. 'We're going to be made for life.'

Alison stared at Fred, thinking she'd misheard him. She thought he'd just asked her to marry him. That couldn't be right.

'Well?' he said. 'I know it's a bit out of the blue but like I said, this way we all win. Think about it, Alison. I can see it's come as a shock and I don't blame you. You don't have to answer right away.'

She'd been standing in his kitchen, wearing yesterday's clothes and wishing she could sneak home for a fresh shirt and then come back here. She'd made herself at home while he'd been out and used the brand-new kettle and toaster, so different to the battered old things she was used to. Now it seemed she could wake up to this every day if she wanted to – but she'd be married to Fred.

'I ... I don't know what to say.' She couldn't say yes. He was old enough to be her father. Worse,

227

he'd been her dad's friend. He was her boss. He was kind to her but she couldn't imagine being married to him. She didn't want to appear ungrateful; he'd saved her life and taken her in when her own family had thrown her out and turned their backs on her. But that didn't mean she wanted to wake up next to him every morning. Yet what choice did she have?

'Take your time,' he said reassuringly. 'It's a big decision, I know.'

Alison stared at him, noticing his balding head, his portly stomach, his podgy face that made his eyes look too small. He was still wheezing slightly from having climbed the stairs. Would she really be able to marry this man? She knew she was no great looker herself but she couldn't imagine him touching her, or worse, trying to touch him back. She shuddered but tried to hide it, not wanting to offend him. From his face she thought he'd seen it though.

'I'm going to go for a walk,' she told him. 'This is all too sudden, I've got to think it through.' She managed a small smile and then bolted through the kitchen door, down the newly painted corridor and down the stairs to Falcon Road.

Fred watched her go. Had he frightened her, asking her so directly, he wondered. Maybe it was all one big mistake. He could tell she found him repulsive and supposed he shouldn't be surprised. He was over twice her age. Yet she didn't have many options. He wouldn't pressurise her into anything. He could only hope that she saw the merits in his plan. He would have to be patient.

As if by instinct he went to the little room he

used as his office, sat down at the desk and pulled the account books towards him. They never let him down.

Alison hardly knew where she was going, her mind was whirling so fast. She couldn't quite believe what had happened in the last twenty-four hours. Her mother had discovered she was pregnant and thrown her out. She had tried to kill herself. Fred had rescued her and taken her back to his home. Now he'd asked her to marry him. She kept thinking she'd wake up and none of it would be real.

Looking down at her oversized creased shirt, she knew that at least the bump was real. However hard she'd tried to imagine otherwise, it wasn't going to go away. She'd heard that shock could make women miscarry but the bump must be immune, as the events of the last day had held more shocks than the rest of her lifetime put together. So she was stuck with it.

She realised she was at one of the gates into Battersea Park, which was buzzing with people out enjoying the Sunday afternoon sunshine. There was a bench free a little way along the path and she sat down, shielding her eyes from the glare. Everyone around her didn't seem to have a care in the world. What would they think of her if they knew the truth? She'd just got used to the idea of being an outcast when suddenly she'd been offered a way out. But which would be worse – being reviled or ignored, or married to someone she didn't love? At least she was used to being the butt of everyone's jokes and being on the receiving end of abuse. She didn't enjoy it but she didn't expect any better.

A group of young women wandered past, in bright sundresses, some with their hair tied back in patterned scarves. Alison had never owned a frock like that; she was too tall for the ones on sale at the market, and she hated showing more of her body than she absolutely had to. A few of them had bobby socks rolled around their tanned ankles. Others had smart sandals, the sort that didn't fit her own long feet. One of them was waving at her. Alison squinted harder and saw it was Vera. Surprised, she waved back.

'Isn't it a scorcher?' Vera came across to the bench, fanning her face with her hand. 'I don't know what to do with myself. Budge up,' she added, calling out to her friends that she'd catch up with them. 'Ta. How are you? Haven't seen you for a while.'

'I was going to pop in to see you yesterday,' Alison said. 'But then it all went wrong. I know it had to happen but I was hoping to get away with it for a while longer. Anyway Mum's found out about the baby and thrown me out.'

'Oh no!' Vera's hands flew to her face. 'What happened exactly? What did you do?'

Alison explained, leaving out the part about wanting to kill herself, and then laid out her dilemma. 'What would you do, Vera? You're braver than me. Would you risk having the baby out of wedlock and never seeing your family again? I can't see you settling for marrying someone old enough to be your dad.'

'Don't you believe it,' said Vera. 'I know they all

used to call you names and you never complained. You're tougher than you think. But what's he like, this boss of yours? I know my mum thinks he's a good butcher but that's not telling me much.'

'He's kind. He listens to me and takes me seriously. He's got a nice flat. I think he's quite good with money.'

'Sounds perfect,' said Vera, rolling her eyes.

'But I don't ... you know. He's not...'

'You don't fancy him, you mean?' Vera asked. 'That's not everything, you know.'

Alison shot a surprised look at her friend.

'Come on,' said Vera. 'You know by now that half of what they say about me isn't true. Romance is fine in its place but you can't rely on it. Won't pay the bills or put a roof over your head. So if a kind man with a nice flat and a healthy bank balance asks you to marry him then don't rule it out. What's your alternative?'

'Mother and baby home then hope Mum forgives me, I suppose.' Alison hadn't put it into words before. She'd tried very hard not to think of that option at all.

'So you'd go back to live with your mum if she'd have you?'

'Where else would I go?'

'Well then, that's your choice. Not ideal, I grant you, but that's your choice.'

Alison sat back and tipped her head so the sun fell full on her face. She shut her eyes. As usual Vera had hit the nail on the head. Assuming she didn't try to kill herself again, it was live with Fred, or with her mum and never be allowed to forget she was there on sufferance. At least Fred seemed to want her and didn't call her useless all the time. She just didn't think she could bring herself to touch him.

'Penny for them,' said Vera, adjusting her neckline. 'Oh, will you look at that, I've gone all red. Now I'll have these strap marks all summer. I should be sensible like you and wear a baggy shirt.'

'Yes, but we both know why I'm doing that.'

'True.'

'I'm glad I saw you, Vera,' said Alison after a moment. 'You talk sense, even if I don't like the choices I've got. But it's not much of a decision really, is it?'

'I couldn't say,' Vera replied. 'It's not my life. You've been really unlucky and got caught out when loads of girls have got away with it. Then they think they have the right to look down on you, when really they're just glad it wasn't them. Well, this could be your chance to get one over on them. I know you don't fancy your boss, but if he's as kind as you say then maybe he's a good catch.'

One of Vera's friends ran back and called out to her. 'We're going for an ice cream. You with us or what?'

'Fancy coming along?' Vera asked. 'Do you good, a bit of distraction.' She got to her feet and carefully rearranged the straps on her dress.

Alison shook her head. 'Better not. I should get back. Let him know my decision.'

'Come and tell me how it went as soon as you get the chance.'

'I will.' She quickly hugged her friend. 'Wish

me luck. I just hope I'm doing the right thing.'

Vera tutted. 'You will. It'll be all right. Better go, even though ice cream always ruins my lipstick.' She made a face.

Alison smiled at her and set off back towards the park gates, her heart heavy. She'd better abandon any remaining dreams about meeting Mr Right, and put any thoughts of romance firmly to the back of her mind. This was about survival. She'd go back to the flat and tell Fred she'd marry him. She just hoped he would leave her alone physically. She never wanted to be touched that way again.

Chapter Twenty-Five

Cora's working week started like a dream. For once she didn't mind the early start. The summer mornings made it easier and the birds were singing as she made her way the short distance to the shop, where the paperboys were waiting. She caught their conversation as she rounded the corner.

'Here she comes, horse face's mother.'

'Haven't seen horse face for a while. Wonder where she's gone?'

'Must've raced off somewhere.'

'Morning, boys,' said Cora. 'For your information, my daughter will shortly be marrying a prominent local businessman. I'll give her your regards, shall I?'

She unlocked the door as they pulled faces behind her back. She could guess what they were doing and didn't care. That piece of news would now go all around the area like wildfire. She'd better make sure to tell some adults too though, as it was such an unlikely turn of events that the boys might not be believed.

Even the chore of sorting out the piles of newspapers couldn't dampen her good mood. She sent the boys on their rounds, confident that they'd tell anyone they happened to get into conversation with, and then hunted round for some writing paper. She'd have to get a letter off to Linda via the first post, to bring her up to speed. What a good job she hadn't written anything on Saturday evening. Linda would be delighted at her youngest sister's change of fortune, she was generous like that.

The first customer of the day was Marian Dalby. Cora couldn't have been happier. Mrs Dalby rarely came in as she had her papers delivered, and only occasionally dropped by to settle the bill or pick up something extra. This was perfect timing, as nobody would doubt the word of the foreman's wife.

'Hello, Mrs Butler.' Marian nodded politely. 'I'm looking for the latest edition of *Woman and Home*. My neighbour tells me there's a lovely dress pattern in it and I thought it might be suitable for your daughter's wedding. So kind of her and Neville to invite us. My Frank was very flattered.'

'Neville's only got good things to say about his boss,' Cora assured her. 'They're delighted you're both coming. Here you are, this is the one. Mind you, we've got another wedding to look forward to.'

'Oh, really?'

'Yes, my youngest daughter just got engaged to her boss. They're keen to get married right away – it's all been a whirlwind romance.' Cora thought she'd better present it this way as the actual truth had to be kept quiet for as long as possible. Alison had returned the evening before, far from thrilled at the prospect of marrying Fred, but Cora didn't care. She'd agreed and that was that.

'Fancy that,' said Marian. 'Well, you'll have your work cut out for you with all that to arrange. When will it be?'

'They haven't chosen the exact date yet but it'll be before Hazel and Neville.'

'Won't that upset Hazel?' asked Marian, who had heard all about the plans for that wedding. Strong rumours of Neville being under the thumb had also got back to her, but she took them with a pinch of salt. She knew some of the men at the factory resented any kind of interference from a woman.

'No, she is delighted for her sister,' Cora insisted firmly, though that wasn't exactly what Hazel had said. When Cora told Alison she'd better get married before the summer was over, Hazel had flown into a temper and accused her sister of stealing her thunder and conning Fred into the whole thing on purpose. Cora had had to shut the windows in the hope none of the neighbours could hear. She didn't want anyone, especially the Parrots, to witness another Butler family row.

'How lovely for them both.' Marian handed over

235

the money and put the magazine in her shopping bag.

'Let me know how you get on with the dressmaking,' Cora smiled as Marian made for the door. That couldn't have gone better. A few more customers like that and her job would be done for her.

Luck was on her side, as one of the women she knew slightly from church came in to buy some peppermints. Cora made sure to pass on her news. 'And to think there was I yesterday at the morning service, with no idea that my daughter's boss was knocking on my front door at that very moment to ask for my permission to propose,' she laughed.

'Is your future son-in-law not a church-going man, then?' the woman asked disapprovingly.

'He goes to St Mary's, where the services have different times,' Cora assured her, though she had never asked Fred what his religious habits were. 'And Sunday's his only day off, what with running his business. He's such a hard worker. Alison tells me he often stays up into the small hours balancing the books.'

'And how would she know that? I trust you don't let her spend the night at his house?'

'Goodness me, no,' said Cora, flustered at the woman's pickiness. 'She checks the books in the morning and can see they've been updated. She asked him when he found time to do it. He sacrifices his own sleep for the good of that business, and he says she'll want for nothing,' she added proudly.

'Then she's a very lucky girl,' said the woman. 'I'll bid you good day, Mrs Butler.'

Thank God she's gone, thought Cora. Presumptuous old bag. Still, she'd no doubt spread the news, and there was a good chance that everyone at church would hear. It was pure inspiration that had made her mention St Mary's. Now no one in the congregation would think it odd that Alison and Fred weren't getting married there, and would assume they'd go to St Mary's. In fact, it would have to be a low-key register office do.

Her good fortune didn't last. Winnie Jewell came in, face red from having been in the sun too long the day before.

'That looks painful,' Cora remarked. 'Have you got any calamine lotion for it?'

'I'll live,' growled Winnie. 'That'll teach me to do a good deed. I was round at Beryl's helping sort out her backyard. Now the rats and rubbish from next door have gone she can make use of it, so we thought we'd try to grow some lettuces and that. Took us ages and then I found I got sunburn. Still, she'll share anything that comes up with me so it'll be worth it.'

'Suppose so,' said Cora, who had never really seen the point of lettuce as it didn't fill you up. 'Your Vera not helping you out, then?'

'No, she was busy with her friends,' said Winnie. 'I don't like to ask her as she's on her feet all week at Arding and Hobbs.' She never missed a chance to drop the name. 'She mentioned she'd seen your Alison, come to think of it.'

'Really? Alison didn't say. Mind you, that's because she has had other things on her mind.' Cora plunged into the official version of the whirlwind romance and yesterday's proposal.

'You're joking!' Winnie began to laugh so hard that her face went even redder. 'Oh that takes the biscuit. You aren't having me on, are you? Your beanpole daughter and fat little Fred! Him with his bald head! What a pair they'll make. She must be twice his height. I can't wait to see it. Better hope they don't have kids, imagine what they'd look like!'

'No need to be like that,' Cora said, affronted. 'He's a very successful businessman, you know. He promised me that Alison will want for nothing.'

'As long as she's happy to look down on his shiny bald spot,' Winnie cackled. 'Well, it must be a relief for you, Cora. You must have thought nobody would ever have her. Suppose beggars can't be choosers and at least he's got his shop. He's a good butcher, I'll give him that. But the thought of them two, you know... Oh, that's priceless. That's the best thing I've heard all day.'

Cora fumed as the other woman left the shop. She knew she'd have to expect more of that sort of reaction. It was exactly what she'd thought herself, but that didn't mean she'd let anyone else get away with saying such things. It reflected badly on the rest of the family. Alison's engagement to Fred was a big success, she reminded herself, and people would have to be reminded to see it that way, rather than commenting how funny it was that two oddballs had found each other. So what if she was young enough to be his daughter and able to see over his head? Looks weren't everything.

Although Alison had realised that Fred wasn't short of money, unlike just about everyone else she knew, she was surprised when he told her about his account at Arding and Hobbs. 'I'm going to put your name on it too,' he said. 'Then you can go in and see if there's anything you think would suit the flat. Or if you wanted anything new to wear.'

'I don't understand,' she said. 'What, I wander in, say "I'll have that", and take it away without paying? Just like that?'

'Well, I end up paying for it later,' said Fred. 'But basically yes. Then you don't have to worry about carrying lots of money around.'

Alison had never been in a position to worry about such a thing before but supposed Fred had. Still, she couldn't get used to the idea. 'What if I go mad and buy heaps of stuff? How would you pay it off then?'

Fred turned to her properly from where he'd been cutting up a chicken at the counter. They were continuing to work together as before, and sometimes it seemed as if nothing had changed. Other times, like now, he was aware of how different life was about to become for both of them. 'Look, I trust you. We're a team now. You wouldn't go mad. You've never done anything rash with money in the shop and you've had plenty of chances. You aren't dishonest, Alison. Just go up there and see if you want anything. Wouldn't you like a new dress for the wedding?'

Alison hadn't really thought about it. She was trying to block it from her mind, as she still dreaded Fred trying to touch her, although he'd made no move in that direction so far. They'd all agreed that the marriage should take place as soon as they could book the register office and a date had been set for the middle of August. That was only three weeks away. She supposed she couldn't wear one of her baggy shirts and it was too late to ask Jill Parrot to make something – not that she ever wanted to go through that again.

'All right,' she said. 'I had better buy a dress. Not a long white one though. That wouldn't be a good idea, would it?' She smiled grimly. Everyone would see the bump soon enough and work out that she wasn't a virgin at her wedding. Perhaps they'd think she and Fred had been carried away by passion beforehand and she cringed at the thought of it. Then again, that wasn't as bad as the prospect of Hazel's fury if Alison brought home a long white wedding dress from Arding and Hobbs. She'd be beside herself with jealousy and would probably hit her once more. Perhaps there were advantages to this new life.

'I'll make sure they have your name on the account and then you go along and choose something,' he said. 'Didn't you say you had a friend who works there? Maybe she can help you choose.'

On Saturday afternoon Alison made her way to the big department store, still not completely convinced it would be as simple as giving her name to the assistant and then walking off with anything she wanted. She'd made sure Vera would be at work and hoped together they could find something that fitted.

Vera was excited to see her. 'We're going to have real fun with this,' she said, taking Alison by the arm and leading her through to where the dresses hung. There were gorgeous displays of the latest summer fashions, from simple sheath dresses to sailor shifts, along with formal short jackets with exquisite linings. 'It's almost as good as shopping for myself. Are you sure you didn't want your mum to come along?'

'God, no. She'd say getting anything special was a waste of money and make me buy something I could then wear in the shop. Besides, I haven't told her about the account or she'd want to have lots of new clothes for herself. And if Hazel got to hear of it she'd buy up the entire shop. You'd be out of a job.'

'Not if I got commission on it,' Vera smirked. 'I could retire. It would be doing me a favour. Over here, let's start with this...' Secretly she was glad to have Alison to herself. She had no time for Cora and Hazel, fully aware they didn't like her. They'd treated Alison badly when she'd needed them and she felt sorry for Neville, marrying into the nest of vipers.

Together they looked at every available dress in Alison's size, of which there were surprisingly many. Alison was impressed. This was very different to shopping at the market, where she had to buy whatever was available whether she liked it or not. She had never been spoilt for choice before, and was glad she had Vera to guide her through the baffling selection. She'd seen girls her age out in tightly waisted frocks with wide skirts and for years had dreamed of having one for herself but it had never been likely she'd find one. She had never been able to afford anything fashionable; when she was little, even if there had been any money to spare in the Butler household, there was

241

rationing in force and only utility wear in the shops. By the time the restrictions were lifted and the swishing skirts of the New Look came in, she was too tall to find anything within their meagre budget.

'Something A-line would be best so if your bump grows over the next few weeks it'll still be disguised,' said Vera, who was familiar with this dilemma from other customers. 'Then it'll fit once you've had the baby so your mum won't go ape and say it's a waste. How about this? The colour's right for you.'

'Too close to the bridesmaid's dress I was to wear to Hazel's do. She'll never forgive me for that, ripping the material.'

'Pity. All right, this is a similar shape.' Vera drew out a grey and cream frock with a V-neck and padded shoulders. 'Look, this is good because it'll make you look broader at the top so people won't notice your height as much. Try it on. And have you thought about shoes? You're not wearing those.' She glanced in horror at Alison's sensible sandals, which had come from the men's stall at the market. 'Didn't you realise you can get proper shoes in big sizes? We'll try that department next. You have to have something with a pointy toe, that's the trend.'

Alison felt as if she was in another world as Vera guided her through what suited her and what didn't. She would never have thought of all the things that apparently mattered. 'Honestly, you've got no idea, have you?' Vera shook her head in mock-exasperation. 'I can see you don't want high heels if he ain't as tall as you to start with but you don't have to wear flat shoes. A kitten heel is what you need. See, these little cream ones will go with your dress and with just about anything else. We'll get you some matching gloves while we're at it.'

'Gloves?' Alison wore them only for warmth in winter.

'Gloves,' said Vera firmly. 'And a matching bag while we're at it. Fred's going to want you to look smart, ain't he? Will you want a hat? How are you having your hair?'

'No idea. Like this, I suppose.'

Vera raised her eyebrows at that. 'You are not. There is no way on this earth that I'm allowing you to get married with hair like that. You have to have it done special. You might as well make the most of it, now it's all shiny.'

'What do you mean?'

'Blimey, don't you ever look in the mirror in the mornings?'

Alison shook her head. She'd avoided mirrors as much as possible for as long as she could remember.

'Your hair gets shinier and thicker when you're having a baby. Do you mean to say you haven't noticed? Has nobody said anything until now? Well, it does. So you can have it cut different if you like. Who usually does your hair?'

'I do.' Alison thought that was a stupid question. 'When it starts getting in the way I chop the ends off.'

Vera almost lost her footing. 'Well not this time. You're going to the hairdresser's to have it done properly, which is how my hair looks like this.' She twirled a curl round her finger. 'You tell me the date of your wedding and I'll book you in to where I have mine done. Don't make that face, it'll be my treat.'

'You don't have to…'

'I know I don't have to, silly, but I want to. Besides.' Vera indicated the pile of goods she had gathered for Alison to buy. The cream kitten heels with their tiny bows at the front were unlike anything she'd ever seen her friend in before and she was particularly proud of having persuaded Alison to have them. 'This lot will give me a nice bit of commission so I can easily afford to treat you. You're not getting out of it, Alison. I'll escort you there myself. You will have a decent hairstyle on your wedding day if it kills me.'

Chapter Twenty-Six

Fred stared at Alison as if he couldn't believe his good luck. 'Hello, Mrs Chapman,' he said.

They had chosen to marry when the shop closed on a Wednesday afternoon, and were now back at the flat after the wedding. There had seemed little point in a honeymoon. Alison thought it would be a waste of money and Fred had been reluctant to shut the shop, even for a couple of days. Besides, it wasn't as if they were rushing to enjoy their wedding night. Or at least Alison hoped not. The way Fred was looking at her she wasn't sure. Suddenly she felt nervous. She told herself not to be stupid – she'd been on her own with Fred for months and he'd never given her a reason to be afraid. Yet now they were married things would be different. Anxiously she turned the ring on her finger.

The ceremony had gone smoothly, with just Cora, Hazel and Linda there as witnesses. Terry and Neville hadn't been able to get time off and June had stayed with one of her little friends. 'It's too confusing for her,' Linda explained. 'We've spent months telling her what a wedding is like, and how she gets special clothes, we all go to church, the bride wears a big white dress and says special words. She won't know what to make of this.'

Alison understood and didn't blame her sister. It wasn't as if she really wanted to be there herself, and the fewer people who saw it the better. Hazel however was delighted, crowing that hers was the proper wedding and hadn't had to be organised in a hurry. It was her way of getting back at Alison for coming home with the new outfit. Hazel's eyes had nearly popped out of her head when she saw it. She was jealous beyond words and furthermore couldn't see the point of putting such beautiful clothes on her ugly sister. It was like wrapping a pig in silk.

Alison had endured having her hair done at the parlour Vera had recommended and had steeled herself for the usual insulting comments. Instead the hairdresser had taken a close look at her hair and then her face, turning her head this way and that, making humming noises. Vera had stood by, observing it all. 'What do you think?' she'd asked.

'Lots of potential,' the hairdresser had replied.

Her own hair was cropped and made her look like Audrey Hepburn. 'Her hair's on the fine side but it could be given more body if I cut it shorter and gave it some waves. That would offset the length of the face. Good cheekbones though. Yes, we can definitely do something with this.'

Alison had blushed furiously, wishing they wouldn't talk about her as if she wasn't there.

Vera had nodded in agreement and got out of the way as the hairdresser had set to work, washing and cutting and spraying. Alison wasn't keen on the spray – it smelt odd and made her want to sneeze. And yet Vera insisted she had to get some.

'You won't get those waves to stay in without it. Besides it'll keep your hair away from your face, which will be useful at work.'

Alison gave way reluctantly, conceding it would be better not to be tucking her long hair behind her ears all the time. She'd have to learn what to do with the spray. Some of the women at the factory had used it but she'd never seen the point before.

Finally the woman had finished, and swung Alison round in the black vinyl swivel chair to see the result. 'What do you think?'

Alison had stared at her reflection, totally taken aback. The girl staring out at her was unrecognisable. Her hair swung in waves, making her face look broader, and it was sleek, as Vera had said. Nervously she patted it. 'It's amazing. How did you do that?'

'It's called a proper haircut,' said Vera, delighted with the result. 'See, I told you it would be a good idea. Now we've got to get you home without spoiling it, and into your new dress. Thanks, Babs, that's just what I wanted for her. I reckon you've just got yourself a repeat customer.'

The combination of smart new clothes and the hairdo had caused plenty of comment. Even Hazel had to admit it was an improvement, though she was quick to point out that just about anything would be. Cora had to bite back the remark that it was a waste of money, pleased that Alison wouldn't be letting down her new husband.

Linda took genuine pleasure in her little sister's transformation and insisted on taking pictures on the camera Terry had recently bought her. 'Then I can show June later and explain that there are different sorts of wedding. She'll love your hair.'

Linda had been more concerned about Alison's pregnancy, careful not to reveal that she was desperately trying for another child herself. 'Why didn't you say anything?' she'd asked in one of the rare moments the two of them could talk privately, as the others rearranged themselves for photos. 'You could have told me, I wouldn't have shouted at you.'

Alison had nodded, remembering how she'd tried to find a way of doing just that. 'I did want to but there was never the time. I couldn't bear to write it down in a letter, it was all too hard. I know you'd have been kind but you couldn't have made it go away. I just wanted someone to wave a magic wand and sort it all out for me but I've had to grow up a bit since then.' She shook her head. 'Look, we'd better pose for the family group. You will come and see me, won't you?'

'Of course,' Linda had said, smoothing the skirt

247

of her well-cut new blue suit, although she knew how hard it would be to see a small baby in her sister's arms. 'You are all right about this whole thing now, aren't you? Fred'll look after you.'

'I know,' Alison had agreed.

As for Fred, he'd smiled so broadly his round face almost split in two. He'd always suspected the girl just needed a helping hand. His chest had swelled with pride as they repeated the words the registrar spoke to them. Linda took more photos as they emerged into the August sunshine, then persuaded Hazel to take one with her in it. It was almost like a proper church wedding.

Now Fred stood in the kitchen of the flat, opening a cupboard and taking out two slender glasses. 'I thought you might like to celebrate,' he said, 'I bought some champagne. Do you like it?'

'I've never tried it,' Alison said cautiously. Nobody she knew drank champagne. Linda drank sherry and she knew Hazel was trying to learn to like it too; Cora would have port and lemon at Christmas. The men drank beer. Champagne was something rich people drank in films.

'Well, time you did,' said Fred, taking a green bottle from the fridge. 'It's only right that we celebrate, isn't it? This is the start of our lives together.'

Alison flinched. She couldn't help it. Was this part of his ploy – would he make her drunk and then get her into his bed? She didn't think she could bear it. When he came over to hand her a glass she recoiled. 'I don't know... I'm not sure...'

Fred set the glass down on the counter. 'What's wrong?' he asked. 'Was it all too much for you, earlier today?'

'No, no, that's not it.' She couldn't tell him. Suddenly she was tongue-tied, too nervous to say anything. Her hands shook. She was afraid she might start to cry.

Fred finally realised what was going on and took a step back. 'No need to worry,' he said, then paused. 'Look, I better say one thing. We didn't talk about it before, but I hope you know me well enough by now to see that I won't ask you to do anything you don't want to do. I'm not going to touch you. You've got a baby on the way and it would be wrong. You didn't seriously think I'd make a grab for you, did you? I'm not that kind of man. I respect you too much for that.'

She looked across the room at him, and sagged with relief. 'I ... don't know. I wasn't sure what to think. I mean, we're married now. But after what happened before, I couldn't... I couldn't...' She began to sob, unable to stop, even though she wasn't afraid any more.

Fred reached into the pocket of his suit trousers and brought out a new white hanky. 'Here. Dry your eyes. Don't get me wrong, you're a lovely young girl and I'm proud to have you as my wife. Really, I am. I thought I was the luckiest man alive today. Don't look so surprised, it's true, and it's about time you started to believe it. But I'm not completely heartless. I know what you've been through. Why would I make that worse? You mean too much to me, you do. We're a team, remember? We're companions.'

He slowly came over to her and gave her a gentle squeeze around the shoulders then stepped back. 'Don't go spoiling your new things by crying all over them. Here. Take this glass and see what you think.'

She lifted her glass and smelt the strange golden liquid. Bubbles stung her nose and she swiftly put it down again. Then she thought how silly it was after all that had happened to be beaten by one small drink.

Gingerly she lifted it once more and sipped. 'It's … it's … not bad. Takes a bit of getting used to.'

'That's my girl.' Fred picked up his own glass and chinked it against hers. 'Cheers. To our life together.'

'To our life together,' Alison repeated. This was it – there was no going back now. She had married Fred and she was now Mrs Chapman. She'd just have to make the best of it.

'Your dad would have been proud of you today,' said Fred. 'Do you know, you sometimes remind me of him. I never said so before, it must be the drink talking, but you do.'

'Really?' Alison couldn't have been more surprised. 'But Mum's always saying she can't see anything of him in me at all. I think it's one of the reasons she doesn't like me much. We've only got a few old pictures and I can't spot any resemblance.'

Fred twisted the glass in his hand. 'Well, maybe it's more like she loved him so much she still can't bear to think he's gone. You'd never know it now but she was lively and fun when he was alive. It was a tragedy he was killed and never even knew you was on the way.'

Alison gulped. 'Would you tell me a bit about him?'

Fred thought for a moment. 'Well, you've got his hair colour. Now you've got it cut different it's more obvious. But what I really meant was you're like him in character. I know I can trust you. I never had any doubts even on that first day in the shop. It's how you are. He was like that too. Once he decided he was your friend, on your side, he stuck to it. He used to keep an eye out for me as he was a couple of years older and believe it or not I was a skinny little thing at school.'

Alison smiled. It was hard to picture that. 'Go on. Mum never says anything about him and my sisters can't really remember.'

'He was fun to be around. He always had his own opinions about things, never took anyone else's view unless he'd reasoned it out for himself. So when he was called up he thought it was the right thing to go and fight. That's a comfort to me, knowing he believed in the cause. I missed him dreadful for years, so heaven knows what it was like for Cora.' He took a sip of the cool drink. 'That's why I know we'll make a good team. You're so like him.'

Alison gave a small smile. It was the best thing he could have said to her. 'Thank you, Fred,' she managed to say. 'I'm so glad to know that. Thank you.'

'How did it go?' asked Terry. He'd got back from his shift in time to collect June from her friend's, and was now bouncing the little girl on his knee. 'Did the camera work?'

'I think so,' said Linda as she put down her bag and swept off the matching hat with its little veil.

She was exhausted, having got up early to get to the wedding, and then getting a crowded train back. Her feet were killing her and she flopped onto a chair before pulling her daughter into her arms. 'Have you had a good day, June? It's past your bedtime. Daddy's being very naughty, spoiling you.' She sent her husband a meaningful look.

'June didn't want to go to bed without seeing you,' he said easily. 'We'll go up now. Then you can tell me all about it.'

Linda sank into an armchair as Terry carried their daughter upstairs. She was glad of the break, and June was such a daddy's girl it would be a treat for her. She wondered how to explain it to her that she'd have a cousin soon. She could hardly believe it herself.

She'd been shocked to hear of Alison's pregnancy and then the hasty wedding. She'd only had her mother and Hazel's full side of the story but however you told it, it was a sorry tale. Yet her little sister had seemed determined to go ahead and marry old Fred. Maybe if her much-improved looks were anything to go by, things were going to get better for her at last. Linda sighed. She was very fond of her youngest sister, and had always seen it as her place to stand up for her. Now she was too far away to make much difference. Clearly events had moved on without her. Defending her sister had been quite a responsibility and now Fred could take on that job. While on the one hand she would have loved to stay around for longer to see if she could help out, she reminded herself that she had more than enough on her plate at home. It wasn't her place to interfere, not any longer.

But Alison was pregnant. It was so unfair. If Fred hadn't stepped in she wouldn't have been able to cope with or keep the baby. Yet she and Terry couldn't conceive a brother or sister for June. Another month had passed with her monthlies being late and again she'd got her hopes up, but it was a false alarm. Terry had taken another risk and accepted an even bigger illicit delivery, which had given her many sleepless nights, but still, they were now well set up to move house and provide for another child. It must be the worry of what Terry was doing that made her unable to conceive. Linda felt trapped in the cycle with no way out. She had to have another baby, she simply had to.

Chapter Twenty-Seven

Cora had worked hard to spread the word of Alison's whirlwind romance to explain the hasty marriage, but not everyone was fooled. Only a couple of weeks later the bump was impossible to disguise and tongues began to wag. Cora was furious – she'd wanted to keep their secret at least until Hazel's wedding was over, so the family could have their moment of glory. Yet again she cursed her youngest daughter for being a nuisance and a burden.

'Didn't think he had it in him,' said Winnie Jewell as she bumped into Cora at the market. 'He must have hidden talents. Who'd have thought it?

Had you any idea, Cora?'

Cora decided she'd better play it down. 'They did seem to hit it off as soon as she started at the butcher's,' she said. 'Working together all day like that, it's bound to bring you closer. I admit I was worried about the age difference at first but not any longer. Alison's never been one to fool around with the boys. She's very mature for her age.'

'If you say so, Cora. As long as she's happy. And you'll soon be a grandma again.'

'And how are you keeping, Winnie?' Cora deliberately changed the subject. 'Still helping out Beryl with her backyard? Did you get many lettuces out of it?'

'Lettuces, cucumbers and some radishes. Made a lovely change, that did. I'm going to try it myself next year, see what I can do,' Winnie said, chatting on. 'The landlord has done up the flat next to Beryl now, and she's just hoping she gets decent neighbours this time. She doesn't want another rough lot like the Lannings.'

Cora didn't want to think about one particular Lanning, but struck by an idea she asked, 'Has the landlord found new tenants already?'

'I don't know, I'd have to ask Beryl, but why are you asking? Have you got someone in mind?'

'Hazel and Neville had their eye on somewhere round our way but the people decided not to move out after all,' Cora explained. 'They aren't desperate, as now that Alison's moved out they could live with me, but young people like their own space, don't they?' In truth she didn't want the lovebirds under her feet, although she hadn't said as much to Hazel, who'd been bitterly disappointed not to get the place they'd looked at. 'They'd like to stay near Ennis Street but it's not too far to walk to Beryl's. It might be just what they are looking for.'

'If you like I could ask Beryl to have a word with her landlord. After what she had to put up with, with those Lannings, he's sure to owe her a favour.'

Cora hated hearing the Lanning name yet again, but worse, she loathed being beholden to anyone. However, if it got Hazel a flat she was prepared to suck up to Winnie. 'Thank you so much, Winnie,' she enthused. 'That's really good of you.'

Winnie preened and said, 'Think nothing of it, Cora. I'll let you know as soon as I can.'

'All right, Mrs Butler?' a stallholder who had been on the market for years shouted out. 'Hear your daughter's got a very big honeymoon baby on the way. Who'd have thought it? I didn't know Fred Chapman had it in him.'

There were laughs from other stallholders, but somehow Cora gave a wooden smile. She was going to have to put up with a lot of this. Winnie was looking at her sympathetically, but, unwilling to show how hurt she was, Cora said, 'I look forward to hearing from you, Winnie,' and then after a hasty goodbye, she hurried off.

As she neared home, Cora had calmed down and begun to cheer up. Hazel would be really pleased to hear about the flat. She also had to get on with the wedding plans, with a myriad of last-minute details that still needed sorting out. It was going to be a wonderful do, sure to divert attention from Alison. It would give all the gossips something else to talk about and for that Cora knew she would be thankful.

The weeks seemed to speed by and now it was Hazel's big day.

'You all ready, Neville?' Jill Parrot called up the stairs to her elder son. For once the house wasn't shaking to the sounds of Little Richard. Richie himself was standing at the front door, looking uncomfortable in a smart new suit. 'The car's here. Time to go.'

Neville emerged from the room he'd shared with his brother and stood at the top of the stairs. Jill's heart missed a beat. She'd always known he was good-looking but he'd surpassed himself this morning. She could hardly believe this was her little boy and after today he wouldn't be living at home any more. Blinking away a tear, she told herself not to be stupid. He was marrying the woman he loved. She brushed aside any feelings of misgiving. She'd never looked at Hazel quite the same after the day they'd learnt about Alison's pregnancy, but had made allowances as it had been such a shock.

Lennie, her husband, came up the garden path. He also looked slightly uncomfortable in his best suit. 'Off we go,' he said. 'All right, son? It's not too late to back out, you know.' He nudged Neville in the ribs.

'Get off, Dad.' Neville could see the net curtain twitching in the house opposite and guessed his sister, Kathy, was watching them to make sure they left on time. She'd gone across the road earlier to get ready with Hazel, Linda and little

June. He was glad she was there – she'd calm them down. He knew what the Butlers could be like once they got together.

Neville waited in the front pew, grinning anxiously at his best man. There had been a row when Richie had wanted to perform this role, but Neville had said he was too young. Lennie had agreed and Richie had stormed off and played his records at full volume until half the street came round to complain. Neville had asked Bill Stevens from the factory instead. He could be relied upon to flirt with the bridesmaids and make a funny speech without overdoing it. He'd also been re-assuring the evening before when some of the lads had taken him down the pub for a stag night. Dennis had been full of filthy suggestions, Nobby had been morose and finally downright offensive, saying no man should have to put up with a woman telling him what to do. But Bill had been lighthearted, and had taken him aside towards the end of the evening. 'Don't pay them no heed,' he'd said. 'They're just jealous. As am I, young Nev. You're marrying the best-looking bird in Battersea. So you just thank your lucky stars and don't take any advice from Dennis. Just keep it simple. Like the birds and the bees.'

Now Bill was standing beside him, probably even more hung-over than the bridegroom, one hand in his pocket where Neville hoped he'd got the ring. He grinned broadly as the organ struck up 'Here Comes the Bride'.

Neville glanced round and there was Hazel, in the dress he'd heard so much about but hadn't been allowed to see – which in a house their size had caused plenty of problems. It had been hidden in his parents' room for safekeeping, and it was a miracle he hadn't laid eyes on it before now. Guiding her up the aisle was Terry, who was the closest thing Hazel had to a male relative. Had things been different she might have asked Fred, but under the circumstances Cora had deemed it unwise. Fred and Alison were to sit at the back of the church where no prying eyes could be distracted by the now very visible bump.

Behind Hazel and Terry came Kathy, Linda and little June, who was enjoying being the centre of so much attention. Linda had her firmly by the hand. The little girl smiled as if butter wouldn't melt in her mouth. Neville turned to face the front as the vicar stepped forward and began the familiar order of service.

The words blurred into each other and all he could think about was Hazel, so beautiful at his side, her bouquet shaking slightly as her hands trembled. There was a slight interruption as the vicar asked if anyone knew of a reason why they may not lawfully marry and in the tense silence June whispered, 'Is this a real wedding then?' so that the whole congregation could hear. Linda shushed her and the vicar went on, but Neville could imagine this was one more thing for which Alison would get the blame. In a matter of moments he was being told he could kiss the bride. Bill winked at him as he quickly pecked Hazel's cheek. It was over. They were married and Hazel was Mrs Parrot. His heart soared.

Walking down the aisle to the 'Wedding March'

he nodded to all the friends and family who had packed out the church. There were the Dalbys, next to Hazel's bosses from the café. Right at the back were Alison and Fred. Fred looked delighted as he took the chance to make a quick exit, so that he was ready to take pictures as the newlyweds stepped into the churchyard. He'd been given Terry's camera for the day and started snapping as other guests came out and threw confetti.

Hazel held on to her husband's arm and beamed at him. 'We've done it, Neville. This is the happiest day of my life.'

'Mine too,' he said. He couldn't believe how lovely she looked and he couldn't wait to get her alone. Somehow he had to get through the reception and then the journey over to Richmond, where they were going to spend the night at a hotel. Cora had been aghast at the idea but Neville had explained it was run by Marian Dalby's sister and all his workmates had chipped in to give them the night as a present. He hadn't repeated what Dennis suggested they do when they got there. Still the very thought made him hot under the collar.

But now there was no time to do anything about it as they were photographed from every angle, then with family, then with friends, until his face ached from smiling. 'My feet are killing me,' hissed Hazel. 'Can't wait to take these shoes off.'

'Can't wait to take off more than that,' he whispered. Then they were being led into the church hall where their mothers and sisters had been hard at work earlier that morning, decorating the place

259

and arranging trestle tables. A big banner hung over the door: 'Congratulations, Hazel and Neville'. As they went through into the hall, everyone cheered.

Hazel's bosses from the café had been very generous and helped out with the catering, for which Fred had provided lots of cold cuts of chicken and ham. Hazel appreciated their kindness but found she was too nervous to eat. Even though the ceremony was over and she hadn't fluffed her words, there were still the speeches to get through before she could finally be alone with Neville. She could hardly wait. Her wedding night in a hotel! She'd secretly dreaded spending it in her new flat, wondering if every sound could be heard by her new neighbours. In her mother's house, Hazel had heard everything that went on in her neighbour's bedroom: the thud-thud-thud of the headboard and the squeaking bedsprings. She might still be a virgin, but one of her friends had given her graphic details of what went on, so the sounds never failed to make her blush, even though they fascinated her. She wanted her first night with Neville to be private and special and now thanks to his workmates and Marian's kindness it would be.

It had been silly of them to have their first real row just a few days ago. She put it down to wedding nerves. Cora had told them about the flat next to Beryl's and they'd gone to see it. Neville had been upset that it was so far from his mum. Hazel knew it wasn't the step up she'd hoped for, but it was a big, newly decorated flat and it was far enough from Ennis Street for them to have time

260

alone but close enough to pop over if they wanted to. So she played down the fact it was closer to the power station, which she hated. She knew in her heart of hearts it was far from what she imagined but she thought they could make the best of it, fill it with things they'd choose together to make it their first home, and hope they could ignore the power station. The location was far from ideal but she told herself the trade-off was the generous size of the rooms and the way it had just been done up. 'I just hope that Beryl doesn't have that tarty niece of hers round too often,' she'd said, looking out of the back window of the flat to Beryl's backyard, full of plants in all manner of containers: buckets, paint tins, an old sink. It wasn't a view to shout about, and the people in the road behind them would be able to see straight into their kitchen, they were so close. She'd have to find a blind down the market.

'I don't know why you all hate Vera so much,' Neville had protested. That had really got on Hazel's nerves. Here she was, prepared to live near to the smelly power station so they could have a good start together, and he was defending that trollop. They'd ended up screaming at each other, all over someone they didn't really know. She hoped Beryl hadn't heard. They'd gone ahead and signed the lease anyway, even though it was more expensive than they'd wanted. It didn't matter, they had been given the keys and had managed to buy some second-hand furniture, enough to enable them to move in as soon as they married. They would carry on saving, and replace the old stuff bit by bit. She'd got a few bits and pieces –

items Jill had given them, some wedding presents, those kitchen knives she'd got at the market which Cora kindly insisted she take with her. The rest would come in time.

Hazel forced herself to eat some chicken as she gazed at her new husband. There was no doubt in her mind that they'd done the right thing, row or no row. They'd make the place their first home and move on when they were ready. He was the man for her, no two ways about it. She was startled out of her thoughts by the tapping of a spoon on glass. The speeches were starting.

People laughed and clapped affectionately as the good wishes flowed. Bill kept his comments just about on the right side of decency, though she could see her mother's eyes glancing round the room, checking nobody was offended. Several of Cora's acquaintances from church were pursing their lips but everyone else was laughing along, taking it all in the spirit in which it was intended. Finally Bill shut up and the music started. People began to clear the tables and push them back so that there could be dancing.

After Neville had led Hazel onto the dance floor, and had waved for others to join them, Fred had pulled an obviously reluctant Alison forward. He was a good dancer though and all eyes seemed to rest on the couple.

'I don't know how she has the nerve,' hissed Cora. 'Look at her up there, big as a balloon already. Does she have to flaunt it? Shameless hussy.'

'Ah, but she's a married woman now,' said Terry, patting her arm. He had had a few drinks and all was well in his world. 'Not a bad mover, old Fred, is he? He's kept his talents under a bushel.'

Cora had a sudden flashback to Fred in the dancehalls when they'd been young and she'd started courting Jack. He'd been a keen dancer then and had known all the steps. Of course things were different now; the teenagers liked rock and roll. But Fred could keep up with any of them. She hoped he wasn't going to swing Alison round to 'Rock Around the Clock'. With her huge bump she'd probably fall over.

Alison was in another new outfit, with a little jacket that had fancy piping around the edges that matched the colour of her pretty pointy shoes. Cora sighed. Fred was treating her well, just like he'd promised. She had to admit the new hairstyle and smart clothes made a difference. She wasn't ashamed to be seen with her youngest daughter any more, but she wished that telltale bump wasn't so obvious, or at least not yet. The church stewards had clearly been shocked but hadn't wanted to show it. Stuff them, Cora thought suddenly. Let them think what they liked. This day belonged to Hazel and she made a lovely bride. All eyes were on her as Neville smooched with her to an Elvis love song.

'Well done, Cora.' Jill came across to pull up a chair beside her. 'We did all right, didn't we? They look so happy. Made for each other.' Jill quickly wiped away a tear. Now the excitement was over she felt very weepy again.

'Yes, they make a perfect pair.' Cora wasn't weeping. She was happy for Hazel, but was looking forward to having the house to herself – or at least after Linda, Terry and June left tomorrow. 'Those dresses look a treat. We'll soon have all the photos to look forward to – I hope they turn out all right.'

Jill nodded, twisting her hanky in her hands, as Bill danced in front of them with Kathy in her gorgeous turquoise frock. She was pleased with the way it had all gone. She should be glad that Neville was so fortunate. Maybe Kathy would be next? But no, she reminded herself. Kathy looked happy enough to dance with Bill but he'd never meet her exacting standards. It would take a very special man to distract her from her career.

A shout went up. The car had arrived to take Hazel and Neville to the hotel, and everyone gathered round to see them off. Cora allowed herself to be pushed to the front and beamed with pride as Hazel hugged her.

'Thanks for everything, Mum. It's been a truly special day.'

'You go and enjoy yourself,' Cora said. 'You deserve a bit of fun, my girl. You worked hard for this. You have a lovely time and we'll see you soon.'

Hazel waved and disappeared into the back seat of the car, followed by Neville, as his friends heckled him.

Jill had another quick sob as she watched them go. Her little boy, all grown up. How had it happened so fast? It seemed like only yesterday that he'd been born. However, before she could dwell on it, Richie was at her elbow.

'We don't have to go yet, do we?' he asked. 'It's only just getting started. Did you see how Bill danced with Kathy? Do you think she'll go out with him?'

'You can forget about that, your sister's far too sensible,' Jill told him. 'But no, we don't have to go yet. Just don't put on anything too noisy. Remember we're not all as young as you.'

Richie raced off and put on Bill Haley. Fred was first out on the dance floor.

Chapter Twenty-Eight

Hazel lay on her back, gazing up at the ornate ceiling in the moonlight. Neville snored beside her. She'd just had the biggest disappointment of her life.

It had begun so well. Marian's sister had greeted them with the news that the evening meal was on the house, and once they'd freshened up she'd shown them to the best table, nestled in a bay window overlooking the park. The cutlery shone in the candlelight and they could hear birds singing through the open window. Hazel suddenly found she was starving, having eaten very little apart from cold chicken all day. She and Neville had three courses of the most delicious food and even had wine with it, which she decided she liked better than sherry. It was the most romantic evening she had ever had.

Then her new husband had kissed her hand and led her up the stairs. Their room was perfect, spacious and with gilt-framed mirrors and elegant lamps, with a big soft bed in the centre. No danger of anyone overhearing them here, Hazel realised with delight. This was how married life should begin. With a secret smile she edged into the bathroom to change into the satin nightdress she'd saved up for. It was peach-coloured, with lots of lace around the edges. She stroked the fabric as she smoothed it over her body. She was so excited she almost tore it as she tugged down the hem. If she had her way it wouldn't stay on for long.

Neville was waiting for her, stretched out on the bed in his suit trousers and wedding shirt, which he'd undone. 'Come here,' he breathed, his eyes shining with appreciation. 'Oh my God, Hazel, I've waited for this moment since I first saw you.'

'Mmmm, me too.' She lay beside him and reached for him, drawing him down to her neck. He kissed it then kissed her face, gently and then more forcefully, his breath getting faster and faster. She could feel him pulling down the straps of her nightdress, exposing her breasts, kissing them, pulling up the hem, reaching between her legs. She thought she would burst with excitement. He had struggled out of his trousers and she helped him off with his shirt. 'Oh Neville, yes, yes, yes. Come on, I want you.' She held him tightly, but then gasped in pain as he suddenly thrust himself inside her. It soon passed and she started to moan in pleasure.

Then, nothing. He stopped moving. 'Neville, what is it? Is something wrong?' She tried to sit up but he had collapsed on top of her, pinning her to the bed. 'Neville, what's going on?'

He rolled over and turned away. 'Sorry. I'm so

sorry. I must have had a bit too much to drink or something.' She could tell he was embarrassed. 'It won't be like that next time.'

She realised her legs were wet and slimy. 'Neville? What do you mean?'

But he wouldn't look at her. After a while he began to snore, leaving her to cross the gorgeous room to the elegant bathroom, where she cleaned herself up. She caught sight of herself in the mirror.

Her hair was dishevelled and her lovely night-dress was rumpled and to her eyes now looked cheap. She pulled it round so it was less notice-able. Was something wrong with her? Had she said something, done something? If so she didn't know what it was.

She went back to the bed and crawled under the covers, trying to work out what had happened. Neville had got it up all right but then had finished almost at once. Why hadn't he carried on, when she was having such a good time? She'd saved herself for this, had dreamed of this, and all for nothing. What a let down.

Shaking with disappointment, she rolled over and stared at the silhouette of the window. What a waste of all these fancy surroundings. They might as well have stayed at their new flat if that was all Neville could manage.

Cora had allowed Fred to get her a few drinks at the reception and now she was home Terry had poured her a port and lemon. She felt quite tipsy, but very pleased. When all was said and done, the day couldn't have gone better. Hazel had been a

267

radiant bride, Neville a handsome groom and the bridesmaids were beautiful. As for Fred, he'd turned into the life and soul of the party. He'd even got some of the more staid church members up on their feet and dancing, wiping their sour expressions off their faces. Cora could have hugged him with relief. Now they'd be less likely to gossip about Alison behind her back. One had even come over to her to praise him. 'I can quite see what your daughter saw in your son-in-law,' she'd whispered. 'If I was forty years younger myself... Not that I approve, you understand, but these things will happen. What a pleasure it must be to have someone like that in your family.'

Talk about a turn-up for the books. Cora sipped her drink, watching as Linda poured herself a very small sherry. 'I think I might go upstairs,' she said. 'You and Terry stay up as long as you like. I'm out for the count. I've been running round like a blue-arsed fly these last few days and now it's all catching up with me.'

Linda looked up, thinking it was more a case of several port and lemons catching up with her. 'Yes, you do that. We won't be long.'

Terry came through from the kitchen, a bottle of beer in his hand. 'I'll just have this, the rewards of giving the bride away.' He grinned at them both. 'I wonder what they're up to now. Making the most of that posh hotel bed, I hope.'

'Terry!' Linda pretended to swipe his arm. She hated it when he spoke like that in front of her mother.

'Well, maybe they are,' said Cora generously. 'Bit of time to themselves after all the pressures of the big day. Just as long as it don't give them a taste for luxuries beyond their means.' She stiffly raised herself from the armchair. 'Good night, then. See you in the morning.' She tottered unsteadily to the stairs and began to climb.

Terry stretched out on the rug in front of the unlit fire, resting his head against Linda's legs.

'What are you doing down there?' she demanded. 'There's a perfectly good chair over here, you know. You'll get dirt over your good suit and who's going to get that clean?'

'I'll take it off if that's any better.' He smiled up at her. 'Come down here and join me.'

'Terry, I can't do that!'

'Course you can.' He reached up for her hand. 'Come down here and let's have some fun. I was staring at you all day in that posh dress. I could have ripped it off you in front of everybody.'

'Glad you didn't,' said Linda, but she was weakening. She knew she shouldn't but what harm would it do? 'Quiet, Terry, what if Mum hears us?'

'She's had that many port and lemons, she wouldn't hear a bomb go off next to her head,' he said. 'And what if she does hear something? We ain't single. We're a respectable old married couple.' He pulled her gently down onto the rug. 'You were the most gorgeous creature there today, do you know that? And you're mine, all mine. Let me show you how much I love you.'

'I think I can feel that,' giggled Linda.

'You certainly can. Wouldn't it be funny if we made June a baby brother or sister right here on your mum's old rug?'

'I'd never be able to tell anybody,' she said,

pulling off his trousers.

'Maybe not,' he breathed, 'but we'd know, wouldn't we?'

Alison put her feet up on the delicate little three-legged stool that Fred had found specially for her. She was finding her legs ached more and more as the bump grew bigger. God knows what they would be like by the time it was full size. She flopped against the padded back of the sofa, glad to be home. She shook herself at the thought. She'd called this place home in her head. Maybe she was getting used to it.

'Do you want a milky drink?' Fred asked. She'd expected him to be tired out after the long day, particularly as he'd been dancing so much, but instead he seemed livelier than ever. She'd noticed there'd been no sign of his wheezing. Maybe dancing was good for you. The grumpy old ladies had certainly seemed to enjoy it.

'No, you go ahead and have one.' She smiled weakly up at him.

'Do you know, I think I might have a drop of Scotch,' he said. 'After all, it's a special day, isn't it? Not often your sister gets married.'

'Not often you get a chance to dance with half the seventy-year-olds in Battersea either.'

'You didn't mind, did you?' Then he realised she was teasing. 'Well, I thought it wouldn't do any harm. They was sitting there, faces like lemons, they needed a bit of help to get into the party spirit. I was only doing my bit.'

'Very kind of you.' She rolled her ankles from side to side. 'I couldn't have been on my feet a moment longer. But I'm glad I didn't deprive you of your fun.'

He sipped at his whisky and nodded. 'No, it was a good day. I hope it's the start of a happy future for them. Who knows, it might make your sister a bit kinder.'

Alison raised her eyebrows. 'Not sure how that would happen. Hazel's Hazel.'

He sat down beside her. 'I know, I know. But it might … I don't know. This is the whisky talking. I just thought, having a proper bit of loving in her life might soften her a little. Make her less inclined to hit out. Sorry, I'm being a soft old sod.'

'Neville's got his work cut out to make her happy,' Alison predicted. 'She won't be content with that flat for long. You think Mum's harsh when she says some of those things about Hazel but she's right. My sister likes the good things in life.'

'I can't blame her for that,' said Fred, gazing round the living room that Alison had begun to add little touches to.

Alison shrugged. She did like the comforts that came with living with Fred. She loved the fact that everything was new, unlike the depressing worn-out stuff in her mother's house that had been poor quality to start with. She liked the way the toaster worked without her having to fiddle with the plug, that there was hot water whenever she wanted it, that there was a proper bath and no more old tin tub. It seemed crazy that there was another room on the top floor with a shower in it – and yet she was getting used to all this luxury fast. She loved the items that made life easier. They just weren't the main thing. Fred provided for her in the material sense but more than that, he gave her confidence and she was beginning to feel that she could be herself. The flat and the furnishings and the money were extras. It was different for Hazel, and suddenly she had the feeling that something would go badly wrong for her sister. She shivered.

'You cold?' asked Fred, immediately on his feet. 'Shall I get you something?'

Alison smiled. 'No, I'm all right. But I think I'll turn in.' She heaved herself to her feet and faced him. 'See you in the morning. We've got that delivery of pork arriving first thing, remember.'

She headed for the room Fred had first put her in that night he'd found her in the churchyard. It was hers now. She'd begun to buy things for it that were to her taste, knowing Hazel would have given her eye teeth for soft bedding and new furniture, but they didn't really matter. The main thing was she was safe here. Nobody would call her names, insult her, attack her in the street. This was her haven, a room facing the backyard of the butcher's shop.

She hoped Hazel felt as safe in the arms of her new husband, but she couldn't shake off the sensation that something terrible was going to happen.

Chapter Twenty-Nine

'How did the wedding go?' called Joe as Hazel walked along through the market stalls. 'Everyone admire the dress, did they? And how was the wedding night? he asked as she drew closer.

'Enough of your cheek,' said Hazel, pretending to be outraged. 'Yes, everyone loved the frock, you done me proud. Got to dash, I'm on my lunch hour.' She sped up and walked on, as Joe shook his head.

'What's got into her?' he said aloud.

'Thought you said she just got married,' leered Barry from the stall opposite. 'She'll have had plenty into her, won't she.'

Hazel knew they were talking about her behind her back but she ignored them. Everyone was being friendly and interested but she didn't want to speak to any of them. Here she was, back shopping at the market, as if her special day had never happened. The only difference was all their savings were gone and they had to scrimp even more. Her fantasies about transforming the new flat into their first beautiful home had been short-lived. Most of their wages would have to go on rent and food, leaving them little to save.

She wouldn't even be able to rely on decent cuts of meat from her sister but would have to return to the butcher's market stall instead, to get scrag ends. Fuming, she stood in the queue, her fierce

273

expression putting anyone off talking to her.

That hadn't been the biggest disappointment though. Things hadn't improved in bed. She couldn't believe she'd spent so long saving herself for Neville only for it all to be such an anti-climax. He'd tried and failed every night since the wedding, and last night she'd lost her temper, telling him not to bother. She couldn't believe he was getting any enjoyment out of it. She certainly wasn't. Was this really what it was like for most people?

'Good to see you back, Hazel,' said the butcher. 'Or do I say Mrs Parrot now?'

'No need,' said Hazel with gritted teeth. 'A pound of that, please. And half of sausages.'

Her sister's good fortune added to her anger. How come Alison had nearly disgraced them all and yet she'd landed in the lap of luxury when she, Hazel, had done everything right but ended up as poor as ever and with a husband who couldn't satisfy her? It was enough to make her weep. If she wasn't careful she might have to concede that her mother had been right after all about Neville. No, she wasn't ready to believe that quite yet. But he was threatening to be a disappointment in every sense.

'Penny for 'em,' said the butcher.

Hazel realised she'd been standing staring into space and the women in the queue behind her were starting to mutter. Bloody interfering old bags, she thought, paying for her meat and then turning back towards the café. She was back to working five days a week, but sitting alone in the flat on her days off when Neville was at work only

274

reminded her of how little money they had to spend on it. Maybe she'd go back to working the extra day. It wasn't as if she had to sleep in after long nights of unbridled passion.

It's early days yet, she reminded herself, you got to give it time. In one way she should be pleased; it showed that Neville hadn't been at it with loads of other women before he met her or, worse, behind her back while they were engaged. That had happened to some girls she knew and she'd always prided herself that her Neville would never have done that. He'd never betray her. Yet now she found herself wishing that he had – at least he might have picked up a few useful tips.

She'd never admit what was happening to anyone. It was too shameful. To think that she, talked about as one of the best-looking girls in Battersea, had chosen someone who couldn't make love to her was too painful to put into words. She deserved better than this. Life had cheated her. Meanwhile her sister was living the life of Riley with her new clothes and what sounded like a huge new flat. She had no intention of going round to visit – she was far too envious.

Head held high, Hazel strode back to the café, where at least she'd be too busy to worry about what was going on at home.

The next few weeks were too hectic for Linda to even think about how her sisters were doing. Terry had heard of a bigger house coming up and persuaded her to go to see it.

'Isn't it too soon?' she'd asked him. 'We don't want to rush into anything.'

He'd won her round and when she caught sight of it she knew why. It wasn't modern but it was an end of terrace, with a big garden. Whoever had had it last had installed a proper inside bathroom, for which she was glad – she wasn't going back to outside lavs and tin baths for anyone. The kitchen was as up to date as it could be and there were gas fires in every room. Best of all there was a third big bedroom and a small box room. When she looked out from the box-room window she could see the downs in the distance.

'Oh Terry,' she'd said, turning to him. 'Are you thinking what I'm thinking? What this could be?'

Terry didn't have to be asked. He knew the way his wife's mind worked. 'It'll be the nursery,' he said. 'It's big enough for a cot and a cupboard and a comfy chair. You can sit here with June's little brother or sister and nurse him or her and look out at the view.' He smiled at her. 'You'd like that, wouldn't you?'

'Yes, and June's room all pink.'

'Whatever you want,' he agreed. 'But it will have been worth it, won't it?'

'Don't remind me,' she'd muttered.

They'd never have managed to live in such a place if Terry hadn't taken those risks, she told herself, as she cleaned up in the old kitchen for the last time. Terry hadn't let the grass grow under his feet but had signed for the new house the day after viewing it. Now after several weeks of frantic planning, packing and organising, they were moving later that afternoon. She gazed around her kitchen with a pang of sadness. She'd thought it was luxury beyond her wildest dreams the first time she'd set foot in it. Now it seemed poky and old-fashioned in comparison to the new place. Pull yourself together, she murmured, as she finished mopping the floor. Nobody was going to be able to find fault with the way they left the house. She wouldn't have anyone saying she was a slob.

Finally satisfied, she twisted the mop to wring the water from it and emptied the bucket into the outside drain. The floor in the new kitchen would be easier to clean too – it had beautiful checked lino tiles, freshly laid by the looks of them. She'd have to make sure her friends didn't wear stilettos when they came to visit.

She quickly ran through the checklist she'd memorised. Boxes packed and labelled, the one with the kettle, teapot and cups on the top. June to be picked up to spend the afternoon after nursery with her best friend. Keys to be posted through the landlord's letterbox. Last-minute items – coat, hand towel, cleaning things – to go into the big shopping bag. At last, everything was ready to go. She could sit down and take a breather, even if she couldn't make a cup of tea.

As she sank onto the one remaining kitchen chair, she began to relax. Anything that hadn't been done by now would just have to stay un-done, she could do no more. Satisfied with her work, she sighed with pleasant exhaustion. Then the thought struck her.

When had she last had her monthlies? Before Hazel's wedding, surely. Yes, the more she thought about it, the more definite she was. What if Terry's prediction had come true and they had managed to conceive a baby that night on her mother's rug, as they tried in vain to stifle their shouts of passion? The harder they'd tried to be quiet, the worse it got. She blamed the sherry. Her mother had looked at her strangely the next morning but hadn't said anything.

Linda tutted. Here she was, getting her hopes up all over again. Don't even think about it, she warned herself. Don't jinx your first days in your new house. This is a fresh start – no more deliveries of dodgy boxes, no waking in the night wondering what's in them or if they've been stolen. Don't set yourself up for disappointment. Forget you've counted back on your fingers and worked out it's possible.

Linda couldn't help it though. As she went to answer the doorbell to the removal van, a little flicker of hope burst into flame in her heart. She knew she was clutching at straws but what if this time she wasn't mistaken? What if their new life in their new home was to be blessed by a new baby?

'Not long now,' said Vera as she ran in through the door and pulled out a chair. 'What are you having? Don't suppose you can fit much in any more.'

'Thanks a lot.' Alison had been waiting for over fifteen minutes in the café by the station but she didn't blame her friend. The ladies' wear supervisor had been stricter than ever recently and had taken to keeping Vera behind to punish her for the smallest fault, real or imagined. 'It's worse than doing detention at school,' Vera had scowled. 'It's only because she's jealous. She's got the hots for the head of menswear and he's not interested. She thinks it's cos he fancies me. It isn't, I can tell you.' Vera had pulled a face. 'He's much keener on the fellow who's head of haberdashery but I ain't telling her that. Let her work it out for herself.'

'It's good of you to come to see me,' Vera said now, hanging her coat on the back of her chair. She began to unwrap a bright paisley scarf from her neck – it was late November and the winds were cold. 'Aren't you tired out?'

'A bit,' Alison admitted. She was completely exhausted but didn't intend to let that stop her seeing Vera. 'Doesn't matter. Who knows if I'll be able to do this for much longer? Can't see me bringing a baby in here. It's hard enough getting between the chairs and tables as it is.'

Vera waved at the waitress to order their usual and sat back in her chair. 'Saw your brother-in-law the other day. He was rushing down the road and hardly had time to say hello. Not the best advert for wedded bliss, is it?'

Alison shrugged. 'I wouldn't know. I've only seen them when I've gone round to visit Mum. Fred told me I should ask them over to the flat so I did, but they haven't come.'

'Probably they think it'll be too much for you now it's so close to your time,' said Vera generously. Alison shook her head. She knew it was much more likely to be sheer envy. Alison knew she wouldn't be able to hide her growing contentment at the flat, with all its wonderful new fixtures and fittings, and could honestly say that she didn't miss her old house at all. As for not seeing her sister, she was only too glad. She'd had enough of her bullying, verbal lashings and shoves and pinches to last a lifetime.

'Have you got everything ready? Just in case it comes early?'

'Fred's got it all sorted out.' Alison raised her eyebrows. 'He won't let me lift a finger. He's packed a bag to take to the hospital. He's even gone out and bought a car, one that's big enough to let me push the seat back. He parks it in the yard and all the delivery lorries have to make do as best they can.'

'Thought you said you weren't working any more?' asked Vera.

'I'm not. Fred stopped me weeks ago, said it was too much for me. I watch it all happening from the back window. I tell you, if he could have this baby for me, he would. I knew he was generous but I hadn't realised quite how far he'd go. He's got a list of all the things to buy once it's here, although he won't do so until the birth in case it brings bad luck.'

'But that's good, isn't it?' Vera looked approving. 'Most men disappear at the very mention of a baby.'

'It's just as well. I wish I could disappear. He's going to be far better at all this than I am.' Alison gazed at the ceiling, suddenly wanting to cry. She usually tried not to admit this to herself and here she was, coming out with it in the middle of a crowded café, windows steaming up, draughts spiralling through every time someone opened or shut the door. 'What if the baby looks like Paul, Vera? What'll I do then? Every time I see it I'll think of ... you know. What he did that night. I

280

won't be able to hold it, I'll want to throw it away. What if I hurt it? I'm meant to love it, aren't I? What if I can't? I don't think I'll be able to manage to. And then all those things I'll have to do – what if I get it wrong? How am I meant to know what to do? I won't exactly have Mum rushing round to show me, and Linda's too far away, and she's just moved house.' She gave a small sob, only just catching herself in time.

'Stop it.' Vera's voice was firm. 'You stop that right now. Stop getting yourself all het up. That won't do you no good. Nobody knows what to do when their first baby comes, that's what my auntie Beryl said. Deep down everyone's frightened. They still cope though. You just get on with it. Don't start worrying about what might never happen.'

'Linda never said that.'

'Why would Linda say that? You were only a girl when she had June. And, not being funny or nothing, I wouldn't admit anything was wrong in front of your mum or Hazel if I could help it. I bet Linda's the same.'

'No, you're right, she'd never hear the end of it.' Alison grew calmer. 'I don't know, I'm all over the place at the moment. It's sitting around all day with nothing to do when I'm used to running round the shop. Too much time to think.'

'Well, make the most of it cos you won't have that for much longer.' Vera smiled as their order arrived. 'And enough of your miserable face. If this is going to be one of our last visits to the café for a bit, we're damn well going to enjoy it. If you're not going to finish that, I'll have it.' She

281

speared the end of Alison's vanilla slice before her friend had had a chance to start.

'You will come and visit, won't you?' Alison was suddenly seized with fear that she'd lose contact with Vera. All at once she realised how much she'd come to rely on her good advice and irreverent attitude. Of all the people she might have ended up making friends with, Vera was the least likely – and yet now she couldn't do without her. 'Fred said you'd be welcome any time. Promise you'll come.'

'Try and keep me away.' Vera put down her fork. 'Don't be daft, of course I'll come round. I want to see Fred change a nappy for a start. Might sell the story to the papers and make my fortune. You could rent him out to all the tired mothers of Battersea.' She reached out and took Alison's hand. 'And as for the rest, we'll take it as it comes, won't we? That's what we've done so far. So let's carry on.'

Alison nodded. Maybe she had got herself into a state over nothing. Maybe the baby would look nothing like Paul at all.

Chapter Thirty

'How was your day?' asked Neville as he came into their small kitchen. It overlooked their back-yard, and they could see Beryl's pots and tubs next door, now empty of vegetables.

'It was all right.' Hazel forced herself not to

flinch as he kissed her, as his face was so cold. 'Busy for a weekday.'

Neville rubbed his hands. 'I could murder a cuppa. It's brass monkeys out there.'

Hazel didn't move. 'The kettle's behind you.'

Neville turned and went to fill it. 'Fancy one?'

'Yeah, go on then.'

He set it to boil. 'What's for tea?'

'Nothing. I haven't made anything. I'm sick of the smell of cooking, I was running in and out of the kitchen at work all day.'

Neville nodded in sympathy. 'I know you work hard, love. They don't let you rest for a minute. Don't worry about it, I had my lunch late.' He grinned as he had an idea. 'Why don't we go out for a meal? It's been ages since we done that.'

Hazel shut her eyes for a second, as if she couldn't quite believe what she was hearing. 'No, Neville! You know how much eating out costs! We're supposed to be saving to buy new furniture. I'm sick of looking at this second-hand stuff!'

'All right,' he said, backing away from her. 'It was only a suggestion. Thought you wouldn't have to cook or anything.'

'Well, it looks as if I do have to flaming cook,' snapped Hazel. 'Unless you can make do with a sandwich. You aren't going to rustle up a meal, are you? Not like Fred, who can make all sorts of meals for himself.'

'Yeah but Fred's been on his own for ages. It's different. I'm not like Fred.' Neville thought it was a daft thing for her to say. As if he wanted to be like the wheezy old butcher, cooking eggs and bacon out the back.

'No, because Fred can buy his wife whatever she wants from whatever shop she wants, and drive her round in a new car, and give her a big flat, and still cook her a meal when he gets in. Of course you're not like Fred.' Hazel's eyes were glittering dangerously as she got up from her chair.

'Hey, steady on, Hazel,' said Neville, beginning to get alarmed. 'You knew I couldn't cook when we got married. None of my friends can cook. You never said it was important.'

'Of course I never said.' Hazel drew closer until Neville was backed up against a cupboard. 'Lots of things we never said, Neville. Lots of things I thought were so important that we wouldn't even need to talk about them.'

It dawned on Neville that this wasn't just about cooking. 'Come on, Hazel. We're only just starting out. We need a bit of time to ... to get used to each other.'

'Oh, that's what you call it, is it?' She was screaming into his face. 'Get used to each other? When night after night you come near me and then can't get it up and I'm left there like something washed up on the beach? Is that what I'm meant to be getting used to?'

'No, no.' He raised his hands again to try to keep her off.

Hazel wished he'd shout back rather than stand there and take it. What was wrong with him? Didn't he love her enough to get upset and argue with her?

'Then what, Neville? Get used to this smelly flat and our pathetic wages and knowing that if we carry on as we are we'll never have children?

Is that it?'

'No, now look, Hazel, we...'

Suddenly she couldn't bear his weakness any more. She drew back her hand and hit him hard around the face.

A few streets away Alison was pacing around what she was getting used to calling their kitchen rather than Fred's kitchen. He'd brought some nice chicken up from the shop and she was just about to start cooking it when she felt a strange sensation. It wasn't quite like the pain she used to have with her monthlies but that was the closest she could think of.

She waited, wondering if she'd imagined it, then lined up the vegetables she was going to chop to have with the chicken. Just as she sliced through an onion the pain struck again, stronger this time. She gripped the counter to steady herself, afraid her knees might give way. This must be it. It was happening at last. Where was Fred?

He'd gone out after the shop had shut to see about some new equipment for the storeroom. Typical Fred, she thought, if there was an improvement to be had then he wanted to be the first one with it. Usually she liked this about him. Tonight she wished he was home.

Fred had shown her how to work the telephone in the hall and she had to admit it was a useful thing. The trouble was nobody she knew had a phone. Linda was talking about getting one in the new house but hadn't done so yet. Cora didn't hold with them, saying they were a waste of money, and wouldn't have been able to afford one anyway. Even if Hazel had had one Alison wouldn't have wanted to speak to her. Vera would have loved one but Winnie had put her foot down, complaining her daughter would use it for gossip and leave her mother to pay the bill.

The doctor's number was pinned up next to the phone but Alison didn't want to bother him yet. She remembered Linda saying this bit could go on for hours, days even, so she didn't like to make a fuss. Besides, Fred would be home soon; he wouldn't want to miss his chicken. She just had to wait till he got back then he'd know what to do. He'd been reading all about it, and she'd been happy to let him, thinking the less she knew the less she'd have to worry about.

Another pain came, much stronger than the one before. She held on to the wall, breathless with the intensity of it. Was that meant to happen or did it mean something was wrong? Guiltily she thought she wouldn't mind if something happened to the baby. Then she thought of how disappointed Fred would be. He seemed to have decided that if he was to be a father then he'd throw himself into it, and had been taking note of where he could buy good toys, and what new things they'd need once the baby was born. She just wanted to get it over with.

All at once her legs were wet. She started to panic, but got herself into the bathroom and began to clean herself up. What was this? She hadn't wet herself since she was a very little girl – she'd taught herself not to as Hazel had picked on her so violently every time, pinching her and teasing her. She tried to get back to the kitchen to wipe the floor but another spasm gripped her. They were getting more frequent. Even though she finally made it to the kitchen she couldn't bend over to reach the cleaning cupboard. She was afraid that if she did manage to get to it she'd never stand up again. The mess she'd made of the floor was embarrassing but it would have to wait. She'd have to apologise to Fred and hope the doctor didn't see.

The pain was coming in big waves now and she started to lose track of how long they lasted or quite where she was. Instinct made her head for her bedroom, her safe haven. She could hear someone moaning and it took a while to realise it was her. Could anyone hear her? The window faced away from the road and there was nothing on the other side of her bedroom wall so probably not. She was on her own until Fred returned. In between the contractions she remembered she hadn't put the chicken back in the fridge. He'd be cross if it was ruined but she couldn't help it.

Time seemed to stand still. It was all one big tunnel of pain. She rolled around, grasping the pillows, sad that the bedclothes would be spoiled. Maybe she was dying. It felt like her insides were being ripped apart. She'd wanted to die months ago, back in the summer, but now she found she wanted to live. She hadn't got this far only to give up. She held on to her courage as the next contraction hit, making her feel as if she should push. She screamed out in agony.

'Alison? Alison?' Fred was running down the corridor. 'Where are you? What's happening?' He appeared at the doorway and took in the bloody scene. Then he came forward and kissed her forehead. 'I'll be right back. I'm ringing the doctor. The damn car broke down and it looks as if it's too late for you to go anywhere anyway.'

In a moment he was beside the bed again, with a stack of towels under his arm. 'Doctor's on his way. I've left the door open for him. Here, grab hold of my hand. When it hurts you squeeze as hard as you can. Breathe, breathe. You're going to be fine.'

Alison gasped. 'Fred, I'm sorry. There's mess everywhere. I forgot the chicken. I couldn't... I couldn't...'

'Don't be daft. We'll sort that out later. You just stay there till the doctor comes. Keep breathing, come on, you're doing well.'

'Fred, am I dying?' Alison's bright eyes met his. 'Just tell me.' She stopped as an even more terrifying contraction tore through her, and then screamed again.

Fred wiped sweat from his forehead. He'd seen animals being born but this was different. He struggled to stay calm, because he knew one of them had to. He hoped the doctor would make it on time but wasn't convinced he would. How had this happened so fast? All the books he had read said a first baby could take hours, even days. He'd been gone far longer than he intended thanks to the car running out of battery but even so it was only a matter of a few hours. Now the baby looked as if it would arrive any minute.

'Course you aren't dying,' he said, hoping that was true. 'It hurts a lot but you get better. You have to push when you get the urge and rest in

288

between. Let me put more pillows in behind you. There. Big breath. Squeeze my hand, remember. Now push.' He winced as Alison did as she was told and crushed his hand so hard he thought she'd broken a bone in it.

Gently pulling his hand free, he began to help her off with her clothes and into a nightdress. He didn't have time to think that he'd never seen her body before or how strange this was for a husband of four months. She didn't notice. She was in a world of her own now, her eyes tightly shut, gasping for breath, her face red with effort.

She was pushing hard, her feet spread wide. He could see something coming between her legs – it was the top of the baby's head. The doctor wasn't going to make it and he'd have to deliver this baby himself. What did the farmer do when he was there? The animals weren't lying down, it wasn't much help. What did the books say? There was a cord, you had to keep the cord from going round the baby's neck, then it had to be cut. His stomach turned. Even though he was a butcher he wasn't sure if he could cut the cord between his wife and the baby.

As Alison screamed again the baby's head came fully out. 'Push, push, it's here,' he exclaimed, reaching forward as a moment later its shoulders came through and then the whole tiny creature slithered out. Gingerly he checked that the cord wasn't round its neck and then took a look at the rest of it.

'It's a boy.' He gazed at his wife. 'You've done it, he's here, it's a boy.' Tears flooded down his face. 'You clever girl, you've had a boy. He's perfect.'

Alison flopped back on the pillows, too exhausted to care. Between the terror of being alone and all the unfamiliar pain, she was happy for Fred to take charge. She heard a second male voice speaking from the corner of the room and assumed the doctor had finally arrived. She shut her eyes as he examined her and kept them shut as the afterbirth came out, glad that there was someone there who knew what he was doing. She had no idea what was going on. The baby was here and Fred was taking care of it somewhere. That was enough.

'Well done, Mr Chapman.' The doctor clapped Fred on the back. 'Couldn't have done it better myself. If you get tired of the butcher's you should take up midwifery. Of course it helps that you have a healthy young wife.' Privately the doctor thought they were a very odd pair but they had produced a fine-looking son, whose first cries now filled the room. 'You kept your head and everything has gone as well as it possibly could. Doesn't seem to be anything wrong with him even if he did arrive in a hurry. Bring him in to the clinic tomorrow and we'll weigh him, but he looks like a fine specimen. If you fetch some hot water now we'll get him cleaned up and then Mrs Chapman can meet her son. I expect you'd like that, wouldn't you, Mrs Chapman?'

Alison didn't reply, turning her head to face the wall. Let them get on with it. She'd done her bit, delivering the baby safely. She was in no hurry to see him. There would be time enough for all of that.

The doctor didn't worry. He'd seen it all before.

Women often took a while to come round after childbirth, and this was Mrs Chapman's first baby. Nothing had gone to plan and she'd had to cope on her own for most of the time, so clearly she was made of strong stuff. Meanwhile the father was sorting everything out, not rushing to get to the pub unlike so many he knew. The doctor admired that. This father was going to take his responsibilities seriously. The baby was a very lucky little boy, he thought, as Fred carefully washed the tiny hands and feet in warm water. The baby waved them jerkily, clenching and unclenching his fingers.

'He's certainly full of life,' said the doctor. 'How about a cup of tea for your wife? That is often very reviving. I'll hold the little fellow if you like.' The doctor didn't always offer to do this but the baby seemed very content, with a beautiful head of dark brown hair – not at all like Mr Chapman, he reflected, but then again who knew what he'd been like in his younger days?

'Of course, of course. And one for yourself, Doctor? Or would you prefer something a little stronger?'

'If you insist, Mr Chapman. A wee dram to toast the baby's health.' The doctor beamed. He felt he deserved his tot of whisky, rushing round here in such a hurry as he had, leaving his own evening meal unfinished. He approved when his patients appreciated him, and not all of them did. The Chapmans were evidently good sorts all round. He obligingly held the little boy as Fred hurried to the kitchen.

Fred took a moment to clean the floor, where

Alison's waters had broken. He could hardly believe the events of the evening – it had all happened so suddenly and he hadn't had a moment to take it all in. He found he was shaking with emotion. He knew he wasn't the biological father but when he'd held the baby in his arms his heart had beaten faster and he'd wanted to shout from the rooftops that the little boy was here and he was safe. He would do anything to defend this helpless creature that he'd helped bring into the world. If someone tried to hurt the child then they'd have him to answer to. God help anyone who tried to say he wasn't the real father. He was going to be the best father this little boy could ever possibly want.

He was so proud of Alison, and was mortified he hadn't been here when she'd needed him. He'd have some severe words for the garage that had just sold him that car. But she had coped, even though she hadn't really known what was happening, and had obviously been in a lot of pain. She'd been strong and had delivered the baby safely. Now she was entitled to rest. He poured her tea and added some sugar for energy. She didn't usually take it but tonight was an exception.

Moving to the drinks cabinet in the living room he found the whisky bottle and poured two generous glugs into cut-glass tumblers. He deserved to celebrate. It wasn't every day you delivered a baby into this world. Now he thought about it, he could see what a huge achievement it was. He was heartily glad he hadn't had time to think about it while it was all happening, but now he could sit back and take stock. He added the whiskies to the tray with the tea and took it through to the bed-room.

Alison was still turned to face the wall and he wasn't sure if she was asleep. He quietly placed the tea on the nightstand so as not to wake her, then he passed the tumbler to the doctor.

'Cheers,' he said.

'Congratulations again on a job well done,' said the doctor, handing Fred the precious bundle. 'Your very good health, in fact to the health of all three of you.' He raised the glass and sipped. 'A fine whisky if I may say so. You are evidently a man of taste.'

Fred beamed as Alison stirred a little. Slowly he moved across the room, the baby in his arms. 'Are you awake now? Here he is. Don't you want to see him? Here, let me bring him down to the pillow and you can meet him.'

Alison wearily turned over. She supposed she had better do as he asked, although she could happily sleep for a week. Inwardly she tried to prepare herself. This was her baby. It was her duty to take care of it. Maybe it would all be all right.

She steeled herself as Fred pulled back the corner of the blanket around the baby's face. Her body ached but she tried to ignore it as she focused on the little face and then drew back. Gasping, she thought she was going to be sick.

He looked just like Paul.

Chapter Thirty-One

'Whoa, Nev, what happened to you?' Bill couldn't believe the state of his friend's face. 'Who've you been picking on? You got a proper shiner there.'

Neville shrugged, embarrassed. He knew it would be spotted as soon as he unwound his scarf once he got to work. He'd checked himself in the mirror this morning just in case he'd got away with it and it didn't show, but it was there for all to see, deep red and purple. He'd just have to come up with a story and stick to it.

'You know we've not long moved into our flat,' he said. 'I ain't quite got the lay of the land yet and I was in a bit of a hurry, caught my foot, and tripped over a chair. That was that.'

'Aha, in a hurry to get to the lovely Hazel, were we?' Bill raised his eyebrows. 'Running to sweep her off her feet? Can't say I blame you.'

'Something like that.' There was no way Neville was going to tell them what had really happened. He was too ashamed. But he blamed himself for not keeping Hazel satisfied and this was just part of the punishment. He truly felt he deserved it, not being able to please her in bed. He wasn't a real man. It wasn't in his nature to argue back and he thought she had every right to be furious with him. He'd always known she had a fiery temper so he couldn't pretend it was news to him, even though she'd never gone this far before.

'Course, if it was Dennis, we'd all know why he might have a black eye,' Bill went on, as Dennis and Nobby came in and began getting their outdoor coats off and factory overalls on.

'Not more trouble with the ladies, Dennis?' Frank had arrived. 'Don't you ever learn? I can't believe you're still out on the town, collecting angry fathers as you go. You'll grow up one day.'

'Some of us have it, some of us don't.' Dennis shrugged. 'It's not my fault if the birds can't leave me alone.'

'I take it you're not interested in night shifts, then,' said Frank. 'We're short on tomorrow's, but I wouldn't want to cramp your style. Sounds as if you got enough enemies after you as it is.'

Neville brightened up. He hadn't gone back to extra late shifts since the wedding but this would be an ideal way to bring in more money and stay out of Hazel's way until she calmed down. 'I don't mind, Frank,' he said. 'Put me down for it if you like.'

'You sure, Nev?' Frank looked dubious. 'Thought you were just doing lates to pay for your wedding, and a slap-up do it was and all. Won't Hazel mind?'

'Yeah, we don't want to get in the way of love's young dream,' said Bill. 'I'd think twice about working nights if I had her waiting for me at home.'

Neville forced himself to smile and play along. 'No, Hazel will be round at her mum's until late tomorrow anyway,' he said. 'Been arranged for ages. She'll hardly notice I'm not there.'

Nobby stuck his miserable oar in. 'Well, that's

all right then. We don't want you annoying Hazel, do we? As long as it's all right with Hazel, you're allowed to come out.'

Bill turned on him. 'Don't be like that, Nobby. Stands to reason that the newlyweds will want to be together of an evening. Nev's giving up his gorgeous bird's company to put up with ours.'

'Maybe she don't want him indoors with a face like that,' muttered Nobby, who'd always been jealous of Neville's good looks. 'Maybe she's glad to see the back of him. Maybe it puts her right off.'

Frank glanced at the big clock over the door, wondering what had happened to make his balding colleague so surly and why he always seemed to have it in for Neville, who wouldn't hurt a fly. If the lad really did want to work extra shifts he thought he should get credit for it. 'Right, time to make a start,' he said. 'Any more for the late shift? Neville, I'll put your name down and thank Hazel from me. It's good of you to make the effort. Meanwhile, get in there and get stuck in. And enough of the gossip. You're like a load of old women.'

Cora had just got rid of the paperboys for the morning when the message came.

'Baby boy born last night. Both he and mother safe and well at home. Regards, Fred.'

The lad who had brought the piece of paper stood around hoping for a tip but he was out of luck. Cora wasn't going to waste a precious coin on him and sent him packing. She wondered what would be the best thing to do. She wasn't particularly anxious about Alison, now that it appeared she had every comfort lavished upon her, and newborn babies all looked alike to her. But she wanted to do the right thing, and to be seen to be doing the right thing, keeping in with Fred and anyone else who might have heard the news.

It didn't take long for the word to get round. Within the hour, Marian Dalby, Jill Parrot and Winnie Jewell had all stopped by to congratulate her and ask her to pass on their good wishes to Alison. Winnie had to draw attention to the speedy arrival of the baby.

'Well, yes, he's come earlier than we expected,' said Cora, refusing to back down.

'I should say so.' Winnie straightened her shoulders. 'Five months earlier if my maths is correct. Still, as long as he's healthy and his mum's all right then who am I to pick holes?'

'Exactly,' said Cora. 'I'll be going out to get him a little something at lunchtime. My first grandson, you know. Don't suppose you got any grandchildren on the way yet, Winnie?'

'Good lord, no.' Winnie pretended to be horrified. 'My Vera's got far too good a job to consider such things. I expect she could get you a bit of a discount at Arding and Hobbs if you was to go there for his little present.'

Cora was tempted, but the thought of being beholden to that slapper Vera Jewell didn't appeal. She'd go to the market as usual. If the traders there were going to hear about the baby they'd better do so from her, before they started spreading any more insinuations. 'That's very kind of you, Winnie, but I don't expect I'll have the time

297

to go all the way up there today,' she said. 'Do tell your daughter the good news, though.'

'Oh, I will,' smiled Winnie. 'Tell Alison I was askin' after her, won't you? Congratulate her on not hangin' around.'

Alison woke up to find she hadn't dreamed it all. The baby was still there. He still looked like Paul. She felt a shiver of revulsion at the tiny face. How was she ever going to love this creature who reminded her of the worst night of her life?

Fred was fussing around, making a pile of nappies and little jackets. 'Oh good, you're awake. How are you feeling? Fancy a cup of tea?'

Alison smiled wanly. 'I'd love one. And I'm still exhausted.' That was no lie. She couldn't have moved if she wanted to, her limbs were like lead. Still, it was quite pleasant to feel she had an excuse and to be waited on. That wasn't something she'd ever had at home even when she'd been ill.

Fred came back in with a mug. 'Here you are. Do you want to hold him?'

The baby snuffled from where Fred had laid him in his cot on the other side of the room. His horribly familiar face was turned towards her. She could see it through the bars.

'No, it's all right.' She took a sip of the tea. 'Don't disturb him.'

Fred settled himself on a chair at the foot of her bed. 'He slept well, bless him. I got up and gave him a bit of a carry when he cried. You were out cold and I don't blame you.' He beamed at her. 'He settled down again fast enough. I expect he'll want feeding soon though.'

Alison grimaced. Before the doctor left he'd checked that she knew how to feed him. She didn't but Fred had read about it in a book and told her what to do. To her great embarrassment the doctor had stayed to make sure she did it right. Exposing herself in front of the two men was mortifying. Now she was going to have to do it again, day after day after day. That creature was going to hang off her and look up at her with Paul's eyes. She scowled in disgust. 'Can't he wait a bit?'

'He'll cry when he's ready I dare say.' Fred turned to look at the baby, still snuffling but content enough where he was. 'We ought to think of a name. I didn't want to talk about it before in case it was bad luck but have you had any ideas? Do you want to call him after your dad? He was John really but we all said Jack.'

Alison had never met her father of course, but everyone spoke of him with such fondness that it was almost like having a good memory of him. Fred would tell her about things they'd done together as boys and she was building up a precious picture of him in her mind. She didn't want to taint that by associating him with this new creature. 'No, I don't think so,' she said. 'It would feel odd as I didn't know him. What about your dad? What was he called?'

'Clarence. I'd rather we didn't choose that.'

'God, no. He'd be laughed at.' Alison didn't want that for her child, even if she didn't love it. She knew all too well what it was like to be mocked. Best not to tempt fate. 'Have you got any names you like in particular?'

Fred sat back and thought for a while. 'It's

299

popular to pick a name from the royal family. What about George? Or Charles?'

'But they're such stuffy names,' said Alison. 'Can't we have something more modern?'

'Do you know what I've always liked,' Fred said suddenly. 'I really like the name David. I don't know why. I haven't got anyone in mind, no friend or relation or anything. I just like it.'

Alison nodded. 'I like the idea of calling him something for himself, not after anybody. David Chapman. That sounds good to me.' Better than he deserves, a little voice in her head said.

As if reacting to his new name, the baby began to cry. Fred hurried over to pick him up. 'There, there. Don't worry, David. That's you, that is. Are you hungry? We'll see if Mummy can do something about that, shall we?' He held the baby as if he knew what he was doing.

Alison pulled a face as the little mouth latched on to her and began to suck lustily. 'Ow, that hurts. I'm not sure I'm going to get used to this. Where did you learn to pick up babies like that, Fred? You haven't got any younger brothers or sisters, have you?'

'Oh, it'll get better,' said Fred breezily. 'And I had a fair bit to do with babies in the war, you know. Carrying them out of bombed-out buildings, usually.' He grew quiet. Some of them had lived, some of them hadn't. One had died in his arms. That was something he had tried to forget, but now the sight of David, so healthy and strong, brought it all back. He coughed. He wasn't going to tell Alison about it. Why upset her when there was no need?

'I sent a message to your mum at the paper shop,' he went on. 'Did I do right? I didn't want to wait until we had a name as I wasn't to know we'd agree so quick.'

Alison shifted to try to get more comfortable but it was impossible. 'No, that was the right thing to do. She'd be livid if she wasn't first to know.'

Fred knew that was true and it was partly why he'd done it. 'I expect she'll be round to see you,' he said. 'To see you both, that is.'

Just what I need, thought Alison. 'Maybe. She won't care if I'm all right but she'll want to make sure she's seen the baby so she can tell everyone about her grandson. Bet she doesn't offer to help out though.' David stopped for a moment and she sighed with relief. 'Here, have him back, see if he'll sleep again.' But she spoke too soon. Before Fred could even get up, the baby started to cry again and only one thing would silence him. Alison turned her head away from those staring, familiar eyes.

Chapter Thirty-Two

That evening Cora made her way along Falcon Road, a parcel under her elbow. Just before she'd been going to leave, Jill had knocked on her door and pressed a bag into her arms. 'Just a little something I had ready for the baby,' she'd said. 'I expect your Alison will be too tired to make anything for a while so I'd like them to have this.'

301

Cora had been surprised. It was news to her that anyone in the street felt anything like affection for Alison. Jill was a good soul, though. She'd be kind to anybody. 'That's very thoughtful of you, Jill,' she'd said. 'I'll make sure she gets it and is grateful.'

'No need for any fuss,' Jill replied. 'We both know what it's like when you've just had a baby. The last thing you want is having to mind your manners. If there's anything I can do, I'd be glad to help.'

'We wouldn't want to impose,' Cora said hurriedly. She had no intention herself of helping her daughter and wasn't going to be outdone by her friendly neighbour. 'I'd best be off, I don't want to keep them up late.' She'd picked up the little romper suit she'd got for a discount at the market and slipped it in the bag.

Now she paused in the streetlight just by the butcher's shop and looked up at the windows above. It was a long time since she'd been to the flat upstairs. The last time she could hardly wait to get out. She had gone there with Jack and been introduced to old Mrs Chapman, who'd given them a piece of her mind about the state of youth and how scandalous young people were compared to in her day, with no reason other than she liked the sound of her own strident voice. She couldn't get out fast enough. The result was, Cora had no idea how big the flat was or what it was really like. She didn't have high hopes of it. Everyone knew men on their own were useless at making a home of a place, and Alison had never shown any signs of interest in that sort of thing.

302

It was growing colder by the minute so she quickly rang the bell. Thankfully it wasn't long before Fred was opening the door, beaming as he said, 'Come inside, come inside. It's blowing a right gale out there.'

Cora followed him up the stairs and was led along to Alison's room. Her daughter was sitting up in bed, propped up by pillows, and a cot was in the corner. Cora looked around in astonishment, taking in the fresh paint, new curtains and counterpane. 'Blimey. You done all right for yourself here,' she breathed. 'Got you set up in a palace, ain't he? No wonder you couldn't wait to marry him.'

Alison raised her eyebrows. Typical. Her mother hadn't even asked how she was, while conveniently forgetting what the truth had been. 'He's over there,' she said, nodding towards the cot. 'Pick him up if you want.'

Cora set down her parcel at the foot of the bed and made her way over to inspect her grandson. She couldn't see much of him – he was bundled up in a knitted jacket and white wool cap, and she could just make out his pink nose. Carefully she reached down for him. He barely stirred.

'Well behaved, I'll say that for him.' She pulled the little cap back and took in his face. 'Doesn't look much like you, does he? That's probably a good thing. But what a shame he's got that bad blood in him.'

'Thanks,' said Alison. 'Is that all you've got to say? Because I don't really need reminding.'

Fred bustled in at that point, bearing a tray with cups of tea and a plate of cake. 'Here you are, Cora, something to warm you up after your cold walk. And one for you too, Alison. What do you reckon, Cora? Isn't he a good baby?'

Cora gazed at her grandson and felt a little tug. This was her blood too, no matter how he'd been conceived. It wasn't really his fault. Despite herself, she couldn't help a rush of excitement. This was a new life after all, and it looked as if he'd be brought up in comfort. She stroked his cheek, as much as she could see of it.

Alison was amazed. Her mother had shown more tenderness to her new grandson in two minutes than she had done for her own daughter's entire life. But she wasn't going to protest. If Cora approved of the baby, in spite of his bloodline, then life would be much easier. 'He's called David,' she said.

'David?' Cora looked up sharply. 'We don't know any Davids, do we?'

'It's my favourite boy's name,' Fred explained. 'We didn't want to name him after anyone. This is a new start for all of us.' He waited to see if Cora would react.

'Well, it's your choice,' she said as she gently lifted the baby. 'At least it isn't too new-fangled. I don't approve of them made-up names. David. Yes, he looks like a David.' She turned to her daughter. 'Shall I pass him to you?'

'No, no,' Alison said quickly, 'I'm still too tired. I hold him all the time when he feeds. Put him back in his cot.'

'I'll have him.' Fred reached for the little bundle. 'I'm getting the hang of this, holding the baby and eating cake at the same time.' He grinned broadly, settling himself in the chair at the end of the bed. David slept on oblivious as Fred helped himself to a slice.

'Oh, I nearly forgot.' Cora picked up the parcel and handed it to Alison. 'This is from me and the other thing inside the paper bag is from Jill. She made it herself.'

Alison felt a lump in the back of her throat. So not everyone on Ennis Street hated her. Jill had every reason to shun her after she'd torn the bridesmaid's dress, but she'd put herself out to make this little padded coat. It was beautifully sewn, with tiny cuffs and a double row of buttons, all in a soft pastel lemon. 'It's lovely,' she breathed. 'Do thank her from me. When I'm up and about I'll come to see her myself. It's perfect.' She had to stop herself from crying.

'What, don't you like the romper suit, then?' Cora was onto her like a shot, taking offence at the least excuse. To think she'd gone all the way to the market specially, when she could have gone straight home to put her feet up – it was sheer ingratitude.

Fred stepped in. 'They're both lovely,' he assured her. 'You're very kind to have brought it. It'll be very useful. We didn't get much beforehand, as it would have been bad luck, so this is just what we need.' He could tell the little suit had come from the market as some of the stitching was already coming undone and there was a button missing but he knew Cora didn't have two spare pennies to rub together, and had no intention of finding fault. 'We're very lucky, aren't we, Alison?'

Alison nodded, but she was already drifting off

305

to sleep. Try as she might she could not keep her eyes open. Fred noticed and got to his feet. 'Tell you what, Cora, why don't we put this little fellow back down again and then I'll give you a tour of the flat. Would you like that?'

Cora's eyes lit up. This would give her something to talk about in the shop tomorrow. 'If it's not too much, Fred,' she said. 'I can see you've got a lot on your hands.'

'My pleasure.' Fred carefully set David in his cot once more and straightened up. 'Follow me.'

Cora couldn't believe it. As she headed back along Falcon Road, she shook her head. Fancy Fred having a flat like that, done up so modern. It was hard to credit. Even more so to think her gormless daughter was sharing it. The girl really had fallen on her feet. The place was huge – she'd never have guessed it from the street, but it went back a long way and there were rooms on the top floor she hadn't known about. Four bedrooms! For one couple and a small baby. And two indoor bathrooms. As for that kitchen with all its up-to-the-minute gadgets – she'd hardly known where to look. She had never seen anything like it.

Part of her couldn't help thinking how different life would have been if she'd had somewhere like that to raise her own family. There would have been none of the fighting between the girls forced to share cramped bedrooms, competing for space for their shabby clothes and the few toys they'd had. Then she shook herself. No point in thinking like that. What was done was done. The important thing now was to make sure everyone knew that

306

her daughter had made a good marriage and was living in the lap of luxury. Fred Chapman might be short and balding but he knew how to do out a home all right.

As for the baby... She'd been determined not to feel anything for it, as it carried the blood of the Lanning family, but somehow he had touched her heart. She'd almost forgotten what that felt like but when she'd held him, so tiny and helpless, she couldn't turn off her emotions. Well, he'd want for nothing. She'd never seen a man so prepared to look after a baby as Fred, who seemed to know everything about it. There would be no lack of new clothes and toys for this little boy. He'd be spoilt rotten. Cora sighed. She hadn't wanted to feel the slightest bit of love for him – and yet she couldn't help it. When all was said and done he was after all her grandson.

'So my useless sister's had her baby.' Hazel stormed around the kitchen, slamming cupboard doors. 'A boy. Mum's gone round there now. Who'd have thought it, she goes and gets herself pregnant, pops out a boy and Mum suddenly can't stay away.'

'Well, she's bound to want to see him,' Neville pointed out. He couldn't understand why Hazel thought it was odd. 'My mum was pleased as punch with the news. She had a little coat all made up for when he arrived.'

This made Hazel angrier than ever. 'Did she now? All ready and waiting?' Her eyes narrowed. 'Well, it's just as well Alison's produced a baby because it doesn't look as if your mum'll have a grandchild of her own any time soon, does it? Not with the way we've been going. No, even my ugly sister can have a baby but there's not much chance of me having one. Not if you can't do the business.'

Neville shifted uncomfortably. 'Now look here, Hazel...' He felt ashamed. He knew he deserved all the blame she heaped on him but now he'd begun to realise just how angry she could get and how long that anger lasted.

'Look at what? There's nothing to look at. That's the bleeding trouble.'

Neville quickly changed the subject and, hoping to pacify her, he said, 'I'm going to do overtime tomorrow. I'll be working all night on the late shift.'

There was a moment of stunned silence, then Hazel's eyes blazed. 'All night!' she yelled. 'You can't satisfy me in bed, so rather than try you're going to work night shifts!'

'No, that's not why I'm doing it,' Neville told her. 'You keep on about wanting new furniture so I thought it would boost our savings. I'm not doing it to keep away from you...'

'I should bleeding well hope not!' Hazel slammed her hands against the table. 'We've only been married three months; it'd be a sad thing if you was trying to avoid me already. What made you say that though? Is that what you really think? Is that what your mates at the factory think?'

'Of course not...'

'Cos if they do you can tell them to mind their own bleeding business. Small-minded interfering busybodies that they are.'

'Hang on, Hazel, they're my friends...'

'Friends who think you should spend more time down the pub with them and less at home with me. Some friends.'

'I'm only doing it for the money...'

'And what am I meant to do while you're away all night? Tell me that, will you? I can't even go round to Mum as she's off seeing that new bloody baby...'

'Well, I wasn't to know your sister was going to have it now, was I?'

'Of course not, Neville. As far as we're all meant to believe, the baby's come early, months early, in fact.' Hazel spoke to him as if he were a child. 'But at least it's come. So she's managed to do something I'll never be able to. Hasn't she?' She advanced towards him. 'Hasn't she?'

'Now, Hazel, don't be like that...'

Neville didn't finish his sentence because Hazel suddenly raised her right hand and hit him hard across the face. She stood there as if willing him to react, then ran towards the bedroom, screaming in frustration.

Neville stayed where he was, lifting his hand to gently touch his cheek. At least it wasn't on top of the first bruise, which had faded considerably anyway. How was he going to explain this? He had to be back at work in under an hour. Slowly he made his way to the kitchen sink and ran the cold water, splashing it onto his aching face. It was all his fault; he was no good in bed. The harder he tried the worse it got. He couldn't blame Hazel. This was no more than he deserved. He had to stand back and put up with it because she was justified – he wasn't a real man. But how was he going to explain this to his mates?

Chapter Thirty-Three

Terry swung open the gate of their new house. It was dark already, but the curtains were still open and he could see the Christmas tree that Linda had insisted they put in the front window. She had made streamers from red and green crêpe paper and she and June had decorated the tree with them, along with some shiny baubles they'd bought in town. He should be full of Christmas spirit just looking at it.

He hesitated before getting out his keys. What should he tell his wife about the conversation he'd just had? He didn't know what to make of it himself. On one level it was no different to how he'd been approached before – a quiet suggestion, the promise of good rewards if he was prepared to bend the law. Yet he could sense there was more urgency this time, combined with a threat.

He'd made it clear for months that he was no longer interested but now they were after him again. He wasn't sure why. There had been a rumour that another member of the team had recently disappeared. Terry had no way of knowing whether that meant they'd moved house, done a runner for a completely different reason or if it was more sinister. Nobody knew the names of who else was involved; it was safer that way. He didn't even know how many others were working for them. You just had the one contact and that was it. He knew only Vincent. That meant he couldn't check out the background or risks he might face if he turned them down again. It had been all smiles to begin with but it hadn't gone down well when he'd tried to sever his connection with the shady business. Should he go ahead anyway, knowing it would comfortably pay for Christmas? Or should he discuss it with Linda, as it would be much worse if she found out he'd agreed to something behind her back?

Before he could open the door Linda flung it back, smiling from ear to ear. 'Thought I heard someone on the front step. Come in and see what June's made.' She bent towards him and he hugged her, giving her a big kiss on the cheek.

'God, you're freezing,' she said. 'Get in beside the fire right now. June, Daddy's home. Where's your angel? He wants to see it.'

Terry threw his coat over the banister and followed Linda into the warm kitchen, where the gas fire was blazing. June stood beside it, a cardboard cone in her arms. It had a ping-pong ball glued to the top on which Linda had drawn a face. 'It's my angel,' she said seriously. 'It's going to go on top of the tree. Do you like it?'

Terry crouched down to her level and solemnly took it from her.

'Mind out,' she said. 'I haven't made her wings. She's going to have white wings. Like a big bird.'

'You're very clever,' he told her. 'It's going to be beautiful.' He met Linda's eyes and she raised her eyebrows, clearly wanting a moment alone with him.

'Why don't you take her into the front room and put her by the tree so she's safe until we make her wings?' she suggested. June took the angel and set off, holding it carefully in front of her. Linda quickly shut the door behind her.

Her smile grew wider. 'I've got something to tell you,' she said, reaching for his hands and drawing him up to full height. 'I've been to the doctor's this afternoon.'

At once Terry was alert. 'And?' He couldn't keep the hope from his voice.

'And...' Linda was enjoying herself, drawing out the moment. 'And ... he says he thinks I'm having another baby. Really. At last, Terry. After all those false alarms.'

He could hardly contain himself. 'That's marvellous, that's bloody marvellous. Oh my God. I can't believe it. Really? You are? Oh my God. That's the best thing ever. Wait, shouldn't you sit down and rest? How are you feeling?'

Linda laughed. 'Stop it, Terry. I'm fine, of course I'm fine. It's early days yet.' She winked at him. 'You were right, it was that rug in front of Mum's fire that did it. The timing fits. I bet that was it. And I haven't even been sick, or anything yet. So don't go treating me with kid gloves.'

Terry drew her into his arms and hugged her tight. 'My precious girl. I'm so happy. I can't wait.'

Linda shook her head. 'I'm afraid you'll have to. It won't be until early summer.' She sighed. 'I'm so glad we've got this house, Terry. Now we really can make the little room a nursery. And I won't have to worry about you bringing home those boxes. I couldn't stand all that again.'

Terry made himself smile back. 'It'll be a lovely nursery,' he said. 'I'll get the paint at the weekend and we can make a start on it.'

He couldn't mention the approach he'd just had. He couldn't take that delight from her face, nor would he ever forgive himself if she lost this longed-for baby through worrying about his activities. For the time being, he'd have to keep the offer to himself and decide what to do without her knowing anything about it.

'Oh, I nearly forgot.' Linda shook her head, amazed the other major news had slipped her mind. 'I got a letter from Mum. Alison's had her baby. It's a boy and they're calling him David. How about that?'

'Looks like your mum's going to be pretty busy being a granny,' Terry said. 'Do you want to go up and see them?'

'I thought we could all go,' Linda suggested. 'Then we could take up the Christmas presents. It'll be lovely to have a little boy to buy things for, won't it?' She felt a little guilty at not being around to help her younger sister more, but knew there was a limit to what she could do from such a distance – and her own news meant that all her attention was needed here, for her own family.

Terry gazed adoringly into her eyes. 'Maybe next Christmas we'll have another little boy to buy things for,' he whispered. 'Or another girl. I don't mind. As long as it's born safe and well and you're all right. That's all I want in life.'

'Oh, Terry.' Linda gazed back at him. 'I don't think I've ever been so happy.'

Vera rushed down the road as soon as her shift finished, keen to get out of the freezing wind. She'd been on the go all day and her feet were aching. Now that it was nearly Christmas, the customers kept her busy from start to finish and her supervisor hadn't allowed her to slack for a minute. She hadn't even had time to go to the babywear department. She was determined to get something for Alison's boy but hadn't had a spare moment. At this rate the little fellow would be into toddler clothes before she managed to finally see him, she thought grimly.

Her eyes were watering so badly from the wind that she nearly crashed into someone coming around the corner. 'I'm so sorry ... oh, it's you.' She wiped her eyes. 'Blimey, Neville, what happened? Been in an accident, have you?'

Neville had been huddling into the upturned collar of his coat with a cap pulled down as far as it would go but now he had to look up and his cover was blown. 'No, it's nothing,' he said unconvincingly. 'How you been, Vera? It's been a while.'

'Cooped up in there.' She nodded back to the department store. 'Everyone wants new togs for their Christmas parties and I've got to wait till the last one's decided what she wants and what to go with it. I shouldn't complain, it's all good for business, but I'm worn out.' She pulled a face. 'How about you?'

'Don't think I'm in the market for any new clothes, 'specially not from your place.' He tried to make light of it. 'No, we're doing all right, thanks.'

Vera looked at him sceptically. 'Walk into a door, did you?'

Neville shrugged. 'It's nothing.'

'Suit yourself,' said Vera. She could tell when a man was lying to her and Neville was hopeless at it. She couldn't help but feel sorry for him – she had a pretty good idea what had happened to his face. It wasn't the first time she'd seen such a thing. 'Don't suppose you fancy a drink, to help keep the cold out? Be doing me a favour. It isn't the done thing for a woman to walk into a pub on her own. If I go home now the house will be freezing but if I leave it a while Mum will have got the oven going.'

Neville looked doubtful. 'I'm not sure that I should…' He was tempted though. Suddenly the thought of a warm pub and friendly company was very appealing. He didn't want to go home to Hazel if she was in one of her moods, and she nearly always was these days. Surely one drink wouldn't hurt.

'Don't look so scared, I ain't forcing you.' Vera looked heavenwards. 'I ain't going to jump you or nothing. It's only a drink, nothing else. If two old friends can't go for a drink when they bump into each other, what's the world coming to?'

Neville made up his mind. 'As long as it's just the one.' He smiled, or as much as his bruised face would let him. 'Better make it somewhere with a dark corner I can hide. No sense in parading my accident, after all.'

Vera beamed. 'I know just the place.'

'Going to be a busy weekend by the looks of it,' said Fred as he came upstairs after shutting up the shop at the end of the day. 'We've got your sister Linda and her family coming round. Plus, I just had Winnie Jewell in, telling me I charge too much for my turkeys, and she said Vera hopes to come round too. Says she's sorry she couldn't come before but they been working her hard in Arding and Hobbs. To hear Winnie talk you'd think Vera ran the place.'

Alison turned off the living-room radio; she hadn't been listening properly anyway. 'That old boss of hers works her into the ground. She always gave me the evil eye when I went in, like she thought I was going to distract Vera from her business. No wonder she hasn't had a moment.' She smiled, glad that her friend was coming to visit. She was looking forward to seeing her friend far more than the thought of seeing her mother again. While she had been relieved that Cora had seemed to warm to the baby, she didn't really want to have to put up with her carping. Sometimes she still had to pinch herself to believe that she'd got away from her mother's house, the constant put-downs, her sister's bullying. She smiled at the thought of how things had changed since she married Fred.

'Well, her boss was probably right,' said Fred. 'You did distract her, didn't you?'

'Not often. And anyway they've done all right out of my custom, haven't they?' Alison stroked the soft new cardigan that Fred had presented her with after David's birth. 'Your custom, I should say.'

'Our custom.' Fred looked at her happily, glad

she liked his gift. The pale grey colour suited her. 'Now, where's the boy? How's he been?'

Alison looked away, and tried to cover her distaste by picking up a book. 'Oh, he's been very good. He's in his cot. I thought it would be quieter for him in there.'

Fred nodded, not fooled for a minute. He knew Alison avoided being in the same room as her baby as much as she could. It worried him but he tried to tell himself it was only to be expected. She'd had a frightening birth as well as an exhausting one and even though she'd been up and about for some days now, it must still be affecting her. He knew too that she must relive the attack every time she saw her son, even though she never mentioned it. Even so, he couldn't wait to see the baby now his work was finished.

To begin with he'd had a few private worries about how he would cope. It was no small thing to take in another man's child, especially a man who had treated Alison the way Paul had. He'd been worried it would be a case of like father, like son, but he'd managed to find some books and read up about how bringing up a baby could influence what sort of child it became, and reassured himself that it wasn't inevitable that the child would turn out bad. Once David had arrived, especially since he'd helped to bring him into the world, he'd been besotted. It wasn't the little boy's fault that he'd been conceived the way he had. He was a helpless creature in need of love and Fred was going to make sure he got lots of it.

'I'll just go and check how he is and then I'll put the kettle on.' He could hear some noise as he set off down the corridor, and it grew louder as he got closer to Alison's room. He opened the door and a full-blooded wail hit him. David was crying as hard as he could, his little face turning red beneath his woolly hat. Fred rushed across to him.

'There, there. Whatever's the matter? Don't you worry, I'm here now.' He reached into the cot and picked up the child, and the smell hit him. The blankets were wet and so was the cotton romper suit. 'Oh, oh, oh. That's it, is it? David needs changing. I expect Mummy didn't hear you with the door shut and the radio on.' He tried to convince himself this was true as he stripped off the wet clothes and dumped them on the floor, then found a clean nappy. Expertly he set about changing the wriggling baby. 'No, you stay still. I know, it's cold, but you'll feel better soon. Where's your new suit? Shall we have this one? That'll be warm, won't it?' Gradually the baby calmed as Fred held him in his new clothes, patting his back gently until the crying stopped. Carefully he balanced David on one shoulder as he picked up the dirty clothes and blankets and bundled them into the laundry bag. 'That's better. Now let's go and see Mummy.'

Alison looked up as they came into the living room, registering that the baby was in a different set of clothes. 'Did you change him, then?' She didn't sound very interested.

'He was sodden, poor little chap.' Fred tickled the baby's cheek. 'I suppose you couldn't hear him from here?'

'No, I didn't hear anything,' she said. 'He must

have just started.'

Fred shook his head, not really believing her, but reminded himself that she was tired and still getting used to everything. 'Tell you what, you hold him and give him a feed and I'll make something to eat.'

'No need.' Alison got up. 'I was feeling lots better this afternoon so I did us a casserole. Shall I get you some now?'

Fred beamed in delight. 'You must be on the mend! You shouldn't have, you know I don't mind cooking. But I'd love some. Maybe in a little while, so I can have a play with the boy. Unless you want to?'

'No, you have him. You've been downstairs all day,' said Alison with relief. The last thing she wanted was to have to play with the baby. That would mean having to look at his face and she still hated doing that. She knew it wasn't David's fault, but those eyes bored into her, torturing her with the memory of how he'd been conceived.

Later that evening, Fred sat at his desk, pleasantly full from the casserole. The baby was settled and Alison had gone to bed early. It looked as if she was getting back to normal, at least as far as cooking was concerned. When it came to the baby he wasn't so sure. Drawing his account books towards him, he admitted he was anxious. She just didn't seem to have any affection for the boy at all. Maybe it was all too much, too soon, but how could she not love such a beautiful baby? What if things didn't improve? He didn't think she would actually harm David – but then he remembered that summer evening when she'd been prepared to kill herself and the unborn child. He shuddered. No, she wouldn't go that far now. He couldn't bear the thought of anything happening to either of them. They were his family, they were his to protect. Somehow he would have to make sure they stayed safe.

With a sigh of relief he turned the page of his account book and began to enter today's figures. At least he knew where he was with them.

Chapter Thirty-Four

It was Saturday teatime before Vera managed to call round. She arrived windblown but glamorous as ever, raincoat belted tight and lipstick bright red.

'Look at you!' She rushed to hug her friend. 'You're still blooming! Your hair's all thick and wavy. Mind you, you haven't been out in that hurricane.'

'I haven't been out at all,' admitted Alison, turning up the gas fire and pulling two armchairs closer. 'But you look like a model with that lipstick. How did you get away with that at work?'

'I don't,' said Vera, patting her hair back into place. 'The dragon won't let me, so I just use Vaseline for a bit of shine. Anything else and she thinks I'll steal her boyfriend. So I stuck this on in the loos before I left. Got to keep up standards.' She gave a huge grin. 'Go on then, where is he?'

'Fred? He's still downstairs.'

'I know that, you daft mare. I waved to him. No, the baby. You're having me on.'

'I'll fetch him,' said Alison, forcing herself not to wince. 'Shall I get you something to drink first?'

'No, I'll make it, I know where everything is.'

So with no further excuses left, Alison went to get David from his cradle. It always surprised her that he reacted to her presence, seeming to hear her approach, and how he blurrily fixed his eyes on her face. She smelt him but thankfully he seemed to be fresh – she hated changing him and had had to do so twice that afternoon already, as Fred had been busy in the shop. Dutifully she carried him back to the living room, where Vera had set out two cups of coffee from the percolator that had already been switched on ready for Fred when he came upstairs.

'Look at him! Look at those little hands!' Vera was cooing over him at once, brushing his face, tickling him. 'Can I hold him? Sure you don't mind?'

'No, please do, go ahead,' said Alison with relief, passing him across.

'Oooh, I'm out of practice, haven't held one this small since my aunt Beryl's kids were born.' Vera shuffled round to support his head. 'Course, she's got your sister living next door now ... sorry, well, you would know that, wouldn't you?' She stopped, seeing the look on her friend's face. 'Is everything all right? What have I said? Oh God, I'm so stupid. It's who lived there before, isn't it? Why did I open my big mouth? I never think. Really, I didn't mean to upset you. Don't take on.'

Alison gulped and looked away. 'No, it's not you. It's every time I catch sight of his face. It's not as if I stand much chance of forgetting, is it? He's the spitting image of his father and I hate it.' She paused and twisted her hands together. 'I mean, what sort of mother am I? Everyone says he's a lovely baby but I can't see it, I just see ... him. It's like a nightmare, all day every day. I don't want to hold him or hug him or anything. I just about manage to feed him though I'm going to get him a bottle as soon as I'm up to going out. Then Fred can do it.' She sank back into her chair, exhausted. 'You'll think I'm a monster.'

'No, not at all.' Vera shook her head, trying not to disturb David. 'It must be awful. We're all excited as can be about him and you can't join in because of how he got here in the first place. It's sod's law he looks like his dad. Not much that can be done about that. Is there any of you in him? What about his mouth? His little cheekbones?'

'At least he'll be better off taking after his dad for looks,' Alison scowled. 'It's a good job you all want to see him because the less I have to do with him the better. Fred loves looking after him, and that makes me feel even worse.'

'Well, he would, wouldn't he? Fred's that sort of man.' Vera jiggled the baby, who gurgled contentedly. 'Things might change, you know. Lots of new mums feel down in the dumps. I can't imagine having the responsibility of such a tiny little baby, so don't be too hard on yourself, that's typical of you, that is. I'll come round and help when I can if you like.'

'Would you? Really?'

'Yeah, why not? I like babies. As long as I can hand them back at the end of the day.' Vera grinned and made silly faces at David. 'Just don't ask me to give him a bottle. Drives me mad when they dribble all over your new clothes.'

'If the baby ruins one thing, Fred gets me another,' Alison said. 'So I should be the happiest woman alive, shouldn't I? I sound so ungrateful. He does everything and never complains. But even that makes me nervous.'

'How d'you mean?' Vera managed to take a sip of coffee while juggling David.

'Well, I keep wondering when he's going to want something in return.' Alison flushed with embarrassment. 'You know. Like we said before I agreed to marry him. I don't think I could stand it if he touched me.'

'Alison, you've not long had a baby,' Vera pointed out. 'Fred's a kind man. He's not going to drag you into bed. He respects you too much. Stop worrying about something that hasn't happened.'

Alison stood up and began to pace in anxiety. 'But one day he will, won't he? We're married. That's part of the bargain. How will I put up with it? I can't even think about it.'

'Then don't,' said Vera firmly. 'I know it's hard, but you have to take things one day at a time. The baby might change in looks as he gets older and Fred's not the sort to force you to do anything, in bed or out of it. So count your blessings.'

Alison sat back down. 'I know. You always talk sense, Vera. Just keep coming round and telling

323

me that.'

Vera beamed. 'Try and stop me. This flat is the bee's knees. One of these days I'm going to have one just like it.' She sighed. 'Not sure how though. Oh, by the way, you seen Neville lately?'

Alison shook her head. 'No, he and Hazel haven't been round here at all, not since I moved in. They're meant to be coming for Sunday lunch tomorrow with Mum, Linda and family so they can all meet David. Well, Mum's been already but the others haven't. Can't see Hazel rushing to congratulate me, can you? Why d'you ask?'

Vera hesitated, now unsure whether she should go ahead and say what state the man had been in. Then she decided Alison should be forewarned. 'I happened to meet him after work the other day and he looked in a right state. His face was all bruised. He said it was nothing but to be honest I didn't believe him. Looked as if he'd been fighting, which took me by surprise.'

'Fighting? Neville?' Alison didn't believe it either. 'He never gets in fights. He just wouldn't. He's not like that. Never.'

Vera sat back, her voice growing cautious. 'No, that's what I thought. But still...'

Alison gazed at her. 'What do you mean?'

'Well, I felt so sorry for him. He seemed so miserable, I got him to come for a drink. He didn't say anything, it was more what he didn't say. It was like he was glad of an excuse not to go home.'

'No, that can't be right,' said Alison. 'Do you mean he was avoiding Hazel? But they're mad about each other. Doesn't make sense. Hang on, you don't mean Hazel had a fight with him? She hit him?'

'He wouldn't be the first,' Vera pointed out.

Alison was having none of it. 'No, you've got that wrong. That wouldn't happen. She's been going on about how wonderful he is ever since she met him, she wouldn't do that. Mind you,' she raised her eyebrows at her friend, 'she'd better not find out that he had a drink with you. You'd better watch it if she gets wind of that. You'll never hear the last of it.'

As it turned out Alison didn't get the chance to see the damage for herself as Neville didn't come on Sunday. Hazel arrived with Cora, full of excuses – he hadn't felt well, had a bit of a cold, and didn't want to give it to the baby. Hazel held the real reason close to her chest, somewhat ashamed that her attacks on him were so visible. But what she had learned that day made her even more angry when she got home to the flat.

Neville had taken advantage of her absence to catch up on sleep he'd missed while working the late shift. He was muzzy-headed when he heard the front door slam hard and barely had time to gather his thoughts when Hazel verbally laid into him.

'So what have you been doing with Vera Jewell?'

'What?'

'Vera Jewell. You've been seen out with her behind my back. Did you think I wouldn't find out? That tart got her claws into you, has she?'

Slowly Neville realised that Vera's private spot for a quiet drink wasn't as private as they'd thought. Maybe they shouldn't have been so careful about it as they'd now run headlong into the very thing they'd wanted to avoid.

'It's nothing like that,' he protested. 'I went for a drink with her, just one drink, just once. It was completely by chance. I saw her outside the department store after work and she said she was cold. She said a drink would warm her up but that she couldn't go into a pub on her own. I felt sorry for her and as I was freezing too I didn't see the harm in having just one drink with her.'

'You must think I was born yesterday,' Hazel fumed. 'I pop out to buy a Sunday newspaper and Ron Small stops me in the street. Ron Small of all people, I ask you. Tells me you was seen hiding away in your cosy little snug with that tart. Could have knocked me down with a feather. I had to make something up on the spot, said I knew all about it. Bet you thought you wouldn't be found out, didn't you? Chose the place special, did you?'

'Yes, of course we did,' Neville snarled back, for once stung by the injustice of it all. 'Because we knew what you'd be like if you heard about it. And sure enough, here you are. Just like we thought. And all over one little drink.' He thanked the stars he'd never told her about Vera helping to choose the ring. That would have been the final straw. 'Seriously, Hazel, one drink. With an old friend. Where's the harm in that?'

'Old friend or old flame? Is there something you haven't told me?' Hazel blazed, flinging off her coat so that it knocked over the vegetable rack in the corner of the kitchen. 'Is that why you can't get it up with me? Guilt is it? Guilt that

326

you've been seeing that tart Vera Jewell behind my back?'

'Don't be daft, Hazel. When would I get the time to do that?'

'Found time to go drinking with her, didn't you? How do I know you've been working late like you said and not sneaking off to be with her all the time?'

'Because you check the bank balance,' Neville pointed out. 'It doesn't grow on its own. So stop being so daft. Come here, don't be silly, I don't give a fig about Vera Jewell.'

Hazel whirled around. 'And do you know what else I found out today? My sister Linda's having another baby. Perfect Linda, always gets what she wants when she wants it, and now she wants a second baby when I can't have even one. And I'm not going to get one, am I?' Tears of frustration began to run down her face. 'Two bloody babies, a husband with a decent wage and just moved to a bigger house. Hasn't a care in the world. And when I says to Mum that it's all unfair, do you know what she tells me? I told you so. That's all I get from her. I told you so.'

'Come on, Hazel...'

'And that's not all!' Hazel screamed. 'Mum told me that Alison's place is like a palace. We had a good laugh, didn't we, my ugly sister marrying old Fred, the ugly butcher. Thought we were so clever. Well, she's had the last laugh. They've got all the latest furniture, like in those shops we saw but better, Mum says. They've got a kitchen full of everything like in a magazine. They've got gas fires everywhere and even spare rooms. It's huge, it's gorgeous, and she's got everything new – her clothes, the baby's clothes. Fred runs round after her like his number's come up on ERNIE. You have never seen anything like it. And that's my sister, my stupid sister who went and got herself pregnant by some no-good runaway. How is that fair? *How is that fair?*' Gasping for breath, she dissolved into a flood of tears.

Neville went to put his arm round her.

'Get off me,' she growled. 'Don't take one step closer. I mean it. Get away from me. Get out of my sight.'

'Hazel...'

'GET OUT!' she screamed. 'Take your useless face out of this room. Get out, get out. You're no good for anything. You can't give me a lovely flat or a new baby or any fun in bed. You're a fake, Neville Parrot, and I can't stand to have you near me.'

'Well.' Neville tried to keep calm, telling himself she didn't mean it. 'If that's how you feel, I'll go for a walk.'

'And don't go running to that tart! I'll hear about it if you do!'

'Hazel,' said Neville with as much dignity as he could, 'keep your voice down. Beryl will hear.'

'See if I care!' she shouted, but as he put on his coat and cap she knew he was right. The door slammed shut behind him and she collapsed at the kitchen table, her head in her hands, as sobs shook her again. What had gone wrong? They had been the golden couple only a few months ago. Now everyone around them had exactly what they'd always dreamed of except for her. She was stuck in

328

this miserable flat with a husband who was useless in every department. She wondered what she'd seen in him for all that time they were courting. Take away his looks, and what was he? And although his looks hadn't changed, they were no good to her if he couldn't put them to use and please her in bed. Grimly she realised that at least one thing he said was right. Beryl would hear. Then Beryl would tell Winnie and soon all of Battersea and beyond would know. They'd see Neville's face and put two and two together. She couldn't have that. She'd better watch her temper in future. She didn't want to get a reputation. But what was she to do? Everything in her whole life was unfair.

'No Neville tonight?' asked Bill on his way in to the main workshop. 'I thought he was down for this shift.'

'No, he had some family do and wasn't sure how long it would go on for,' said Frank, ticking Bill's name off the list on his clipboard. 'They were going to meet the new baby. You know, Hazel's sister's.'

'Oh, the one they were trying to pretend wasn't on the way at the wedding?' Bill grinned. 'She's married to old Fred the butcher, ain't she – the little fat one. And her so tall and skinny.'

'Yep, between them they've got all the angles covered.' Frank yawned. 'Anyway they got a baby boy by all accounts. Marian was in there the other day ordering her turkey and Fred was over the moon, saying how wonderful he was. So just goes to show, you don't need good looks to be happy.'

Dennis wandered in, late but not bothering to hide it. 'Lucky for some of us that manage both. Talking of good looks, what's happened to young Neville's? He's fallen over a lot of steps lately.'

Frank turned round. 'Just going through a clumsy phase.'

'Oh come off it, Frank, you don't believe that,' said Bill. 'He was never like this before. What, as soon as he marries Hazel he can't stand on his own two feet? Not a great advertisement for married life, is it?'

'Maybe he's too tired,' sniggered Dennis. 'He's been trying out all them things I suggested and can't stand up straight after. Don't blame him. Even I get tired sometimes and God knows I've had plenty of practice.'

He picked up his overall and sauntered off to the machines.

Frank stared after him. 'Well, maybe that's what it is.'

Bill looked at his boss. He knew him well enough to be able to tell when he was keeping something back, even if he didn't always realise what it was. 'What are you really thinking, Frank? You got that look on your face that means something's up.'

Frank shrugged, reluctant to voice his suspicions. Sometimes it was hard being the eldest at the factory, knowing what he did of life, surrounded by all the young men with their confidence that nothing bad would ever befall them. Neville, now there was a lad who wouldn't hurt anyone, and yet he sensed there was something going badly wrong there. He didn't want to spell it out. No man would want to admit he'd been beaten up by his wife – he'd be a laughing stock and would never be able to hold his head up with pride again. If Bill couldn't read the signs, he wasn't going to make it easy for him.

'I'm not thinking anything,' he said now, adjusting his overall and putting his pen away. 'Just ... we better keep an eye on him, make sure he's all right. Don't want him to have any worse accidents, do we?'

'What, do you think he's ill?' Bill was suddenly concerned. It had all been a bit of a game before, his mate doing something as stupid as falling over twice in quick succession. He hadn't seriously thought anything was up.

'I'm sure he isn't,' said Frank hastily. Now he'd made it worse as Bill had got the wrong end of the stick. 'No, of course he isn't. He's as healthy as they come. I'm just saying, let's hope he doesn't have any more near misses. We don't have to make a song and dance about it.'

'All right,' said Bill, still feeling he was missing something. 'I'll ask the others, shall I?'

'No,' said Frank instantly. Then he corrected himself. 'I mean, no need. We don't want to make a fuss, we just agreed that. You're his friend, you keep it to yourself.' Bill nodded, still looking baffled, and moved off to start work.

Frank put his paperwork away and sighed. The last thing he wanted was for Nobby to get wind of this. The man worked hard, he'd give him that, but there was something about him he didn't quite trust. He didn't think he was dangerous, but he seemed to enjoy undermining Neville and

Hazel whenever he got the chance. If ever he got to hear about this, heaven knows what he would do.

Chapter Thirty-Five

Cora was thrilled at Linda's news and couldn't wait to see her eldest daughter again. Now that the family had moved to a bigger house she had high hopes of an invitation to spend Christmas with them but none was forthcoming. Linda had explained why they wouldn't be coming back up to Battersea for the day either, as they'd only just been and she was beginning to feel tired. 'You know what it's like, Mum,' she had confided as they were leaving Fred and Alison's flat. 'And on top of that we've still got lots to sort out in the new place, plus June keeps me run ragged. I'm not complaining but I'll be glad of the rest. I might even get Terry to learn how to roast vegetables.'

Terry had smiled at that; in his world, the women did the cooking and the men brought home the wage packet. He wasn't going to trim any Brussels sprouts. Neither did he want his nosy mother-in-law poking around his business.

In the run-up to Christmas Day, Hazel had forced herself to be calm and not lash out any more, worried about what people would think if they saw any more evidence. She and Neville had come to an uneasy truce, which lasted as long as he didn't try to come near her. He was back working lots of late shifts, getting ribbed for it by his mates, and as often as not came back and slept on the sofa. She was relieved. Having him in bed beside her was just a mockery, a reminder of how things should have been.

She had no intention of inviting anyone over to the flat, now that it was tinged with such misery, and so she leapt at Jill's invitation for them to come to Ennis Street. 'We'd love to have you, unless you're desperate to spend your first married Christmas in your own home,' Jill had said, and Hazel had snapped up the offer at once.

'Will your mother be spending the day with Alison and the new baby?' Jill went on. 'I expect they could do with the extra pair of hands.'

Hazel didn't care if they needed help or not, but was pretty certain that Cora wouldn't want to spend the day cooped up with the daughter she disliked, even if it would have meant the most succulent turkey in the area. 'They'll probably want to be by themselves this year, what with the baby being so little,' she said diplomatically. So Jill invited Cora across the road, and they all crammed into the cheerful house, where Richie was persuaded to stop playing rock and roll and to put on Bing Crosby instead.

Cora enjoyed herself with the good-natured Parrot family but was just as glad to get away. It was a pleasant change not to have all the clearing up to do, though she'd offered to help with washing the dishes. Jill had pointed out that there wasn't room in the kitchen and that Hazel and Kathy could share it. So Cora sat in her own living room, which didn't seem as cramped now there

333

was only her there, and poured herself a small port and lemon. What a year 1957 had been. There had been times when she thought her family would never get through it unscathed. Yet they'd all survived it and in better shape than ever before. Yes, she thought as she unsteadily mounted the stairs, things were definitely looking up for the Butlers.

Alison made it her new year's resolution to heed Vera's advice and take things one day at a time. It helped that her friend had some time off over the festive season and came round more often. 'Make the most of me as I'll be on duty for the sales when I go back,' she warned. 'It's going to be mayhem in there. All those stuck-up madams that like to think they're so grand fight like madwomen when it comes to a bargain. You don't want to get in their way. I'm dreading it.'

Alison thought it would take more than a dedicated bargain-hunter to get the better of Vera but didn't say so. 'Maybe I should come along, see if I can get some baby clothes the next size up.'

'You watch yourself,' said Fred, coming into the living room as he was taking a break from the endless accounts. 'Don't you get caught in any ruckus just for the sake of money off. When it comes to David we can get him the best.'

'Who's a lucky boy,' cooed Vera, dandling the baby on her knee. 'Don't even need your auntie Vera's discount, do you? Do try not to dribble on her new skirt though.' She hastily reached for her handkerchief. 'Do you think he's looking different? Is it his hair?'

'Hard to tell when you see him every day,' Fred replied, beaming in adoration at the little face. 'But I reckon he's got his mother's mouth and maybe her hair.'

'My hair?'

'Yes, why not?' said Vera, keen to back Fred. 'Your hair is lovely now it's cut properly and you use the right stuff on it. You are using it, aren't you? I got you those bottles especially for you, so don't go leaving them on the bathroom shelf, I know what you're like.'

'No, I am trying, I really am,' said Alison hastily. She was still getting used to the idea that anyone would praise her hair, for so long the butt of many jokes. But she had to admit that evening when she looked in the mirror, it wasn't bad at all. If it made Vera happy she would carry on with the special shampoo and spray. So maybe it wouldn't be so awful if the boy had her hair. There. She'd done it. She'd thought a good thing about the baby. It was a start.

So a few weeks later when Fred commented on how nice her hair looked she didn't shy away or act embarrassed like she usually did when anyone paid her a compliment. She tried to do as she'd seen Vera do on many occasions, just laugh a little and smile. The truth was, she was beginning to feel better about herself. It had been a long time since anyone had pointed at her in the street and called her horse face. Now when she ventured out, people looked at her differently. The haircut and the stylish clothes helped.

Stepping out of a new car did wonders as well, particularly when it came to the boys who had

335

tormented her for years. They seemed confused more than anything, as if they couldn't quite take in that it was the same person they'd picked on for fun. In fact, Alison realised one day in early spring, she didn't feel like the same person either. The events, good and bad, of the past year had changed her. She was no longer scared to say boo to a goose, or awkward around everyone. She had a proper friend for the first time in her life and a husband who spoilt her. That was another change – somewhere along the line she'd stopped thinking of Fred as her father's friend who was also her boss. Their relationship was altered too.

'I got an idea,' said Fred one evening over dinner. She'd made a chicken pie, something else she couldn't have done a year ago. 'Now the weather's brightening up, why don't we get David a proper pram? That carry-cot is all very well but we can't lug that around all the time, not if we want to take him for walks. I've seen some I like, I was keeping an eye out.'

Alison cut herself another small piece of pie. Ever since she'd had David she seemed to be starving all the time. 'That would be nice. We could take him to the park once it warms up. Where would we buy one? Shall we see if Vera can get us something?'

Fred shrugged. 'We could. But I thought we could go to Peter Jones in Sloane Square instead and make a trip out of it. They do the Silver Cross ones there, and David must have the best.'

Alison put down her fork. 'I've never been there. I'd like to go. Kathy talked about it as it's not far from where she works now, but I've never even thought of it. When were you thinking of?'

'How about tomorrow? It's Monday, it'll be quiet, I could shut the shop for the morning.'

'Really?' He'd never done such a thing before. 'Won't there be deliveries?'

'No, the pork supplier cancelled, he's coming on Thursday instead. It would be perfect. What do you say?'

Alison raised her eyes to meet his and gave a big smile. 'I'd love to. Thank you, Fred. You're very generous.'

Fred pushed away his empty plate. 'Not a bit. It's what the boy deserves, and you do too. I don't want any hand-me-downs for him. I've worked hard for all these years and now I can enjoy spending some of the proceeds on someone special.' He got up. 'Let's have our coffee somewhere more comfortable, shall we?'

Alison agreed, admitting to herself she'd got a taste for coffee which would have baffled her mother, who associated it with unsuitable bars in Soho. She took the plates to the sink while Fred fussed around with the cups and then they took them into the living room. David had already been settled in his cot, although Fred these days insisted on keeping the doors open so they would hear if he cried.

Fred turned the control on the radio until he found some music then settled himself beside Alison. 'No Little Richard,' he said.

'Just as well.'

Fred sighed in satisfaction. 'You know what, I couldn't be happier if I'd won the pools.' Then he shifted slightly. 'Well, maybe I could.' He looked

337

at her directly. 'Can I ask you something?'

'Ask away.'

'May I kiss you, Alison?'

She gasped in surprise. Ever since that conversation with Vera, she'd tried to put these anxieties to the back of her mind. But what had Vera said – take everything one day at a time. So now she had to ask herself, would she really mind?

Fred wasn't Paul. She could trust him. He wouldn't make her do anything suddenly or hurt her. And he was very kind. What harm could it do? It was only a kiss.

'Go on then,' she said quickly, before she could back out of it.

Gently he leant forward and began to kiss her. At first she didn't know what to make of it. Then to her surprise she found it wasn't so bad after all. Something told her he'd done this before and knew exactly what he was about.

After a moment he pulled back. 'All right? You're not going to do a runner?'

'No,' she said shakily. 'No, I'm not.'

Softly he held her to him again and this time the kiss was more insistent. Strangely she didn't want to pull away. She found herself reaching around his neck and kissing him back. It was so unlike anything she'd ever experienced before, and so completely unlike how it had been with Paul, that she forgot to be afraid and let herself be carried away. She stopped worrying and let her body take over, in a way she never could have imagined. All her previous fears were far from her mind. She'd been fretting over nothing. What was happening now felt completely natural, the exact opposite of what she'd needlessly dreaded for all that time.

'Are you sure this is all right?' Fred said at one point. But all she could do was nod, as they fell together once more and slowly sank onto the plush carpet. Don't think any more, she told herself. Just relax. You might enjoy it.

After it was over, she realised she had.

Terry sat in the cab of his lorry, chewing his thumbnail, staring at the darkening sky. The thing that he'd most feared had finally happened. He'd been approached again by Vincent, and had refused to agree to store any more boxes. He didn't want to risk upsetting Linda with the baby on the way, and they didn't need the extra money any longer. It wasn't worth the risk.

Vincent had then piled on the pressure, but Terry hadn't given in. Enough was enough. He'd done what he set out to do. But Vincent hadn't seen it that way. He hadn't been violent but he hadn't needed to be. He simply told Terry that they knew where June went to nursery school and that he might like to reconsider. Then he'd left Terry to think about the implications.

Deep down Terry had known that it wouldn't be as easy to walk away from this business as he'd pretended to Linda, but he hadn't thought they'd stoop so low as to threaten his daughter. The memory of the man who'd disappeared last year came back. Somehow Terry doubted he'd left town of his own accord. He wondered exactly what they'd done to him.

Sitting here panicking wouldn't help. He had to think. So, they knew where he used to live but nobody had come to the new house. That was good. He could tell Linda they had to change June's nursery school – he'd have to find a good reason as she would be onto him immediately to spell out exactly why, but it could be done. They knew where he worked, though. They could easily follow him. He had to hope they hadn't done so already, but then they'd have had no reason to if they thought they could force him to agree. They didn't like to waste manpower. So he reckoned they were safe in the house, at least for the time being. He didn't want to contemplate what it would do to Linda if they had to move again.

Sweating hard even though the night was cold, he switched on the engine and moved off. He wasn't going to let this beat him. Nobody would destroy his family.

'Right you are, David, in you go.' Fred tucked the baby into the new pram and adjusted the hood to keep the chilly breeze off the little face but to allow the boy to look out and his parents to look in. It was the first outing with the pram since the very successful shopping trip, in which they'd also managed to buy more clothes suitable for a three-month-old child and order a new cupboard in which to put them. He'd also treated Alison to a new coat and persuaded her to throw away her old one. He gazed at her in admiration.

He couldn't believe it. She'd let him take her to bed – well, to the carpet – and it had all worked out. She'd confessed afterwards how the idea had frightened her for nearly all of their marriage, as she couldn't bear to endure what Paul had put her through all over again. But he'd shown her it didn't have to be that way. In spite of himself he felt proud. Those wartime widows had taught him a few things about pleasing a woman and it seemed he hadn't lost his touch. There was life in the old dog yet.

This had given him the courage to raise the difficult subject of how Alison was reacting to her son. He'd given her more than enough time to change but there had been little improvement, and it couldn't be down to exhaustion any longer. He was up in the night more than she was now that David was bottle fed. In fact nearly every time David cried it was Fred who went to him and carried him around until he settled again. He really had to say something.

At first Alison had denied it but then she caved in. 'I just don't seem to be able to love him properly,' she admitted. 'I feel awful saying it. I want to love him. I don't want to be like Mum was with me, I don't want him to feel he's unwanted. It's just that he looks like Paul, and I know it's not his fault but I keep remembering that night...'

Fred had gone to her and hugged her, glad that he could now do this without her badly hidden resistance. 'Of course, of course, that's only natural. You've been to hell and back. You've been so brave. But you're right, none of it is his fault. He needs you, he needs us both. At least you've got me to help. Your poor mum had no one. She did her best, but it was all too hard for her. I'll back you up, you'll see, I'll help with everything. Take it one step at a time.'

Alison had wiped her eyes. 'It's better now that

341

I've told you. I really don't want history to repeat itself. I've thought for so long that he'd be better off without me that it's hard to change my mind. I so wanted my mum to love me when I was growing up but she wasn't interested. I can't be like that for David. It's not fair on him.'

'We'll work at it together,' Fred had assured her. He hugged her again. 'That's my girl. If you put your mind to it you can do anything. I'd put good money on it. And you know how careful I am with my money.'

Now Alison took his arm as he began to push the pram along Falcon Road. Halfway there, he was wheezing. 'Must be the smoke in the air,' he gasped. 'That or David's suddenly got heavier.'

'He might have, he drinks enough formula,' she said. 'But when was the last time you walked along here? You go everywhere in the car these days.' She remembered how she'd hurried along here to see Vera after work, even when she was heavily pregnant. 'You have to do it often enough to get used to it. Then maybe you won't wheeze so much. Can't have you getting ill.' She patted him on the arm.

'No, or everyone'll think I'm an old man.' He had to stop and catch hold of the side of the pram. 'Can't have that, not in front of David. I'll have to get fit so his friends don't laugh at me.'

'Well, you've got a while to go then,' she laughed. 'But seriously, we should walk him along here every day if we can. It'll be good for us and for him. The air's not that smoky, you know. Maybe you should give up the Lucky Strikes as well.'

Before he could reply, someone had come up

beside them and was peering into the pram. 'Well, so this is the young man,' said Marian Dalby. 'He's very alert, isn't he? Likes his walks.'

'It's his first real one,' explained Alison. 'We only got the pram yesterday. We thought as long as we wrapped him up he'd be all right.'

'Oh, you can't beat a bit of fresh air for babies,' said Marian. 'My two always loved it. Gets them used to seeing other faces. Well, I must get on, but lovely to meet him at last – and to see you looking so well, my dear.' She nodded appreciatively at Alison. 'Marriage suits you! You're quite transformed. Your mother must be delighted.' She waved and set off in the opposite direction.

'Blimey,' said Alison. 'There must be something in it after all. Mrs Dalby never beats around the bush. Not sure if Mum's noticed or if she'd care if she had, but all the same.'

Fred glowed with pleasure. 'She's right though. You look like a new woman. And I wonder why that might be?' His eyes twinkled.

'You'd better make sure you get fitter fast, then,' said Alison and set off again up the hill.

Chapter Thirty-Six

There were days when Hazel felt like handing in her notice at the café. She'd been run off her feet all morning, carrying heavy trays of fried breakfasts and bacon sandwiches, for precious little reward. She'd broken a nail trying to get a grater out of an overcrowded drawer in the kitchen. Everyone was complaining that service wasn't fast enough, even though it was obvious they were full to capacity and short-staffed. Not a word of thanks, even when she gave some of the regulars extra tomatoes or topped up their tea for nothing. There was no pleasing some people.

Now she slogged through the market, looking for something cheap to eat that evening. She couldn't remember if Neville was doing another late shift or not and didn't really care. She'd make enough for two and if he ate it, he ate it. If not she'd have it tomorrow, warmed up. Let him go running back to his mother's if it wasn't good enough.

'All right, Hazel?' called Joe. 'Give us a smile.'

Hazel scowled at him. 'Give me a break. I've been smiling all morning and a fat lot of good it's done me.' She strode past his stall, buttoning her worn jacket against the biting wind.

'Someone's got out of bed the wrong side this morning,' commented Barry from the stall opposite. 'What's got into her?'

'Not like her to be so miserable,' said Joe, but to be honest he couldn't remember the last time he'd had a bit of a laugh with the young woman. She'd changed over the past few months, her replies getting shorter and sharper until sometimes she didn't answer at all. It was a far cry from the pretty redhead who'd been so excited about her wedding dress. Now she looked haggard and bad-tempered.

'She won't be getting any bargains with a face like that,' Barry predicted. 'I used to have her down as a bit of a looker but not any more. I pity

344

her husband, coming home to that.'

Hazel barged past two friends of Kathy who she couldn't be bothered to speak to. She really didn't want to hear about her sister-in-law's new job as a civil servant. She stopped briefly to buy some sausages. She'd do toad-in-the-hole. Then she fancied something sweet after. Damn, she'd run out of sugar, but she could get some at the newsagent's and maybe her mother would let her have it at cost price.

She wove her way through the back streets to the corner shop where she could see her mother through the glass of the door.

Cora looked up in delight as her daughter came in. 'Well, look who's blown in. Just finished your morning shift, have you? Come inside and we'll have a cuppa.' She turned to fill the kettle.

'It's freezing out there,' complained Hazel. 'You wouldn't think it's meant to be spring. I'd love a cuppa. I was down the market and it's like a wind tunnel. And they all think they're so funny, with the same old jokes every time you go there. It's enough to make you want to scream.'

'But they mean well,' said Cora, who had always got on with the traders and most of the other customers. 'Where would we be without them? They did us plenty of favours out of the good of their hearts over the years. You know that as well as I do.'

'Doesn't mean I have to laugh at their tired old nonsense every time,' said Hazel, gratefully taking her mug. 'All I want is to go there, buy what I need and go away again. But you try doing that and they get all narky.'

'Biscuit?' Cora brought out the packet she kept under the counter for herself and special guests. Maybe it would improve Hazel's temper.

'That reminds me. You couldn't let me have a bag of sugar at cost, could you?'

Cora sighed. Her boss didn't begrudge her this perk but she didn't like to abuse it. Still, her daughter looked as if she needed something to go right for her today. 'Yes, go on. Don't make a habit of it though.'

'Thanks, Mum.' Hazel drank her tea and wondered how soon she could reasonably leave again now she'd got what she came for.

'Don't suppose you've seen anything of your sister lately?' Cora asked, knowing it was unlikely. She realised Hazel was so jealous of Alison's home that she'd never willingly set foot in it again, and she was hardly going to ask her younger sister round to her place.

'No, thank God.'

'I bumped into her and Fred out with the baby earlier in the week. They bought this flash new pram. Apparently they've been out walking with him every day since they got it and I have to say it's doing them some good. Alison's finally losing that awful stoop of hers. Makes the world of difference. And of course he's gone and treated her to a new coat. Blue, bit like the sky ought to be but ain't.'

Hazel banged down the mug so hard that tea slopped over the top and onto a pile of newspapers.

'Here, watch it!' cried Cora, hastily wiping it up with a rag. 'I got to try to sell them.'

'Honestly, Mum, I come in here for a bit of a chat after a morning like you wouldn't believe, and all you do is remind me how bloody marvellous Alison is!' Hazel couldn't understand her mother's change of heart. 'Wasn't so long ago you said what a disgrace she was, and how she'd never darken your door again. Now it's Alison-this, Alison-that, with her fancy flat and new clothes and precious baby. Well, I've had it up to here with her. She let us down big time and don't you forget it. Just because she's got Fred wound around her little finger don't mean she's any different deep down. Don't let her fool you with her new cooker and telephone and God knows what else. She's still the same old Alison underneath. But if you can't see it, I'm off.' She drained what was left of her tea, threw the sugar into her shopping bag and stormed out.

Cora leant against the counter and watched her go. Hazel had always had a hot temper and usually it was best to let it blow over. She couldn't help noticing the changes in the girl though. Her skin had lost its bloom and lines were appearing on her forehead and between her brows, as if she was frowning all the time. She slumped as if she had the cares of the world on her shoulders. There was no way anyone would think her the best-looking girl in Battersea now. She couldn't help but draw the comparison to Alison. The new haircut, the clothes, the improved posture – she was a new woman. She might never be a looker like her sister had been but she wasn't horse face any longer either. Who'd have thought it?

'I can't believe you haven't come down the pub with us once since Christmas.' Nobby blocked Neville's path as he tried to leave the factory door. 'It's a scandal, that's what it is. Don't go saying you've gone off our company as I won't believe you.'

'Out the way, Nobby,' said Neville. He was tired after a double shift and needed aggro from his temperamental colleague like he needed a hole in the head. 'We're saving money, that's all. I still love you all as much as ever.' He tried to raise a smile.

Nobby wasn't having any of it. 'You're always saving money. What for this time? More treats for the little lady? Time you realised you're entitled to spend some of your hard-earned wages on yourself. You hear me, Nev? Entitled.'

'I don't doubt it,' said Neville, getting drawn in against his better judgement. 'But it's not the law, is it? I don't have to spend it on myself if I don't want to. And I want to save money so we can do up the flat a bit.'

'What sort of ambition is that for a young lad like you?' Nobby mocked, rubbing his hand over his balding head. 'Makes my blood boil to hear you come out with crap like that. You're under the thumb, you are.'

'Under the landlord's thumb, more like,' said Neville, but he was angry now. Nobby was an idiot in most ways but he'd got this one right. Maybe he would go for a drink with the lads. It would be more fun than an evening with Hazel.

'What you standing around here for?' demanded Dennis, breezing through from the workshop.

'Aren't you coming out? Even Frank's coming. Aren't you, Frank?'

Frank raised his eyebrows. 'Someone's got to keep an eye on you lot. I don't want the entire morning shift to have hangovers. Besides, Marian's gone to her mother's for the evening so she won't mind me not coming home.'

'She'll have left you something to heat up though, wont she?' asked Bill, always keen to hear about his boss's wife's cooking.

'Oh yes, she's done me a lamb hotpot to warm through,' Frank said, smiling at the thought of it. 'Bet Hazel does the same for you when the need arises, Nev?'

'Yes, of course,' said Neville, remembering how Hazel had slammed down some congealed toad-in-the-hole in front of him only a few days ago, as she snarled something about rude stallholders. 'Can't beat home cooking.' There were times when Neville longed for the comfort of his mother's kitchen, all the hurly-burly of the conversation and banter as they crowded round the extended table. What a let-down married life had been – and yet it was all his fault. He just couldn't shake the feeling that if only he'd been a proper man then there would have been no problems.

'Coming with us, then?' Bill asked, clapping him round the shoulders.

'Yeah, why not,' Neville said.

The black van sped away, leaving Terry shaking. Vincent hadn't accepted it when he'd said he was still thinking about the proposal. He'd known

349

Terry was stalling and hadn't been impressed. He'd delivered his ultimatum: agree to more deliveries by tomorrow or suffer the consequences. Terry knew he wasn't going to agree, and now he had to face the risk of reprisals.

He'd already moved June to another nursery. Fate had played into his hands, as an outbreak of whooping cough had swept through the old one. 'You're not going near that in your condition,' he'd said to Linda, breathing a sigh of relief that she hadn't suspected a thing.

He'd kept his eyes peeled but had noticed nothing out of the ordinary in the vicinity of the house. He'd taken to going to and coming home from work a different way every day, which often made him late and Linda irritated, but it was worth it. He was vulnerable while he was in the lorry but he'd have to deal with that. He could look after himself – before meeting Linda he'd been in enough fights to feel confident that he'd give anyone a run for their money. It was Linda alone in the house, or just with June, that he was worried about. He thought of finding an excuse to get Cora to come to stay, but then they'd never had her down before, and Linda would smell a rat right away. Besides, Cora might be a liability. He couldn't really see her being much use if anyone tried to break in – not unless she attacked them with her scathing tongue.

He'd better make a note of the number plate on Vincent's van. The vehicle itself was common enough but he wanted to be able to recognise it if it turned up anywhere it shouldn't. Maybe he could persuade June to start collecting car numbers as some sort of game – but no, at four she wasn't reliable enough, even though she could count to a hundred. His heart pounded in his chest. If anyone tried to hurt his daughter they would be very sorry.

'You're missing my point, Nev.' Nobby had had a few by now and was getting more and more belligerent, poking Neville with his forefinger. 'You got to get this straight in your head. You are the boss. That's just how it is. That's the natural order of things. You don't mess with that. Go home now and tell her ... tell her...' He swayed and caught hold of the brass rail that ran around the edge of the bar. 'Tell her who's boss. Show her if you have to.'

Frank was still nursing his first pint and was growing worried about tomorrow morning's shift. Everyone else had had at least three. He hated being the one to spoil the party but it looked as if things would turn nasty if Nobby didn't shut his mouth soon. 'Easy now, lads,' he said.

'You want me to show you how it's done?' Nobby ignored his foreman. 'Cos I will. Seems to me you need a lesson in how to do things right, young Nev. Come outside and I'll show yer.'

'You couldn't show a dog how to bark, let alone how to prove who's boss,' crowed Dennis. 'You can't even stand up straight. Stop going on about it. Nev'll do what he wants to do.'

Nobby turned on him. 'You're nothing but a gobby young bastard who can't keep his cock in his trousers,' he began but Dennis just laughed.

'Yeah, who's buying your drinks, and you don't

351

seem to have gone short of those,' he pointed out. 'At least I've got something in my trousers to let out, which is more than I hear can be said for you.'

Neville blushed furiously. He knew the jibe hadn't been aimed at him but it hurt none the less. What if his mates ever got to learn the truth? They'd crucify him. He'd never live it down.

Bill noticed his change of expression and decided to ride to the rescue. 'Come over here and stand by me,' he said, slightly slurring his words. 'Why don't we have a nice tot of whisky together? That'll set you right. Medicinal, whisky is, it's well known.'

'Yeah, why not,' Neville agreed, even though he knew he was at the limit of his capacity. What did it matter? He wasn't going to get a warm welcome at home whatever he did so he might as well enjoy himself. 'Not that I need medicine, Bill. There's nothing wrong with me.' He realised he was slurring as well.

Bill patted his shoulder. 'I'm very glad to hear it. Cos we was worried a while back, wasn't we, Frank?'

Cautiously Frank pushed his way through the others to reach Bill and Neville, who were now propped in a corner next to a huge gilt-framed mirror. He had to stop this conversation in its tracks before it went any further. 'I wouldn't go that far,' he said. 'You got tickets for the game this weekend, then? Bit of a local derby, isn't it?'

But Bill was flooded with affection for his friend and wanted to show how concerned he was. 'Yes, we was worried,' he went on. 'When you had all those bruises before. We thought you was sick, what with falling over like that all the time.'

Neville tried to laugh it off. 'No, no, I wasn't really falling over, I wasn't sick or nothing,' he assured him, his guard well and truly down.

Frank closed his eyes briefly, willing the young man to stop before it was too late.

'What d'you mean, you was in a fight after all?' Bill's befuddled brain couldn't work it out. 'You're not a fighter, Nev. That's what I like about you. You don't take offence.'

Neville caught sight of the reflection of his mates in the mirror and everything seemed to be a blur. 'Not a fight, no. I wouldn't. You know that.' He nodded meaningfully at his friend. 'I never even hit her back...'

'Nev, that's enough now,' said Frank, leaning in to catch the young man's arm, but the damage was done. Bill's mouth hung open as the penny finally dropped.

'What, you mean Hazel hit you?' he gasped, just as the conversation at the bar went quiet. 'Those shiners was from her?'

Nobby lurched forward. 'What's this I hear?' he shouted. 'You let a woman beat you, Nev? A woman? You didn't stand up to her and show her who's boss? You're a disgrace, you are. You let us all down, all of us here, all your mates. You some kind of pansy or something? What's wrong with you? You get back and show her tonight. You let her get away with this and there's no telling what she'll do next.'

'Nobby, shut up,' said Frank bluntly. 'That's stupid talk. It's none of your bloody business. Go home before you make an even bigger fool of yourself.'

'And you can fuck off an' all, Mr high and mighty Dalby,' raged Nobby. 'You let your missus get away with talking back all the time. I wouldn't stand for it.'

'We might be off work premises, Nobby, but one more remark like that and you're sacked,' said Frank, staying calm because someone had to. 'See that door over there? Well, go through it now. Maybe the cold air will sober you up. God knows you need it.'

Nobby flailed around, catching the remains of Frank's pint and sending it crashing to the floor. 'I'll go all right. I can't stand to be near you bunch of poofs any longer. That's all of you. All you lot.' He pointed wildly. 'I'm off, see if I care. But you, young Nev, you go back and show her who's boss.' He staggered to the door, barely managing to keep upright.

'Drunken old pisshead,' laughed Dennis as the door blew shut behind him, its brass finger plates flashing. 'He ain't been with a woman for years. They won't go near him and who can blame them? He's got nothing better to do than insult his friends. Frank, another pint for you, your last one went all over his legs and he didn't even notice. Marian's a diamond, don't let no one say anything different. Three cheers for Mrs Dalby, now.'

Everyone cheered, raising pints and chasers.

Neville leant back against the mirror, his face bright red with humiliation. It didn't matter that everyone seemed more taken up with the insult to the boss's wife than the revelation about Hazel

354

beating him. Nobby's words rang in his ears. 'Show her who's boss.' Even though he was drunker than he'd ever been before, he knew he was ashamed and hurt to the core. He gritted his teeth. 'Maybe I will,' he muttered.

Chapter Thirty-Seven

'Is he asleep?'

'He's just gone off.' Alison pulled the door nearly shut and backed carefully out into the corridor. She held David's bottle in her hand. It had been a big relief to stop feeding him herself, even if she no longer hated the sight of his face. Somehow that emotion had faded, along with her fears of being touched. The confession to Fred and her vow to try to change her attitude had started off the process, and she kept telling herself that it didn't have to happen all at once. She just had to hang on to the idea that history must not repeat itself. Slowly, bit by bit, everything seemed to be falling into place. She wouldn't call herself a perfect mother and there were plenty of times she felt like climbing the walls, but Vera assured her plenty of women felt like that even if they didn't admit it. Her aunt Beryl had been the same and it didn't mean she loved her children any the less. When it came down to it, they were hard work.

'Come and sit down and I'll tell you about my plans for the backyard,' said Fred, slipping an arm around her waist as they went into the living room. 'I've been looking at it and thinking we don't need it all for the deliveries and the car. We could divide it so that we had somewhere to sit outside once it gets warm. We could make a playpen for David once he's old enough.'

Alison turned to face him. 'Yes! Let's do that. We could work out which bit is sunniest and have it there. Somewhere far enough from the storerooms so we won't smell what's in there.'

'I thought you didn't mind that any more?'

'I don't,' said Alison, 'but other people might. I don't think Vera's very keen on it for a start.'

'Fair enough,' said Fred. 'We don't want to stop her coming round.'

'It's funny, I quite miss it,' Alison admitted. 'I think I'd like to come back to work. Maybe not full time but if we put David in the back room, he'd be all right. Either of us could go to him if he cried or needed looking after.'

'Are you sure?' Fred's face lit up. 'I'd love it if you did. I tried that new assistant but she was terrible. She couldn't add up and kept mixing up the orders. I was glad when she told me she'd got another job. As long as you feel you're up to it.'

Alison laughed. 'Why wouldn't I be? I'm not some frail creature who needs wrapping in cotton wool. I've had a baby, not a major illness.' She took his hand and he rested it on his stomach. 'I like it when we work together. I don't want to get out of touch with how the business is going. I haven't seen some of the customers for ages, they must think I've left the country. No, I'm keen to start again. Let's say next week. Then I can go shopping over the next few days and get anything we need.' She stared at where their hands lay. 'Fred Chapman, I do believe you've lost weight. That waistband looks as if it's loose.'

Fred nodded. 'I've noticed that myself. I had to use the next hole on my belt. It must be all that walking you make me do.'

'You enjoy it, don't complain. You would miss taking David out so everyone can stop to admire him. It's the highlight of your day.'

'It is,' he admitted. 'Or at least, it's one of them.' He cast her a glance. 'How about an early bed? What do you say?'

Alison smiled at him. 'I'd say that sounds like a good idea.' She stood up and held out her arms to him. She couldn't believe that she'd spent months terrified that Fred would try to touch her but now spent all day longing for him to do so. Here she was, in a beautiful flat, with a healthy baby, and a good man who loved her. Life was finally coming right for her. She sighed with contentment.

Hazel jumped as the street door slammed. She'd just finished the washing-up from her lonely meal, yesterday's reheated stew. That had better be Neville, home at last. What did he think he was doing, coming in so late? He needn't think she was going to stand for it, being left on her own, which she hated. There were often strange noises coming from the neighbours and she always imagined burglars creeping across the backyard. He had no business deserting her like this. It was bad enough when he was on lates but at least then she knew what time to expect him back. He had no such excuse now.

'Is that you, Neville?' she called.

The kitchen door opened and there he stood, swaying slightly, hanging on to the door frame.

'God, you're drunk!' she said in disgust. 'Where've you been all evening?' Her eyes narrowed with suspicion. 'Who've you been with? Who was so fascinating that you'd rather be with them than me? Who was worth leaving me here on my own for?' She paused to take a breath and caught a strong whiff of alcohol. 'Ugh, that's revolting. Look at the state of you. Who was it, tell me?'

He said nothing.

'It was that tart Vera Jewell, wasn't it? Go on, admit it. You've been meeting up with her behind my back again. Answer me, why don't you? Cat got your tongue? That stopped working as well as everything else?'

Neville stared at her, wondering what he'd ever seen in her. His wife was a monster. She would never forgive him, even for such a small thing as one drink with a friend. She would taunt and torment him every day of his life if he didn't do something about it. Suddenly it occurred to him that Nobby was right. He'd let her get away with it for too long. His confused mind hung on to what his colleague had said.

'How could you go out with that scheming bitch?' she screamed. 'Don't you know what everyone says about her? Think you're special, do you? Is that what she tells you? She says that to everybody. You won't last long with her. Meanwhile I'm stuck in here, waiting, cooking for you, fool that I am. You don't deserve it. That's the last time I do this for you. You're a drunken, cheating bastard.' She threw herself across the room and lifted her arm, ready to slap him.

In a flash he grabbed her, twisting her arm behind her back. 'No you don't, not this time. You keep your hands off me. You want to know where I was? I was down the pub with my mates, because anything's better than being back here with you.'

'Let me go!' She was wriggling around, trying to get herself free, but he had a strong grip, fuelled by the drink and his determination not to give way this time. She turned her head, trying to scream in his ear. 'You lying, cheating scum! I hate you!'

Suddenly she broke away, twisting around, ready to hit him, but her heel caught in the rug on the floor. Unable to stop herself she fell, catching the side of her head on the corner of the table. Before he knew what was happening, she was lying motionless on the ground.

Without fully realising what he was doing, he reached across the sink to where the washing-up was draining and grabbed the carving knife. 'You bitch!' he shouted. 'You mean, evil, conniving bitch! I'll show you who's boss! There! How do you like that?' and he plunged the blade into her, again and again, unable to stop the rage pouring out of him.

Beryl thought she was having a nightmare, dreaming that the Lannings were back and they were fighting, screaming insults she didn't want her children to hear, banging on the wall, crashing over furniture. But then she woke up and realised it wasn't a dream. Something really was happening on the other side of the bedroom wall. She could just about make out what somebody was screaming, and her blood ran cold. 'Roy, wake up!' She shook her husband, who groaned. 'Roy, something dreadful's going on next door! Get the police, quick!'

'What?' Roy sat up, rubbing his eyes, unsure of what was happening. 'Are you sure you aren't imagining it?'

'Listen! Someone's shouting "I hate you, I hate you". That's not right, Roy. It sounds really bad. Go on, get your shoes and coat on and go for the police. What if they break the wall down and come in here? What about the children? Hurry, get on with it, come on, do it for me and the kids. Hurry up, Roy.'

Still groaning, Roy struggled into his trousers over his pyjamas and dragged on a big jumper before finding his keys. He knew he'd have no peace from Beryl until he did as she asked. And, now he was more awake, he had to admit it sounded like someone was committing murder next door.

Jill Parrot was fast asleep when someone started banging on her front door. She turned over towards Lennie, not wanting to wake up after a hard day. But the banging carried on.

Lennie struggled to sit up, shaking his head. 'I'll go. You stay here where it's warm. God almighty, don't some people know what time it is?' he grumbled, making his way to the bedroom door by light of the streetlamp outside.

'I'll come with you, it could be anything.' Jill reached for her faded old dressing gown. Still half-asleep she followed her husband down the steep stairs.

The banging got louder and more frantic as they reached the door.

Jill looked at Lennie. 'Shall we let them in? They could be crazy, making a din like that.'

'Stand back and let me handle it,' said Lennie. He opened the door and they both gasped.

Neville stood there, covered in blood.

'Oh my God, oh my God.' Jill went weak with fright. 'Whatever's happened? Are you hurt? Come in, come into the kitchen and let me have a look.' She switched on the hall light and ran to the kitchen to grab something to clean Neville up with. 'Let's get you clean and we can see the damage.'

'What's happened, son?' asked Lennie. He didn't like this one bit. Neville didn't seem able to talk, he just stared at his father with wild eyes. 'Let your mother sort you out. Whatever it is it can't be that bad.'

Neville threw him a desperate glance and started to sob in great gulping heaves.

Jill was shaking as she poured water into a bowl. 'Let me clean you up a bit. Let's see where it hurts.' She reached for a rag. 'We'll call the doctor. Lennie, you get dressed and go round to his house.'

'N-n-n-o,' Neville managed to say. 'Too late. Doctor's no good.'

Jill gazed up at her husband in horror. Was their boy at death's door?

'What do you mean?' Lennie hesitated. He couldn't work out what was going on here.

Jill helped Neville out of his coat and shirt, washing away what blood she could, and slowly she realised that there was no deep wound on him. That could only mean one thing. 'Neville,' she said quietly, trying to keep calm, 'whose blood is this? It's not yours, is it?'

Neville sobbed again. 'It's Hazel, it's Hazel. It was an accident but I made it worse. Mum, she's dead, she's on the kitchen floor, she's dead.'

'No, Neville.' Jill couldn't take it in. 'She can't be!' she cried, close to hysteria.

Neville bent double in the chair he was sitting in, rocking to and fro. 'I stuck the knife in her. I couldn't take it any more. She's dead, go and see if you don't believe me.'

Tears streaming down her face, Jill hugged her son and tried to stop his desperate rocking. 'Now then, start from the beginning. This doesn't make sense. We'll help you. You know we will. But I don't believe you killed Hazel. You love her, you're only just married, so that can't be right.'

Neville let out a howl. 'I did it, I did it. She was going to hit me, but then she tripped over and fell onto the floor. Then when she was down I got the knife, I couldn't stand any more of it, I hated her. She was a monster!'

Lennie shifted uneasily. 'Did this just happen, son? You came straight here?'

Neville nodded. 'I didn't know what else to do.'

'You did right.' Lennie was thinking hard. 'Listen, we've got to get you away before the police get here. You said it was an accident but

362

who knows what they'll believe. Now that the blood is cleaned up we'll get you new clothes and then you've got to go.'

'Lennie!' Jill gasped in terror. 'He can't just go off like that, what'll he do? We have to look after him, he's our son!'

'We are looking after him,' said Lennie grimly. He was the only one thinking straight. 'Get into some clean clothes and bung some others in a bag. We'll give you what cash we got here and some food, but then you got to go. There's no other way. You make for my brother up north, he can get you away, he's on the trawlers. When it's all died down we can see what's best then, but for now you've got to scarper. Don't just sit there! Come on, Neville!' Lennie yelled in an effort to get through to his son. 'You don't want to be here when the rozzers turn up.'

Trembling, Jill forced herself to step away from her boy. 'Your dad's right, Neville. Come on, you'd better get going. Give me those bloody clothes, I'll get rid of them, and you can have some of your old things. I'll make you up some sandwiches and cut you a bit of cake, that'll keep you going. Stand up, Neville, come on, don't just collapse, we don't have long.'

But Neville couldn't move. His panic had got him this far but now all his energy was gone. He couldn't get out of the chair, let alone start planning an escape.

'Come on, Neville!' Jill shook him frantically. 'This is the only way. Come on, shift yourself, think of your future.'

Neville shook his head, clinging to the back of

the chair, seemingly unable to move.

'Gordon Bennett, I'll carry you if I have to but you got to go.' Lennie stood in front of him, stern now. 'Whatever you did, sitting there like this won't help. Save yourself, boy. Get away up north and wait till we give you the word. It won't be forever. Come on, up you get...'

But it was too late. Someone else was banging on the door, with authority this time.

Jill, Lennie and Neville's blood ran cold as they heard the words: 'Open up. Police.'

Chapter Thirty-Eight

The talk was of nothing else the next day but for once Cora wasn't at the heart of all the gossip. The paperboys turned up only to find the newsagent's was still locked up. One of them ran to find the owner, who complained about staff letting him down as he struggled to remember how to open up, sort out the papers, and do all the jobs he'd relied on Cora to do for so long. She'd better have a good excuse, he thought. It wasn't until later in the day that he realised what had happened and even he had to admit he wasn't surprised the woman hadn't shown up.

Winnie Jewell was desperate to talk about it all to somebody but knew that Cora was unlikely to be at work that day. She wondered if she should go round to give her condolences but decided against it. She was bursting to exchange news, full of importance as it was her own sister who'd got the police involved. She'd tried talking about it to Vera, taking the unheard-of step of visiting her on the shop floor of Arding and Hobbs, but Vera hadn't been interested in Beryl's role in the proceedings. She was more upset to hear that Neville had been arrested and what the shock would do to Alison. 'I'll go round and see her after work so don't expect me back on time,' she told her mother. 'Now you'd better go because the old bag is watching us and she knows you're not a customer. Go on, don't get me into trouble, it's bad enough if she sees I'm upset.'

Winnie was all prepared to get into a row as to why she didn't look good enough to be seen in the department store but Vera wasn't falling for it.

'Just go,' she hissed. 'There's going to be enough trouble about all this, don't add to it.'

Winnie had gone, affronted, but had bumped into Marian Dalby on the pavement outside. Here was her chance. She launched into the story, pleased that Marian hadn't heard yet. 'Of course I only know all this because our Beryl was on the spot and she came straight over to me after breakfast. Worried sick, she was. She thought someone was going to break in and harm her children.'

Marian stopped in her tracks, full of disbelief. 'Neville? Neville Parrot? But he's such a nice boy. I can't believe it. He's never even answered back, let alone attacked and killed someone. Are you sure, Winnie?'

Winnie drew herself up to her full height. 'Of course I'm sure. I heard it from my own sister, who heard it all happening through the wall. He might seem like a nice boy but underneath all that he's a raving maniac. Just goes to show. Well, I must be off.' Offended at having her word doubted, Winnie stormed across the road, determined to find someone else who'd join in the speculation about what Neville Parrot was really like.

Marian slowly made her way along the street, recalling what Frank had said about the night out when he'd got back from the pub. He'd been concerned that Nobby had gone too far and had wound up the lad. She'd better get hold of him fast. If Neville really had cracked and killed his young wife then there must have been a good reason for it, as she didn't believe he'd been a maniac in disguise all along.

Cora checked that her front-room curtains were pulled tight. She didn't want anyone looking in and she couldn't bear to see out, not with the Parrot house directly opposite. To think that she'd been friendly with them, welcomed them into her home, let their boy court her daughter. Her daughter. Blindly Cora caught hold of the back of the sofa as she was assailed yet again by memories of Hazel, her laughing, smiling, beautiful girl. She didn't remember the rows, the lack of consideration, the way Hazel had bullied her younger sister. She didn't think about how the girl had been recently, angry, sullen, losing those famous good looks. All she could do was rerun scenes in her mind where Hazel had been perfect, the life and soul of any party, turning all the men's heads, making her friends wish they were her. She couldn't believe her life had been snuffed out so abruptly. It didn't seem possible. Any moment now, Hazel would come barging in the door, new clothes from the market in her bag, ready to pass on who said what to who at the café, planning to dress up for a night out. Of all the men who'd been interested, why did she have to pick Neville?

Cora bent double with grief, too distressed even to cry. Why hadn't she stopped her daughter from seeing him? She'd known he would never make her happy. But she'd never imagined anything like this. If anything he was too mild-mannered, too polite, too keen to let Hazel have her way. She'd be the first to admit that Hazel could be a handful. But to kill her ... no, there had to be a mistake, she'd be back from work in a minute... Her heart stopped when the door opened.

'Mum!' Alison stood there. 'What are you doing? You can't stay there like that. Can you get up? Take my arm, come on, let's get you sitting down on the comfy chair.'

Cora's heart sank. She knew she should be grateful for Alison's help but she didn't particularly want to see her youngest. The girl was of no comfort. It made the contrast with her sister even sharper, although Alison looked so different these days. All the same it was hard to forget the first seventeen years of her life and she really didn't want to have to put up with her now, of all days.

'I'm all right,' she muttered. 'Don't fuss. Let me go, I'm all right.'

'Really, Mum?' Alison sounded anxious. 'Have you had anything to eat? I brought some ham just

367

in case. Shall I do us a spot of lunch? You've got to keep your strength up.'

Cora almost laughed. 'For what? What could be worse than what's just happened?' Suddenly she grabbed Alison's elbow. 'You know what I just had to do? The police came round and told me he'd killed her then I had to go and identify the body. Can you imagine what that was like? My own child, my little girl, they'd cleaned her up but they only let me see half her face, and I could see her hair ... she had that lovely hair...'

'Oh, Mum.' Alison guided her into the chair and got her to settle. 'You should have asked them to get me to do it.'

'I had to do it myself. I had to see her body before I could believe she's dead.'

'I can understand that,' Alison said. She shut her eyes, recalling the events of the morning, with the knock on the door before the shop was open. She and Fred had stood there in silence as the young police constable had informed them of the news and then asked them to go over the last time they'd seen Hazel and Neville. They'd been astounded, unable to square what they knew of the friendly young man with what he'd been accused of doing. Neville, a murderer? He was the least likely person.

Alison gave herself a mental shake to bring her thoughts back to the present. She had to focus on the practicalities. 'Does Linda know yet? Did the police say they'd be contacting her?'

Cora shook her head. 'I don't know. If they told me, I didn't take it in.'

'I could phone Terry's firm and if he isn't in the

depot, I could ask his boss to pass on a message,' Alison suggested.

Cora stirred herself. 'Yep, sooner the better.' She had to get rid of her youngest. She was making things worse, not better. 'Not being funny or anything but I'm washed out. I think I'll have a little sleep. You go back and get hold of Terry somehow. Don't worry about me. Get back and look after that baby of yours, I'll be fine.'

'Don't you want me to make you a sandwich or something? Wouldn't you feel better coming back with me?'

Cora's stomach heaved at the thought of food. 'No, you leave me that ham and I'll do it myself later,' she said, thinking she'd do no such thing. 'You go on now. I'm going to have a lie-down. I'd rather be in my own home.'

'Well, if you're sure...'Alison hesitated. She didn't think her mother ought to be left alone at a time like this, but she couldn't phone Terry's firm from here and there wasn't even a public box nearby. 'I'll go and make that call now but I'll be back later.'

Cora nodded but could think of nothing worse than the wrong daughter hanging around, cluttering up the place. 'No, you look after Fred and the baby. That's what matters now. Off you go.' She practically pushed the girl out of the door and slammed it swiftly behind her, before anyone could look in or she caught a glimpse of the house across the road. She didn't think she'd ever be able to set foot outside her own door again.

Alison wasn't sure what to think as she made her

way back to the flat. She was worried about her mum who, even though she'd always put on a tough front, had been dealt a blow that no mother should ever have to suffer. As for herself, she didn't know what she felt. She was in shock. Even though she'd often hated her sister she wouldn't have wished this on her. As for Neville, what had got into him? He could hang for this, she realised. And what about his family? They'd always been so kind to her and never let Cora and Hazel's sniping affect the way they treated her. They were some of the friendliest and fair-minded people she knew. What would this do to them?

But she couldn't mind about that now. Linda had to be told. She dreaded making the call and found her legs getting heavy as lead the closer she got to the front door. It would be better to speak to Terry first, though, in case the Kent police hadn't been round. She didn't know how these things worked, but she knew that a shock would be bad for Linda's unborn baby. Grimly Alison remembered how she'd hoped shock would bring on her own miscarriage and how it failed, but she wasn't going to risk it with her sister.

Alison went into the shop and was relieved to find it empty of customers. Fred was wiping down the counter and she could hear David gurgling from the back room.

'How did it go?' he asked, coming across and hugging her.

'Mum's not in a good way,' said Alison, 'but she didn't want me there – said she was going to sleep. They made her identify the body. I don't think she should be left on her own for long but

370

there's no budging her. What's it been like here?'

'This is the quietest it's been all day,' Fred said. 'Word has gone round like wildfire and they're all in here, saying it's to see how we are but really to get more snippets for the gossips. Winnie's been here. She said it was to tell you Vera will be round after work, but after that it was like the Inquisition. I got rid of her as fast as I could. I didn't want her still here when you got back.'

'Thanks, Fred. I couldn't have stood her, not today.' Alison met his eyes. 'I said I'd call Terry at work in case they don't know. I really don't want to.'

'Do you want me to do it?' Fred offered, as she had known he would. She was tempted. Then she shook her head. 'No. Best not. I've got to do it really.' She gritted her teeth. 'I'll go up and get it over with. Wish me luck.'

Fred watched her go, knowing that this would be the first of many unbearable conversations. He wished he could put the clock back to yesterday when they'd been so happy, making plans and having an early night. But he knew things would never be the same again.

Chapter Thirty-Nine

Terry put down the phone and rubbed his eyes. He couldn't take in what he'd just heard. Alison's words had shaken him to the core. He'd known some dodgy characters back in the days before

371

he'd met Linda and sorted himself out but he'd never come across anything like this. He'd have to get back home to tell her at once.

It had been pure luck that he hadn't already set off on his next batch of deliveries when his boss had taken the call. He'd had to get a new bulb for one of the brake lights and by the time it was fitted he was running late, but it had been a blessing in disguise. He could have been anywhere – some days he was away all day and on others he was off overnight.

His boss waved him away, saying he knew what had gone on and to take as much time as he wanted, so Terry rushed home by the most direct route. His mind was whirling. This would cut Linda to the quick. She loved her sisters, different though they were, and felt close to them despite the distance between them. He himself had always got on with Hazel, even if he thought she was a bit rough on Alison most of the time. She couldn't hold a candle to Linda but then nobody could. Yet however unfair she'd been to the youngest in the family she hadn't deserved this. What had possessed Neville?

Linda would have got back from nursery with June, but the little girl might have gone to a friend's house. Or she might have someone back to play with her. He hoped not. He couldn't remember what today's arrangements were – they usually passed him by in a blur in the mornings. He hoped there wouldn't be a house full of four-year-olds waiting when he got back.

As he rounded a corner a police car drew up and two officers got out. He quickened his pace. If

Linda opened the door to find the police on the doorstep, she'd likely imagine it was something to do with the boxes and he didn't want that. Today's news was going to be enough of a shock as it was. He hurried to catch them before they went up the garden path, and explained who he was and that he already knew about his sister-in-law. Once they heard Linda was pregnant they agreed their presence would make things worse and agreed to wait outside in the car while he broke the news to her himself.

None of them noticed a black van pull over on the other side of the road.

Alison finally managed to cry when Vera came round. They settled in the living room while Fred took David for a walk to give them some time on their own. 'I don't know why I'm crying,' she sobbed. 'I didn't even like her most of the time. She was horrible to me but I can't believe she's gone.'

'She was still your sister,' Vera said. 'That goes deeper than liking someone or not. I often don't like my mum much but I'd be heartbroken if anything was to happen to her. That's family for you.'

Alison wiped her eyes with the sleeve of her cardigan. 'I know. And that's another thing. Mum wouldn't be helped earlier, just wanted to be on her own. I don't think that's right, she looked awful, but she was dead set on it.'

Vera sighed deeply. 'You can't force her, she's a grown woman. Give her time. You're all still in shock. Everyone copes in different ways.'

373

Alison nodded. 'You're right, as usual. I'll give her a bit of time. She's got food in, I took her some. Anyway, Linda rang me back from Terry's office and said she and June would be coming up tomorrow. If Mum won't have them at her place they can stay here. There's plenty of room. As if it mattered.' She started sobbing again, digging in her pocket for a handkerchief.

Vera found her own first and passed it over. 'Here. Have this. Staff discount's finest. God, in all of this it's Neville I feel sorry for. You might think it's terrible of me to say that.'

Alison shook her head. 'No, the daft thing is I know what you mean. It's a mess, isn't it? It can't have been much of a picnic being married to Hazel. There was only one way of doing things when she was around, and that was her way, and heaven help anyone who didn't agree... God forgive me for speaking ill of the dead. But it's true. I didn't see much of her but you get to hear things, you know how it is. Everyone was saying how much she'd changed.'

Vera turned to look out of the window. 'She never liked me. She was one of those who believed everything she heard and spoke behind my back every chance she got. So I felt sorry for Neville. But that's all I did, I purposely kept away because I knew if Hazel found out we'd had the one drink it would make things worse for him. From what I heard it wasn't what you'd call a happy marriage.' She stared at the darkening sky outside. 'Poor Neville. It must all have got too much for him.'

'He might get the death sentence,' whispered Alison.

'He might.' Vera turned back to look at her friend. 'I can't begin to think about it. But it'll depend what he's charged with, won't it?'

'The police this morning say he claimed he didn't know what he was doing,' Alison said. 'So it might not be murder. But he still won't get off, will he?'

'No, he might spend years in prison. But you don't want him to get away with it, do you?'

'No. That wouldn't be fair. I just keep thinking about his family. They must be going through hell and I can't help feeling sorry for them, but Neville killed my sister!' Tears rolled down her cheeks again.

'I know,' said Vera. 'It's such a terrible mess.'

Linda arrived the next day, not her usual efficient self and very shaky. Her bump was very visible; the baby was due in about three months and she was beginning to struggle to get around. It didn't help that June was hopping up and down with excitement at the thought of seeing David. She was too young to understand what had happened to Hazel and as far as she was concerned it was another trip to Battersea, where she usually got lots of attention and presents.

Alison did her best to welcome her niece, showing her where David slept and where he kept his toys. June was delighted and started making up a story for her baby cousin, so Linda sighed with relief. The two sisters went into the kitchen, and hugged. Alison couldn't help crying again. Then she felt bad because Linda was so heavily pregnant and she didn't want to upset her further.

'I went round to see Mum before I came here,' Linda said, 'but she just seemed to want rid of us.'

'She was the same with me, but that isn't surprising. You know how she doesn't really like to be in the same room as me, even now.' Alison knew it was true – even though she'd done as her mother wanted, married Fred, produced a grandson, and been a constant source of top-quality free food, her mother still didn't enjoy her company. Cora was beginning to be more understanding of Alison, now she was a mother herself, but it didn't change how she reacted to her youngest daughter. 'Also, she probably did need to sleep after the shock of it all. I'm worried about her though.'

'I'd better go round there right now,' said Linda. 'I won't take June this time. If she's all right, we can both go over there later and stay there. June'll be all right here, won't she?'

'Of course,' said Alison. 'She can get to know her cousin and get used to what babies are like. I can show her how he takes his bottle – that'll be useful for her to learn. If Mum still wants to be on her own you can both stay here, there's plenty of room.'

'Thanks.' Linda hugged her again and then set off, the sound of her daughter's voice floating out from the baby's room. She didn't say goodbye. She felt she needed all her emotional energy to face what was to come.

Rounding the corner of Ennis Street, she could see a big removal van pulled up opposite Cora's house. She stopped to see what was going on, and found herself face to face with one of the women from down the road who she'd known since she was a girl. 'It's Linda, isn't it?' said the woman, eagerly turning bright eyes on her. 'Come to see your mum, I expect? Terrible business. Do give her my condolences. Just as well that lot are going.' She nodded towards the van.

'What! Is that for the Parrots?' asked Linda. 'Are they moving house?'

'Gone already,' said the woman, 'and more's the pity they ever came here in the first place. This lot are just collecting their stuff. Won't say where they're going, but they aren't wanted round here, that's for sure.' She sniffed and drew her threadbare cardigan around her. 'We won't see no more of them.'

Linda didn't know what to think. She had liked the Parrots, but now that their son had killed Hazel she never wanted to see them again.

'I'd better see how Mum is,' she said. 'Don't let me keep you.'

She turned and stood at her old front door. Now that she had her lovely new house in Kent this one seemed even shabbier, with its tired, peeling paintwork and narrow window facing directly onto the street. She noticed the curtains were still firmly shut. Usually there would be a twitching of the nets, but not today.

She knocked and tried the door. It was locked. She hadn't brought her own key, and cursed her lack of forethought.

'Mum, it's me. Linda. Open up, will you?'

A minute passed.

'Come on, Mum, I'm dying for a cuppa. Let

me in and I'll put the kettle on.'

It was another few minutes before she heard a shuffling on the other side of the door and then it opened. Cora drew her in and shut the door behind her firmly again, and she found herself in the gloomy front room, the only light coming from the kitchen at the back.

'I was sleeping,' said Cora. 'It's all I seem to be able to do.' She sighed. 'Good of you to come, Linda, but I'm all right, as you can see.'

Linda couldn't see very much at all, but strode through to the kitchen and took out two cups. 'You'll be glad of some tea, then, to wake you up a bit. I know I will.'

Now that she could see her mother properly she thought how gaunt she was. Her eyes were dead, her skin was slack, and she was hunched over like a woman twice her age. No wonder Alison was worried. 'You had anything to eat, Mum? Alison said you had some food in.'

'Spying on me, is she?' snapped Cora. 'None of her business. If I feel like eating then I'll eat. Don't you go talking about me behind my back.'

Linda took out the milk and sniffed it. 'This is off, Mum. You can't drink this. I certainly can't.' She picked up her bag again. 'I'll run to the corner shop and get more. Here, bung the tea cosy round the pot and it'll do for when I get back. Do you want anything else? What about some bread?'

'No thanks.' Cora wouldn't look at her.

Linda dashed out, turning her gaze away from the lorry that was now nearly full of the Parrots' belongings.

It took longer than she'd planned as she kept bumping into people who knew her and who wanted to talk. By the time she got back, the tea was cold. Cora complained as she set about making more. 'It's a waste, that's what it is. I don't need no tea. I'm all right as it is.' She stopped and glanced suspiciously at her daughter. 'You didn't talk to no one, did you? They all want to know what went on but I ain't telling them nothing. And did you shut the door tight? I won't have that family,' she almost spat, 'them lot opposite looking in here. To think I thought of them as friends. Just goes to show.'

'Mum, they're gone. There's a dirty great lorry out there taking everything away and they've gone already.'

Cora pursed her lips. 'You sure? You aren't havin' me on?'

'Honestly, Mum. Why would I lie?'

Cora seemed to come to her senses. 'Thank God for that. I couldn't stand to see any of their ugly faces ever again. To think they were all smile, smile, smile and they brought up that murderer, that killer, that bastard what did for our lovely Hazel.' At the name she stopped and broke down, great heaving sobs shaking her tiny body. 'Our Hazel. Who never did no harm to anyone. That beautiful girl. So pretty, especially at her wedding – to that bastard.'

Linda hugged her mother as best she could against her bump, thinking it was probably a good thing that she cried. 'That's right, Mum, you let it all out. Here, have my hanky. You don't have to worry about them now, they've gone. You can open those curtains and let some light in.'

'No.' Cora sat upright, her sobs subsiding. 'No, I don't want any of them nosy busybodies looking in here. You mind you keep them shut. They want entertainment, they can go elsewhere.'

'Mum, that's not fair. People are worried about you. Everyone's asking after you.'

'I hope you told them to mind their own business.'

'Mum, come on. People are concerned.'

'Well, I don't want their concern.' Cora slammed down her cup. 'I'm doing very well on my own without any help from them, thank you very much. I won't be no laughing stock for them. You can tell them that when they ask.' Tea sloshed over the kitchen table. Linda went to wipe it up.

'I'll tell them no such thing, Mum. You need good neighbours at a time like this.'

'Neighbours? What good have they done me? I thought them lot opposite were friends, see how wrong I was then. No, they can all keep off. I won't have them interfering.'

Linda sat back and took all this in. She supposed it was still the shock talking, as this wasn't like her mother at all. 'Don't suppose you'd like to come and stay with us for a bit, until it all calms down?'

Cora immediately shook her head. 'Thanks, Linda, but no thanks. I belong here. This is where ... I feel closest to Hazel. I don't want to be away. You got your own life down where you are. My life is here.'

Linda felt slightly relieved at this. She didn't know how she'd cope with her mother in this mood as well as settling June into the new nursery and the last stages of her pregnancy. She hadn't discussed it with Terry either. 'Well, how about I go and collect June from Alison's and then we both stay here tonight? I can make up the beds and everything.'

Cora stiffened. 'No, no, don't do that. I don't want her to see me like this. She's at an impressionable age, I don't want her to think of her old granny in a state like this.' She sighed. 'Linda, I know you mean well but I'd rather be on my own. I'm closer to Hazel then, can't you see? I don't want no one around. And you can stay with Alison, can't you? God knows she's got enough room in that grand flat.'

Linda shook her head. 'I'd rather stay with you here. June can stay there, she loves it with David. But I'd be happier with you, to make sure you're all right.'

Cora's eyes blazed. 'I keep telling you I'm fine. I'm telling you again. And I want to be on my own, is that clear? I don't want help from you or anyone else.' Cora reared to her feet. 'Just go will you. I want to be left in peace to grieve for my Hazel.'

Chapter Forty

Terry waited on the platform for the train from London. He knew Linda didn't have much to carry after only one night away but with June and the bump, he wanted to be there to meet her. Nervously he chewed on a thumbnail. He'd noticed a black van just outside the station car park, but hadn't got close enough to check the number plate. Relax, he told himself. There are hundreds of vans like that. He'd heard no more from Vincent over the past couple of days but didn't fool himself that this meant he was off the hook.

The train pulled in and Linda waved as June ran to meet him. He scooped her up and she laughed in delight. 'I saw baby David and played with him,' she said. 'I helped give him his bottle. Auntie Alison said I was very good at it.'

'Did you?' he said, tickling her and making her squeal. 'So when your little brother or sister arrives, you'll know exactly what to do.'

Linda raised her eyebrows. 'We'll see about that.'

'How was your mum?' he asked her.

She shook her head. 'I'll tell you later. June had a lovely time, didn't you, Junie? Saw how a nappy gets changed and everything.'

June wrinkled her nose. 'I didn't like that bit.'

'I know what you mean,' said Terry, setting her down. 'Here, walk like a big girl. Only big girls can give babies their bottles.' He lifted the small overnight case and headed out of the station, past the car park.

June pointed. 'Look, there's that van.'

Terry's blood ran cold. 'What van's that? There are lots of vans.'

'That black one. It was outside my old nursery where they all got sick.'

'You must have made a mistake,' he laughed, as the van's engine purred into life.

'No, it's the letters,' June said, skipping along the street. 'I didn't tell you I knew them, it's my secret. But look, it's A for Alison, F for Fred and D for David, just like baby David. So I remembered, it's easy.'

It was the same number plate.

The engine purred to life, and trying not to panic, Terry looked round. The van began to move towards them. He tried to see who was behind the wheel. He was pretty sure it was Vincent.

It started to speed up. It was heading straight for them.

Terry threw the case to the ground and shoved Linda and June into the nearest doorway as hard as he could, shouting 'Sorry, stay there', but with no time to explain. The van carried on aiming for him. It was only half a block away. He knew he had to draw it away from his wife and daughter but had no time to think of how he could save himself. It was hard to believe that Vincent was prepared to run him over right outside a busy station and yet it seemed that this was exactly what was going to happen. Terry ran, his legs pumping and his heart pounding with fear.

There was a small side road coming up and he darted into it at the last minute, giving the van driver no warning of what he was doing. What Terry knew, and he was banking on Vincent not knowing, was that there was a newly installed massive concrete bollard in the centre of the narrow street, stopping it being used as a rat-run. Everything depended on it being big enough, and solid enough, to stop the speeding van. If it wasn't then that would be the end of him.

The setting sun was full in Terry's face, and as the van screeched around the corner, it must have blinded the driver who, unable to see the obstruction ahead, hit the bollard head on. There was a sickening crash, the sound of metal crunching, and Terry froze in his tracks. Heart still pounding, he ran back to look through the windscreen. The driver was slumped over the steering wheel, blood pouring from his face and head where he'd hit the windscreen. But it was the eyes that held Terry. They were open but lifeless, and he knew the man was dead.

Time seemed to stand still but then Terry could hear screaming. To his dismay Linda had followed him and she was staggering towards him, holding her arm. June was cowering behind her, shielded by her mother's body. 'I'm hurt, I'm hurt,' gasped Linda. Terry thought he was going to be sick. But he tried to summon words of comfort. 'There, you're going to be fine. Junie's all right, aren't you? She's safe behind you.'

'I didn't know what was happening ... why you pushed me into the doorway... I wanted to see where you'd gone ... and that van clipped me.'

Linda was having trouble speaking. 'I nearly fell, I banged my head on something. Maybe a wall. My arm ... I can't feel it properly. Oh God, what about June, I didn't realise she'd come after me...'

Terry kept on talking, trying to calm them down, trying not to think of what might have happened. That van really had been out to kill him. If it hadn't been for the way the sun was setting .

Gradually he was aware that people had come out of the houses that surrounded the station. Somebody must have called for help as finally ambulances arrived. Linda was escorted into one of them, tearful now, worried about her husband and daughter. 'We're fine,' Terry assured her. 'You caught the worst of it. I'm so sorry. I'm so sorry.'

'Not your fault,' she whispered.

But Terry knew that it was.

Linda was kept in overnight and when Terry went in the next day, the doctor took him to one side. 'We want to keep her in,' he said. 'The arm will heal as long as she takes care of it but her blood pressure is very high. That's not good in her condition. Has she been under stress lately?'

'Her sister just died,' Terry said shortly. He couldn't face explaining the full circumstances of Hazel's death. 'So there's that and she's worried about how her mum's taking it.' He still didn't know exactly what had happened in Battersea but he'd seen enough from Linda's expression when she got off the train to understand that it must have been an ordeal.

'That might be it, then.' The doctor pushed his glasses up his nose. 'We'll have to see, take it day by day. She's better off staying here for the time being. You can visit her for a few minutes but don't tire her out.'

Terry felt a lump in his throat. Here was his wife, coping with the murder of her sister, her mother's collapse, and a pregnancy, and he'd put her in danger from a criminal who'd tried to kill them all. What had he been thinking of? He carefully made his way to her bed on the ward and drew back one of the curtains around it. She looked up at him, her dark hair spread out on the pillow, and smiled weakly. It was the loveliest smile in the world.

'I won't stay long,' he said, taking her hand. 'Just checking you're all right.'

'Don't worry, I'm fine. I'm sure the doctor told you it's just a bit of blood pressure.'

'Yes, he did and they want you to rest.'

'Terry, what happened? Why was that van trying to run us down?'

'Don't be daft, love. Of course it wasn't,' Terry lied. 'The brakes failed and the poor sod of a driver couldn't stop.'

Linda managed a smile. 'The brakes. I should have realised. I've got too much of a vivid imagination, that's the trouble. Terry, I want to come home.'

'You can't, not at the moment. You've had a bit of a shock and they want to keep you in until your blood pressure comes down.'

He squeezed her hand as he told the lie. 'You have a proper rest and June and me'll look after the house for you. She's in charge.' He tried to

386

raise a smile.

'I was worried about Mum,' Linda whispered. 'I asked her to come down here for a bit but she wouldn't. Just as well. I couldn't have her now, if I'm stuck in here.'

Terry closed his eyes for a moment. That had been a narrow escape. He realised he was safe now; it had been reported that Vincent had died in the crash and he was the only one who knew Terry's name or what his family looked like. There was no need to worry any more.

'She's not on her own,' he said. 'Alison's there, she'll keep an eye on her. You concentrate on getting better. Keep that baby safe. I love you very much, you know.' He swallowed hard. 'I just want you to be all right. You're my world, you are.'

'I know. And you're mine.' Her voice was very quiet and he could tell she was about to fall asleep.

'See you tomorrow.' He dropped a kiss on her forehead and backed away from the bed, faint with guilt and relief.

Chapter Forty-One

Alison fell into a routine over the following weeks of working in the shop for most of the day, with David in the back room where she or Fred could go to him if he needed anything. In the afternoon she would go round to her mother, taking her something to eat, but it was always a struggle to persuade her to open the door. She was more likely to shout 'Leave me alone' through the letterbox. On the occasions when she did manage to set foot inside the house, Alison was horrified to find that her mother had completely let things go. The once-immaculate front room was a shambles, with dust gathering, bits of clothing strewn over the furniture, and mouldy cups left on the side table or shelves.

It didn't help that they couldn't hold Hazel's funeral until the post-mortem had been completed and then they had to wait for all the paperwork to be sorted out before the body could be released. Cora was totally incapable of making any decisions, and Linda was still in hospital, too ill with her high blood pressure to be asked what she thought should happen. So it fell to Alison and Fred to arrange everything. Of course Hazel had never said what she wanted for such an occasion, and Alison felt out of her depth trying to imagine what her sister might have approved of. Fred decided it would be best to play it safe and be very traditional. They didn't feel anyone would be able to face the funeral in the same church where Hazel had married Neville, so with much sadness they opted for a service at a different one.

When the sad day arrived, it was a sombre procession to the church and, unlike Hazel's wedding, there were no bright flowers decorating the pews this time – just the spray of white lilies on top of Hazel's coffin. It wasn't a huge gathering, just some of Hazel's friends and her workmates from the café, along with a few market traders who had known her.

Alison fought back tears. She had suffered at Hazel's hand, but now that her sister had gone, all she could feel was grief.

Cora had closed in on herself. She felt distant, barely aware of being in the church or of the service, but when the curtain closed around Hazel's coffin to take her for cremation, her feelings returned. She felt a well of anguish rising. Sobs racked her body, and though she felt Alison trying to take her hand, she wrenched it away. Fred put an arm around her shoulder and gently urged her to her feet before leading her outside the church. He led her over to where the flowers lay, but she didn't want to look at them or read the accompanying cards with condolence messages. She just wanted to go home – to be left alone to grieve.

'Fred, I want to go home,' she said, her voice strangled.

Thankfully, he led her to the black limousine, and as he held the door for her, she was aware of Alison getting in behind her. She didn't want Alison. She wanted Hazel and closed her eyes rather than look at her youngest child.

When they arrived at her house, Cora refused any offers of company, adamant that she would be better off on her own. With a gathering of Hazel's friends due at the flat for tea and sandwiches, Alison had to let her have her way, but she was far from happy about it.

The only good thing to happen was that the results of the post-mortem came out. It was highly likely that Hazel had not been killed by the knife wounds but had died instantly from a blow to the head. Neville had been overcome with remorse

389

during his imprisonment but still couldn't remember what had happened that night. He was distraught at Hazel's death, and wasn't interested if he himself lived or died. He didn't care that he wasn't going to be sentenced to be hanged for murder, and would be facing a lesser charge. For Alison and Vera, though, this was a relief. He'd done an unspeakable thing in causing his wife's death, but they also knew what Hazel was like, and how she could make someone's life hell. However, Cora, when she said anything about it at all, still referred to him as 'that murderer'.

At least that meant Cora was drinking something, Alison thought one afternoon in early June as she collected the latest batch of mouldy cups and washed them in boiling water. There was a funny smell in the kitchen and she traced it to some beef that had gone off. It was worse than offal, she decided, as she gingerly threw it into the rubbish and set the bin outside. She glanced around the small yard, only to find her mother hadn't put the rubbish into the alley for collection and it too was stinking in the tiny backyard. Grimly she tidied up some of it that had spilt, trying not to think about rats, and counted on her fingers what day it was. Tomorrow was bin day so at least she could get rid of this lot. 'Mum, you have to bring the dustbin in tomorrow,' she called. 'Promise me you will.'

Cora grunted in what sounded like reluctant agreement.

But the next afternoon when Alison went round, Cora had forgotten or hadn't bothered. There was also an unpleasant smell coming from upstairs.

'Here, where do you think you're going?' Cora protested as Alison ran into her bedroom.

'Mum! You haven't washed your clothes, have you? There's a big pile here.'

Cora set her face. 'So what? There's no one to see except you, and you don't count. Mind your own business, this is my home and I'll do what I want.'

Pulling a face, Alison gathered the dirty clothes into a bag and carried them downstairs. 'I'll do them. Fred's got me a new washing machine.'

'Of course he has.' Cora looked at her daughter with disgust. 'Got everything, you have. God forbid you have to work at anything.'

Alison bit her lip, not replying that she'd been on her feet in the shop since half past seven. She remembered how, even when they were at their poorest, her mother had never sent them out in dirty clothes. She'd taken in washing for years and would have been ashamed to send her daughters out in anything but the cleanest things, even if they were hand-me-downs and patched and worn.

'He's put up a new clothesline for me in the backyard as well. We've rearranged it to give us somewhere to sit out and for David to play, now summer's almost here. You'll have to come round and see it.' Alison thought that might do the trick – she might want to visit her grandson.

Cora wasn't interested. 'Very nice, I'm sure. Now you'll want to be getting back to them, I dare say. Don't let me keep you.' She practically bundled Alison out of the door.

Fred was pacing around the kitchen when she

got back, with David crying on his shoulder. 'He just started when we came up,' he said. 'I don't know what's wrong with him but he doesn't need changing or feeding.'

'Here, let me.' Alison reached out for the little boy. It was strange how natural this felt now. 'Maybe he just wants a good cry. I know how he feels.' She rocked him up and down and he snuffled against her hair. 'Honestly, Mum's getting worse, not better.'

'Ah, well.' Fred looked uncomfortable. 'I don't want to make things even worse but I had better tell you. Just after you left, her boss came in. He's not very happy.'

'What did he want?' Alison felt a sense of dread.

'He wanted you or me to take a message to Cora. He doesn't want to go round there himself. She hasn't been to work since ... since Hazel died, so he's given her the sack.'

'Oh no.' If she was honest Alison knew this was coming but she'd hoped her mother would get better and go back to the job she'd enjoyed so much. 'Then how will she pay the rent? She hasn't got any savings. Did you ask him to think again?'

'Of course,' said Fred. 'But as a business owner I have to say he's got a point. He's had to take on someone new. Your mum won't like it.'

'Who is it?'

'Beryl. Winnie Jewell's sister. She jumped at the chance apparently. She's moved to a new flat after all the trouble first with the Lannings and then with Hazel and Neville, and it's even closer to the newsagent's. Her new neighbour will take her children to school and she'll be finished in

392

time to pick them up. She's already started and the paperboys love her.'

Alison groaned. 'I'll talk to Mum again when I take her laundry back, but a fat lot of good it'll do. She's in no state to get herself another job. Oh, now, now, don't start crying again.' She began to walk around, trying to comfort the baby. 'He's usually so good. I hope he's not going to start doing this a lot. What'll we do in the shop?'

Fred went over and gave them both a hug. 'It'll pass. We'll worry about that if we need to. Got enough on our plates at the moment as it is.'

'I suppose you're right.' Yet she knew David wouldn't stay quietly in the back room for much longer. They'd have to come up with something soon. For the moment, though, Fred was right – they had enough on their plates.

It took Alison quite a while to persuade Cora to open the door the next day, even though she had the bag of clean laundry with her. Alison tried to reason with her mother through the letterbox, aware that several of the neighbours were watching from behind their curtains. Just what Cora wouldn't want. 'Open up, Mum, they're all looking and you'll get a reputation,' Alison called, crouching down to call through the slit. That worked. There was the sound of a key turning and Cora stood there, her expression stony. 'Come on then, don't just stoop there.'

Alison followed her in, dragging the heavy bag. 'Here you are, all fresh and ironed. What's this?' She almost tripped over a pile of paper, pushed to the side of the door. 'Oh, Mum, it's your post.

You haven't been opening it, have you?'

Cora threw her a look. 'Why would I? Nobody's got anything good to say.' She turned her back and went through to the kitchen.

Alison flicked through the envelopes, opening them and growing more anxious as she did so. 'Lots are letters of condolence, Mum.'

'I don't want them.'

'Well, I'll keep them in case you do later. Hang on, what's this?' She reread the final letter. 'Oh Mum. Looks like you've got behind with your rent.'

'What if I have?'

'But this isn't the first letter from the landlord. What did you do with that? Did you read it?'

Cora stood in the kitchen doorway and shrugged. 'Can't remember. I might have burnt it.'

'Mum! This is serious. You'll get evicted.' Alison did her best to stop her voice from rising. 'You've got, let's see, three days to pay the back rent or you're out. Mum! Listen to me.' Cora had wandered into the kitchen. 'You haven't got the money, have you? And you won't be getting any in, because you haven't been going to work. Mum, look at me. You haven't got a job any more. Your boss came round and told Fred he's had to take on somebody else.'

For a moment Cora showed a spark of interest. 'Who?'

'Beryl, Winnie's sister.'

'Oh, her.' Cora turned away again. 'Good luck to her. She'll need it. People coming by and pestering you all the time. Winnie will be pleased. That bloody family.'

'Steady on, Mum,' Alison protested. 'Vera's my friend.'

'Might have known it.' Cora sounded triumphant. 'A right pair you make. Well, you've said your piece. Time for you to go.'

Alison couldn't keep the despair from her voice. 'Mum, haven't you been listening? You're going to be evicted and you haven't got a job to pay any rent. What are you going to do?'

Cora shrugged again. 'Sleep on the street. What does it matter?'

'But you love this house. We've lived here for as long as I can remember. You said it made you feel closer to Hazel. Linda told me.'

'Well, I was wrong,' said Cora. 'That was just after she died, but I don't feel like that now. I might have been a bit crazy then. I know she's not here any more, God love her. Not here nor anywhere else. So it doesn't matter where I go. Anyway, what's going on with Linda? She ain't been round for ages.'

'Mum, you know she's in hospital,' Alison sighed. 'I told you. She's got high blood pressure and they're worried she'll lose the baby. So she's there until it comes down again, or the baby's born. You know that already.' She didn't mention the car crash. Terry had rung to tell them what had happened but asked them to keep quiet about the accident as there was no point in upsetting Cora any further.

'So she is.' Cora lost interest in that as well. 'Right, time you were off. There's nothing you can do here.'

Alison cried all the way back to Falcon Road and had to pretend it was hay fever when an old neighbour stopped her. When she got back home, Fred rushed to her as soon as he saw how distraught she was. He held her hand as she gulped out what had happened in the little house which had been the only home she'd known as a child. 'And the worst thing is, Mum doesn't seem to care, not about anything. Not losing her job, the house, Linda being ill, nothing. I don't know what to do.'

Fred rubbed his forehead. He'd never come across anything like it. It was so far from the Cora he knew, the proud fighter with a scathing tongue, and before that the young woman full of hope and life, yet was it surprising when she'd lost a daughter? 'Do you think...' he began, but then a wail came from the back bedroom. 'Sorry, love, he's been like this more or less since you left. I thought he'd gone quiet at last but there he is again.'

'I'll go,' said Alison, glad that at least here was somebody she could do something for.

'As soon as I finish up and close the shop, we'll take him for a walk,' Fred suggested. 'We can have our dinner after that.'

'Yes, all right,' Alison agreed as she hurried to see to David, lifting him tenderly into her arms. To think she had once rejected him. It didn't seem possible when she loved him so much now.

At least if she kept going all day she fell asleep easily. She dreaded lying awake with all the worries flying around her head.

As soon as Fred closed the shop, David was tucked into the big Silver Cross pram and they

396

set off along Falcon Road. Slowly the trundling along did its work and David grew quiet, leaving Fred to start putting his thoughts into words. 'I was just wondering,' he said. 'Maybe it would help if your mum felt needed. She's sat there all day, doing nothing, and now someone else is even doing her job at the shop. It's not like her to give up. She could have done that when Jack died but she didn't, because she had you three to look after.'

Alison stopped for a moment. 'Yes, I can see that, yet she always said that she wished I hadn't come along, but maybe I was good for something, after all. Funny, isn't it?' Before Fred could comment David let out another yell. 'Oh no, do you suppose he's teething? But isn't it too soon?'

Fred knotted his brow. 'He could be. That book said they usually start at six months and that's not so far off now. If that's the case we aren't going to get many quiet days in the shop.'

She looked at him. 'Well, that's the answer, isn't it? If only she'll agree, we could ask her to come round to care for him while we're working.'

'In fact,' said Fred carefully, not wanting to push things too far, 'what would make sense is if she moved in and looked after him that way. Then you could do more with the business. I'd love it if you did. It could do with your new ideas and you enjoy all the work behind the scenes. We're a team, we need to work together. How about it?'

Alison nodded slowly. Not long ago if anyone had made that suggestion she would have panicked, hating the very thought of being under the same roof as her mother once more. But things were different now; she was a different person, and she knew how much help her mother needed. However she knew what Cora's answer would be. 'I've asked her to come to us before, Fred. When it all happened and several times since. I've given up trying. We've got room, she'd be close to her friends and everything she knows. She won't have it.' She gulped again, holding tight to the pram handle. 'I don't know how to get her to change her mind.'

Fred rubbed her back. 'Come on, keep moving, that'll send him to sleep if we walk for long enough. You know, maybe it would help if I went round instead. Tell you what, give me your door key in case she objects.'

'Would you, Fred? That might make a difference. But careful if you let yourself in, she really doesn't like it. I tried it once and thought she was going to hit me. Try to get her to let you in. It might take a while but it'll be easier in the long run.'

Fred smiled. 'I always take your advice, Alison. You know that.' He turned the pram to the left. 'Let's go down this way. I like the winding old lanes.' He steered them down the narrow street, and before long they found themselves facing St Mary's. There was the graceful spire with the clock. 'Look where we are. Do you remember...'

Alison blushed. 'I try not to. Whatever was I thinking of?' She took his arm. 'I'm glad I didn't jump. You saved me, Fred, me and David.'

'Well...' Fred was blushing as well. 'Maybe I knew I loved you then. I just didn't want to admit it.'

'I'm glad you did.' She sighed and met his eyes. 'Now look what we've got. How well things have worked out for us. All because you came along at the right time and saved me.' She turned and looked out to the river and her lip trembled. 'Fred, do you think you can save my mum as well?'

Fred drew up in the car around the corner from Ennis Street. He didn't want his arrival to cause a fuss but he had every intention of driving Cora back in it, as long as she agreed to come. Somehow he had to persuade her. Alison had such faith in him that he couldn't let her down. He thought that Cora had more loyalty from her youngest daughter than she deserved. Then he remembered what Cora had been like as a young woman and how life had dealt her such bitter blows. No wonder she'd finally given up.

He walked with purpose to the shabby front door, fingering the key in his pocket. It looked as if someone was moving into the house across the road, once the home of the Parrots. He wondered if they knew the history of the family who'd lived there. If they didn't now, they would soon enough. He gathered his courage and knocked. Nothing happened.

'Cora,' he called, 'it's me, Fred. I know you're in there. Come on, open up.'

He waited a few moments and knocked again. 'I'm not going away without seeing you, Cora. So don't think you can hide from me.' Still nothing happened.

He was going to have to let himself in after all.

With Alison's warning ringing in his head, he brought out the key and was just going to insert it when the door was flung open.

'What are they doing back?' Cora hissed.

'What?' Fred was totally taken aback but then he realised what she meant. 'It's not the same people, Cora. They're new. They're just moving in. Shall we talk inside?'

Cora turned abruptly and he followed her in. Even though Alison had told him about the state of the place it still came as a shock. Cora herself was nothing but a stick, with wild hair and bright eyes boring into him. 'What do you want, then, Fred Chapman?' Her expression was hostile.

He stood gazing around, taking in the changes. He couldn't believe this was where he had come to ask for permission to marry Alison. He'd been nervous then but now he was seized with anxiety. Looking at Cora he could tell this was a woman driven to the edge. He had to get this right or he'd never forgive himself. He couldn't crush Alison's hopes.

Even though he'd known her for so many years, he found it impossible to judge how Cora might react. She had the look of someone who was past reason and there was even a bit of him that wondered if she was going to let fly. He shook himself. Come on, he thought. She's only small, just look how thin she's got. She can't harm you. Sadness overcame him, thinking of what she'd been like in her young days. Nobody who'd known her then would have recognised her now.

'Oh Cora.' He swept his arm around. 'What's all this? How's it come to this?' His eyes misted up, but he blinked the tears away. They'd do no good. All he could say was what was uppermost in his mind. He hadn't planned it. 'What would Jack have thought?'

It was the best thing he could have come out with. Cora's eyes shot up to meet his. 'No call for that,' she barked. 'He ain't here, more's the pity, and he can't help me now. No one can. You just take yerself off and don't come meddling where you're not wanted. You keep your do-gooding to yerself.'

'Cora, he wouldn't have let me do that,' Fred persisted, sensing that this was the one way to get through to her. 'He would have expected more of me. He was my best mate, you know that, and I can't begin to tell you how much I owe him. I looked up to him like I've never looked up to anyone else before or since. So how could I leave you here? Do you really think that's what he would have wanted? No, Cora, you're coming home with me.'

He could see she was struggling to take this in, almost as if she didn't want to hear it, but all at once she crumpled, as if someone had cut her strings. 'No, don't ask me that,' she whispered. She shook her head as if trying to escape the sound of his voice. She stared at the worn-out rug on the floor, her hands trembling.

'Think, Cora.' He pressed his advantage. 'You came through all that. You never gave up. You brought his girls up on your own and did a damn good job. You kept going all those years through the war and rationing and all the rest of it. Even when there didn't seem to be enough to go round

401

you managed it somehow. Nobody knew how you did it, but somehow you kept them all fed and clothed and held the household together. You can't stop now. We need you.'

'No, nobody needs me,' said Cora, glancing up again, adamant that she was right. 'Linda doesn't, she's got Terry. Alison's got you. Even the shop's got Beryl now. And as for Hazel...' She started to sob. 'Hazel doesn't need anyone now. She thought she had her man and her big wedding and all that but it did for her in the end. So I'm finished. I've had enough. I tell you, Fred, I'm tired of it all. Struggling to make ends meet for all those years and for what? So my eldest can think I'm not good enough, my youngest can manage very well without me and my beautiful Hazel can get killed by that useless man of hers. What's the point?'

'Come on, Cora, you can't think like that.' Fred moved across and put his hand on her shoulder. 'We all miss Hazel. It's terrible. But we do need you. We want your help.'

'What help can I be? Just look at me.' Cora wiped her eyes, clearly unable to believe that such a thing would be possible. 'I don't have the strength to squash a fly, Fred. I used to heave around those big tubs of laundry and now I can hardly get up the stairs. My back and my hands give me gyp all day long. I don't want no more of this, I really don't.'

'Then come and stay with us,' said Fred. 'No wonder you get arthritis in a place like this. It's damp enough to grow mushrooms. We got nice fires, it's warm as toast. You'd get proper food – you know what a good cook I am.' He tried to force a smile. 'We'd love you to come. We need your help with David. We think he's teething already and he needs someone there all the time, but it takes two of us to run the shop. Would you help us?'

Cora said nothing.

'Is it leaving this house that's bothering you?' he asked. 'Is it because this is where Hazel used to live?'

Cora snorted. 'You been listening to Linda and Alison? I know I said some stupid stuff when she died. I thought I'd feel her here, but it's not true. She's not here, she's gone, I know that now. It's worse. And having that house opposite, I can't bear to look out.'

'Ah, Cora.' Fred sat back. 'It's hard, isn't it? But we can't leave you here. Come back with me and live with us. We're at the end of our tether trying to think what to do with David. We don't want some stranger looking after him, he's too precious. You know all about babies. He needs his granny.'

She looked at him doubtfully.

'Come on, Cora. You've raised three children and helped with a granddaughter. What do me and Alison know about bringing up a baby, especially when he starts getting difficult? What chance have I ever had to get to look after a baby before? Been too busy running the shop all hours of the day and night. And Alison, well, it's only natural she gets tired. And being the youngest herself, she never had no sisters to practise on, did she?'

'Should hope not,' growled Cora. 'Didn't want no more after her, that's for sure. And you being a man, Fred, I don't blame you for not knowing which end of a baby is which, it's not your place.'

'Well, then.' He rubbed his hands over his face. 'You can see the pickle we're in. Fact is, David needs you. Your grandson needs you.'

Cora finally softened. 'Does he? Well, maybe, Fred.' She cast her eyes around the sorry state of her once-immaculate room. She seemed to become a little taller as her resolve grew. 'I could maybe help you out. They don't want me here anyway. I'm not paying that cheat of a landlord a penny more. That's a waste of good money.'

Fred perked up. If Cora was starting to talk about waste, it was a sure sign she was more like her old self.

'Would you come with me now, Cora? When I left he was screaming his lungs out, and there was Alison trying to cook, and then we got to do the accounts before we open up tomorrow. We don't have enough pairs of hands, that's the truth.' He held his breath. She was holding herself straighter and her expression had lost its wild edge. He knew he had to go carefully. If she didn't agree now, he couldn't guarantee that she'd feel the same in the morning. He had to strike while the iron was hot. He'd keep it practical, avoid any more appeals to her dead husband's memory. 'Do you need me to pack anything for you?'

'What, let a man handle my underwear? Wash your mouth out, Fred Chapman.' Now she'd made the decision Cora suddenly grew lively. 'No, I got a bag of clean stuff what Alison brought back yesterday.' She looked around. 'Most of this furniture is a load of rubbish. Not like all that new modern business that you got.' She got to her feet. 'No time like the present. I'll make sure the gas is turned off and we can go.'

Fred picked up the laundry bag and held open the front door for her, locking it behind them. 'Wait here, Cora, I'll get the car.'

'Nonsense, Fred.' She slapped his arm. 'I can walk that far. Not dead yet, you know.'

Chapter Forty-Two

It took a while for everyone to settle in to the new living arrangements. Alison was relieved to see that her mother was safe, but a lifetime of them not getting along could not be put right overnight. Cora was still offhand with her or downright rude about Vera after she made one of her regular visits. What made it easier was the way David loved having his grandmother there. He gurgled when she looked over the bars of his cot and cooed when he heard her voice. He allowed her to comfort him when his new teeth hurt and sucked happily on a plastic ring that Cora recommended. 'He has to have something to bite on,' she said. 'An old spoon will do, you don't have to go spending on something special.' But Fred was adamant and bought the ring from Peter Jones.

More and more it made Fred remember the way he'd put up with his own mother for so long, and he knew he'd lost some of the best years of his life by not sorting that out. He didn't want another case of history repeating itself. He was relieved that Cora and Alison seemed to be edging their way to a better understanding, and knew he had to give them time. Besides, his mother had been a domineering bully and he knew Cora had a different side to her. When she was with David she was like another person. How sad she hadn't been like that when Alison was little and needed her. He knew how Jack's death had knocked her for six and she never really got over it, taking the easy way out and blaming her innocent daughter for all the hardships that followed. He could only hope that she'd come to see how Alison had changed, how she'd blossomed now that she was loved and respected, and had become a loving mother herself. He made sure he praised his wife as much as possible in her mother's hearing and trusted the message might begin to get through.

Alison thought she noticed some shift in her mother's attitude but couldn't be certain. She was so used to dismissive comments that she didn't expect her mother to treat her any other way. So when she began to try David on solid food, mashing up carrots and attempting to get him to eat it, she couldn't quite believe her mother's reaction.

Cora stood watching them from the kitchen door. 'Not bad,' she said, nodding her head.

Alison waited for the barb that inevitably followed. None came.

'He likes it, don't he?' Cora went on. 'Knows what's good for him. Help him see in the dark, that will. Here, you don't want to be getting your blouse dirty if you got to go down to the shop. Let me do it. Mummy's got to go to work, hasn't she? Clever Mummy gave you some nice orange dinner before running her shop. You'd like your granny to give you some more carrots, wouldn't you?'

David bashed his hand in the food in reply, happily kicking his legs.

'All right, thanks,' said Alison, not quite believing it could be that easy or that her mother had said something good about her. She wiped her gooey hands on a tea towel and stood back as Cora took the baby on her knee, not seeming to mind the mess that was flying everywhere. This arrangement might work after all, she thought with relief – and it meant she could be of more use to Fred as well if she could count on Cora at a moment's notice in this way.

News came from Kent towards the middle of June that Linda had finally been allowed home from hospital. Cora was delighted that Terry had arranged for a telephone to be installed in their house so they could talk whenever they wanted. That meant she was first to know when the new baby, a boy this time, arrived, none the worse for what his mother had been through while carrying him. 'He's gorgeous, Mum,' Linda said. 'And his big sister is over the moon. She chose his name: he's going to be Tommy. Thomas Terrance Owens. I'd love to have you down to see him but we're bursting at the seams now. When he's a little bit older we'll bring him up to see you.'

'You do that,' said Cora. It would be nice to see them all. She made a face as she remembered telling Linda not to bring June round last time. She wouldn't make that mistake again.

The other big news was that the date of Neville's trial was announced and he intended to plead guilty to stabbing Hazel, even though that hadn't been the cause of her death. Frank had come forward to testify that the lad hadn't been in his right mind that night, having been wound up by a colleague and having suffered at the hands of his wife over the course of many months, as well as that same evening. Dennis had somehow retained enough memory to back Frank up on this. Bill hadn't been able to recall much about the evening, other than to feel he'd somehow let his friend down by not realising how badly Hazel had been treating him. It was all too little, too late. At least it meant Neville was spared the death penalty but it looked as if he'd spend years in prison.

Marian was able to pass on this news when she saw Alison in the shop. She was a little hesitant to start with, not knowing if any word of Neville would be welcome. Alison assured her that she'd rather know than be kept in the dark. 'We didn't even know for sure where he was,' she told the kindly older woman. 'Even though he did what he did we can't pretend he doesn't exist. We'd be grateful if you passed on any news.'

'Well, he's being held in Brixton prison,' Marian said, hefting her bulging shopping bag. 'It's not too bad there, I heard. At least he's nearby – his family can visit. You won't be going there, I take it?'

Alison shook her head. Knowing where he was, was one thing. She thought it best to leave it at that.

Alison was quietly relieved that he'd had the

grace to plead guilty, the more so because Vera didn't have to give a statement. 'I wish I'd acted sooner though,' Vera said one sunny day when the young women were sitting out in the backyard, now divided into two sections by a row of potted plants. Alison was trying her hand at nasturtiums, mainly because David loved the colour. 'I mean, I knew she must have been hitting him. He was such a happy-go-lucky bloke – he must have been pushed that bit too far.'

'Come off it, if you'd tried to say anything everyone would have got the wrong end of the stick and come down on you like a ton of bricks,' Alison said. 'At least you listened to him. Like you listened to me.' She shook her head, chasing away the vision of the cheerful young man who'd been her brother-in-law, and changed the subject. 'So what do you think of my idea? Are you going to say yes?'

'Of course I'm going to say yes,' said Vera, adjusting the straps on her tightly belted sundress. She was being careful of sunburn marks this year. 'Look, I must be going, I've got a new date, and before you ask, no, you don't know him. Let me know what they say.'

She ran out of the back gate as fast as she could on her high heels, just as Cora and the baby emerged from the storeroom door.

'Look who it is. Mummy's looking after your flowers.' Cora lifted David round so the sun didn't shine full in his face. 'You done a good job there, my girl.'

Alison raised her head at the compliment from her mother. She still wasn't used to her praise but

409

she was beginning to feel less on her guard. 'Th ... thanks,' she managed. 'Well, they're pretty easy, you just remember to water them and pick off the dead heads, and they do the rest themselves. He really likes them, look how he's reaching for them.'

Cora shifted slightly. 'That wasn't what I meant.' She glanced at her feet in their comfy old sandals. 'Look, I'm not one for being soppy but I just wanted to say sorry. I can see what a good mum you are and you didn't have no example to follow from me. I wish things had been different, but times was hard. Now you're giving me a home and maybe I don't deserve it. I might not say so very often but I can see how far you've come.'

Alison didn't know what to say. She cleared her throat and looked away. But then she realised she couldn't let the moment pass. 'The thing is,' she began slowly, trying to choose her words carefully, 'now I've had David I know how hard it can be trying to work and look after him, and I'm one of the lucky ones.' She had to stop to swallow hard as a lump was forming in her throat. She'd never thought she'd hear her mother say those words. Somehow she made herself continue. 'We've got a big flat, there's no war on so we can buy what we want when we need it, and most of all I've got Fred.' She turned at the sound of footsteps. 'Here he is now.'

Cora nodded. 'You got a diamond there. Who'd have thought it?'

'What have I been missing?' Fred demanded, coming over to ruffle the top of David's head in its small sun hat. 'Talking about me behind my back, were you?'

410

Alison caught his eye and grinned. 'Something like that. We had something to tell Mum, didn't we? Might as well get it all over in one go, don't you think? That all right with you, Fred?'

'Of course,' said Fred, shielding his eyes to gaze at his wife. Nobody would have dreamt she'd ever been called horse face. Her hair was beautifully cut, her hunched back was gone, her sundress was elegant. She might not be pretty but she had grown into a striking young woman. He still couldn't believe his luck, and things were set to get even better.

'Two things, then,' she said. 'We want to get David christened at St Mary's. Fred and I have always liked it there.' She paused, but didn't explain why that particular church was so special. 'I've asked Vera to be godmother. No, don't say anything, I know how you feel about her but she's my closest friend and without her, David might not be here. Second thing. David's going to have a little brother or sister in the New Year. What do you think of that?'

Cora's eyes nearly popped out of her head. Somehow she'd still hung on to the idea of this marriage as one of convenience, even though she'd seen how they were around each other. But she couldn't forget that old image of the beanpole girl with the fat balding man. Now she took in the pair before her – the elegant young woman and the man, admittedly much shorter, but much slimmer now, with his big smile and kind face – and realised that all her ideas about them were wrong. For all those years she'd ignored her youngest daughter, mistreated her, sniped at her and belittled her to all and sundry, when in fact she was a fine and caring young woman. Now she could finally admit to herself that she was indeed like her father, not in looks but in her manner and her attitude to life. She'd always thought Linda was her most reliable daughter, but her eldest hadn't rushed to intervene in her hour of need. Her friends hadn't made the effort to get through to her when she'd been shut in her house, unable to face the world. It had taken Alison and Fred to do that. What a remarkable couple they'd turned out to be. Who'd have thought it?

'One more thing,' said Fred. 'We thought if it's a boy we'd like to call him Jack. Would that be all right with you, Cora?'

Cora was lost for words for once. She stared at the ground, overcome with emotion. Then she stepped forward and for the first time in her life she hugged her youngest daughter with affection. Alison held her tightly in return. 'You're a lovely girl, Alison, and don't let no one tell you different,' she said, choking with happiness. 'And I can't wait to meet little Jack.'

The publishers hope that this book has given you enjoyable reading. Large Print Books are especially designed to be as easy to see and hold as possible. If you wish a complete list of our books please ask at your local library or write directly to:

Magna Large Print Books
Magna House, Long Preston,
Skipton, North Yorkshire.
BD23 4ND

This Large Print Book for the partially sighted, who cannot read normal print, is published under the auspices of

THE ULVERSCROFT FOUNDATION

THE ULVERSCROFT FOUNDATION

... we hope that you have enjoyed this Large Print Book. Please think for a moment about those people who have worse eyesight problems than you ... and are unable to even read or enjoy Large Print, without great difficulty.

You can help them by sending a donation, large or small to:

**The Ulverscroft Foundation,
1, The Green, Bradgate Road,
Anstey, Leicestershire, LE7 7FU,
England.**
or request a copy of our brochure for more details.

The Foundation will use all your help to assist those people who are handicapped by various sight problems and need special attention.

Thank you very much for your help.